Nathan Willey

A Treatise on the Principles and Practice of Life Insurance

Nathan Willey

A Treatise on the Principles and Practice of Life Insurance

ISBN/EAN: 9783337338480

Printed in Europe, USA, Canada, Australia, Japan

Cover: Foto ©Andreas Hilbeck / pixelio.de

More available books at **www.hansebooks.com**

A TREATISE

ON THE

PRINCIPLES AND PRACTICE

OF

LIFE INSURANCE:

BEING AN ARITHMETICAL EXPLANATION OF THE COMPUTATIONS
INVOLVED IN THE SCIENCE OF LIFE CONTINGENCIES,
TO WHICH ARE ADDED

VALUABLE TABLES FOR REFERENCE.

By NATHAN WILLEY, ACTUAR..

NEW YORK:
Offices of THE SPECTATOR,
J. H. AND C. M. GOODSELL, PUBLISHERS.
1872.

PREFACE.

The design of this work is to furnish the public with a means of clearly understanding the fundamental principles of Life Insurance, and to enable agents to present them in a concise and forcible manner. To accomplish this result, the author has attempted to explain the mathematical laws which the study and experience of the past two centuries have shown to lie at the foundation of the science. In this undertaking he has endeavored to confine himself strictly to those topics which the experience of American companies, during the last few years, has shown to be absolutely necessary to an intelligent and successful prosecution of the business, and to illustrate them in such a manner that they may be comprehended by any one who is willing to give the subject a careful investigation. Those who still remain prejudiced against Life Insurance are confirmed in their opinions more by a want of correct information than by any solid argument which they can produce against it, and the sooner it is stripped of forbidden technical nomenclature and formulæ, and adapted to the comprehension of the average intellect of business men, the greater will be the popular appreciation of its merits. Both officers and agents of companies should be able to meet any objections raised against Life Insurance, and to explain its principles so clearly that the public may see that it is a plain financial transaction, giving support to the families of thousands of claimants every year, and throwing its mantle of protection around nearly a million of its living patrons.

CONTENTS.

CONTENTS.

DEFINITIONS IN LIFE INSURANCE.

Accumulation—The annual premiums and interest during the first years of a policy are largely in excess of the annual cost of carrying the risk ; which is necessary in order to establish a fund to pay the amount insured when it becomes a claim. Hence, to provide for the payment of future claims, this excess increases by compound interest and additions from the annual premium, and is called accumulation. The *accumulation formula* expresses, in algebraic language, the law by which this increase takes place.

Actuary—One who is proficient in that branch of life insurance, which is strictly of a scientific and mathematical nature, as the preparation of tables and formulæ, calculation of policy liability, distribution of surplus, etc.

Annuity—A sum of money payable at regular intervals. An annuity contingent is dependent for its termination upon an event which may or will occur, as the death of the annuitant or person who receives it.

An annuity certain is a sum payable during a definite term of years, and which does not cease in the meantime in the event of any contingency. The interest on a six per cent bond of one thousand dollars is an annuity certain of sixty dollars per annum during the time which the bond has to run.

A perpetual annuity is a sum of money payable at regular intervals during an unlimited series of years.

A deferred annuity is one in which the regular payments are to commence at some future period.

A joint annuity is one which depends upon the joint existence of two or more lives from year to year.

A survivorship annuity is one which continues during the lifetime of the survivor of two or more lives.

Assets—All the funds and available property of any kind belonging to a company.

Bonus—A dividend paid to policyholders from the surplus of a company over and above the liabilities. "Bonus addition" to a policy is another term for reversionary insurance.

Brokerage—A commission on the first premiums paid to solicitors of life insurance companies in lieu of all future commissions on the renewal premiums.

Commission—A percentage given to a solicitor or agent on premiums collected by him.

Commutation Columns—Columns formed from a given table of mortality and rate of interest, and used in the computation of premium rates and other life insurance calculations.

Company, Insurance—A number of persons associated together for the purpose of effecting insurance against risks of any kind. A stock company has for its basis a capital stock, and insures at lower premium rates than those of mixed or mutual companies, so that whatever surplus may then accrue belongs exclusively to the stockholders. In a mutual company the surplus is returned to the insured. Mixed companies partake of the nature of stock and mutual companies; a certain portion of the profits are paid to the stockholders, and the remainder is distributed among the insured.

Contribution—A term used to denote the method of distributing the surplus of a company, according to the amount each policyholder has contributed to produce it.

Discount—The difference between a sum of money payable at any future time and the present value if paid immediately, computed according to a given rate of interest.

Dividend—The surplus or profit distributed to each stock or policyholder after the liabilities of the company are reserved. Dividends to policyholders are practically a misnomer. They are mainly a restitution of the over-payments which have been made in the premises. Reversionary dividends, the allotment of the surplus converted into single premiums to purchase additional insurance payable according to the terms of the policy. Deferred dividends, those which are payable after a certain number of years. Tontine dividends, those which are payable on the tontine method.

Endowment—A sum of money assured and payable when the policyholder arrives at a certain age. This is usually called "Simple Endowment."

For "Endowment Insurance" see "Policy."

Expectation of Life—A term applied to the mean or average duration of the life of individuals, after any specified age and according to a given table of mortality.

Experience—The data upon which different life insurance tables are made.

Forfeiture—The violation of some of the conditions of a policy which enables the company to cancel the contract made with the policyholder.

Insurance, Life—An agreement by a life insurance company, in consideration of a stipulated premium, to pay a certain sum of money on the death of a policyholder or upon his attaining a certain age. *Cost of Insurance*—The annual tabular expense which the company incurs upon a policy in force, or the amount at risk multiplied by the probability of dying that year. *Insurance Value*—The present value of the future cost of insurance assured by the company when it gives a policy upon the life of another. *Self Insurance*—The amount of reserve which is in the hands of the company, or the amount upon which the company does not assume any risk of being obliged to pay from the premiums of other policyholders. *

Interest—A stipulated amount per annum paid for the use of money.

Lapse—The expiration of the contract of insurance occasioned by the non-payment of premiums.

Liabilities—Actual losses unpaid, expenses and contingent debts of a company, for the payment of which its assets are held liable. The whole amount insured is a contingent debt, but it is regarded as a liability only to the extent of the " reserve " on the policy.

---

* *Assurance and Insurance.* "I do not accept the distinction laid down by some writers as to the use of the words *assurance* and *insurance*, by which the former is restricted to life and the latter to fire risks. The more correct distinction I believe to be that a man *insures* the life of himself or of some other person, or his house, or his ships, or the fidelity of his servants, and that the office *assures* to him in each of these cases a sum of money payable in certain contingencies. Hence the office is the *assurer* or *assurers* and the man the assured; while we may speak of *the life assured* or *the life insured* or *the sum assured* or *the sum insured*, according as we take the point of view of the office or the individual. So also we may speak either of ' Life Insurance' or ' Life Assurance,' as, for instance, we may say that a man believes in the duty and advantage of life insurance, in that a certain company finds the business of life assurance very profitable." *Thomas Bond Sprague, Vice-President Institute of Actuaries, London.*

Loading—A percentage added to the net premium in order to defray expenses and provide for an excess of mortality.

Loss—The payment of a claim upon the death of a policyholder. Matured endowments, strictly speaking, are not losses.

Margin—The same as " loading."

Mortality—Having a given number of persons of the same age living at the beginning of a year, the mortality is the number dying during that year. The *rate* of mortality is the ratio of the dying to the number of living. A *table* of mortality is a tabulated exhibit of the number of survivors and the number of dying each year, among a number of persons taken at a given age.

Policy—The contract effected between the insurer and the insured, or the instrument containing the terms and conditions on which a company undertakes to indemnify a person in whose favor a policy is issued against the loss of the life of the policyholder, or upon his attaining a certain age. *Life Policy*—When the sum insured is payable on the death of the policyholder. *Term Policy*—One taken for a limited number of years, the sum insured payable only in case of the death of the policyholder during this period. *Endowment Insurance Policy*—One payable when the policyholder attains a certain age or at death if it should take place before that time. *Limited Payment Policy*— One in which the number of payments is not to exceed a certain limit. *Joint Life Policy*—One payable on the death of the first of two or more persons insured. *Survivorship Policy*—One payable on the death of the survivor of two or more persons.

Premium—The sum required to keep a policy in force according to its conditions. *Net Premium*—The lowest rate, according to a given table of mortality and interest at which an insurance can be effected. *Gross, or Office, Premium*—The premium increased by the loading or margin. *Single Premium* —A sum of money paid for insurance and in consideration of which all future premiums are forborne. The *Net Single Premium* is the present value of all future net annual premiums, diminished by the probability of dying each year.

Premium Notes and Loans—Notes given by policyholders in lieu of a part of the cash payment of the premium; *Loans* are granted by the company for the same purpose. These notes or loans are never intended to be paid in cash, but to be cancelled by dividends, or deducted from the amount insured in case of death.

Present Values—The present value of a given sum payable at a certain future time is the amount which, placed at interest, will equal this sum in the time specified. The present value of an *annnity* is the sum of money which will purchase, at a given rate of discount, all the future payments. The present value of a *perpetual annuity*, is that sum which, invested at a given rate of interest, will always produce the amount required. The present value of a *deferred annuity* is that sum which, invested at a given rate of interest, will, at the end of the period during which the annuity is deferred, amount to the sum which will then purchase all the future payments.

Reserve—That part of the premiums of a policy, with the interest thereon, which is reserved or set aside as a fund for the payment of the policy when it becomes due.

Reversion—A sum payable on the occurrence of some event, as the death of a policyholder. It is usually applied to annuities and surplus on policies, when payable in this manner.

Risk, Amount at—The difference between the sum insured and the reserve, or the amount of hazard which the company assumes.

Scrip—A certificate entitling the policyholder to certain profits or surplus, when payable.

Solvency, Test of—A rule to determine the ability of a company to pay all the losses, which, according to a given table of mortality and rate of interest, may occur.

Surplus—The sum left, after providing for the liabilities, claims and expenses of a company.

Tontine—A fund purchased jointly by a number of persons, the profits divided among the oldest survivors. *Tontine Dividend*—A distribution of surplus among the diminished number who are entitled to it after a certain period.

Valuation—A method of finding the necessary reserve on a policy.

Value of a Policy—The Reserve. The *net value* of a policy is the difference between the net single premium for the sum insured at the age of the policyholder when the policy is valued, and the present value of all future net premiums calculated to be received on the life of the party insured.   The *gross value* of a policy is the difference between the net single premium, as given above, and the present value of all future gross premiums to be received on the policy.

INTEREST AND DISCOUNT.

In many life insurance calculations, a great amount of time and labor is often saved by a familiarity with the use of interest and discount tables, there being many operations which can be done in a much more accurate and expeditious manner by them than by the seriatim method, and therefore a clear understanding of them is of great importance.

COMPOUND INTEREST.

1. In compound interest the interest of a given sum is added to the principal, increasing it at the end of each year or period when it becomes payable, instead of being paid as often as it becomes due.   Thus, at 6 per cent, the amount of $1 for one year is $1.06; the amount at compound interest for two years is $1.06 × $1.06 = $1.1236; for three years it is $1.06 × $1.1236 = $1.1910.

2. Tables of compound interest are made by multiplying $1 by the amount of $1 for one year at the given rate per cent, and this product by the amount of $1 for one year which gives the amount of $1 for two years, and so on for the number of years required.   The last product gives the amount for the given number of years.   The compound interest is found by subtracting $1 from it.   Thus the compound interest of $1 for 3 years, at 6 per cent, is $1.1910—$1 = .1910.

3. To find the amount of any sum at compound interest for any number of years at a given rate per cent, by the use of the tables, we have only to look in the tables, under the given rate per cent, and opposite to the required number of years for the amount of $1 and multiply this amount by the given sum.

Thus, the amount of $1 for 20 years, at 4 per cent, is $2.1911, and at 7 per cent for the same period is $3.8697. The amount of $200 at 4 per cent would be $200×$2.1911=$438.22, and at 7 per cent, $200×$3.8697=$773.94. The compound interest is found by substracting the principal from the amount of the principal and interest; thus, $438.22—$200=$238.22= the compound interest in the first case given above.

4. The above rule gives the compound interest for a whole number of years. To find the compound interest for a number of years and a fractional part of a year, we first find the amount by the tables for the entire years, and then the interest for the part of the following year, by subtracting the amount for the entire years required from the amount of the next year in the tables, and this result gives the interest for the entire year of which the fractional part is required. The next step is to find this fractional part, and add it to the amount of the entire year's principal and interest.

Thus to find the amount at compound interest, 4 per cent, or $1 for 20 years and 6 months, we have :

Amount of $1 for 20 years, - - - - - - - $2.19112
" $1 for 21 years, - - - - - - 2.27876
Compound interest, 21st year, - - - - - - .08764
" " for 6 months, - - - - - .04382
Amount of $1 for 20 years and 6 months, $2.19112+$04382=$2.23494
Compound interest=$2.23495—$1= - - - - - $1.23494

To find the compound interest of $1 for 20 years and 73 days, at 4 per cent, we have : $2.19112+.08764×$\frac{73}{365}$=$2.19112+ .01753—the amount of $1 for the given time=$2.20865, and the compound interest is $2.20865—$1=$1.20865

5. To find the time in which a given sum will increase to a given amount at a given rate per cent, divide the given amount by the given sum, and the result is the amount of $1 in the time required. By comparing this result with the amounts of $1 during a series of years and at the given rate per cent. the time required can easily be obtained.

Example. The number of years required for $200 to double itself at compound interest, 4 per cent, is found as follows : 400÷200=2. The amount of $1 for 17 years, at 4 per cent, according to Table No. I, is $1.9479, and for 18 years is $2.0258 ; consequently the exact time required is between these two periods, or $2.0258—$1.9479=.0779, which is the compound interest on $1 during the eighteenth year. The difference between 1.9479 and 2 is .0521, and we have this proportion. If it requires 365 days for $1 during the eighteenth year at compound interest to earn .0779, how long is required for it to earn .0521? By the rule of three .0779 : .0521 :: 365 : 244 days. Hence, the time required is 17 years and 244 days.

6. The rate per cent is very nearly determined by a similar method.

Example. If $1 increases to $2 in nine years, what is the rate per cent? By inspecting Table No. VI, we find, by running the eye along the columns opposite to 9 years, that $1, at 8 per cent per annum, will amount to $1.999, which shows that 8 per cent is the nearest rate required.

7. To find the principal which will amount to a certain sum at compound interest, the time and rate per cent being given, divide the given amount by the amount of $1 increased at compound interest, according to the required conditions of the principal.

Example. To find the principal, which will amount to $2.000 in 10 years, at 6 per cent compound interest, we find, by Table No. IV, that the amount of $1 during this term, at 6 per cent, is $1.7908, and consequently we have the proportions 1.7908 : 1.00 :: 2,000 : 1,116.79=the principal required.

8. It sometimes happens, in making calculations of considerable accuracy, that the amount of compound interest of a certain sum is required when the interest is added to the principal semi-annually or oftener.

When the interest is added semi-annually, the following rule is a very expeditious one to use, provided the proper tables are at hand:

In the column giving the amounts of $1 at one-half the annual rate of interest given, take double the number of years and proceed as when the interest is payable annually.

Example. To find the amount at compound interest of $1 for 10 years, at 10 per cent interest, added semi-annually, find the amount at compound interest of $1 for 20 years at 5 per cent, which is $2.6533, the answer required. To find the amount at compound interest of $1 for 20 years at 8 per cent, interest added semi-annually, find the amount at compound interest of $1 for 40 years, at 4 per cent, which is $4.8010, the answer required.

9. If the interest is added tri-annually, select the column giving the amounts of $1 at one-third the rate of interest, and take three times the number of years; if added quarterly, select the column giving the amounts of $1 at one-fourth the rate of interest given, and take four times the number of years.

10. In the last example the amount at compound interest of $1 for 20 years, at 8 per cent interest, added annually, is $4.660957 ; semi-annually, $4.801021 ; quarterly, $4.875430.

To find the amount at compound interest, added semi-annually or quarterly, in cases where the ordinary interest tables do not apply, multiply the principal by the proper amounts of $1 as given in the following table, for the required number of years :

THE AMOUNTS OF $1 IN ONE YEAR, WITH INTEREST ADDED ANNUALLY, HALF YEARLY AND QUARTERLY.

Rate of Interest.	How Payable.	Am't of $1 in one year.	Rate of Interest.	How Payable.	Am't of $1 in one year.
4 per cent.	Annually. Half Yearly. Quarterly.	1.040000 1.040400 1.040604	7 per cent.	Annually. Half Yearly. Quarterly.	1.070000 1.071225 1.071859
4½ per cent.	Annually. Half Yearly. Quarterly.	1.045000 1.045506 1.045765	8 per cent.	Annually. Half Yearly. Quarterly.	1.080000 1.081600 1.082432
5 per cent.	Annually. Half Yearly. Quarterly.	1.050000 1.050625 1.050946	9 per cent.	Annually. Half Yearly. Quarterly.	1.090000 1.092025 1.093083
6 per cent.	Annually. Half Yearly. Quarterly.	1.060000 1.060900 1.061364	10 per cent.	Annually. Half Yearly. Quarterly.	1.100000 1.102500 1.103813

ANNUITIES CERTAIN AT COMPOUND INTEREST.

1. In the Tables we have the amount of $1 per annum, paid in advance, and improved at different rates of interest, for any number of years not exceeding 50. At the end of the first year the amount of $1 at 4 per cent interest is $1.04. At the beginning of the second year $1 is added to this amount, making $2.04 ; and the interest on this sum at the end of the second year increases it to $2.1216. This increased by $1 at the beginning

of the third year is $3.1216, and at the end of the year it amounts to $3.2465. By continuing this process the columns of annuities certain are formed.

2. These columns may also be formed from the compound interest columns, as illustrated by the following examples:

The amount of $1 for 4 years at 4 per cent compound interest is $1.1698585. Subtracting the amount of $1 for 1 year, we have $1.1698585 − 1.04 = .1298585, and, dividing by .04, the rate of interest, we have .1298585 ÷ .04 = $3.24646, the amount of $1 per annum for 3 years. The explanation of this operation is in the fact that .1298585 is the annuity of .04 for 3 years, improved at 4 per cent interest. And hence we have the proportion, .04 : 1.00 :: .1298585 : 3.24646.

3. To find the amount of $1 per annum for 49 years, take the amount of $1 at 4 per cent compound interest for 50 years, which is $7.1066833, then (7.1066833 − 1.04) ÷ .04 = 151.66708.

Hence, to find the annuity certain of $1 per annum for any number of years, we have the following rule: From the amount of $1 in the compound interest columns at the given rate per cent, and taken at the given number of years plus one, subtract the amount of $1 for one year at the given rate, and divide the remainder by the rate per cent.

4. When the annuity is payable at the end of the year, as in the old English tables, instead of at the beginning, the rule is as follows:

From the amount at compound interest in the tables, at the given rate per cent, and taken at the given number of years, subtract $1, and divide the remainder by the rate per cent, and the quotient is the amount of an annuity of $1 for that term.

Thus, in the last example, the amount of $1 for 50 years is 7.1068833; subtracting $1, we have 6.1068833 ÷ .04 = $152.66708, the amount of $1 per annum for 50 years, instead of 49 years, as in the previous rule.

In this example, deducting $1 from the amount, we have the annuity certain of .04 for 50 years at compound interest; therefore, .04 : $1 :: $6.1066833 : $152.66708.

5. In life insurance it is cften necessary to make such calculations as the following, in order to estimate the probable advantages of accepting a risk:

If an annual net premium on a life policy of $1,000 is $23.68, how long will it be necessary for the insured to live, in order that the company may realize the amount insured?

Dividing $1,000 by $23.68, we have $42.2297; therefore, it would require the same time which it takes $1 per annum at 7 per cent compound interest to amount to this sum. By Table V, we find that $1 per annum, for 19 years, at 7 per cent, amounts to $39.9955, and for 20 years the amount is $43.8652. It is evident, then, that the time required is between 19 and 20 years. The exact date is thus found. At the beginning of the twentieth year, as the premiums are payable in advance, the amount of $1 per annum would be $39.9955+$1=$40.9955. The difference between this and $42.2297 is $1.2342, which is the amount of interest required to be earned after the beginning of the twentieth year. The total amount of interest earned during the twentieth year is $43.8652−$40.9955=$2.8697. Therefore, we have the proportion, if it requires 1 year for $40.9955 to earn $2.8697 interest, how long does it require to earn $1.2342, or $2.8697 : $1.2342 :: 365 : 157 days. That is, it would require 19 years and 157 days, or twenty premiums and the interest thereon for 157 days after the twentieth premium is paid.

PRESENT VALUES AND DISCOUNT.

A familiarity with the present values of sums payable, is quite as important as that of interest.

1. The present value of $1 for one year at 6 per cent discount, is the sum which, placed at 6 per cent interest for 1 year, will amount to $1. This quantity is found by the following proportion: if $1 will amount to $1.06 in 1 year, what sum is required to amount to $1? or $1.06 : $1 :: $1 : .943396, or $\frac{\$1.00}{\$1.06}$=.943396. The present value of $1 for 2 years is $\frac{\$1.00}{\$1.06 \times \$1.06}$=$\frac{\$1.00}{\$1.236}$= .889996; and for 3 years $\frac{\$1.00}{\$1.06 \times \$1.06 \times \$1.06}$=$\frac{\$1.00}{\$1.191016}$=.839619. In this manner the columns of present values are found.

2. To find *the number of years* which the payment of a sum of money must be deferred in order that it may have a certain present value, divide the given present value by the amount and the result is the present value of $1 for the time required. By comparing this result with the present values of $1 during a series

of years and at the given rate per cent, as given in the tables, the time required can be obtained.

Let it be required to find the number of years which the payment of $1 must be deferred to have a present value of .50 at 6 per cent discount. By referring to Table IV, we find in the 6 per cent column that the present value of $1 for 11 years is .526788, and at 12 years it is .496969; the difference between these two quantities is .029819. The difference between .526788 and .50 is .026788. To find the number of days required in addition to the 11 years, we have the following proportion: if it requires one year for the present value of $1 at the end of 11 years to diminish .029819, how long will it require to diminish .026788? and the ratios are stated as follows: .029819 : .026788 :: 365 : 328 days. Hence the time required, 11 years and 328 days.

3. To find *the rate per cent* of discount required for a given sum to have a certain present value in a given number of years, we find the present value of $1 according to the terms given, and compare this result with the present values of $1 in the tables at the required number of years.

Thus to find the rate per cent required for $1, payable 14 years hence, to have a present value of .50, we divide .50 by $1, and we have the result .50, then, by inspecting the columns of present values along the lines representing the values of $1, payable 14 years hence, we find, under the 5 per cent column, that the present value of $1 is .505068, which indicates that 5 per cent is very nearly the rate required.

4. The present value of $1 per annum, at the end of each year for any number of years, is the present value of $1 for one year, plus the present value of $1 for two years, plus the present value of $1 for three years, and so on. By referring to Table II, we find the present value of $1, at $4\frac{1}{2}$ per cent for one year, is .956938, and for two years, is .915730. Adding these together, we have 1.872668= the present value of $1 per annum for two years. The present value of $1, per annum, for three years, is .956938+.915730+.876297=$2.748965.

5. The present value of $1, per annum, for any number of years, at any given rate per cent, may be easily found by the following rule: Subtract the present value of $1, as found in the **tables,** for the given time and rate, from unity, or $1,

and divide this difference by the given rate for $1, the result will be the required present value of $1, per annum. Thus, in the last example we have $1−.876297=.123703÷.045=$2.74896.

The quantity .123703 becomes the present value of 4 1-2 cents, payable annually for three years, and hence .123703+.045= 2.74896, or .045 : 123703 :: 1.00 : 2.74896.

6. The present value of a perpetual annuity is the sum which, paid now and invested at a given rate per cent, will produce the annuity. To find the present value of the perpetual annuity of $1 at 5 per cent interest, we have the following proportion: .05 : .1 :: 1 : 20, or $1 divided by the given rate per cent, will give the present value of the perpetual annuity of $1, and from this the present value of any other sum may be found.

7. In making calculations by means of these tables, care should be taken to examine whether the annuity is payable at the beginning or at the end of the year. In the above example the present value of $1 payable at the beginning of the first year is $1 ; for the second year $1.9569; for the third year $2.8727 ; for the fourth year $3.7490, and so on. This caution becomes the more necessary as all life insurance premiums are regarded as being paid at the beginning of each year, while annuities are usually payable at the end.

8. The present value of the premium $23.68 for twenty years, at seven per cent discount, the first premium being paid in advance, is computed thus : ($10.335595+1) × $23.68=$268.427.

DEFERRED ANNUITIES.

1. The present value of a deferred annuity certain of $1, payable at the end of the year, deferred for four years, and then to continue six years, at 6 per cent discount, is found by taking the difference between the present value of $1 for the whole annuity term and the present value of $1 for the deferred term ; thus, by Table IV, 7.360087−3.465106=$3.894981.

2. To find the present value of an annuity certain to continue a given number of years, after a given term, multiply the difference of the present value of $1 per annum for the whole term, and of $1 per annum for the deferred term by the given annuity ; the result will be the required value.

TABLE No. I.

MONETARY TABLES, 4 PER CENT.

N Years.	Amount of $1 in N years.	Present Value of $1 due N years hence.	Amount of $1 per annum in N years.	Present Value of $1 per annum for N years.	Sinking fund that will amount to $1 in N years.
1	1.0400	.961538	1.0400	.9615	.96154
2	1.0816	.924556	2.1216	1.8861	.47134
3	1.1249	.888996	3.2465	2.7751	.30802
4	1.1699	.854804	4.4163	3.6299	.22643
5	1.2167	.821927	5.6330	4.4518	.17753
6	1.2653	.790315	6.8983	5.2421	.14496
7	1.3159	.759918	8.2142	6.0021	.12174
8	1.3686	.730690	9.5828	6.7327	.10435
9	1.4233	.702587	11.0061	7.4353	.09086
10	1.4802	.675564	12.4864	8.1109	.08009
11	1.5395	.649581	14.0258	8.7605	.07130
12	1.6010	.624597	15.6268	9.3851	.06399
13	1.6651	.600574	17.2919	9.9856	.05783
14	1.7317	.577475	19.0236	10.5631	.05257
15	1.8009	.555265	20.8245	11.1184	.04802
16	1.8730	.533908	22.6975	11.6523	.04406
17	1.9479	.513373	24.6454	12.1657	.04058
18	2.0258	.493628	26.6712	12.6593	.03750
19	2.1068	.474642	28.7781	13.1339	.03475
20	2.1911	.456387	30.9692	13.5903	.03229
21	2.2788	.438834	33.2480	14.0292	.03008
22	2.3699	.421955	35.6179	14.4511	.02808
23	2.4647	.405726	38.0826	14.8568	.02626
24	2.5633	.390121	40.6459	15.2470	.02460
25	2.6658	.375117	43.3117	15.6221	.02309
26	2.7725	.360689	46.0842	15.9828	.02170
27	2.8834	.346817	48.9676	16.3296	.02042
28	2.9987	.333477	51.9663	16.6631	.01924
29	3.1187	.320651	55.0849	16.9837	.01816
30	3.2434	.308319	58.3283	17.2920	.01714
31	3.3731	.296460	61.7015	17.5885	.01621
32	3.5081	.285058	65.2095	17.8736	.01534
33	3.6484	.274094	68.6579	18.1476	.01452
34	3.7943	.263552	72.6522	18.4112	.01376
35	3.9461	.253415	76.5983	18.6646	.01306
36	4.1039	.243669	80.7022	18.9083	.01239
37	4.2681	.234297	84.9703	19.1426	.01177
38	4.4388	.225285	89.4091	19.3679	.01119
39	4.6164	.216621	94.0255	19.5845	.01064
40	4.8010	.208289	98.8265	19.7928	.01012
41	4.9931	.200278	103.8196	19.9931	.00963
42	5.1928	.192575	109.0124	20.1856	.00917
43	5.4005	.185168	114.4129	20.3708	.00874
44	5.6165	.178046	120.0294	20.5488	.00833
45	5.8412	.171198	125.8706	20.7200	.00794
46	6.0748	.164614	131.9454	20.8847	.00758
47	6.3178	.158283	138.2632	21.0429	.00723
48	6.5705	.152195	144.8337	21.1951	.00691
49	6.8333	.146341	151.6671	21.3415	.00659
50	7.1067	.140713	158.7738	21.4822	.00630

TABLE No. II.

MONETARY TABLES, 4½ PER CENT.

N Years.	Amount of $1 in N years.	Present Value of $1 due N years hence.	Amount of $1 per annum in N years.	Present Value of $1 per annum for N years.	Sinking fund that will amount to $1 in N years.
1	1.0450	.956938	1.0450	0.9569	.95695
2	1.0920	.915730	2.1370	1.8727	.46795
3	1.1412	.876297	3.2782	2.7490	.30505
4	1.1925	.838561	4.4707	3.5875	.22368
5	1.2462	.802451	5.7169	4.3900	.17494
6	1.3023	.767896	7.0192	5.1579	.14247
7	1.3609	.734828	8.3800	5.8927	.11933
8	1.4221	.703185	9.8021	6.5959	.10202
9	1.4861	.672904	11.2882	7.2688	.08859
10	1.5530	.643928	12.8412	7.9127	.07788
11	1.6229	.616199	14.4640	8.5289	.06914
12	1.6959	.589664	16.1599	9.1186	.06188
13	1.7722	.564272	17.9321	9.6829	.05577
14	1.8519	.539973	19.7841	10.2228	.05055
15	1.9353	.516720	21.7193	10.7395	.04604
16	2.0224	.494469	23.7417	11.2340	.04212
17	2.1134	.473176	25.8551	11.7072	.03868
18	2.2085	.452800	28.0636	12.1600	.03563
19	2.3079	.433302	30.3714	12.5933	.03293
20	2.4117	.414643	32.7831	13.0079	.03050
21	2.5202	.396787	35.3034	13.4047	.02833
22	2.6337	.379701	37.9370	13.7844	.02636
23	2.7522	.363350	40.6892	14.1478	.02458
24	2.8760	.347703	43.5652	14.4955	.02295
25	3.0054	.332731	46.5706	14.8282	.02147
26	3.1407	.318402	49.7113	15.1466	.02012
27	3.2820	.304691	52.9933	15.4513	.01887
28	3.4297	.291571	56.4230	15.7429	.01772
29	3.5840	.279015	60.0071	16.0219	.01667
30	3.7453	.267000	63.7524	16.2889	.01569
31	3.9139	.255502	67.6662	16.5444	.01478
32	4.0900	.244500	71.7562	16.7889	.01394
33	4.2740	.233971	76.0303	17.0229	.01316
34	4.4664	.223896	80.4966	17.2468	.01242
35	4.6673	.214254	85.1640	17.4610	.01174
36	4.8774	.205028	90.0413	17.6660	.01111
37	5.0969	.196199	95.1382	17.8622	.01051
38	5.3262	.187750	100.4644	18.0500	.00996
39	5.5659	.179665	106.0303	18.2297	.00943
40	5.8164	.171929	111.8467	18.4016	.00894
41	6.0781	.164525	117.9248	18.5661	.00848
42	6.3516	.157440	124.2764	18.7235	.00804
43	6.6374	.150661	130.9138	18.8742	.00764
44	6.9361	.144173	137.8500	19.0184	.00725
45	7.2482	.137964	145.0982	19.1563	.00689
46	7.5744	.132023	152.6726	19.2884	.00655
47	7.9153	.126338	160.5879	19.4147	.00623
48	8.2715	.120898	168.8594	19.5356	.00592
49	8.6437	.115692	177.5030	19.6513	.00563
50	9.0326	.110710	186.5357	19.7620	.00536

TABLE No. III.

MONETARY TABLES, 5 PER CENT.

N Years.	Amount of $1 in N years.	Present Value of $1 due N years hence.	Amount of $1 per annum in N years.	Present Value of $1 per annum for N years.	Sinking fund that will amount to $1 in N years.
1	1.0500	.952381	1.0500	.9524	.95238
2	1.1025	.907029	2.1525	1.8594	.46458
3	1.1576	.863838	3.3101	2.7232	.30211
4	1.2155	.822702	4.5256	3.5460	.22097
5	1.2763	.783526	5.8019	4.3295	.17236
6	1.3401	.746215	7.1420	5.0757	.14002
7	1.4071	.710681	8.5491	5.7864	.11697
8	1.4775	.676839	10.0266	6.4632	.09973
9	1.5513	.644609	11.5779	7.1078	.08637
10	1.6289	.613913	13.2068	7.7217	.07572
11	1.7103	.584679	14.9171	8.3064	.06704
12	1.7959	.556837	16.7130	8.8633	.05983
13	1.8856	.530321	18.5986	9.3936	.05377
14	1.9799	.505068	20.5786	9.8986	.04859
15	2.0789	.481017	22.6575	10.3797	.04414
16	2.1829	.458112	24.8404	10.8378	.04026
17	2.2920	.436297	27.1324	11.2741	.03686
18	2.4066	.415521	29.5390	11.6896	.03385
19	2.5270	.395734	32.0660	12.0853	.03119
20	2.6533	.376889	34.7193	12.4622	.02880
21	2.7860	.358942	37.5052	12.8212	.02666
22	2.9253	.341850	40.4305	13.1630	.02473
23	3.0715	.325571	43.5020	13.4886	.02299
24	3.2251	.310068	46.7271	13.7986	.02140
25	3.3864	.295303	50.1135	14.0939	.01996
26	3.5557	.281241	53.6691	14.3752	.01863
27	3.7335	.267848	57.4026	14.6430	.01742
28	3.9201	.255094	61.3227	14.8981	.01631
29	4.1161	.242946	65.4388	15.1411	.01528
30	4.3219	.231377	69.7608	15.3725	.01434
31	4.5380	.220359	74.2988	15.5928	.01346
32	4.7649	.209866	79.0638	15.8027	.01265
33	5.0032	.199873	84.0670	16.0025	.01190
34	5.2533	.190355	89.3203	16.1929	.01120
35	5.5160	.181290	94.8363	16.3742	.01055
36	5.7918	.172657	100.6281	16.5469	.00994
37	6.0814	.164436	106.7095	16.7113	.00937
38	6.3855	.156605	113.0950	16.8679	.00884
39	6.7048	.149148	119.7998	17.0170	.00835
40	7.0400	.142046	126.8398	17.1591	.00788
41	7.3920	.135282	134.2318	17.2944	.00745
42	7.7616	.128840	141.9933	17.4232	.00704
43	8.1497	.122704	150.1430	17.5459	.00666
44	8.5572	.116861	158.7002	17.6628	.00630
45	8.9850	.111297	167.6852	17.7741	.00597
46	9.4343	.105997	177.1194	17.8801	.00565
47	9.9060	.100949	187.0254	17.9801	.00535
48	10.4013	.096142	197.4267	18.0772	.00506
49	10.9213	.091564	208.3480	18.1687	.00480
50	11.4674	.087204	219.8154	18.2559	.00455

TABLE No. IV.

MONETARY TABLES, 6 PER CENT.

N Years.	Amount of $1 in N years.	Present value of $1 due N years hence.	Amount of $1 per annum in N years.	Present Value of $1, per annum for N years.	Sinking fund that will amount to $1 in N years.
1	1.0600	.943396	1.0600	0.9434	.94340
2	1.1236	.889996	2.1836	1.8334	.45796
3	1.1910	.839619	3.3746	2.6730	.29633
4	1.2625	.792094	4.6371	3.4651	.21565
5	1.3382	.747258	5.9753	4.2124	.16735
6	1.4185	.704961	7.3938	4.9173	.13525
7	1.5036	.665057	8.8975	5.5824	.11239
8	1.5938	.627412	10.4913	6.2098	.09532
9	1.6895	.591898	12.1808	6.8017	.08210
10	1.7908	.558395	13.9716	7.3601	.07157
11	1.8983	.526788	15.8699	7.8869	.06301
12	2.0122	.496969	17.8821	8.3838	.05592
13	2.1329	.468839	20.0151	8.8527	.04996
14	2.2609	.442301	22.2760	9.2950	.04489
15	2.3966	.417265	24.6725	9.7122	.04053
16	2.5404	.393646	27.2129	10.1059	.03675
17	2.6928	.371364	29.9057	10.4773	.03344
18	2.8543	.350344	32.7600	10.8276	.03053
19	3.0256	.330513	35.7856	11.1501	.02794
20	3.2071	.311805	38.9927	11.4699	.02565
21	3.3996	.294155	42.3923	11.7641	.02359
22	3.6035	.277505	45.9958	12.0416	.02174
23	3.8197	.261797	49.8156	12.3034	.02007
24	4.0489	.246979	53.8645	12.5504	.01857
25	4.2919	.232999	58.1564	12.7834	.01720
26	4.5494	.219810	62.7058	13.0032	.01595
27	4.8223	.207368	67.5281	13.2105	.01481
28	5.1117	.195630	72.6398	13.4062	.01377
29	5.4184	.184557	78.0582	13.5907	.01281
30	5.7435	.174110	83.8017	13.7648	.01193
31	6.0881	.164255	89.8898	13.9291	.01112
32	6.4534	.154957	96.3432	14.0840	.01038
33	6.8406	.146186	103.1838	14.2302	.00969
34	7.2510	.137912	110.4348	14.3681	.00905
35	7.6861	.130105	118.1209	14.4982	.00847
36	8.1473	.122741	126.2681	14.6210	.00792
37	8.6361	.115793	134.9042	14.7368	.00741
38	9.1543	.109239	144.0585	14.8460	.00694
39	9.7035	.103056	153.7620	14.9491	.00651
40	10.2857	.097222	164.0477	15.0463	.00610
41	10.9029	.091719	174.9505	15.1380	.00572
42	11.5570	.086527	186.5076	15.2245	.00536
43	12.2505	.081630	198.7580	15.3062	.00503
44	12.9855	.077009	211.7435	15.3832	.00472
45	13.7646	.072650	225.5081	15.4558	.00443
46	14.5905	.068538	240.0986	15.5244	.00417
47	15.4659	.064658	255.5645	15.5890	.00392
48	16.3939	.060998	271.9584	15.6500	.00368
49	17.3775	.057546	289.3359	15.7076	.00346
50	18.4202	.054288	307.7561	15.7619	.00325

TABLE No. V.

Monetary Tables, 7 per cent.

N Years.	Amount of $1 in N years.	Present Value of $1 due N years hence.	Amount of $1 per annum in N years.	Present Value of $1 per annum for N years.	Sinking fund that will amount to $1 in N years.
1	1.0700	.934579	1.0700	.9346	.93458
2	1.1449	.873439	2.2149	1.8080	.45149
3	1.2250	.816298	3.4399	2.6243	.29071
4	1.3108	.762895	4.7507	3.3872	.21050
5	1.4026	.712986	6.1533	4.1002	.16251
6	1.5007	.666342	7.6540	4.7665	.13065
7	1.6058	.622750	9.2598	5.3893	.10799
8	1.7182	.582009	10.9780	5.9713	.09109
9	1.8385	.543934	12.8164	6.5152	.07803
10	1.9672	.508349	14.7836	7.0236	.06764
11	2.1049	.475093	16.8885	7.4987	.05921
12	2.2522	.444012	19.1406	7.9427	.05224
13	2.4098	.414964	21.5505	8.3577	.04640
14	2.5785	.387817	24.1290	8.7455	.04144
15	2.7590	.362446	26.8881	9.1079	.03719
16	2.9522	.338735	29.8402	9.4466	.03351
17	3.1588	.316574	32.9990	9.7632	.03030
18	3.3799	.295864	36.3790	10.0591	.02749
19	3.6165	.276508	39.9955	10.3356	.02500
20	3.8697	.258419	43.8652	10.5940	.02280
21	4.1406	.241513	48.0057	10.8355	.02083
22	4.4304	.225713	52.4361	11.0612	.01907
23	4.7405	.210947	57.1767	11.2722	.01749
24	5.0724	.197147	62.2490	11.4693	.01606
25	5.4274	.184249	67.6765	11.6536	.01478
26	5.8074	.172195	73.4838	11.8258	.01361
27	6.2139	.160930	79.6977	11.9867	.01255
28	6.6488	.150402	86.3465	12.1371	.01158
29	7.1143	.140563	93.4608	12.2777	.01070
30	7.6123	.131367	101.0730	12.4090	.00989
31	8.1451	.122773	109.2182	12.5318	.00915
32	8.7153	.114741	117.9334	12.6466	.00848
33	9.3253	.107235	127.2588	12.7538	.00786
34	9.9781	.100219	137.2369	12.8540	.00729
35	10.6766	.093663	147.9135	12.9477	.00676
36	11.4239	.087535	159.3374	13.0352	.00628
37	12.2236	.081809	171.5610	13.1170	.00583
38	13.0793	.076457	184.6403	13.1935	.00542
39	13.9948	.071455	198.6351	13.2649	.00503
40	14.9745	.066780	213.6096	13.3317	.00468
41	16.0227	.062412	229.6322	13.3941	.00435
42	17.1443	.058329	246.7765	13.4524	.00405
43	18.3444	.054513	265.1209	13.5070	.00377
44	19.6285	.050946	284.7493	13.5579	.00351
45	21.0025	.047613	305.7518	13.6055	.00327
46	22.4726	.044499	328.2244	13.6500	.00305
47	24.0457	.041587	352.2701	13.6916	.00284
48	25.7289	.038867	377.9990	13.7305	.00265
49	27.5299	.036324	405.5289	13.7668	.00247
50	29.4570	.033948	434.9860	13.8007	.00230

TABLE No. VI.

MONETARY TABLES, 8 PER CENT.

N Years.	Amount of $1 in N years.	Present Value of $1 due N years hence.	Amount of $1 per annum in N years.	Present Value of $1 per annum for N years.	Sinking fund that will amount to $1 in N years.
1	1.0800	.925926	1.0800	.9259	.92593
2	1.1664	.857339	2.2464	1.7833	.44516
3	1.2597	.793832	3.5061	2.5771	.28522
4	1.3605	.735030	4.8666	3.3121	.20548
5	1.4693	.680583	6.3359	3.9927	.15783
6	1.5869	.630170	7.9228	4.6229	.12622
7	1.7138	.583490	9.6366	5.2064	.10377
8	1.8509	.540269	11.4876	5.7466	.08705
9	1.9990	.500249	13.4866	6.2469	.07414
10	2.1589	.463193	15.6455	6.7101	.06392
11	2.3316	.428883	17.9771	7.1390	.05563
12	2.5182	.397114	20.4953	7.5361	.04879
13	2.7196	.367698	23.2149	7.9038	.04308
14	2.9372	.340461	26.1521	8.2442	.03824
15	3.1722	.315242	29.3243	8.5595	.03410
16	3.4259	.291890	32.7502	8.8514	.03053
17	3.7000	.270269	36.4502	9.1216	.02744
18	3.9960	.250249	40.4463	9.3719	.02472
19	4.3157	.231712	44.7620	9.6036	.02234
20	4.6610	.214548	49.4229	0.8181	.02023
21	5.0338	.198656	54.4568	10.0168	.01836
22	5.4365	.183941	59.8933	10.2007	.01670
23	5.8715	.170315	65.7648	10.3711	.01521
24	6.3412	.157699	72.1059	10.5288	.01387
25	6.8485	.146018	78.9544	10.6748	.01267
26	7.3964	.135202	86.3508	10.8100	.01158
27	7.9881	.125187	94.3388	10.9352	.01060
28	8.6271	.115914	102.9659	11.0511	.00971
29	9.3173	.107328	112.2832	11.1584	.00891
30	10.0627	.099377	122.3459	11.2578	.00817
31	10.8677	.092016	133.2135	11.3498	.00751
32	11.7371	.085200	144.9506	11.4350	.00690
33	12.6760	.078889	157.6267	11.5139	.00634
34	13.6901	.073045	171.3168	11.5869	.00584
35	14.7853	.067635	186.1021	11.6546	.00537
36	15.9682	.062625	202.0703	11.7172	.00495
37	17.2456	.057986	219.3159	11.7752	.00456
38	18.6253	.053690	237.9412	11.8289	.00421
39	20.1153	.049713	258.0565	11.8786	.00387
40	21.7245	.046031	279.7810	11.9246	.00357
41	23.4625	.042621	303.2435	11.9672	.00330
42	25.3395	.039464	328.5830	12.0067	.00304
43	27.3666	.036541	355.9496	12.0432	.00281
44	29.5560	.033834	385.5056	12.0771	.00259
45	31.9204	.031328	417.4261	12.1084	.00240
46	34.4741	.029007	451.9002	12.1374	.00221
47	37.2320	.026859	489.1322	12.1643	.00204
48	40.2106	.024869	529.3427	12.1891	.00189
49	43.4274	.023027	572.7702	12.2122	.00175
50	46.9016	.021321	619.6718	12.2335	.00161

TABLE No. VII.

MONETARY TABLES, 9 PER CENT.

N Years.	Amount of $1 in N years.	Present Value of $1 due N years hence.	Amount of $1 per annum in N years.	Present Value of $1 per annum for N years.	Sinking fund that will amount to $1 in N years.
1	1.0900	.917431	1.0900	0.9174	.91743
2	1.1881	.841680	2.2781	1.7591	.43896
3	1.2950	.772184	3.5731	2.5313	.27987
4	1.4116	.708425	4.9847	3.2397	.20061
5	1.5386	.649931	6.5233	3.8897	.15330
6	1.6771	.596267	8.2004	4.4859	.12195
7	1.8280	.547034	10.0285	5.0330	.09972
8	1.9926	.501866	12.0210	5.5348	.08319
9	2.1719	.460428	14.1929	5.9952	.07046
10	2.3674	.422410	16.5603	6.4177	.06039
11	2.5804	.387533	19.1407	6.8052	.05225
12	2.8127	.355535	21.9534	7.1607	.04555
13	3.0658	.326179	25.0192	7.4869	.03997
14	3.3417	.299247	28.3609	7.7861	.03526
15	3.6425	.274532	32.0034	8.0607	.03125
16	3.9703	.251870	35.9737	8.3125	.02780
17	4.3276	.231073	40.3013	8.5436	.02481
18	4.7171	.211993	45.0185	8.7556	.02221
19	5.1417	.194489	50.1601	8.9501	.01994
20	5.6044	.178431	55.7645	9.1285	.01793
21	6.1088	.163697	61.8733	9.2922	.01616
22	6.6586	.150182	68.5319	9.4424	.01459
23	7.2579	.137781	75.7898	9.5802	.01319
24	7.9111	.126405	83.7009	9.7066	.01195
25	8.6231	.115967	92.3240	9.8226	.01083
26	9.3992	.106392	101.7231	9.9290	.00983
27	10.2451	.097608	111.0866	10.0266	.00893
28	11.1671	.089548	123.1354	10.1161	.00812
29	12.1722	.082155	135.3075	10.1983	.00739
30	13.2677	.075371	148.5752	10.2736	.00673
31	14.4618	.069148	163.0370	10.3428	.00613
32	15.7633	.063438	178.8003	10.4062	.00559
33	17.1820	.058200	195.9823	10.4644	.00510
34	18.7284	.053395	214.7108	10.5178	.00466
35	20.4140	.048986	235.1247	10.5668	.00425
36	22.2512	.044941	257.3759	10.6117	.00389
37	24.2538	.041230	281.6298	10.6530	.00355
38	26.4367	.037826	308.0665	10.6908	.00325
39	28.8160	.034703	336.8824	10.7255	.00297
40	31.4094	.031838	368.2919	10.7573	.00272
41	34.2363	.029209	402.5281	10.7866	.00248
42	37.3175	.026797	439.8457	10.8134	.00227
43	40.6761	.024584	480.5218	10.8379	.00208
44	44.3370	.022554	524.8587	10.8605	.00191
45	48.3273	.020692	573.1860	10.8812	.00174
46	52.6767	.018983	625.8628	10.9002	.00160
47	57.4176	.017416	683.2804	10.9176	.00146
48	62.5852	.015978	745.8656	10.9336	.00134
49	68.2179	.014659	814.0836	10.9482	.00123
50	74.3575	.013448	888.4411	10.9617	.00113

TABLE No. VIII.

MONETARY TABLES, 10 PER CENT.

N Years.	Amount of $1 in N years.	Present Value of $1 due N years hence.	Amount of $1 per annum in N years.	Present Value of $1 per annum for N years.	Sinking fund that will amount to $1 in N years.
1	1.1000	.909091	1.1000	0.9091	.90909
2	1.2100	.826446	2.3100	1.7355	.43290
3	1.3310	.751315	3.6410	2.6849	.27465
4	1.4641	.683013	5.1051	3.1699	.19588
5	1.6105	.620921	6.7156	3.7908	.14891
6	1.7716	.564474	8.4872	4.3543	.11783
7	1.9487	.513158	10.4359	4.8684	.09582
8	2.1436	.466508	12.5795	5.3349	.07949
9	2.3579	.424098	14.9374	5.7590	.06695
10	2.5937	.385544	17.5312	6.1446	.05691
11	2.8531	.350494	20.3843	6.4951	.04906
12	3.1384	.318631	23.5227	6.8137	.04251
13	3.4523	.289664	26.9750	7.1034	.03707
14	3.7975	.263331	30.7725	7.3677	.03250
15	4.1772	.239392	34.9497	7.6061	.02861
16	4.5950	.217629	39.5447	7.8237	.02529
17	5.0545	.197845	44.5992	8.0216	.02242
18	5.5599	.179859	50.1591	8.2014	.01994
19	6.1159	.163508	56.2750	8.3649	.01777
20	6.7275	.148644	63.0025	8.5136	.01587
21	7.4002	.135130	70.4027	8.6487	.01420
22	8.1403	.122846	78.5430	8.7715	.01273
23	8.9543	.111678	87.4973	8.8832	.01143
24	9.8497	.101526	97.3471	8.9847	.01027
25	10.8347	.092296	108.1818	9.0770	.00924
26	11.9182	.083905	120.0999	9.1609	.00833
27	13.1100	.076278	133.2099	9.2372	.00751
28	14.4210	.069343	147.6309	9.3066	.00677
29	15.8631	.063039	163.4940	9.3696	.00612
30	17.4494	.057309	180.9434	9.4269	.00553
31	19.1943	.052099	200.1378	9.4790	.00500
32	21.1138	.047362	221.2515	9.5264	.00452
33	23.2252	.043057	244.4767	9.5694	.00409
34	25.5477	.039143	270.0244	9.6086	.00370
35	28.1024	.035584	298.1268	9.6442	.00335
36	30.9127	.032349	329.0395	9.6765	.00304
37	34.0039	.029408	363.0434	9.7059	.00275
38	37.4043	.026735	400.4478	9.7327	.00250
39	41.1448	.024360	441.5926	9.7570	.00226
40	45.2593	.022095	486.8518	9.7791	.00205
41	49.7852	.020086	536.6370	9.7991	.00186
42	54.7637	.018260	591.4007	9.8174	.00169
43	60.2401	.016600	651.6408	9.8340	.00153
44	66.2641	.015091	717.9048	9.8491	.00139
45	72.8905	.013719	790.7953	9.8628	.00126
46	80.1795	.012472	870.9749	9.8753	.00115
47	88.1975	.011338	959.1723	9.8866	.00104
48	97.0172	.010307	1056.1896	9.8969	.00095
49	106.7190	.009370	1162.9085	9.9063	.00086
50	117.3909	.008519	1280.2994	9.9148	.00078

LIFE CONTINGENCIES.

The first fundamental basis of all life insurance calculations is the law of mortality, or inversely the duration of human life. The age which any individual will attain is always a matter of great uncertainty, as death in a thousand different ways is liable to take away human life; and yet there is a certain uniform death rate when applied to a large number of people of any given age which would be truly astonishing, were it not one of the recognized laws which govern human affairs. The uniformity of these occurrences, which many regard as entirely fortuitous, is one of the most interesting discoveries of modern science. The statistics of our fire insurance companies show that the ratios of losses to premium receipts occur from year to year with surprising uniformity; the aggregate number of suicides and murders annually occurring from year to year in a civilized country vary but very little; the prevailing direction of the winds and the fall of rain during the corresponding seasons of each year display almost uniform results in their yearly aggregates. It is on the same principle, by collecting the statistics of the deaths of a large number of persons, that the different tables of mortality have been formed.

According to the American table of mortality, which is adopted by the state of New York, and several other states, as the official standard for making the valuations of the Insurance Department, out of a class of 100,000 persons living at the age of 10 years, 92,637 will be living at 20, 85,441 at 30, 78,106 at 40 years of age, and so on; or the percentage of mortality in a class of 100,000 at the age 20 is 780; at 30, 843; at 40, 979.

This rate of mortality does not have a uniform increment; but if we represent the probability of dying from 10 to 95 years of age by a line, it will describe a curve very nearly the same as a cycloid.

The various tables of mortality, constructed in different countries and periods, show a great degree of uniformity in the probability of life at the same age ; and yet it is an interesting and encouraging fact, that each successive century is slowly lengthening the average duration of human life. Improvements in civilization, more abundant supply of food, new discoveries in medicine, and a more general knowledge of the laws of physiology and hygiene, are having a favorable influence in lessening the rate of mortality.

TABLES OF MORTALITY.

The value of life insurance calculations depends in a great degree upon accurate and reliable tables of mortality, since it is this and the assumed rate of interest which determines the net premiums, the proper reserves, and, to some extent, the margin for expenses, and distribution of surplus to policyholders. Without a reliable and well adjusted table of mortality, conforming very closely to actual experience, it would be impossible for these terms to be correctly computed, or the policyholders to be equitably treated. It was not till tolerably correct tables were made that life insurance rose to the dignity of a science. Previous to this it was all conjecture. In its early history statistics of mortality were almost entirely neglected. In a few parishes of England there were registers of the living and the dying, but they were so imperfectly kept as to be almost wholly unreliable. And the best informed public men could not tell whether the population of the country was increasing or decreasing. The great truth, reserved for discovery in later times, that there are certain laws to which the average duration of human life conforms, was never thought of. It was for this reason that when life insurance companies were first organized in England the rates were the same for all ages, as the fees and dues for cooperative associations, burial clubs, workingmen's unions and friendly societies are at the present day. But a short period of observation revealed the fact, which is now regarded as self-evident, that the aged are much more likely to die than the young, and the necessity for a different guide to determine the probable length of human life became evident.

THE AMERICAN EXPERIENCE TABLE.

This table, first adopted by the state of New York, in the year 1868, as a basis for the valuation of policies, was constructed by

Mr. Sheppard Homans, from the experience of the Mutual Life Insurance Company, of New York, who also availed himself of other statistics, to ascertain the laws of mortality as applicable to healthy insured lives in this country. All the standard European tables were used in adjusting it. This table of mortality, with 4 1-2 per cent rate of interest, is now made the legal standard of valuation in several of the states.

In the illustrations and explanations given in this part of the work, the American Table of Mortality and 4 1-2 per cent interest will be used as a basis, unless some other table and rate are expressly named.

THE COMBINED EXPERIENCE, OR ACTUARIES' TABLE.

This table was prepared by a committee of eminent actuaries, on the data afforded by the combined experience of seventeen of the principal life insurance offices in England. It was deduced from 62,537 assurances, first published by Mr. Jenkin Jones, in 1843, and furnishes a very accurate graduation of assured lives. Some of the objections advanced against it are that certain lives, having been more than once assured, have appeared twice or oftener as elements of the calculation, and that the data for the older ages were insufficient. The mortality amongst assured females, taking all ages together, is greater than amongst assured males. A more careful comparison of the different classes insured reveals the fact that the average duration of male lives under 36 years of age is greater than that of females, and from 36 to 61 years of age the average duration of the lives of females is greater than that of males; but after the age of 61 the male lives have a greater expectation than female lives. The average duration of all the policies was a little less than 8 1-2 years.

RATE OF INTEREST.

The second principal element of all the calculations in life assurance is the rate of interest assumed by the companies to be realized on their assets. A contract of insurance made between the company and the policyholder is designed to exist as long as the policy can be continued in force, either during a term of years or the lifetime of the policyholder. In contracts extending over a long series of years, the continued and ultimate solvency of the company is of the highest importance, and the adoption of any erroneous principles of calculation, and increased from year to year at each renewal of the premiums, and moreover multiplied by thousands of policies in force, cannot fail to work out a disastrous result in time. Hence it is of the highest importance that the primary elements of mortality and of interest should be such as are perfectly safe to the insured. The company assumes that the adopted rate of mortality will be experienced in the future, and in each annual premium there is a certain part set aside or reserved to pay the claim of the policyholder when it becomes due ; and this reserve, according to the laws and assumptions of life insurance, accumulates at compound interest as long as the policy remains in force. The question now arises, what rate of interest must be assumed as the one which these reserves will earn during the years that intervene between the payment of the first premium and the final settlement of the claim? The opinions of Hon. Elizur Wright on this subject are worth quoting here :

"A very large part of the immense sums promised to be paid in the distant future is to be produced by the accumulation of interest, and the premium, being fixed at the outset and unalterable, it will make a life or death difference with the company whether six per cent interest is always to be received on investments, or the rate is to fall occasionally or permanently to four or three per cent. If the interest is to be more, the premium may be less, and if it is to be less, the premium *must* be more. The only safety is to assume a rate of interest so low that the profits on investments may always exceed it, and to divide at short intervals the surplus that may result from the excess."

"It is historically certain that all experiments of life insurance that have been tried long enough to test results, without reserving premium on an assumption of interest lower than the current interest on investments, have proved failures."—*Mass. Report*, 1865, *p.* 305.

The standard rate of interest adopted by the state of New York and several other states, is 4 1-2 per cent ; in Massachusetts, Illinois and some other states it is 4 per cent.

PROBABILITY OF LIFE.

The probability of life is the likelihood which a person has, according to the table of mortality, of living a certain number of years. The probability of death is the likelihood a person has of dying within a given period. As it is absolutely certain that a person will always be dead or alive, the probability of death is found by subtracting the probability of life from unity, and *vice versa.*

Example. Required, the probability that a person aged thirty will live to be fifty years old, American table.

The number living at the age 50 is 69,804.

The number living at the age 30 is 85,441.

Therefore $\frac{69,804}{85,441}$=.81698 the probability.

As there are 85,441 chances in all of the persons aged 30 attaining to fifty years, and as the probability is that only 69,804 will live, the contingency that each individual will live, is, .81698, and hence the contingency of his dying is, $1-.81698$=.18302, or $85,441-69,804$=15,637, and $\frac{15,637}{85,441}$=.18302.

These operations are sometimes useful in making estimates upon endowment policies, as to whether a person will live to complete his payments, and on term policies, whether the party will die during the period of insurance.

COMMUTATION COLUMNS.

The commutation columns are now universally used in the computation of premium rates, annuities and many other calculations. The four principal columns are denoted by the capital letters D, N, C, M. In increasing insurance S and R are used. The column D, usually written D_x, denotes the number of living at any age x, discounted by such a power of 1.045, or whatever rate of interest is assumed, as corresponds to the age x. For the sake of convenience and uniformity we use that power of $\frac{1}{1.045}$ which corresponds to the age of the insured. It would make no difference in the result if we took the first power of $\frac{1}{1.045}$ to discount the living at the age 10, and the second power for the age 11, &c., since the ratio between the different numbers in the column is not changed by taking a different exponent of discount. The first number in the column D against the age 10 is found by multiplying 100,000, the tabular number living at that age, by $\left(\frac{1}{1.045}\right)^{10}$ or .64392768, which gives D_{10} = 64392.768. The second number, or D_{11}, is found by multiplying 99,251 by

$\left(\frac{1}{1.045}\right)^{11}$ or .6162087, which gives 61158.341. In this manner all the remaining terms in column D are found. C denotes the number of dying at the age x, discounted by the $x+1$ power of $\frac{1}{1.045}$, for the reason that the deaths are computed as taking place at the end of the year, while the premiums are paid at the beginning. Thus, at the age 10, $C=749 \times \left(\frac{1}{1.045}\right)^{11}=749 \times .6162087=$ 461.5329, and at the age 11, $C=746 \times \left(\frac{1}{1.045}\right)^{12}=746 \times .58966385=$ 439.8892, and so on with the remainder of the column. The N column is found by taking the sums of the numbers in the D column beginning with the oldest age, as follows: D at the age $95=3 \times \left(\frac{1}{1.045}\right)^{95}=.045822$, and is the same as N at the same age, or $N95=.045822$. $N94=D95+D94=.045822+.335188=$ .381010. $N93=D95+D94+D93=N94+D93=381010+1.317687$ $=1.698697$. Continuing this process through all the ages in the mortality table, we have the N column complete. The M column is found by adding together the terms of the C column in the same manner as the N column. The S and R columns are found by adding together the numbers in the N and M column respectively, in the same manner as N and M were obtained from D and C.

EXPLANATION OF LIFE INSURANCE.

The table of mortality enables us to determine the ratio there is between the number living at a given age at the beginning of a year and the number dying during that year. At the age 30 there are 85.441 living, and during that year there are 720 deaths, and, therefore, the probability that a person aged 30 will die during that year is $\frac{720}{85,441}=.0084269$. If 1,000 persons aged 30 insure for $1 each for one year, the net premium required of each, without reckoning interest, will be one thousandth part of the total losses at the end of the year. As the total losses are 8.4269, the net premium required of each policyholder will be .0084269. But as the premiums paid at the beginning of the year are increased by 4 1-2 per cent interest, and the losses are reckoned to take place at the end of the year, this amount of premiums required must be discounted at 4 1-2 per cent, which reduces the total amount of premiums required to $8.0640, and the amount required to insure $1 for one year at the age above given is .0080640. At the age 31 the net premium for one year is .0081438, and at 32 it is .0082365.

The foregoing explanation relates entirely to temporary insurance from year to year, and, if carried on through life, the premium would have to be changed each successive year. In order to find the uniform annual premium required on a policy payable at death, and to simplify the explanation we will take an example in which the element of interest is omitted.

At the age 95, according to the American Experience Table of Mortality, there are three persons living, all of whom die during the year. Consequently, if each of these were insured to the amount of $1, there would be three claims of $1 each to pay during the year. At the age of 94 we have 21 persons living, 18 of whom die during the first year and 3 during the next, hence there are $21 + 3$ premiums paid, and only 21 claims to be met; and, therefore, the amount of each premium would be $\frac{21}{24} = .875$. At the age of 93 there are 79 living, and the first year there are 79 premiums paid, the second 21, and the third 3, making 103 premiums to 79 losses, and the annual premium to insure $1 is $\frac{79}{103} = .76699$.

From the above example it will be seen that the fundamental principle for finding the premium to insure $1 through life for any given age (without regarding interest) is as follows: Divide the number of living, or future deaths, at any given age, by the total number of premiums to be paid till the death of the last survivor.

It is clear from the above example that in life insurance some persons insured pay much more than the company returns, and others less. At the age 93 there are 79 living, of whom 58 pay .76699 each, and the company returns $1 for each loss. At the age 94 there are 18 claims of $1 each, for which 18 persons have paid $1.53398 each in two annual premiums. At the age 95 there are 3 losses of $1 each, on which 3 persons insured have each paid premiums amounting to $2.30097.

In computing the net annual premium at 4 1-2 per cent interest, the same general principles given above are applicable. In the foregoing example we have 3 persons living at the age 95. According to the mortality table there would be 3 premiums to be paid at the beginning of the year, and 3 claims of $1 each at the end of the year; and, therefore, the premium required to insure $1 for one year would be the present value of $1 for one year, or $\frac{1}{1.045} = .95694$.

At the age 94 there are 21 living, and the annual premium to be paid is found as follows:

Premiums at the beginning of the first year, - - - -	21
Premiums at the beginning of the second year discounted=	
3 × .95694= - - - - - - - - -	2.87082
Total premiums discounted, - - - - - -	23.87082

The next step is to find the present value of the future losses.

Losses of the first year, present value, 18 × .95694= - -	17.22492
Losses second year, present value, 3 × .91573= - - -	2.74719
Total losses, present value, - - - - -	$19.97211

Annual premium, age 94=19.97211+23.87082=.83667.

At the age 93 there are 79 living.

Premiums at the beginning of the first year, - - - -	79
Premiums second year, 21 × .95694= - - - - -	20.09574
Premiums third year, 3 × .91573= - - - - -	2.74719
Total number discounted premiums, - - - -	101.84293

Losses first year, present value, 58 × .95694= - - -	55.50252
Losses second year, present value. 18 × .91573= - - -	16.48314
Losses third year, present value, 3 × .87630= - - -	2.62890
Total losses, present value, - - - - -	$74.61456

Annual premium=$74.61456÷101.84293=.732643.

In each of the above examples the number of premiums to be paid and the number of losses to be met are discounted by a different power of $\frac{1}{1.045}$. It is easy to see that in computing premiums for the younger ages this would be an exceedingly difficult and tedious operation, were not some more expeditious method discovered. The commutation columns enable us to perform these operations with much greater facility.

Under the head of "Commutation Columns," page 36, we found that N is the sum of the numbers in the D column, or the discounted numbers of the living, and M is the sum of the C's or discounted numbers of the dying. In the last example we have the quantity 101.84293 equals the total number of discounted premiums, or number of living at the beginning of each year, and therefore it corresponds to N_{93}, discounted by a different power of $\frac{1}{1.045}$. The quantity 74.61456 is the discounted number of the losses or dying each year, and corresponds to M_{93}. Therefore, the annual premium $74.61456 \div 101.84293 = \frac{M_{93}}{N_{93}} = .73264$. And generally the annual premium for one dollar on a whole life policy is found by dividing the discounted number of future losses by the discounted number of future premiums to be paid. Hence the formula for finding the annual premium on a whole life policy is $\frac{M_x}{N_x}$.

By referring again to the commutation columns, we find that $\frac{M_{93}}{N_{93}} = \frac{1.2445367}{1.698696} = .73264$. In the same manner the net annual premium for the age 30 is $\frac{M_{30}}{N_{30}} = \frac{5990.8434}{390642.05} = .015336$; that is, at the age 30 the discounted number of future death claims, according to the table is 5990.8434, and the discounted number of future premiums is 390642.05, making the average value of each premium .015336 on an insurance of $1. Hence the rule for finding the net annual premiums by means of the commutation columns is: Divide the discounted sum of the dying at the given age in the M column by the discounted sum of the future premiums to be paid as found in the N column at that age, and multiply the quotient by the sum insured.

In the commutation columns N_{93} is the sum of the D's discounted by the ninety-third, fourth and fifth power of $\frac{1}{1.045}$, and the M column is the sum of the C's multiplied into one higher power of $\frac{1}{1.045}$. The reason why these figures give the same result, as when we take the living and dying in the mortality table and discount them by the first, second and third powers of $\frac{1}{1.045}$, is that it makes no difference in the result what power of $\frac{1}{1.045}$ we use to discount by, provided we take a power higher by one at each successive age. In the first case we have $\left[C93 \times \frac{1}{1.045} + C94 \times \right.$

$\left. \left(\frac{1}{1.045}\right)^2 + C95 \times \left(\frac{1}{1.045}\right)^3 \right] \div \left[D93 + D94 \times \frac{1}{1.045} + D95 \times \left(\frac{1}{1.045}\right)^2. \right]$ In

the latter we have $\left[C93 \times \left(\frac{1}{1.045}\right)^{94} + C94 \times \left(\frac{1}{1.045}\right)^{95} + C95 \times \left(\frac{1}{1.045}\right)^{96} \right]$

$\div \left[D93 \times \left(\frac{1}{1.045}\right)^{93} + D94 \times \left(\frac{1}{1.045}\right)^{94} + D95 \times \left(\frac{1}{1.045}\right)^{95} \right] = \left(\frac{1}{1.045}\right)^{93} \times$

$\left[C93 \times \frac{1}{1.045} + C94 \times \left(\frac{1}{1.045}\right)^2 + C95 \times \left(\frac{1}{1.045}\right)^3 \right] \div \left[D93 + D94 \times \frac{1}{1.045} + \right.$

$\left. D95 \times \left(\frac{1}{1.045}\right)^2 \right].$ Since both numerator and denominator are

multiplied by the same quantity $\left(\frac{1}{1.045}\right)^{93}$ the result is not changed.

The net single premium is the sum which, paid in advance, will insure a person during life. Were it not for the discount the net single premium would be equal to the sum insured at all ages. To find the net single premium we give the following illustration : At the age 93 we have 79 lives to insure in the sum of $1 each. The present value of all the future annual premiums which they would pay is (page 40) 74.61456, consequently the single premium which would be required of each is $\frac{74.61456}{79} =$

.94449. Here the numerator represents Mx, and we have seen that the denominator represents Dx; therefore the formula is

$\frac{Mx}{Dx}$. By the commutation columns we have $\frac{M93}{D93} = \frac{1.2445367}{1.317686} =$

.94449. At the age 30 $\frac{M30}{D30} = \frac{5990.8434}{22812.75} = .262609.$

The general rule given on page 40, for finding the net annual premium on a whole life policy, will also apply to find the annual premium on a policy with a limited number of annual payments. A person insures in the sum of $1 at the age 30 on the ten payment plan. The discounted number of future claims at this age is 5990.8434, and the discounted number of future premiums during ten years from the age 30 is N30−N40=390642.02−208640.18= 182001.87 ; therefore, if it requires 182001.84 premiums to meet 5990.8434 claims of $1 each, what will be the amount of each premium? It is evident that 5990.8434÷182001.84=.032916 the annual premium. Here, as before, we divide the discounted number of future claims by the discounted number of future premiums to be received during the years in which these premiums are to be paid.   The formula for limited premium life policies is $\frac{M_x}{N_x - N_{x+n}}$, in which $n=$ the number of years during which the annual payments are made.

In term or temporary insurance the premiums are payable during a limited number of years, and the amount insured is paid only in case the policyholder dies during this period.   The premium is the ratio which the discounted number of premiums in the column N, during the period of insurance, bears to the discounted number of claims in the column M for the same time, and multiplied by the sum insured ; and is found by dividing the difference between the number of deaths in the M column, at the time when the insurance commences, and the number when the policy ceases to be in force, by the difference between the corresponding N numbers at the same ages.   The term insurance for a policy of \$1, issued at the age 30, for ten years, is $(M_{30}-M_{40})+$ $(N_{30}-N_{40}) = (5990.8434-4444.1583)+(390642.05-208640.18)$ $=1546.6851+182001.87=.0084982$; that is, we assume that there will be 1546.6851 deaths to 182001.87 premiums paid, and therefore each premium required would be .0084982.

Simple endowment is a form of insurance in which the sum insured is payable only in case the policyholder is alive at the time when the policy expires by limitation.   The annual premium is the ratio between the number of payments made by the living during this term and the number living at the end of the term.   Thus the simple endowment on a person aged 30, payable at 40, if living, is the ratio between the tabular number of payments for ten years, commencing at 30, and the number of living at the age 40, or $D_{40}+(N_{30}-N_{40})=13428.663+(390642.02- 208640.18)=13428.663+182001.84=.073783$.   In this example, according to the commutation columns, the discounted number of premiums to be paid during ten years is 182001.84, and the discounted number of claims is 13428.663.

Simple endowments are very seldom issued, for the reason that the policyholder assumes all the risk, and the company is merely a depository of the premiums paid.   The death of the policyholder allows the company to retain all the premiums, and, as a general rule, the same amount of money can be realized from the premiums by the ordinary methods of investment.   " Children's endowments" usually come under this form of so-called insurance.

Endowment insurance consists of two parts, the simple endowment and term insurance. We have seen how these are found separately; it remains only to unite them in one expression. It will be noticed that in the last two examples the denominators are the same, $N_{30}-N_{40}$, and that the numerators are D_{40} and $M_{30}-M_{40}$; that is, the denominator comprises the discounted number of premiums to be paid during the ten years the policy is in force, and the numerator is D_{40}, the discounted number of survivors at the age 40, and $M_{30}-M_{40}$, the discounted number of losses during the period the policy is in force. Hence the whole number of claims divided by the whole number of premiums gives the annual premium for $1 of insurance. Carried out by figures, the operation is $(13428.66+5990.8434-4444.1583)\div$ $(390642.05-208640.18=14975.345\div182001.83=.082281.$

For an endowment insurance policy with a less number of premiums than the policy has years to run, we apply the same principle as before, dividing the discounted number of claims by the discounted number of premiums. In a ten year endowment policy, issued on a life aged 30, premiums payable in five years, we have the same numerator as before, $D_{40}+M_{30}-M_{40}$; and for a denominator, $N_{30}-N_{35}$, or $(13428.66+5990.8434-4444.1583)$ $\div(390642.05-287677.63)=.14544.$

The single premium in these endowments is found by dividing the numerator, as given above, by the discounted number of living in the D column at the age of insurance. Thus the net single premium on a ten annual endowment policy of $1, issued at the age 30, is $(D_{40}+M_{30}-M_{40})\div D_{30}=14975.3451\div22812.75=.656446.$

Since all premiums are simply the ratio of the discounted number of premiums payable during life or a given number of years to the discounted number of claims during the time the policy is in force, the general rule for finding the net premium for any kind of a policy is simply this: Divide the number of claims, as represented in the commutation columns during the time when the risk is in force, by the number of premiums during the period of their payment, and multiply the quotient by the sum insured.

LIFE ANNUITIES.

The duration of any life annuity depends upon the existence of the person called the nominee, and according to the American

Experience Table of Mortality this must cease in every case at or before attaining the age of 95.

Let us take 847 persons at the age 90, according to the American Experience Table, and compute the present value of an annuity of $1 per annum, payable at the end of the year, on the lives of each of them. At the end of the first year 385 will have died; hence the probability that each person will pay one dollar at the end of the year is $1-\frac{385}{847}=\frac{462}{847}$. The present value of $1 payable at the end of the year, at 4 1-2 per cent discount, is .956938; hence $\frac{462}{847}\times.956938=.52197$, the present value of the contingent payment of $1 from each of the members living at the end of the first year. The present value of $1 to be paid at the end of the second year by each of the 847 members is $\frac{216}{847}\times.915730=.23353$.

Third year, $\frac{79}{847}\times.876297=.08173$.

Fourth year, $\frac{21}{847}\times.838561=.2079$.

Fifth year, $\frac{3}{847}\times.802451=.00284$.

Placing these in a series, we have for the present value of $1 per annum, payable at the end of the year through life, on a person aged 90 years, $\left(\frac{462}{847}\times.956938\right)+\left(\frac{216}{847}\times.915730\right)+\left(\frac{79}{847}\times.876297\right)+\left(\frac{21}{847}\times.838561\right)+\left(\frac{3}{847}\times.802451\right)=.52197+.23353+.08173+.02079+.00284=.86086$.

If the first payment is to be made at the beginning of the first year, it is evident that the present value of the life annuity is $1+.86086=1.86086$, and the terms would read thus: $\frac{847}{847}+\frac{462}{847}\times\frac{1}{1.045}+\frac{216}{847}\times\left(\frac{1}{1.045}\right)^2$, etc. By inspecting these fractions we find that the numbers 847, 462, 216, etc., are the numbers of the living at the beginning of each year, and, when discounted by the proper powers of $\frac{1}{1.045}$, their sum corresponds to the number opposite 90 in the N column, with this difference, that a different rate of discount is used, and that the denominator 847 is the same as D90 before it is discounted. Now, if, instead of multiplying the numerators by the first, second, third, etc. powers of $\frac{1}{1.045}$, we multiply them by the ninety-first, ninety-second, ninety-third, etc. powers of $\frac{1}{1.045}$ and the denominator 847 by the ninetieth power, the relative value of these fractions will not be altered, and we shall have for the denominator, D90 or · 16.12194 and for the numerators 16.12194, 8.415104, etc., or D90 + D91 + D92, etc. The sum of these numerators is N90, which is placed over the denominator D90 thus, $\frac{D90}{N90}$=1.86086= the present value of a premium of \$1 per annum on a person aged 90; or, in other words, the present value of a life annuity of \$1 on a life aged 90, the first payment made at the beginning of the first year. If the first payment is made at the end of the first year, leave out the D90 from the sum of the numerators and we have $\frac{N91}{D90}$=13.87871÷16.12194=.86086. If the first payment is deferred for two years, the present value of the deferred annuity is $\frac{N92}{D90}$=5.463610÷16.12194=.33889. The general expression for an annuity is $\frac{Nx}{Dx}$ and for a deferred annuity is $\frac{Nx+n}{Dx}$.

The difference between the present value of an annuity for life and the single premium is this: The annuity is the present value of \$1 multiplied by the probability of living at the end of each year, because the annuity is payable only in case the nominee is living. Since all deaths are supposed to take place at the end of the year, the payment of each policy is regarded as taking place then, and hence the single premium is equal to the present value of \$1 payable at the end of each year, multiplied by the probability of dying that year. It is evident that the greater the probability of dying the greater will the premium be, while on the other hand, the greater the probability of living the greater the annuity.

VALUATION OF POLICIES.

We have seen (page 40) that the net annual premium to insure a person aged 30 in the amount of \$1 during life is $\frac{M30}{N30}$=.015336. If he should postpone insuring for one year he would not save this amount, for at the age of 31 the net annual premium is .015787, and the difference between these two premiums is .000451. By insuring at age 30 he pays .000451 less premium every year of his life, and the present value of this is found by multiplying it by the then present value of the life annuity of $1, or .000451 × 16.9926=.00766366. If he should postpone insuring till he reaches the age of 32, his net annual premium will be .016265 and the difference between this and the premium at 30 is .016265—.015336=.000929. Multiplying this by the life annuity at age 32, we have .000929 × 16.85573=.01565897. This is called the net value of the policy. If the sum insured is $1.000, the net values are $7.66366 and $15.65897. It is clear from this illustration that if he insures at the age of 30, instead of deferring it one or two years, he does not lose all the premiums he has paid. These net values are the same as so much ready money at 4 1-2 per cent interest, to be used for paying future premiums. As we proceed further, we shall find that no part of the net premium is lost, strictly speaking.

The net value of a policy is also found by taking the difference between the net single premium at the age when the policy is valued and the present value of the future net premiums to be paid on it. At age 31, the net single premium for $1 is .268261, and the then present value of all the net premiums on a life aged 30 is the net premium at 30 multiplied by the life annuity at 31 or .015336 × 16.9926=.260598, and the difference .268261—.260598=.007663, the net value.

The premium on a policy of $1 to insure it for one year only at age 30 is .008064. This is the reserve at the beginning of the year; at the end of the year this premium is entirely absorbed in carrying the annual risk. At the end of six months this premium is half gone, and therefore the reserve is .008064÷2=.004032.

In the gross valuation of a policy the present value of the future gross premiums receivable is considered as an asset, and the present value of the future net premiums taken at the age of valuation as a liability. If the latter is greater than the former the difference is the gross value of the policy, otherwise there is a surplus in the hands of the company. If the net single premium for $1 at age 31 is .268261, and the gross annual premium at age 30 is .0227, then the present value of the future gross premiums receivable will be .0227 multiplied by the present value of the annuity of $1, or .0227 × 16.9926=.385732. The difference between .385732 and .268261 is .117471 the surplus. That is, the present value of the future receipts is .117471 greater than the present value of the future liabilities.

At age 40, multiplying the gross premium by the present value of the annuity, we have .0227 × 15.5369=.352688. But the single premium at age 40 is .330946, and there is still a surplus of .021742. At age 50 we have the present value of the future premiums =.0227 × 13.2358=.300453, and the net single premium at that age is .430037, leaving a gross value of .129584.

The defect in this method of valuation is that no provision is made for future expenses.

A modified form of this method of valuation is sometimes practised by taking off a percentage of the gross premiums for expenses, and proceeding as before.

AMOUNT AT RISK.

When a person takes out a policy of insurance, the risk which the company assumes as liable to lose is not the whole amount insured, but the amount of the policy less the reserve. For the sake of uniformity, the reserve at the end of the year is taken. Hence the sum insured may be divided into two parts, the insurance which the company carries and that assumed by the policyholder. In this last example of a policy of $1 issued at age 30, it is clear that the policyholder has a deposit in the hands of the company of .007663, thus insuring himself for this amount, while the company insures the balance or .992337. This is what the company would lose if he should die at the end of the first year. At the end of the second year the risk which the company assumes is .984341, and that of the policyholder .015659.

The reserve on a policy when compared with the amount at risk is called by Hon. Elizur Wright "self insurance," since it is the unearned and unexpended part of the premiums which the policyholder has on deposit in the company to provide for the future payment of his claim. For this reason Hon. Gustavus W. Smith, Insurance Commissioner of Kentucky, calls it the "trust fund deposit."

The amount at risk varies greatly in different kinds of policies, and it is owing to the want of a proper understanding of this subject that many people find themselves greatly mistaken in their opinions of the benefits of short term endowments. Thus a person paying a premium on a whole life policy of $1,000 is insured at the end of each of the first ten years for $992.34, $984.34, $976.01, $967.34, $958.31, $948.89, $939.10 $928.91, $918.33, $907.33 ; average amount, $952.09.

On a ten annual payment endowment for the same age and same amount he is insured at the end of each year as follows : $921.78, $839.42, $752.69, $661.34, $565.11, $463.71, $356.83, $244.16, $125.34, $0.00 ; average insurance, $493.04. That is in a ten year endowment a man insures himself on an average for more than one-half of the amount of the policy. The annual net premium on a ten annual endowment for this age and amount is $82.29, and on the whole life policy given above $15.34. On the endowment plan as above described, during the ten years the policy-holder pays between five and six times as much net annual premium and gets only about half the insurance as on the whole life plan. But there is a partial offset to this, as the premiums in the former case cease in ten years when the amount insured is paid, and in the latter they may continue till the policyholder is 95 years old, according to the assumptions of the American mortality table.

COST OF INSURANCE.

We have seen that the amount at risk is the sum insured less the reserve at the end of the year. On an ordinary life policy of $1, issued at age 30, the amount insured at the end of the first year is .99234. The expense of insuring $1 for one year at age 30 is $\frac{720}{85.441}$=.0084269, and therefore the cost of insuring .99234 for one year is .99234 × .0084269=.0083623. This is the net cost of insurance, and is found by multiplying the amount at risk by the probability that the insured will die that year.

The cost of insurance at age 31 is found in the same manner.

Amount of policy, - - - - - - - - -	$1.
Reserve at end of second year, - - - - - -	0.01566
Amount at risk, - - - - - - - - -	.98434
Number of dying, age 31, - - - - - - -	721
Number of living, " - - - - - - - -	84.721
Probability of dying, 721÷84721= - - - - -	.0085103
Cost of insurance, .98434 × .0085103 - - - - - -	.0083377

The cost of insurance on an ordinary life policy at age 95 and on an endowment insurance in the last year of its duration is nothing, because in these cases the reserve equals the amount insured.

Having the net premiums and reserves, the cost of insurance can be found very easily by adding 4 1-2 per cent interest to the net premium and subtracting the reserve, and the remainder is the cost of insurance for the first year. For the second and subsequent years, the cost of insurance is obtained by adding the net premium to the reserve of the previous year, increasing this amount by the interest and subtracting the reserve for that year. In the example above given—

First year—Net premium,　　- - - - - - - - .015336
　　Interest 4½ per cent,　　- - - - - - - - .000690

　　Amount,　　- - - - - - - - - - .016026
　　Reserve first year, - - - - - - - - .007664

　　Cost of insurance,　　- - - - - - - - .008362

Second year—Reserve first year, - - - - - - .007664
　　Net premium,　　- - - - - - - - - .015336

　　Amount,　　- - - - - - - - - .023000
　　Interest 4½ per cent, - - - - - - - - .001035

　　Amount,　　- - - - - - - - - .024035
　　Reserve second year,　　- - - - - - - .015657

　　Cost of insurance, - - - - - - - - .008378

From this view of the subject we see that there is an actual expense incurred in carrying a risk in life insurance in case the policyholder survives, since in the example above given the 720 losses which occur at the age 30 must be met by the 85,441 premiums, and in this respect life insurance adopts the same law which runs through all other kinds of insurance. At any age the greater the reserve the less the cost of insurance, and conversely. In the case of a whole-life policy issued at age 30, the 'cost of insurance during the first year of issue is greater than the reserve, and therefore a company would not be justified in paying a surrender value of even one-half the net premium, while in a ten-payment endowment it could return nearly the whole.

DISTRIBUTION OF SURPLUS.

Having explained the method of finding the reserve and the

cost of insurance, we are now prepared to examine the methods of distributing the surplus.

The method of distribution now almost universal in this country is called the " Contribution Plan," because it returns to each policyholder the amount of surplus contributed by him.

There are three sources of surplus, and each of these will have to be considered separately. There is a surplus from loading, when this is greater than the expenses, or the expenses and mortality, over the tabular rate. If the loading on ordinary life policies is 40 per cent and the average expense is but 15, we have a surplus of 25 per cent on the net premium to return to the policyholder. The second source is from excess of interest. If the tabular rate of interest on reserves is 4 1-2 per cent, and the actual rate of interest on assets is 6 1-2, then here is a gain of 2 per cent on the reserves, and a further gain of 6 1-2 per cent on that part of the loading not taken for expenses. The third source is from diminished mortality. If the actual mortality during the year does not equal the tabular mortality, the difference is so much gained and goes to swell the surplus ; but if, on the other hand, it is greater, then its deficiency must be made up from the loading.

The arithmetical explanation of this plan will be best understood by taking the example of a whole-life policy for $1,000, issued at age 30 ; gross premium, $22.70. We will assume that the experience of the company at the end of each year shows that the expenses are 15 per cent of the gross premiums, that the average rate of interest realized is 6 1-2 per cent, and that the mortality is only three-quarters of the tabular rate. The three sources of surplus will be as follows :

First Source—From loading,

Gross premium, - - - - - - - - - $22.70
Net premium, - - - - - - - - - 15.34

Loading, - - - - - - - - - - - $7.36
Expenses $22.70 × 15= - - - - - - - 3.41

Difference, - - - - - - - - - - $3.95
Interest at 6½ per cent, - - - - - - - .25

Surplus from loading, - - - - - - - $4.20

Second Source—Interest on reserves.

Reserve at end of first year, - - - - - - $7.66
Difference between the actual and assumed rate of interest 2 per cent × $7.66= - - - - - - - - - .15

Third Source—Cost of insurance, - - - - - - $8.39
    Gain of one-fourth, - - - - - - - - 2.09
    Total surplus $4.20+.15+$2.09= - - - - - 6.44

SECOND YEAR.

First Source—Surplus from loading same as before, - - - $4.20
Second Source—Interest on reserves, $15.66 × .02= - - .31
Third Source—Gain from mortality $\frac{8.38}{4}$= - - - - 2.09

    Total surplus, - - - - - - - - - $6.60

This method of distributing the surplus can also be illustrated by opening a debit and credit account with the policyholder :*

Cr.—Gross premium, - - - - - - - - $22.70
    Interest on net premium, 4½ per cent, - - - - .68
    Interest on loading, 6½ per cent, - - - - - - .25
    Surplus interest on reserves, 2 per cent, - - - - .15
    Gain from mortality, - - - - - - - - 2.09
                     $25.87

Dr.—Reserve, - - - - - - - - - - $7.66
    Expenses, - - - - - - - - - - 3.41
    Cost of insurance, table rate, - - - - - - 8.36
    Dividend to balance, - - - - - - - - 6.44
                     $25.87

This explanation shows that the policyholder is credited with
all the contributions he makes and is charged with only the necessary expenses, mortality and reserves. What remains after
these deductions belongs to him.

By adding the net premium and interest together, $15.34+
.68=$16.02, we have the reserve and cost of insurance=$7.66 +
$8.36=$16.02, which explains the presence of the .68 interest
in the above credit account.

The principal objection to the contribution plan is that under
certain circumstances it shows a deficiency in the assets. If
a deficiency actually exists, it would be difficult to show a
surplus. To illustrate how the plan operates in case of a deficiency, take the example of a whole-life policy of $1,000, age

* For this illustration I am indebted to my friend, Mr. Henry W. Smith,
Actuary of the Hope Mutual Life Insurance Company, of New York.

30, annual premium $16.55, no gains from favorable mortality, and the account will stand:

Cr.—Gross premium, •   •   -   •   •   •   •   • $16.55
    Surplus interest of 2 per cent on actual reserve of
    $6.52, -   -   -   -   -   -   -   -   -   .13
    Interest on net premium -   -   •   -   -   •   .68
       Total, •   -   -   -   -   -   -   - $17.36

Dr.—Reserve required by law, -   -   -   -   - $7.66
    Cost of insurance, -   -   -   -   -   -   -   8.36
    Expenses, 15 per cent, -   -   -   -   -   -   2.48
       Total, -   -   -   -   -   -   -   - $18.50
       Balance against the company, -   -   -   -   1.14

Here is a difference of $1.14, which equals the difference between the actual and the required reserve, $7.66−$6.52=$1.14.

There are other methods of distributing surplus, such as the percentage plan, by a percentage on the gross premiums, or a percentage on the reserves, or on the amount insured; and they are so simple as to require no particular explanation. But none of these can be adapted to different kinds of policies and to premiums with different percentages of loading, and make an equitable adjustment of surplus, like the contribution plan.

Surplus may be applied in several different ways to benefit the policyholder, but they may all be reduced to two: the reduction of premium, and the increase of insurance. It may be deducted from the next premium, the policyholder paying the difference, or it may be applied to the permanent reduction of the premium in the following manner: Divide the surplus by the present value of an annuity of $1 at the present age of the policyholder. If a man aged 50 has a surplus of $100 on a continued-payment life policy, divide $100 by 13.2358, the present value of $1 at age 50, and the result is $7.5553, the annual reduction. To find what would be the temporary reduction for ten years, we have the present value of a temporary annuity of $1 for ten years, which is $\frac{N_x - N_{x+10}}{D_x}$ = A50.10 =7.7393 and $100÷7.7393=$12.921. To find how much this surplus will give a permanent increase to the policy, taking the net premium as a basis, we have the ratio, if .43037 will purchase $1 insurance, $100 will purchase $100÷.43037=$232.538; that is, we divide the surplus by the single premium of $1 for the given age. The temporary increase of the policy for ten years is found by dividing the surplus by the single premium of $1 for ten years, or $100÷.132498=$754.73.

TONTINES AND TONTINE DIVIDENDS.

Tontines are a kind of life annuity which were first brought into public notice in Europe by Lorenzo Tonti, a Neapolitan, in the year 1648. The members of a tontine were divided into classes according to their ages, and each individual subscribed a certain sum which was invested so as to produce an annual revenue to be divided among the survivors. Each succeeding year the numbers of the living became less and the revenue was concentrated upon a smaller number of survivors until the last one passed away, when the capital subscribed reverted to the crown.

The first association of this kind in France was founded in 1653, under the administration of Cardinal Mazarin, and called the "Royal Tontine." The total sum subscribed was 1,025,000 francs, and the members were divided into ten classes paying 102,500 francs each. Each individual subscription was 300 francs and the subscriber received the interest on this sum which was annually increased by the dividend arising from the subscriptions of other members who had died during the year. In France in 1726, a widow, the last surviving member of a tontine died at the advanced age of ninety-six. She had been the wife of a poor surgeon who had invested her little capital of 300 francs in a tontine, and at her death she enjoyed a revenue of 79,000 francs.

The Tontine Association of New York was established in 1794 by several prominent merchants of that city, who were desirous of having an exchange where they could meet and transact business. They formed a Tontine Association and issued 203 shares of stock valued at $200 each, and with this fund, amounting to $40,600, they purchased a piece of property on the corner of Wall and Water streets and erected a building known as the Tontine Coffee House. The members of the association agreed that each could nominate some one person during whose life the interest in the funds would be paid, and in most cases the nominees were their own or a friend's children. By a recent arrangement, it was agreed by the surviving members that when their number should be reduced to seven the property would be divided among them and the old Tontine Association be brought to a close. The members having been reduced by death to the required number in 1870, the preliminary steps were taken to have the property, amounting to $300,000, divided among the survivors.

Life insurance and tontines are opposed to each other in the advantages which they offer. In the former the gain, if we may use the expression, is on the part of him who dies early, and the earlier the policyholder dies the greater is the amount of insurance obtained on a given kind of policy. In the tontine the advantage is altogether on the side of him who survives the longest.

To illustrate the nature of tontines, we will suppose that 69,804 persons at the age of fifty, contribute one dollar each at the beginning of each year to form a tontine fund, and this to be equally divided among the survivors, at age 60. If the money is placed at compound interest, 7 per cent, and the mortality is the same as the American Experience Table, the following will be the result:

Living at the beginning of 1st year	•	•	$69,804 \times 1.9672 = 137,318.10$
"	"	2d "	•	$68,842 \times 1.8385 = 126,566.01$
"	"	3d "	•	$67,841 \times 1.7282 = 116,564.42$
"	"	4th "	•	$66,797 \times 1.6058 = 107,262.65$
"	"	5th "	•	$65,706 \times 1.5007 = 98,605.00$
"	"	6th "	•	$64,563 \times 1.4026 = 90,556.06$
"	"	7th "	•	$63,364 \times 1.3108 = 83,057.54$
"	"	8th "	•	$62,104 \times 1.2250 = 76,077.40$
"	"	9th "	•	$60,779 \times 1.1449 = 69,585.89$
"	"	10th "	•	$59,385 \times 1.07 = 63,541.96$

Total amount to be distributed - • • • • •	$969,135.03
Survivors at the end of the tenth year, - - -	57,917
Share of each surviving member. • - • - •	$16.73
Amount of $1 per annum at 7 per cent compound interest for ten years - - - - - - - - -	$14.78
Gain from the tontine system • - - • •	$1.95

The application of the tontine principle to the distribution of surplus or bonus in life insurance companies has long been the subject of practical and scientific investigation in England, and in a modified form it has been adopted by several companies in this country. All the different methods of applying dividends, in which the main idea is to defer them for a number of years, and then to pay them to those policyholders only who have persisted in keeping their policies in force usually for ten or more years, while all the premiums and surplus of those who have allowed their policies to lapse, or who have died, is concentrated upon those policies which remain in force, involve the principle of the tontine system. Considering the large number of policies which lapse after one or two premiums are paid, and the prospect there is of realizing a much larger dividend than by the ordinary method, it is not strange that this feature should have some attractions, for those who can afford to assume the risk that they will live to enjoy its benefits.

EXPECTATION OF LIFE.

" The Expectation of Life expresses the true average duration in years of a certain number of individuals at a certain age."— *Neison.*

The calculation of a life expectancy is very simple. In the American Experience Table of mortality, at age 95, there are 3 living at the beginning of the year, and all die during the year; and, therefore, assuming that the deaths of each year are equally distributed throughout that year, we have the average expectation of these 3 persons to be half a year each, or .50, and the number of years which the aggregate of these three lives will amount to will be 1.50. At the age 94 there are 21 living at the beginning of the year, and 18 dying during the year. The 18 who die during the year live in the aggregate 9 years, and there are 3 who live during the whole of this year and half of the next, making the total number of years lived by these 21 to be $9+3+1.50=13.50$, and this divided by $21=.64$, the expectation. For the age 93 we have 79 living and 58 deaths during the year.

Hence, $\left(\frac{58}{2}+21+13.50\right) \div 79 = 63.50 \div 79 = .80$, or $\frac{1}{2}+\left(\frac{21+3}{79}\right) = .80$.

For age 91 we have $\frac{1}{2}+\left(\frac{216+79+41+3}{462}\right) = .50+\frac{319}{462} = 1.19$.

To find the expectation of life for any age we have the following rule:

Divide the sum of the tabular numbers of the living at all the

TABLE No. IX.

EXPECTATION OF LIFE BY DIFFERENT TABLES.

Age.	North-ampton.	Carlisle.	Farr, No.3, Males.	Combined Experience.	American Experience.	Age.	North-ampton.	Carlisle.	Farr, No.3, Males.	Combined Experience.	American Experience.
1	32.74	44.67	46.65	....	....	53	16.54	18.97	17.67	18.16	18.79
2	37.79	47.55	48.83	....	....	54	16.06	18.28	17.06	17.50	18.09
3	39.55	49.81	49.61	....	....	55	15.58	17.58	16.45	16.86	17.40
4	40.58	50.76	49.81	....	....	56	15.10	16.89	15.86	16.22	16.72
5	40.84	51.24	49.71	....	....	57	14.63	16.21	15.26	15.59	16.05
6	41.07	51.16	49.39	....	....	58	14.15	15.55	14.68	14.97	15.39
7	41.03	50.79	48.92	....	....	59	13.68	14.92	14.10	14.37	14.74
8	40.79	50.24	48.37	....	....	60	13.21	14.34	13.53	13.77	14.09
9	40.36	49.57	47.74	....	....	61	12.74	13.82	12.96	13.18	13.47
10	39.78	48.82	47.05	48.36	48.72	62	12.28	13.31	12.41	12.61	12.86
11	39.14	48.04	46.31	47.68	48.08	63	11.81	12.81	11.87	12.05	12.26
12	38.49	47.27	45.54	47.01	47.44	64	11.35	12.30	11.34	11.51	11.68
13	37.83	46.50	44.76	46.33	46.82	65	10.88	11.79	10.82	10.97	11.10
14	37.17	45.74	43.97	45.64	46.16	66	10.42	11.27	10.32	10.46	10.54
15	36.51	44.99	43.18	44.96	45.50	67	9.95	10.75	9.83	9.96	10.00
16	35.85	44.27	42.40	44.27	44.85	68	9.50	10.23	9.36	9.47	9.48
17	35.20	43.57	41.64	43.58	44.19	69	9.05	9.70	8.90	9.00	8.98
18	34.58	42.87	40.90	42.88	43.53	70	8.60	9.15	8.45	8.54	8.48
19	33.99	42.16	40.17	42.19	42.87	71	8.17	8.65	8.03	8.10	8.00
20	33.43	41.46	39.48	41.49	42.20	72	7.74	8.16	7.62	7.67	7.54
21	32.90	40.75	38.80	40.79	41.53	73	7.32	7.72	7.22	7.26	7.10
22	32.39	40.03	38.13	40.09	40.85	74	6.92	7.33	6.85	6.86	6.68
23	31.87	39.31	37.46	39.39	40.17	75	6.54	7.00	6.49	6.48	6.28
24	31.36	38.58	36.79	38.68	39.49	76	6.18	6.69	6.15	6.11	5.88
25	30.85	37.86	36.12	37.98	38.81	77	5.83	6.40	5.82	5.76	5.48
26	30.33	37.13	35.44	37.27	38.11	78	5.48	6.11	5.51	5.42	5.10
27	29.82	36.40	34.77	36.56	37.43	79	5.11	5.80	5.21	5.09	4.74
28	29.30	35.68	34.10	35.86	36.73	80	4.75	5.51	4.93	4.78	4.38
29	28.79	34.99	33.43	35.15	36.03	81	4.41	5.20	4.66	4.48	4.04
30	28.27	34.34	32.76	34.43	35.33	82	4.09	4.93	4.41	4.18	3.71
31	27.75	33.68	32.09	33.72	34.62	83	3.80	4.65	4.17	3.90	3.39
32	27.24	33.02	31.42	33.01	33.92	84	3.58	4.39	3.95	3.63	3.08
33	26.72	32.36	30.74	32.30	33.21	85	3.37	4.13	3.73	3.36	2.77
34	26.20	31.68	30.07	31.58	32.50	86	3.18	3.90	3.53	3.10	2.47
35	25.68	31.00	29.40	30.87	31.78	87	3.01	3.71	3.34	2.84	2.19
36	25.16	30.32	28.73	30.15	31.07	88	2.86	3.40	3.16	2.59	1.93
37	24.64	29.63	28.06	29.44	30.35	89	2.66	3.47	3.00	2.35	1.69
38	24.12	28.95	27.39	28.72	29.62	90	2.41	3.28	2.84	2.11	1.42
39	23.60	28.27	26.72	28.00	28.90	91	2.08	3.26	2.69	1.89	1.19
40	23.07	27.61	26.06	27.28	28.18	92	1.75	3.37	2.55	1.67	.98
41	22.56	26.97	25.39	26.56	27.45	93	1.37	3.48	2.41	1.47	.80
42	22.04	26.34	24.73	25.84	26.72	94	1.05	3.53	2.29	1.28	.64
43	21.54	25.71	24.07	25.12	25.99	95	.75	3.53	2.17	1.12	.50
44	21.03	25.09	23.41	24.40	25.27	96	.50	3.46	2.06	.99	....
45	20.52	24.45	22.76	23.69	24.54	97	....	3.28	1.95	.89	....
46	20.02	23.81	22.11	22.97	23.80	98	....	3.07	1.85	.75	....
47	19.51	23.17	21.46	22.27	23.08	99	....	2.77	1.76	.50	....
48	19.00	22.50	20.82	21.56	22.36	100	....	2.28	1.68	....	....
49	18.49	21.81	20.17	20.87	21.63	101	....	1.79	....	....	....
50	17.99	21.11	19.54	20.18	20.91	102	....	1.30	....	....	....
51	17.50	20.39	18.90	19.50	20.20	103	....	.83	....	....	....
52	17.02	19.68	18.28	18.82	19.49	104	....	.50	....	....	....

ages greater than the given age by the given age, and increase the quotient by one-half.

The expectation of life is never used in any exact calculations in life insurance, but it is often referred to for the sake of making off-hand estimates on the probable duration of a lifetime. Its want of adaptation to the computation of premiums is easily illustrated by the following table:

TABLE No. X.

A.	B.	C.	D.	E.
Age.	Expectation of Life.	Net Annual Premium, $1,000.	Amount of $1.00, per Annum during Expectation, 4½ per cent.	Net Annual Premium, multiplied by Annuity = C × D.
10	49	9.973	177.5030	1770.19
15	46	10.843	152.6726	1655.50
20	42	11.965	124.2764	1487.08
25	39	13.423	106.0303	1423.29
30	35	15.336	85.1640	1306.07
35	32	17.877	71.7562	1282.75
40	28	21.301	56.4230	1201.84
45	25	25.986	46.5706	1210.20
50	21	32.490	35.3034	1146.99
55	17	41.527	25.8551	1073.68
60	14	54.141	19.7841	1071.13
65	11	71.898	14.4640	1039.93

Column A gives the age of the insured, B the expectation in even years, C the net premium for $1,000 on the whole life rate, D the amount of $1 per annum at 4 1-2 per cent, and E the net premium multiplied into the amount of $1.00 per annum, or C×D. If the sum insured were equal to the net premium multiplied by the amount of $1 per annum during expectation, as many people suppose, then the amounts in the last column would be $1,000 each, whereas they vary from it by considerable differences.

EQUATION OF LIFE.

This is a term used by Mr. T. G. P. Neison to represent the number of years for which there is an equal probability of living, and which he regards as the best mode to determine the comparative value of life within this period, as the expression is affected by the mortality within these years only. The expectation of life, which is often confounded with a chance of living an equivalent number of years, merely expresses the true average duration in years of a class of individuals at a certain age : it involves a consideration of the decrements of life at every superior age, and, consequently, at even younger ages, it is affected by the irregularities of mortality at the older ages.

The equation of life is illustrated by the following example: At age 20, according to the American Experience Table of mortality, there are 92,637 persons living, and the equation of life represents the period when one half, or 46,318, will be surviving. At age 66 there are 47,361 alive, and the difference between these two numbers, 47,361−46,318=1043; hence the equation will fall between the ages 66 and 67. The number dying between these ages is 2,070; hence we have the proportion, 2,070 : 1,043 :: 1 : .50; that is, the equation of life will be reached

TABLE No. XI.
EQUATION OF LIFE.

Age.	Amer-ican Ex-perience.	Com-bined Ex-perience.	Age.	Amer-ican Ex-perience.	Com-bined Ex-perience.	Age.	Amer-ican Ex-perience.	Com-bined Ex-perience.
10	54.65	53.34	40	29.79	28.47	70	7.86	7.75
11	53.85	52.52	41	28.96	27.64	71	7.38	7.29
12	53.05	51.69	42	28.12	26.83	72	6.91	6.86
13	52.23	50.87	43	27.28	26.02	73	6.48	6.44
14	51.42	50.06	44	26.46	25.21	74	6.05	6.04
15	50.61	49.23	45	25.62	24.40	75	5.65	5.66
16	49.79	48.38	46	24.79	23.59	76	5.26	5.30
17	48.98	47.55	47	23.97	22.80	77	4.87	4.96
18	48.15	46.72	48	23.14	22.01	78	4.51	4.64
19	47.33	45.89	49	22.33	21.23	79	4.16	4.33
20	46.50	45.06	50	21.52	20.46	80	3.83	4.03
21	45.68	44.22	51	20.72	19.70	81	3.52	3.77
22	44.85	43.39	52	19.92	18.95	82	3.21	3.51
23	44.03	42.50	53	19.14	18.21	83	2.92	3.26
24	43.19	41.72	54	18.35	17.48	84	2.64	3.01
25	42.36	40.89	55	17.58	16.76	85	2.36	2.79
26	41.53	40.06	56	16.82	16.04	86	2.07	2.57
27	40.69	39.22	57	16.08	15.35	87	1.81	2.35
28	39.86	38.39	58	15.34	14.67	88	1.59	2.12
29	39.02	37.56	59	14.62	14.00	89	1.38	1.91
30	38.18	36.73	60	13.91	13.34	90	1.16	1.72
31	37.34	35.90	61	13.22	12.70	91	.94	1.54
32	36.51	35.07	62	12.55	12.08	92	.79	1.35
33	35.67	34.24	63	11.89	11.47	93	.69	1.15
34	34.83	33.41	64	11.25	10.88	94	.58	.97
35	33.99	32.58	65	10.63	10.31	95	.50	.86
36	33.15	31.76	66	10.03	9.76	96	....	.77
37	32.31	30.93	67	9.46	9.23	97	....	.72
38	31.47	30.11	68	8.90	8.71	98	....	.67
39	30.63	29.29	69	8.37	8.22	99	....	.50

at 66.50 years of age; and, subtracting the age of the person from this quantity, we have 66.50−20=46.50, the equation of life.

The expectation of life at age 20 is 42:20 years, and would be reached at age 62.20, when there are 54,400 living, or 8,082 more than half the tabular number at the age 20.

The equation of life may be found by the following rule: Take half the tabular number living at the given age, divide the difference between this quotient and the tabular number of the living at the next preceding age where the number of living is greater than this quotient, by the number of dying in that age where the equation occurs, the result is the fractional part of the year required. The integral part of the equation may be found by subtracting the given age from the age in which the equation is found, as in the preceding example.

JOINT-LIFE POLICIES.

Joint-life policies, as issued in this country, are made payable to the survivor on the death of one of two lives, both parties being insured under the same policy. In this class of policies the probability that either one of two persons will survive a given period of time is less than the probability that each separate life will continue the same length of time. It is evident, with very little demonstration, that if A aged 60 and B aged 70 were insured on the same joint-life policy the probability that one of the two will die within a year is greater than the probability that either of the two taken separately will die during that time. If the probability that A will live for one year be $\frac{9}{10}$ and B's probability of living is $\frac{8}{10}$ then the probability that both of them will survive this period is $\frac{9}{10} \times \frac{8}{10} = \frac{72}{100}$ and the probability of one of the two dying during year is $1 - \frac{72}{100} = \frac{28}{100}$. In making this calculation we assume that A has only $\frac{9}{10}$ of a certainty of living one year and B only $\frac{8}{10}$, therefore the chance of both living would be in A's case not $\frac{9}{10}$ of a year but $\frac{9}{10}$ of B's $\frac{8}{10} = \frac{72}{100}$, and in B's case the chance would be $\frac{8}{10}$ of $\frac{9}{10} = \frac{72}{100}$. As the supposed mortality on A's single life is only $\frac{10}{100}$ and on B's $\frac{20}{100}$ the risk on their joint lives would be much greater than upon either life taken separately, and since the premiums on policies increase with the probability of dying, though not exactly in the same ratio, it is easy to see from this illustration that the premiums on joint life policies should be considerably larger than those on policies for single lives.

It is not intended in this place to enter upon a full explanation of the intricate calculations involved in the computation of joint life premium rates, but we propose to give only such tables as will be of value to the public. As a general rule, joint-life policies are not regarded with much favor by American companies. Many of the most prominent companies have refused to issue them or have abandoned them after a few years' trial, while other companies have large numbers upon their books.

Required the probability that two lives aged 25 and 35 will both live one year. The probability of the life age 25 = $\frac{88314}{89032}$ = .991936. The probability of the life aged 35 = $\frac{81090}{81822}$ = .991054. Multiplying, .991936 × 991054 = .983062. The probability that one of the two will die within a year is 1 − .983062 = .016938.

THE RETURN-PREMIUM PLAN.

By·this plan a company contracts to return to the policyholder the whole amount of the sum insured at death or expiration of the policy when the full number of premiums have been paid, and also to return the whole amount of premiums without interest.

We assume that the legitimate object of life insurance is to obtain the greatest amount of insurance at the least cost, that is, to throw as great a burden as possible upon the company with a due regard to the length of the time in which the payments will be made and exercising a reasonable caution against making the payments too heavy in the unproductive period of old age.

In order to enable the company to afford to return the whole amount of premiums paid when the claim is due, it is necessary to charge a larger annual premium during the continuance of the policy. The company cannot afford to return all the premiums without being repaid for this obligation by a greater reserve, a greater accumulation of interest, and a less amount at risk for the same money than in the ordinary methods of insurance. It is plain that he who chooses this form of policy seeks a future good by paying a greater premium and obtaining less insurance.

As an illustration of the workings of the return-premium plan we take the columns as given in the following table:

TABLE No. XII.

RETURN PREMIUMS, AMERICAN EXPERIENCE, 4½ PER CENT.

A. Age.	B. Net Annual Premium to insure $1.000 for whole life. premiums returned at death, without interest.	C. Amount of Insurance for the first year on the Return-Premium Plan.	D. Amount of Insurance on the ordinary whole life plan purchased by a net annual premium equal to that charged in the Return-Premium plan at the same age.	E. No. of Premiums to be paid before C=D
10	$13.584	$1013.584	$1362.078	27
15	15.247	1015.247	1406.161	27
20	17.472	1017.472	1460.137	27
25	20.496	1020.496	1526.931	26
30	24.687	1024.687	1609.742	25
35	30.630	1030.630	1713.375	24
40	39.284	1039.284	1844.233	22
45	52.261	1052.261	2011.121	20
50	72.313	1072.313	2225.700	17
55	103.986	1103.986	2504.058	15
60	155.365	1155.365	2869.637	13
65	241.331	1241.331	3356.575	10
70	389.633	1389.633	4017.001	8

Column A gives the age of the policyholder; B, the net annual premium on the return-premium plan; C, the amount of insurance the first year on this plan; D, the amount of insurance which could be purchased by the premiums in column B if the party were insured on the whole-life plan; and E, the number of premiums necessary to be paid in order that column C may equal D. At age 30 the net annual return premium is $24.687 which secures for the first year $1024.687 insurance, but insured on the whole-life plan with the same amount of premium the policyholder would get $1609.742 insurance and the policyholder insured by the first method has to make 25 payments before his policy increases to $1609.742, the amount to be obtained on the whole-life plan. At age 55 the policyholder in the return-premium plan pays an annual premium $103.986 and obtains the first year $1103.986 insurance but on the whole-life plan he could have $2504.058 or $1400.072 more insurance the first year and not till he has made 15 payments or till he has reached the age of 69 will his policy be larger than if he had adopted the whole life plan.

FORFEITURE OF POLICIES AND PAID-UP INSURANCE.

A policy of life insurance is a contract whereby the company, for a certain consideration, agrees to indemnify the policyholder, his heirs or assigns, in case of his death or at a certain period if living, according to the terms expressed therein. One part of the contract is that the premiums shall be regularly paid during the time specified. The company cannot violate this contract, until the policy becomes payable, except by refusing to receive the premiums and keep the policy in force upon the books. But it is comparatively easy and a frequent practice for the policyholder to violate his part of the contract and to refuse or neglect to pay the premiums due. In the meantime, the company holds an unearned deposit or reserve, to accumulate and meet the future claim. The neglect to pay the premium constitutes the first violation of the contract, and the policyholder cannot legally claim any favors from the company after this. But there may be a moral injustice done to the policyholder in refusing to make any compromise with him. Since he has paid money for insurance which he has not got, it is but just that he should have all the company can afford to restore.

With a limited payment life or endowment policy, the rule usually adopted is to issue a paid-up policy for such a fractional part of the sum insured as the number of payments made bears to the whole number promised. But in the case of a continued premium life policy, the case is different. In this form of insurance, there is the least for the policyholder to sacrifice, and therefore the temptation to allow the policy to lapse is often very strong. Although the policyholder, by violating the conditions, has forfeited all claim upon the company unless otherwise agreed upon, yet public opinion naturally frowns upon a company which absorbs the unearned premiums for the benefit of other policyholders. Beyond protecting itself from loss, the company should derive no undue advantage from the inability of a policyholder to pay the annual premium. It is this which has made the non-forfeiture law of Massachusetts and the non-forfeiture regulations of some companies of other states, a means of removing, to some extent, one of the harsh features of life insurance. In life insurance more than in almost any other business, the public need the most perfect confidence, not only that the legal obligations of the companies will be fulfilled, but that they or their legal representatives will be equitably dealt by, and this has become one of the first conditions to the prosperity of the business.

The forfeiture of policies for the non-payment of premiums was quite common ten years ago, when the whole-life plan of insurance was the one usually adopted, and the sacrifices which policyholders were sometimes compelled to make, in losing not only the whole of the reserves, but reversionary paid-up insurance, was a hardship which loudly demanded a reform. In the year 1859, the subject was first brought before the legislature of Massachusetts by Hon. Elizur Wright, the insurance commissioner, which resulted, in 1861, in the passage of the non-forfeiture law of that state.

In England also, previous to this time, non-forfeiture policies had been strenuously advocated by Dr. Farr. It is highly probable that this eminent actuary was the first to propose and advocate the payment of a definite cash surrender value to a policy. Many years ago he demonstrated what was the portion of yearly premium which was necessary to secure the company against loss and what might be withdrawn by the policyholder in anticipation of his future claim. The plans of Dr. Farr were adopted by the British Imperial Life Association, where any policyholder has a right to withdraw from the company a definite proportion of the premiums he has paid. The Massachusetts non-forfeiture law, above alluded to, compels the company, in case the policyholder neglects to pay the premiums, to continue the policy in force as a paid-up policy of temporary insurance so long as four-fifths of the cash reserve computed according to the Actuaries' Table of mortality and 4 per cent interest would sustain it.

This law was intended to apply exclusively to whole life policies. At the time when the law was proposed in 1859, there were very few endowment or limited-term life policies in force in the companies doing business in Massachusetts—the policies issued up to that time having been almost entirely confined to the whole-life plan. The clause in the law which allows the companies to deduct from the amount insured, when the policy became a claim, the unpaid premiums and interest thereon at 6 per cent interest, weakens its force to a great extent when applied to short term endowments and life policies with a limited number of payments.

This peculiarity of the law is easily shown by taking the example of a fifteen-payment endowment for $1,000, issued at age 40, payable at death or 55, annual premium $69.49. Suppose that after five annual payments have been made, the payment of premiums is discontinued, and then, according to the operation of this law, a term policy for twenty-two years is allowed. At the end of the fifteen years from the date of the policy, or ten years after the payment of premiums ceased, the policyholder, in the event of death, would leave to his heirs only the amount of $1,000 less the unpaid premiums and interest, or $1,000 − $970.89 = $29.11, and the greater the loading on the premiums the less the insurance which is obtained. That is, the amount insured constantly decreases, and decreases faster under mutual than under non-participating rates. In another part of this work we give some tables for the calculation of insurance due on lapsed policies, according to this law.

SURRENDER VALUES.

No subject in life insurance is more thoroughly discussed at the present day than the proper rule for determining the surrender value of a policy. The common method of computing the surrender value is to deduct from the reserve 25 to 50 per cent, as a surrender charge, and pay the remainder as an equitable surrender value. But this method is held to be wrong in principle, for the longer a policyholder remains in a company, and consequently the less benefit he can confer upon it by the payment of his annual premium, the greater will be his surrender charge. In other words, the longer he stays in the company the more it will cost him to get out.

Every policyholder when he comes into a company is expected

to confer a benefit upon it by his annual contributions; and, if he leaves the company by allowing his policy to lapse, he inflicts an injury upon it equal to the present value of the future profit which the company would receive from the transaction. What is the measure of this injury, or what basis shall we adopt for ascertaining it? Mr. Wright says that the present value of the future cost of insurance, which he calls "insurance value," should be the basis, and that the surrender charge should be a percentage on this insurance value. Prof. Bartlett, Actuary of the Mutual Life, of New York, takes similar ground, when he says that "the company's interest in any particular policy is the present value of the sums the policy would, if continued in the company in its present condition, contribute from year to year to pay death claims on other policies." Upon this basis some very ingenious formulæ for computing surrender values have been made. This theory of "insurance value" may be correct so far as the policyholder is concerned, but it fails to do justice to the companies. The "cost of insurance," as regards the companies, is, in addition to the policyholder's contribution to losses, as given in the cost-of-insurance tables, all his proportion of office expenses, salaries, license fees, etc.,—everything required to sustain the company as an efficient working organization. When the company receives an application for a policy of insurance, it receives also a virtual pledge that the applicant will make his annual contributions to the support of the company as a corporation, besides what is necessary to pay death claims and endowments. This view of the subject seems the more reasonable, because under this new rule the company is supposed to cut off all profits from lapsed policies as a source of income, and make only such a surrender charge as will prevent the company from incurring any loss. Now these two things are perfectly clear, the policyholder has agreed to make certain contributions towards the future losses of the company and the running expenses, and by paying a percentage on the insurance value he has recompensed the company for only one of them. A surrender charge, made by taking a percentage of the present value of the unexpired gross premiums from the reserve, has been proposed as a method of finding an equitable surrender value for all kinds of policies. Some of the advantages of this method are that it gives a better practical adjustment of the surrender charges on

whole-life and short-term endowment policies, than by taking a
percentage on the insurance value, and that the surrender charge
each subsequent year is less than the one preceding.

AVERAGE DURATION OF POLICIES.

This is a subject which has always been ignored in life insurance calculations, since all policies are issued upon the assumption that the future premiums are to be promptly paid, while in
practice the average duration of policies is much less than the
tabular duration. In every company a large number of policies
lapse after a few payments, but as most companies give either a
surrender value on being released from the contract, or a paid-up
policy for a fractional part of the sum insured, this result makes
but little change in the ratio of liabilities and assets. But cases
sometimes arise when agents wish to know the present value of
their future commissions, and then the future duration of the
policies must be estimated. Unfortunately no statistics on this
subject derived from the experience of American companies
have been published.

The combined statistics returned by fifteen life offices in
England show that the average lifetime of a policy in these
companies, up to the year 1843, was less than five and-a-half
years ; in the Gotha Life, of Germany, it was a little over eight
years ; and in the Equitable Life, of London, twelve and-a-half
years. In the seventeen life offices the average duration of life,
after insuring, of the policyholders who died was 6.413 years.

In the Massachusetts Report for 1861, we find that on 2,180
policies which had been forfeited in companies doing business
in that state, 7.646 premiums had been paid, making the average
duration of each lapsed policy 3.51 years.

LIFE INSURANCE TABLES.

TABLE XIII.

AMERICAN EXPERIENCE MORTALITY TABLE.

Age.	Number surviving at each age.	Deaths in each year.	Age.	Number surviving at each age.	Deaths in each year.
10	100,000	749	55	64,563	1,199
11	99,251	746	56	63,364	1,260
12	98,505	743	57	62,104	1,325
13	97,762	740	58	60,779	1,394
14	97,022	737	59	59,385	1,468
15	96,285	735	60	57,917	1,546
16	95,550	732	61	56,371	1,628
17	94,818	729	62	54,743	1,713
18	94,089	727	63	53,030	1,800
19	93,362	725	64	51,230	1,889
20	92,637	723	65	49,341	1,980
21	91,914	722	66	47,361	2,070
22	91,192	721	67	45,291	2,158
23	90,471	720	68	43,133	2,243
24	89,751	719	69	40,890	2,321
25	89,032	718	70	38,569	2,391
26	88,314	718	71	36,178	2,448
27	87,596	718	72	33,730	2,487
28	86,878	718	73	31,243	2,505
29	86,160	719	74	28,738	2,501
30	85,441	720	75	26,237	2,476
31	84,721	721	76	23,761	2,431
32	84,000	723	77	21,330	2,369
33	83,277	726	78	18,961	2,261
34	82,551	729	79	16,670	2,196
35	81,822	732	80	14,474	2,091
36	81,090	737	81	12,383	1,964
37	80,353	742	82	10,419	1,816
38	79,611	749	83	8,603	1,648
39	78,862	756	84	6,955	1,470
40	78,106	765	85	5,485	1,292
41	77,341	774	86	4,193	1,114
42	76,567	785	87	3,079	933
43	75,782	797	88	2,146	744
44	74,985	812	89	1,402	555
45	74,173	828	90	847	385
46	73,345	848	91	462	246
47	72,497	870	92	216	137
48	71,627	896	93	79	58
49	70,731	927	94	21	18
50	69,804	962	95	3	3
51	68,842	1,001	96	......	.....
52	67,841	1,044	97	......	.....
53	66,797	1,091	98	......	.....
54	65,706	1,143	99	......	.....

TABLE No. XIV.

COMBINED EXPERIENCE MORTALITY TABLE.

Age.	Number surv:- ving at each age.	Deaths in each year.	Age.	Number surv:- ving at each age.	Deaths in each year.
10	100,000	676	55	63,469	1,375
11	99,324	674	56	62,094	1,436
12	98,650	672	57	60,658	1,497
13	97,978	671	58	59,161	1,561
14	97,307	671	59	57,600	1,627
15	96,636	671	60	55,973	1,698
16	95,965	672	61	54,275	1,770
17	95,293	673	62	52,505	1,844
18	94,620	675	63	50,661	1,917
19	93,945	677	64	48,744	1,990
20	93,268	680	65	46,754	2,061
21	92,588	683	66	44,693	2,128
22	91,905	686	67	42,565	2,191
23	91,219	690	68	40,374	2,246
24	90,529	694	69	38,128	2,291
25	89,835	698	70	35,837	2,327
26	89.137	703	71	33,510	2,351
27	88,434	708	72	31,159	2,362
28	87,726	714	73	28,797	2,358
29	87,012	720	74	26,439	2,339
30	86,292	727	75	24,100	2,303
31	85,565	734	76	21,797	2,249
32	84,831	742	77	19,548	2,179
33	84,089	750	78	17,369	2,092
34	83.339	758	79	15,277	1,987
35	82,581	767	80	13,290	1,866
36	81,814	776	81	11,424	1,730
37	81,038	785	82	9,694	1,582
38	80,253	795	83	8,112	1,427
39	79,458	805	84	6,685	1,268
40	78,653	815	85	5,417	1,111
41	77,838	826	86	4,306	958
42	77,012	839	87	3,348	811
43	76,173	857	88	2,537	673
44	75,316	881	89	1,864	545
45	74,435	909	90	1,319	427
46	73,526	944	91	892	322
47	72,582	981	92	570	231
48	71,601	1,021	93	339	155
49	70,580	1,063	94	184	95
50	69,517	1,108	95	89	52
51	68,409	1,156	96	37	24
52	67,253	1,207	97	13	9
53	66,046	1,261	98	4	3
54	64,785	1,316	99	1	1

TABLE No. XV.

COMMUTATION COLUMNS, AMERICAN EXPERIENCE, 4½ PER CENT.

Age	$D_x.$	$N_x.$	$C_x.$	$M_x.$	$R_x.$
10	64,392.77	1,214,144.09	461.5329	12,109.051	322,708.03
11	61,158.34	1,149,751.32	439.8893	11,647.519	310,598.98
12	58,084.84	1,088,592.98	419.2538	11,207.629	298,951.46
13	55,164.32	1,030.508.14	399.5799	10,788.375	287.743.83
14	52,389.25	975,343.82	380.8230	10,388.796	276.955.46
15	49,752.43	922,954.57	363.4350	10,007.973	266,566.66
16	47,246.~~	873,202.15	346.3651	9,644.538	256,558.69
17	44,865.~~	825,955.60	330.0915	9,298.173	246.914.15
18	42,~~.53	781,089.96	315.0104	8,968.081	237,615.98
19	~~,453.92	738,486.43	300.6161	8,653.071	228,647.90
20	38,411.27	698,032.51	286.8773	8,352.455	219.994.83
21	36,470.32	659,621.24	274.1440	8,065.577	211,642.37
22	34,625.68	623.150.92	261.9754	7,791.433	203,576.79
23	32,872.65	588,525.23	250.3465	7,529.458	195.785.36
24	31,206.73	555,652.58	239.2333	7,279.111	188,255.90
25	29,623.67	524,445.85	228.6130	7,039.878	180,976.79
26	28,119.40	494,822.18	218.7684	6,811.265	173.936.91
27	26,689.75	466,702.78	209.3478	6,592.497	167,125.65
28	25,331.08	440.013.04	200.3328	6,383.149	160,533.15
29	24,039.93	414,681.96	191.9730	6,182.816	154,150.00
30	22,812.75	390,642.02	183.9617	5,990.843	147.967.19
31	21,646.42	367,829.28	176.2844	5,806.881	141.976.34
32	20,537.99	346,182.86	169.1612	5,630.597	136.169.46
33	19,484.42	325,644.86	162.5484	5,461.436	130.538.87
34	18,482.83	306,160.44	156.1915	5,298.887	125,077.43
35	17,530.73	287.677.61	150.0806	5,142.696	119.778.54
36	16,625.73	270,146.89	144.5988	4,992.615	114.635.85
37	15,765.20	253,521.15	139.3108	4,848.016	109.643.23
38	14,947.00	237.755.96	134.5695	4,708.706	104.795.22
39	14,168.78	222,808.96	129.9781	4,574.136	100,086.51
40	13,428.66	208,640.18	125.8617	4,444.158	95.512.375
41	12,724.53	195,211.51	121.8588	4,318.296	91.068.217
42	12,054.73	182,486.98	118.2685	4,196.438	86.749.920
43	11,417.36	170,432.25	114.9057	4,078.169	82.553.483
44	10,810.79	159,014.90	112.0271	3,963.263	78.475.314
45	10,233.23	148.204.10	109.3153	3,851.236	74.512.050
46	9,683.250	137.970.87	107.1347	3,741.921	70.660.814
47	9,159.133	128,287.62	105.1810	3,634.786	66.918.893
48	8,659.540	119,128.49	103.6597	3,529.605	63,284.107
49	8,182.981	110,468.95	102.6278	3,425.946	59.754.502
50	7,727.976	102,285.96	101.9164	3,323.318	56.328.556
51	7,293.276	94.557.989	101.4815	3,221.401	53.005.239
52	6,877.730	87,264.713	101.2831	3,119.920	49.783.837
53	6,480.277	80,386.982	101.2850	3,018.637	46.663.918
54	6,099.937	73,906.705	101.5431	2,917.352	43.645.281

TABLE No. XV—(CONTINUED.)

COMMUTATION COLUMNS, AMERICAN EXPERIENCE, 4½ PER CENT.

Age.	D_x.	N_x.	C_x.	M_x.	R_x.
55	5,735.717	67,806.768	101.9312	2,815.809	40,727.929
56	5.386.794	62,071.052	102.5043	2,713.877	37.912.121
57	5,052.322	56,684.258	103.1504	2,611.373	35,198.243
58	4,731.607	51,631.936	103.8488	2,508.223	32,586.870
59	4,424.005	46,900.329	104.6523	2,404.374	30.078.647
60	4,128.846	42,476.324	105.4668	2,299.722	27,674.274
61	3,845.582	38,347.478	106.2782	2,194.255	25.374.552
62	3,573.704	34,501.897	107.0117	2,087.977	23,180.297
63	3.312.801	30,928.193	107.6044	1,980.965	21,092.320
64	3,062.540	27,615.392	108.0620	1,873.361	19,111.356
65	2,822.598	24,552.851	108.3902	1,765.299	17,237.995
66	2,592.661	21,730.253	108.4373	1,656.908	15,472.697
67	2.372.578	19,137.592	108.1792	1,548.471	13,815.788
68	2,162.230	16,765.014	107.5983	1,440.292	12,267.317
69	1,961.522	14,602.784	106.5454	1,332.694	10,827.025
70	1,770.509	12,641.263	105.0323	1,226.148	9,494.3319
71	1,589.234	10,870.754	102.9055	1,121.116	8,268.1839
72	1,417.893	9.281.520	100.0430	1,018.210	7,147.0681
73	1,256.792	7,863.627	96.42778	918.1673	6,128.8578
74	1,106.244	6,606.834	92.12806	821.7395	5,210.6905
75	966.4790	5,500.590	87.27957	729.6114	4,388.9510
76	837.5807	4,534.111	82.00317	642.3319	3,659.3395
77	719.5095	3,696.530	76.47059	560.3287	3,017.0077
78	612.0552	2,977.021	70.76821	483.8581	2.456.6789
79	514.9306	2,364.966	64.91260	413.0899	1,972.8208
80	427.8438	1,850.035	59.14724	348.1773	1,559.7309
81	350.2727	1,422.191	53.16253	289.0301	1,211.6536
82	282.0267	1,071.9185	47.03961	235.8675	922.52352
83	222.8424	789.89177	40.84970	188.8279	686.65598
84	172.3966	567.04938	34.86844	147.9782	497.82805
85	130.1044	394.65274	29.32659	113.1098	319.84982
86	95.17523	264.54837	24.19736	83.78319	236.74004
87	66.87942	169.37314	19.39314	59.58583	152.95684
88	44.60631	102.49372	14.79868	40.19269	93.37101
89	27.88676	57.88742	10.56396	25.39401	53.178320
90	16.12194	30.00064	7.012586	14.83005	27.784310
91	8.415104	13.87871	4.287819	7.8174590	12.954265
92	3.764915	5.463611	2.285102	3.5296396	5.136862
93	1.317687	1.698697	.9257566	1.2445372	1.6071665
94	0.335188	0.381009	.2749318	.3187806	.36262938
95	0.045822	0.045822	.0438488	.0438488	.04384878

TABLE NO. XVI.

COMMUTATION COLUMNS, COMBINED EXPERIENCE, 4 PER CENT.

Age.	D_x.	N_x.	C_x.	M_x.
10	67,556.41	1,381,771.74	439.1167	14,411.3725
11	64,519.00	1,314,215.33	420.9784	13,972.2557
12	61,616.50	1,249,696.33	403.5858	13,551.2772
13	58,843.07	1,188,079.83	387.4858	13,147.6913
14	56,192.36	1,129,236.76	372.5825	12,760.2055
15	53,658.54	1,073,044.40	358.2524	12,387.6229
16	51,236.51	1,019,385.86	344.9868	12,029.3704
17	48,920.90	968,149.35	332.2118	11,684.3835
18	46,707.10	919,228.45	320.3837	11,352.1716
19	44,590.30	872,521.35	308.9740	11,031.7878
20	42,566.31	827,931.05	298.4068	10,722.8137
21	40,630.73	785,364.74	288.1955	10,424.4069
22	38,779.81	744,734.01	278.3283	10,136.2113
23	37,009.94	705,954.20	269.1839	9,857.8830
24	35,317.31	668,944.26	260.3311	9,588.6992
25	33,698.63	633,626.95	251.7611	9,328.3681
26	32,150.76	599,928.32	243.8120	9,076.6069
27	30,670.39	567,777.56	236.1021	8,832.7948
28	29,254.65	537,107.17	228.9451	8,596.6926
29	27,900.53	507,852.52	221.9894	8,367.7475
30	26,605.44	479,951.99	215.5266	8,145.7580
31	25,366.64	453,346.55	209.2325	7,930.2313
32	24,181.76	427,979.91	203.3779	7,720.9987
33	23,048.32	403,798.15	197.6641	7,517.6207
34	21,964.18	380,749.83	192.0889	7,319.9565
35	20,927.31	358,785.65	186.8939	7,127.8675
36	19,935.52	337,858.34	181.8143	6,940.9735
37	98,986.96	317,922.82	176.8491	6,759.1591
38	18,079.84	298,935.86	172.2134	6,582.3100
39	17,212.25	280,856.02	167.6727	6,410.0966
40	16,382.57	263,643.77	163.2265	6,242.4238
41	15,589.24	247,261.20	159.0669	6,079.1972
42	14,830.58	231,671.96	155.3561	5,920.1302
43	14,104.82	216,841.38	152.5857	5,764.7740
44	13,409.74	202,736.56	150.8258	5,612.1882
45	12,743.16	189,326.82	149.6357	5,461.3623
46	12,103.41	176,583.66	149.4188	5,311.7282
47	11,488.47	164,480.25	149.3031	5,162.3094
48	10,897.30	152,991.78	149.4143	5,013.0062
49	10,318.76	112,094.48	149.5775	4,863.5918
50	9,781.92	131,765.72	149.9131	4,714.0142
51	9,255.78	121,983.80	150.3918	4,564.1010
52	8,749.40	112,728.02	150.9873	4,413.7091
53	8,261.90	103,978.62	151.6753	4,262.7218
54	7,792.46	95,716.72	152.2026	4,111.0465

TABLE No. XVI.—(Continued.)

Commutation Columns, Combined Experience, 4 per cent.

Age.	D_x.	N_x.	C_x.	M_x.
55	7,340.55	87,924.26	152.9100	3,958.8437
56	6,905.30	80,583.71	153.5515	3,805.9337
57	6,486.17	73,678.41	153.9175	3,652.3821
58	6,082.78	67,192.24	154.3249	3,498.4644
59	5,694.50	61,109.46	154.6633	3,344.1394
60	5,320.82	55,414.96	155.2044	3,189.4760
61	4,960.97	50,094.14	155.5630	3,034.2715
62	4,614.60	45,133.17	155.8334	2,878.7084
63	4,281.28	40,518.57	155.7717	2,722.8749
64	3,960.85	36,237.29	155.4841	2,567.1031
65	3,653.02	32,276.44	154.8380	2,411.6189
66	3,357.68	28,623.42	153.7227	2,256.7808
67	3,074.82	25,265.74	152.1862	2,103.0580
68	2,804.37	22,190.92	150.0063	1,950.8717
69	2,546.50	19,386.55	147.1266	1,800.8653
70	2,301.43	16,840.05	143.6909	1,653.7385
71	2,069.22	14,538.62	139.5893	1,510.0474
72	1,850.05	12,469.40	134.8485	1,370.4580
73	1,644.05	10,619.35	129.4424	1,235.6094
74	1,451.37	8,975.298	123.4610	1,106.1668
75	1,272.087	7,523.928	116.8853	982.7057
76	1,106.275	6,251.841	109.7545	865.8203
77	953.972	5,145.566	102.2484	756.0657
78	815.0323	4,191.594	94.3904	653.8171
79	689.2945	3,376.5616	86.2047	559.4266
80	576.5783	2,687.2671	77.8415	473.2219
81	476.5607	2,110.6888	69.3925	395.3803
82	388.8389	1,634.1281	61.0154	325.9878
83	312.8680	1,245.2892	52.9205	264.9724
84	247.9142	932.4212	45.2153	212.0519
85	193.1637	684.5070	38.0931	166.8365
86	147.6411	491.3433	31.5838	128.7433
87	110.3786	343.7022	25.7091	97.1594
88	80.4243	233.3236	20.5139	71.4503
89	56.81712	152.8993	15.9734	50.9363
90	38.65848	96.08221	12.0336	34.9630
91	25.13852	57.42373	8.7255	22.9294
92	15.44572	32.28521	6.0188	14.2039
93	8.83283	16.83949	3.8833	8.1851
94	4.60983	8.006655	2.2885	4.3018
95	2.14399	3.396825	1.2045	2.0133
96	.85704	1.252835	.5345	.8088
97	.28954	.395795	.1927	.2743
98	.085663	.106255	.0618	.0816
99	.020592	.020592	.0198	.0198

TABLE No. XVII.

COMMUTATION TABLES, AMERICAN EXPERIENCE, 6 PER CENT.

$Age.$	$D_x.$	$N_x.$	$C_x.$	$M_x.$	$R_x.$
10	55,839.47	853,966.39	394.5637	7,501.7416	155,968.97
11	52,284.18	798,126.92	370.7391	7,107.1779	148,467.23
12	48,953.97	745,842.74	348.3474	6,736.4388	141,360.05
13	45,834.65	696,888.77	327.3027	6,388.0914	134,623.61
14	42,912.92	651,054.12	307.5243	6,060.7887	128,235.52
15	40,176.36	608,141.20	289.3300	5,753.2644	122,174.73
16	37,612.90	567,964.84	271.8388	5,463.9344	116,421.46
17	35,212.03	530,351.94	255.4006	5,192.0956	110,957.53
18	32,963.50	495,139.91	240.2830	4,936.6950	105,765.43
19	30,857.35	462,176.41	226.0584	4,696.4120	100,828.74
20	28,884.66	431,319.06	212.6743	4,470.3536	96,132.327
21	27,037.00	402,434.40	200.3587	4,257.6793	91,661.974
22	25,306.24	375,397.40	188.7558	4,057.3206	87,404.294
23	23,685.06	350,091.16	177.8245	3,868.5648	83.346.974
24	22,166.57	326,406.10	167.5260	3,690.7403	79,478.409
25	20,744.33	304,239.53	157.8236	3,523.2143	75,787.669
26	19,412.30	283,495.20	148.8902	3,365.3907	72,264.454
27	18,164.60	264,082.90	140.4624	3,216.5005	68,899.064
28	16,995.72	245,918.30	132.5117	3,076.0381	65,683.563
29	15,901.41	228,922.58	125.1852	2,943.5264	62,607.525
30	14,876.14	213,021.17	118.2635	2,818.3412	59,663.999
31	13,915.84	198,145.03	111.7243	2,700.0777	56,845.658
32	13,016.42	184,229.19	105.6926	2,588.3534	54,145.580
33	12,173.95	171,212.77	100.1237	2,482.6608	51,557.226
34	11,384.72	159,038.82	94.84670	2,382.5371	49,074.566
35	10,645.47	147,654.10	89.84627	2,287.6904	46.692.029
36	9.953.050	137,008.63	85.33960	2,197.8441	44.404.338
37	9.304.330	127,055.58	81.05522	2,112.5045	42,206.494
38	8,696.614	117.751.25	77.18859	2,031.4493	40,093.990
39	8,127.166	109,054.63	73.49997	1,954.2607	38,062.540
40	7,593.635	10,027.47	70.16506	1,880.7607	36,108.280
41	7,093.643	93,333.831	66.67222	1,810.5956	34,227.519
42	6,625.144	86,240.188	64.07927	1,743.6234	32,416.923
43	6,186.057	79,615.044	61.37623	1,679.5442	30.673.300
44	5,774.525	73.428.987	58.99186	1,618.1679	28,993.756
45	5,388.674	67,654.462	56.74930	1,559.1761	27,375.588
46	5.026.906	62.265.788	54.83025	1,502.4268	25,816.412
47	4,687.532	57,238.882	53.06862	1,447.5965	24.313.985
48	4,369.133	52,551.350	51.56092	1,394.5279	22,866.388
49	4,070.263	48,182.217	50.32530	1,342.9670	21,471.861
50	3,789.544	44,111.954	49.26926	1,292.6417	20,128.894
51	3,525.773	40.322.410	48.36477	1,243.3724	18,836.252
52	3,277.836	36.796.637	47.58714	1,195.0077	17,592.879
53	3,044.711	33,518.801	46.91461	1,147.4205	16,397.872
54	2,825.455	30,474.090	46.36856	1,100.5059	15,250.451

TABLE No. XVII—(CONTINUED.)

COMMUTATION COLUMNS, AMERICAN EXPERIENCE, 6 PER CENT.

Age	D_x.	N_x.	C_x.	M_x.	R_x.
55	2,619.154	27,648.635	45.88711	1,054.1373	14.149.945
56	2,425.013	25.029.481	45.49213	1,008.2502	13,095.808
57	2,242.257	22,604.468	45.13107	962.75810	12,087.558
58	2,070.205	20,362.211	44.79368	917.62703	11;124.800
59	1,908.230	18,292.006	44.50145	872.83335	10,207.173
60	1,755.716	16,383.776	44.21317	828.33190	9.334.3394
61	1,612.122	14,618.060	43.92288	784.11873	8,506.0075
62	1,476.947	13,015.938	43.60014	740.19585	7,721.8887
63	1,349.746	11,538.991	43.22123	696.59571	6,981.6929
64	1,230.124	10,189.245	42.79084	653.37448	6,285.0972
65	1,117.703	8,959.121	42.31342	610.58364	5,631.7227
66	1,012.124	7.841.418	41.73278	568.27022	5,021.1391
67	913.1013	6,829.2936	41.04427	526.53744	4,452.8688
68	820.3721	5,916.1923	40.24618	485.49317	3.926.3314
69	733.6897	5,095.8202	39.28841	445.24699	3,440.8382
70	652.8716	4,362.1305	38.18240	405.95858	2,995.5912
71	577.7344	3,709.2589	36.87985	367.77618	2,589.6327
72	508.1524	3,131.5245	35.34659	330.89633	2,221.8565
73	414.0425	2,623.3721	33.58719	295.54974	1,890.9601
74	385.3208	2,179.3296	31.63543	261.96255	1,595.4104
75	331.8748	1,794.0088	29.54641	230.32712	.1,333.4479
76	283.5430	1,462.1340	27.36739	200.78071	1,103.1207
77	240.1261	1,178.5910	25.15983	173.41332	902.3400
78	201.3741	938.4649	22.95417	148.25349	728.92670
79	167.0214	737.0908	20.75693	125.29932	580.67321
80	136.8105	570.0694	18.64571	104.54239	455.37389
81	110.4208	433.2589	16.52192	85.89668	350.83150
82	87.64860	322.83809	14.41216	69.37476	264.93482
83	68.27522	235.18949	12.33856	54.96260	195.56016
84	52.07201	166.91427	10.38290	42.62404	140.59756
85	38.74165	114.84226	8.609106	32.241142	97.973523
86	27.93962	76.10061	7.002851	23.632036	65.732381
87	19.35528	48.16099	5.533062	16.629185	42.100345
88	12.72664	28.80571	4.162468	11.096123	25.471160
89	7.843789	16.079072	2.929308	6.933655	14.375037
90	4.470494	8.235283	1.917022	4.004347	7.441382
91	2.300426	3.764789	1.155568	2.087325	3.437035
92	1.014645	1.464363	.6071208	.9317566	1.3497102
93	.3500915	.4497184	.2424804	.3246358	.4179536
94	.0877947	.0996269	.0709930	.0821554	.0933178
95	.0118322	.0118322	.0111624	.0111624	.0111624

TABLE No. XVIII.

Net Premiums per $1,000, American Experience, 4½ Per Cent.

Age.	Single life.	Whole life.	Ten payment life.	Endowment 10 years.	Endowment 15 years.	Endowment 20 years.	Endowment 25 years.	Endowment 30 years.	Endowment 35 years.
20	217.45	11.97	27.17	81.90	50.55	35.43	26.80	21.42	17.89
21	221.16	12.23	27.64	81.93	50.58	35.47	26.86	21.49	17.97
22	225.02	12.50	28.13	81.96	50.62	35.52	26.91	21.56	18.07
23	229.05	12.79	28.64	81.99	50.66	35.57	26.98	21.64	18.17
24	233.26	13.10	29.18	82.04	50.70	35.62	27.05	21.72	18.28
25	237.64	13.42	29.73	82.06	50.75	35.68	27.12	21.82	18.41
26	242.23	13.77	30.32	82.10	50.80	35.74	27.20	21.93	18.55
27	247.01	14.13	30.92	82.14	50.85	35.81	27.28	22.04	18.70
28	251.99	14.51	31.56	82.19	50.91	35.89	27.38	22.16	18.87
29	257.19	14.91	32.22	82.24	50.97	35.97	27.48	22.31	19.05
30	262.61	15.34	32.92	82.29	51.04	36.06	27.61	22.47	19.26
31	268.26	15.79	33.64	82.35	51.12	36.16	27.74	22.64	19.49
32	274.16	16.27	34.40	82.41	51.20	36.27	27.89	22.84	19.74
33	280.30	16.77	35.19	82.48	51.29	36.39	28.05	23.06	20.03
34	286.69	17.31	36.01	82.55	51.39	36.52	28.24	23.30	20.34
35	293.35	17.88	36.87	82.64	51.51	36.68	28.44	23.57	20.68
36	300.29	18.48	37.77	82.73	51.63	36.85	28.67	23.87	21.07
37	307.51	19.12	38.71	82.83	51.77	37.04	28.93	24.21	21.49
38	315.03	19.81	39.69	82.94	51.92	37.25	29.21	24.58	21.96
39	322.83	20.53	40.72	83.07	52.10	37.49	29.53	25.00	22.48
40	330.95	21.30	41.79	83.21	52.30	37.76	29.90	25.46	23.05
41	339.37	22.12	42.90	83.36	52.52	38.06	30.29	25.97	23.68
42	348.12	23.00	44.07	83.54	52.77	38.40	30.74	26.54	24.37
43	357.19	23.93	45.29	83.74	53.05	38.79	31.24	27.18	25.10
44	366.60	24.92	46.57	83.97	53.37	39.22	31.81	27.88	25.96
45	376.35	25.99	47.90	84.23	53.73	39.70	32.43	28.65	26.87
46	386.43	27.12	49.30	84.52	54.14	40.25	33.13	29.51	....
47	396.85	28.33	50.76	84.86	54.60	40.86	33.90	30.46	......
48	407.60	29.63	52.29	85.24	55.13	41.52	34.77	31.50	......
49	418.67	31.01	53.89	85.67	55.71	42.30	35.74	32.64	......
50	430.04	32.49	55.57	86.17	56.36	43.15	36.79	33.89	......
51	441.70	34.07	57.31	86.69	57.09	44.09	37.96	......	......
52	453.63	35.75	59.13	87.30	57.90	45.14	39.25	....	
53	465.82	37.55	61.03	87.97	58.80	46.30	40.66	......	
54	478.26	39.47	63.02	88.73	59.80	47.58	42.22	......	
55	490.93	41.53	65.10	89.55	60.92	49.00	43.91	......	
56	503.80	43.72	67.27	90.48	62.15	50.57	......	......	
57	516.87	46.07	69.55	91.51	63.53	52.29	......		
58	530.10	48.58	71.94	92.65	64.05	54.19	......		
59	543.48	51.27	74.45	93.92	66.74	56.28	......		
60	556.99	54.14	77.08	95.33	67.61	58.57	......		
61	570.59	57.22	79.86	96.90	70.69	......			
62	584.26	60.52	82.79	98.64	72.95	......			
63	597.97	64.05	85.89	100.58	75.47	......			
64	611.70	67.84	89.17	102.52	78.23	......			
65	625.42	71.90	92.66	104.49	81.24				
66	639.08	76.25	96.35	......	......				
67	652.65	80.91	100.28	......	......				
68	666.11	85.91	104.46	......					
69	679.42	91.26	108.90	......					
70	692.54	97.00	113.63	......					

TABLE No. XIX.

NET ANNUAL PREMIUMS PER $1,000, COMBINED EXPERIENCE, 4 PER CENT.

Age.	Single life.	Whole life.	Ten payment, life.	Endowment, 10 years.	Endowment, 15 years.	Endowment, 20 years.	Endowment, 25 years.	Endowment, 30 years.
20	251.91	12.95	30.81	83.87	52.27	36.97	28.19	22.68
21	256.56	13.27	31.40	83.91	52.33	37.05	28.28	22.79
22	261.37	13.61	32.00	83.97	52.40	37.12	28.37	22.90
23	266.36	13.96	32.63	84.02	52.47	37.21	28.47	23.01
24	271.50	14.33	33.27	84.08	52.54	37.29	28.57	23.15
25	276.82	14.72	33.94	84.15	52.62	37.38	28.68	23.29
26	282.31	15.13	34.64	84.22	52.70	37.48	28.81	23.44
27	287.99	15.56	35.35	84.29	52.79	37.59	28.94	23.61
28	293.86	16.01	36.09	84.37	52.88	37.70	29.08	23.79
29	299.91	16.48	36.86	84.45	52.98	37.82	29.24	24.00
30	306.17	16.97	37.66	84.54	53.08	37.95	29.40	24.21
31	312.63	17.49	38.48	84.63	53.20	38.09	29.59	24.44
32	319.29	18.04	39.33	84.71	53.31	38.25	29.79	24.70
33	326.17	18.62	40.21	84.82	53.43	38.41	30.04	24.98
34	333.27	19.23	41.12	84.93	53.57	38.59	30.26	25.29
35	340.60	19.87	42.06	85.03	53.72	38.80	30.52	25.63
36	348.17	20.54	43.04	85.15	53.88	39.02	30.81	26.01
37	355.99	21.26	44.05	85.28	54.07	39.28	31.14	26.42
38	364.07	22.02	45.10	85.42	54.27	39.55	31.50	26.87
39	372.42	22.82	46.20	85.58	54.51	39.87	31.90	27.37
40	381.04	23.68	47.33	85.76	54.77	40.22	32.35	27.92
41	389.96	24.59	48.53	85.97	55.07	40.60	32.84	28.53
42	399.18	25.55	49.77	86.22	55.40	41.05	33.38	29.20
43	408.71	26.58	51.08	86.51	55.79	41.53	34.00	29.94
44	418.52	27.68	52.44	86.84	56.23	42.08	34.67	30.76
45	428.57	28.85	53.86	87.02	56.70	42.68	35.42	31.63
46	438.86	30.08	55.33	87.61	57.22	43.34	36.23	.....
47	449.35	31.39	56.85	88.06	57.80	44.06	37.12	.....
48	460.02	32.77	58.43	88.55	58.43	44.85	38.08	.....
49	470.88	34.23	60.05	89.07	59.11	45.71	39.13	.....
50	481.91	35.78	61.74	89.66	59.86	46.65	40.27	.....
51	493.11	37.41	63.49	90.29	60.68	47.68	.....	.....
52	504.46	39.15	65.30	90.97	61.57	48.81	.....	.....
53	515.95	41.00	67.17	91.73	62.55	50.03	.....	.....
54	527.57	42.95	69.12	92.55	63.63	51.37	.....	.....
55	539.31	45.02	71.14	93.45	64.80	52.84	.....	.....
56	551.16	47.23	73.25	94.43	66.09	.....	.....	.....
57	563.10	49.57	75.44	95.51	67.51	.....	.....	.....
58	575.14	52.07	77.75	96.74	69.06	.....	.....	.....
59	587.26	54.72	80.15	97.99	70.77	.....	.....	.....
60	599.43	57.56	82.68	99.47	72.64	.....	.....	.....
61	611.63	60.57	85.34	101.07	.....	.....	.....	.....
62	623.83	63.78	88.13	102.81	.....	.....	.....	.....
63	635.99	67.20	91.07	104.73	.....	.....	.....	.....
64	648.12	70.84	94.16	106.83	.....	.....	.....	.....
65	660.17	74.72	97.43	109.12	.....	.....	.....	.....
66	672.13	78.84	100.88	......	.....	.....	.....	.....
67	683.96	83.24	104.53	......	.....	.....	.....	.....
68	695.65	87.91	108.39	......	.....	.....	.....	.....
69	707.19	92.89	112.48	......	.....	.....	.....	.....
70	718.57	98.20	116.85	......	.....	.....	.....	.....

TABLE No. XX.

NET ANNUAL PREMIUMS PER $1,000 FOR TERM INSURANCE POLICIES.

Age.	AMERICAN EXPERIENCE, 4½ PER CENT.				COMBINED EXPERIENCE, 4 PER CENT.			
	Three years.	Five years.	Seven years.	Ten years.	Three years.	Five years.	Seven years.	Ten years.
20	7.50	7.55	7.61	7.68	7.09	7.18	7.27	7.41
21	7.57	7.61	7.66	7.74	7.18	7.27	7.36	7.51
22	7.62	7.67	7.72	7.80	7.27	7.37	7.47	7.63
23	7.67	7.72	7.78	7.87	7.37	7.47	7.58	7.75
24	7.72	7.78	7.84	7.94	7.47	7.58	7.69	7.87
25	7.78	7.84	7.91	8.01	7.58	7.70	7.82	8.01
26	7.84	7.91	7.98	8.10	7.70	7.82	7.95	8.15
27	7.91	7.98	8.06	8.19	7.82	7.95	8.09	8.30
28	7.99	8.06	8.15	8.28	7.96	8.09	8.24	8.46
29	8.07	8.15	8.24	8.39	8.10	8.24	8.39	8.62
30	8.15	8.24	8.34	8.50	8.25	8.40	8.56	8.80
31	8.24	8.33	8.44	8.63	8.41	8.57	8.73	8.98
32	8.34	8.45	8.57	8.77	8.57	8.74	8.91	9.17
33	8.45	8.57	8.69	8.91	8.75	8.92	9.10	9.38
34	8.57	8.70	8.84	9.08	8.93	9.11	9.30	9.59
35	8.70	8.84	9.00	9.26	9.12	9.31	9.50	9.83
36	8.84	9.00	9.17	9.47	9.31	9.51	9.72	10.10
37	9.00	9.18	9.36	9.70	9.52	9.73	9.96	10.41
38	9.18	9.37	9.58	9.94	9.74	9.96	10.23	10.75
39	9.37	9.58	9.81	10.22	9.96	10.21	10.53	11.15
40	9.58	9.81	10.08	10.54	10.21	10.51	10.89	11.59
41	9.81	10.07	10.37	10.90	10.49	10.86	11.31	12.09
42	10.07	10.36	10.70	11.29	10.83	11.28	11.80	12.67
43	10.37	10.69	11.08	11.77	11.25	11.77	12.35	13.30
44	10.69	11.07	11.50	12.29	11.76	12.34	12.98	14.03
45	11.06	11.50	12.00	12.88	12.34	12.98	13.68	14.81
46	11.49	11.99	12.57	13.55	12.99	13.69	14.45	15.69
47	11.98	12.55	13.19	14.30	13.71	14.47	15.29	16.63
48	12.55	13.19	13.91	15.13	14.48	15.31	16.20	17.65
49	13.19	13.91	14.73	16.07	15.32	16.23	17.20	18.76
50	13.92	14.72	15.60	17.12	16.24	17.23	18.28	19.97
51	14.73	15.62	16.62	18.28	17.25	18.31	19.45	21.28
52	15.63	16.63	17.73	19.56	18.34	19.50	20.72	22.71
53	16.64	17.75	18.97	20.98	19.53	20.78	22.10	24.27
54	17.77	19.00	20.34	22.56	20.81	22.16	23.60	25.96
55	19.02	20.38	21.86	24.29	22.21	23.67	25.24	27.80
56	20.40	21.91	23.54	26.20	23.71	25.31	27.03	29.81
57	21.94	23.60	25.39	28.31	25.35	27.10	28.99	32.00
58	23.64	25.47	27.44	30.63	27.15	29.08	31.13	34.39
59	25.52	27.54	29.60	33.18	29.13	31.24	33.47	36.99
60	27.60	29.82	32.19	35.99	31.31	33.62	36.04	39.81

VALUATION TABLES.

NET VALUES.

The following tables, from page 82 to 119 give the net values of a policy of $1,000, according to various plans of insurance and ages, and also according to the two standards of mortality and interest generally adopted in the United States.

The states of New York, California, Kansas, Kentucky, Missouri, Michigan, and Wisconsin, have adopted the American Experience Table and 4½ per cent interest, while Massachusetts, Connecticut, Maine, New Hampshire and Illinois, use the Combined Experience 4 per cent.

The net values are given to the end of each policy year, to the 15th and also of the 20th year, where the number of annual premiums is sufficient.

Although there has been an endless amount of discussion about the relative merits of the two standards of valuation, very few persons have taken the trouble to investigate for themselves the actual difference there is between the valuations of the same policy made upon both of them. Thus the value of a whole life policy issued at age 20, and having been in force 5 years, has a value 29 per cent greater by the Combined Experience 4 per cent standard than by the other. In the older ages, and when the policy has been in existence a greater number of years this difference diminishes. A life policy with the same conditions, issued at age 35, has a reserve 15 per cent greater by the Combined Experience 4 per cent table, and at 50 only 4 per cent greater. Also, the longer a policy is in force the less the difference, and we see that a policy issued at age 50, and in force 20 years, has a larger reserve by the American Experience 4½ per cent standard than by the other. Similar differences, though in a less degree, are seen in the Ten payment Life and Endowment policies.

The difference in the valuation of endowments by the two standards is very slight. In the Ten Year Endowments it is almost nothing, but increases with the length of the policy term.

TABLE NO. XX. *a.*

SHOWING THE DIFFERENCE BETWEEN THE VALUES OF THE SAME POLICY ACCORDING TO THE AMERICAN EXPERIENCE 4½ PER CENT, AND THE COMBINED EXPERIENCE, 4 PER CENT. STANDARDS.

WHOLE LIFE.

Age 20.

Year of Policy.	Premium American Experience, 4½ per cent.	Premium Combined Experience, 4 per cent.	Ratio.
1	4.74	6.22	1.31
5	25.81	33.30	1.29
10	57.71	72 53	1.26
15	97.00	118.56	1.22
20	145.04	172.61	1.19

Age 35.

Year of Policy.	Premium American Experience, 4½ per cent.	Premium Combined Experience, 4 per cent.	Ratio.
1	9.82	11.48	1.17
5	53.20	61.34	1.15
10	117.45	133.41	1.13
15	193.42	214.30	1.11
20	279.59	301.35	1.08

Age 50.

Year of Policy.	Premium American Experience, 4½ per cent.	Premium Combined Experience, 4 per cent.	Ratio.
1	20.45	21.62	1.05
5	106.83	110.79	1.04
10	222.74	226.84	1.02
15	342.79	344.07	1.00
20	460.56	456.79	.99

TEN PAYMENT LIFE.

Age 20.

Year of Policy.	Premium American Experience, 4½ per cent.	Premium Combined Experience, 4 per cent.	Ratio.
1	20.75	24.94	1.20
5	114.91	136.30	1.19

Age 35.

Year of Policy.	Premium American Experience, 4½ per cent.	Premium Combined Experience, 4 per cent.	Ratio.
1	29.85	34.78	1.16
5	164.99	190.23	1.15

Age 50.

Year of Policy.	Premium American Experience, 4½ per cent.	Premium Combined Experience, 4 per cent.	Ratio.
1	44 90	49 06	1.09
5	245.54	265.87	1.08

TEN-YEAR ENDOWMENT.

Age 20.

Year of Policy.	Premium American Experience, 4½ per cent.	Premium Combined Experience, 4 per cent.	Ratio.
1	78.39	80.51	1.027
5	435.59	442.17	1.015

Age 35.

Year of Policy.	Premium American Experience, 4½ per cent.	Premium Combined Experience, 4 per cent.	Ratio.
1	78.10	78.89	1.010
5	434.32	439.79	1.013

Age 50.

Year of Policy.	Premium American Experience, 4½ per cent.	Premium Combined Experience, 4 per cent.	Ratio.
1	77.31	78.56	1.016
5	429 38	432.60	1.008

FIFTEEN-YEAR ENDOWMENT.

Age 20.

Year of Policy.	Premium, American Experience, 4½ per cent.	Premium, Combined Experience, 4 per cent.	Ratio.
1	45.37	47.42	1.045
5	251.86	260.01	1.032
10	577.52	586.80	1.016

Age 35.

Year of Policy.	Premium, American Experience, 4½ per cent.	Premium, Combined Experience, 4 per cent.	Ratio.
1	45.27	47.02	1.039
5	251.09	257.94	1.027
10	575.69	583.58	1.013

Age 50.

Year of Policy.	Premium, American Experience, 4½ per cent.	Premium, Combined Experience, 4 per cent.	Ratio.
1	45.74	47.07	1.029
5	250.28	254.64	1.013
10	568.47	572.42	1.007

TWENTY-YEAR ENDOWMENT.

Age 20.

Year of Policy.	Premium, American Experience, 4½ per cent.	Premium, Combined Experience, 4 per cent.	Ratio.
1	29.45	31.39	1.066
5	163.27	171.80	1.052
10	373.82	386.71	1.035

Age 35.

Year of Policy.	Premium, American Experience, 4½ per cent.	Premium, Combined Experience, 4 per cent.	Ratio.
1	29.64	31.36	1.058
5	163.81	171.29	1.045
10	373.59	385.17	1.031

Age 50.

Year of Policy.	Premium, American Experience, 4½ per cent.	Premium, Combined Experience, 4 per cent.	Ratio.
1	31.74	33.11	1.043
5	170.88	175.76	1.028
10	377.08	382.92	1.015

TWENTY-FIVE-YEAR ENDOWMENT.

Age 20.

Year of Policy.	Premium, American Experience, 4½ per cent.	Premium, Combined Experience, 4 per cent.	Ratio.
1	20.36	22.19	1.089
5	112.72	121.18	1.075
10	257.57	271.90	1.056

Age 35.

Year of Policy.	Premium, American Experience, 4½ per cent.	Premium, Combined Experience, 4 per cent.	Ratio.
1	20.95	22.67	1.082
5	115.33	123.21	1.068
10	261.32	275.11	1.052

Age 50.

Year of Policy.	Premium, American Experience, 4½ per cent.	Premium, Combined Experience, 4 per cent.	Ratio.
1	25.00	26.36	1.054
5	132.64	137.64	1.038
10	284.94	291.35	1.022

TABLE No. XXI.

NET VALUE PER $1,000 OF AN ORDINARY LIFE POLICY, AT THE END OF VARIOUS YEARS, AMERICAN EXPERIENCE, 4½ PER CENT.

Age.	First year.	Second year.	Third year.	Fourth year.	Fifth year.	Sixth year.	Seventh year.	Eighth year.
20	4.74	9.68	14.83	20.20	25.81	31.66	37.77	44.14
21	4.96	10.14	15.54	21.17	27.06	33.19	39.59	46.17
22	5.20	10.63	16.29	22.20	28.37	34.80	41.51	48.51
23	5.46	11.15	17.09	23.29	29.76	36.50	43.53	50.86
24	5.72	11.70	17.93	24.43	31.22	38.29	45.66	53.34
25	6.01	12.28	18.82	25.64	32.75	40.16	47.89	55.95
26	6.31	12.88	19.75	26.90	34.36	42.13	50.24	58.68
27	6.62	13.53	20.72	28.23	36.06	44.21	52.71	61.55
28	6.95	14.20	21.75	29.63	37.85	46.39	55.30	64.58
29	7.30	14.91	22.84	31.11	39.72	48.69	58.03	67.75
30	7.66	15.66	23.99	32.66	41.69	51.11	60.90	71.09
31	8.06	16.45	25.19	34.29	43.78	53.64	63.91	74.58
32	8.46	17.27	26.45	36.01	45.96	56.31	67.06	78.24
33	8.89	18.14	27.79	37.82	48.26	59.10	70.37	82.08
34	9.34	19.07	29.19	39.72	50.67	62.04	73.85	86.11
35	9.82	20.04	30.67	41.72	53.20	65.12	77.50	90.34
36	10.32	21.06	32.21	43.81	55.84	68.34	81.31	94.77
37	10.85	22.12	33.84	46.00	58.63	71.74	85.33	99.40
38	11.40	23.24	35.54	48.31	61.56	75.30	89.52	104.25
39	11.98	24.42	37.34	50.74	64.64	79.03	93.92	109.30
40	12.59	25.66	39.23	53.29	67.86	82.93	98.50	114.57
41	13.24	26.98	41.23	55.97	71.24	87.01	103.28	120.04
42	13.92	28.36	43.31	58.78	74.76	91.25	108.23	125.67
43	14.64	29.80	45.49	61.70	78.42	95.64	113.33	131.46
44	15.38	31.31	47.75	64.72	82.20	100.15	118.56	137.39
45	16.17	32.87	50.11	67.86	86.09	104.78	123.92	143.47
46	16.98	34.50	52.54	71.07	90.07	109.51	129.39	149.66
47	17.82	36.18	55.03	74.35	94.14	114.35	134.98	155.98
48	18.69	37.88	57.56	77.70	98.28	119.28	140.66	162.40
49	19.56	39.61	60.14	81.11	102.51	124.30	146.45	168.92
50	20.45	41.39	62.78	84.61	106.83	129.42	152.34	175.56
51	21.37	43.21	65.49	88.18	111.24	134.64	158.35	182.32
52	22.32	45.08	68.27	91.83	115.75	139.97	164.46	189.18
53	23.29	47.00	71.11	95.56	120.34	145.39	170.67	196.14
54	24.28	48.96	74.00	99.36	125.01	150.90	176.97	203.17
55	25.30	50.96	76.95	103.24	129.77	156.49	183.34	210.28
56	26.33	53.00	79.97	107.19	134.60	162.15	189.79	217.45
57	27.39	55.09	83.05	111.20	139.50	167.88	196.29	224.68
58	28.48	57.22	86.17	115.26	144.44	173.66	202.84	231.92
59	29.58	59.38	89.32	119.36	149.43	179.47	209.40	239.14
60	30.70	61.56	92.51	123.50	154.46	185.29	215.94	246.33

TABLE No. XXI—(CONTINUED.)

NET VALUE PER $1,000 OF AN ORDINARY LIFE POLICY, AT THE END OF VARIOUS YEARS, AMERICAN EXPERIENCE, 4½ PER CENT.

Age.	Ninth year.	Tenth year.	Eleventh year.	Twelfth year.	Thirt'nth year.	Fourt'nth year.	Fifteenth year.	Twentieth year.
20	50.78	57.71	64.93	72.46	80.31	88.49	97.00	145.04
21	53.23	60.48	68.05	75.94	84.15	92.70	101.61	151.78
22	55.80	63.40	71.33	79.58	88.18	97.13	106.45	158.84
23	58.51	66.47	74.77	83.41	92.41	101.78	111.52	166.21
24	61.35	69.69	78.38	87.43	96.85	106.65	116.83	173.91
25	64.34	73.08	82.18	91.65	101.51	111.74	122.39	181.94
26	67.47	76.63	86.16	96.07	106.37	117.08	128.19	190.30
27	70.77	80.36	90.34	100.70	111.48	122.66	134.28	199.00
28	74.23	84.27	94.71	105.56	116.82	128.51	140.64	208.03
29	77.86	88.37	99.29	110.63	122.41	134.63	147.30	217.39
30	81.67	92.67	104.10	115.96	128.26	141.03	154.24	227.05
31	85.67	97.18	109.13	121.53	134.40	147.71	161.49	237.02
32	89.84	101.90	114.40	127.37	140.79	154.69	169.04	247.26
33	94.23	106.84	119.92	133.46	147.47	161.94	176.88	257.78
34	98.83	112.03	125.69	139.83	154.43	169.50	185.02	268.56
35	103.66	117.45	131.72	146.46	161.67	177.34	193.43	279.59
36	108.69	123.11	137.99	153.36	169.18	185.43	202.09	290.85
37	113.96	129.01	144.53	160.51	176.93	193.77	211.00	302.32
38	119.45	135.15	151.31	167.91	184.92	202.34	220.14	313.99
39	125.18	141.52	158.31	175.53	193.15	211.16	229.53	325.85
40	131.11	148.11	165.53	183.36	201.59	220.18	239.11	337.86
41	137.25	154.89	172.95	191.41	210.24	229.41	248.91	350.00
42	143.55	161.86	180.56	199.64	219.07	238.83	258.87	362.25
43	150.02	168.99	188.34	208.05	228.08	248.40	268.99	374.58
44	156.64	176.28	196.28	216.61	237.23	258.13	279.26	386.96
45	163.41	183.72	204.37	225.32	246.54	268.00	289.65	399.37
46	170.30	191.29	212.58	234.15	255.96	277.98	300.14	411.76
47	177.33	198.98	220.93	243.12	265.51	288.06	310.72	424.11
48	184.45	206.79	229.38	252.18	275.14	298.22	321.36	436.38
49	191.69	214.71	237.94	261.34	284.85	308.44	332.06	448.54
50	199.04	222.74	246.60	270.59	294.64	318.73	342.79	460.56
51	206.51	230.87	255.36	279.92	304.51	329.07	353.54	472.41
52	214.08	239.09	264.19	289.32	314.42	339.42	364.27	484.08
53	221.73	247.40	273.10	298.77	324.34	349.76	374.96	495.61
54	229.45	255.76	282.05	308.23	334.26	360.05	385.55	507.07
55	237.25	264.19	291.02	317.69	344.13	370.27	396.04	518.57
56	245.09	272.62	299.98	327.11	353.92	380.37	406.37	530.21
57	252.95	281.06	308.92	336.45	363.61	390.22	416.55	542.08
58	260.81	289.45	317.77	345.69	373.15	400.12	426.61	554.26
59	268.62	297.77	326.51	354.77	382.53	409.80	436.65	566.77
60	276.36	305.98	335.11	363.71	391.81	419.47	446.78	579.68

TABLE No. XXII.

NET VALUE PER $1,000 OF A TEN-PAYMENT LIFE POLICY, AT THE END
OF VARIOUS YEARS, AMERICAN EXPERIENCE, 4½ PER CENT.

Age.	First year.	Second year.	Third year.	Fourth year.	Fifth year.
20	20.75	42.56	65.48	89.58	114.91
21	21.20	43.47	66.89	91.51	117.39
22	21.66	44.43	68.36	93.53	119.98
23	22.15	45.43	69.90	95.63	122.67
24	22.66	46.48	71.51	97.82	125.48
25	23.19	47.57	73.18	100.11	128.41
26	23.74	48.69	74.92	102.48	131.46
27	24.32	49.88	76.73	104.96	134.63
28	24.92	51.10	78.62	107.54	137.94
29	25.54	52.38	80.59	110.23	141.38
30	26.19	53.72	82.63	113.02	144.95
31	26.87	55.10	84.76	115.92	148.67
32	27.58	56.54	86.96	118.94	152.53
33	28.30	58.02	89.26	122.07	156.54
34	29.06	59.58	91.64	125.32	160.69
35	29.85	61.20	94.12	128.68	164.99
36	30.66	62.86	96.66	132.17	169.45
37	31.51	64.58	99.31	135.77	174.06
38	32.38	66.36	102.03	139.49	178.83
39	33.28	68.20	104.86	143.35	183.76
40	34.21	70.11	107.78	147.33	188.84
41	35.18	72.08	110.81	151.44	194.09
42	36.17	74.12	113.91	155.66	199.46
43	37.20	76.20	117.10	159.99	204.98
44	38.25	78.34	120.36	164.41	210.60
45	39.33	80.53	123.70	168.93	216.32
46	40.43	82.76	127.08	173.49	222.09
47	41.55	85.02	130.49	178.09	227.92
48	42.67	87.28	133.91	182.72	233.78
49	43.79	89.53	137.33	187.33	239.66
50	44.90	91.98	140.76	191.96	245.54
51	46.02	94.04	144.18	196.58	251.41
52	47.13	96.28	147.58	201.17	257.25
53	48.24	98.50	150.95	205.73	263.04
54	49.32	100.70	154.27	210.22	268.76
55	50.39	102.85	157.53	214.64	274.39
56	51.44	104.96	160.73	218.95	279.89
57	52.46	107.02	163.85	223.17	285.25
58	53.47	109.02	166.86	227.23	290.42
59	54.42	110.93	169.74	231.11	295.39
60	55.33	112.75	172.48	234.82	300.13

TABLE No. XXII—(CONTINUED.)
NET VALUE PER $1,000 OF A TEN-PAYMENT LIFE POLICY, AT THE END OF VARIOUS YEARS, AMERICAN EXPERIENCE, 4½ PER CENT.

Age.	Sixth year.	Seventh year.	Eighth year.	Ninth year.	Tenth year.
20	141.56	169.57	199.03	230.02	262.61
21	144.61	173.22	203.32	234.97	268.26
22	147.79	177.03	207.79	240.13	274.16
23	151.11	181.00	212.44	245.51	280.30
24	154.56	185.14	217.30	251.12	286.69
25	158.17	189.46	222.36	256.96	293.35
26	161.92	193.95	227.62	263.04	300.29
27	165.83	198.62	233.10	269.37	307.51
28	169.89	203.48	238.81	275.95	315.03
29	174.12	208.55	244.74	282.80	322.83
30	178.52	213.81	250.91	289.92	330.95
31	183.09	219.28	257.31	297.31	339.37
32	187.84	224.95	263.96	304.97	348.12
33	192.76	230.83	270.85	312.93	357.19
34	197.87	236.93	278.00	321.18	366.60
35	203.15	243.25	285.40	329.73	376.35
36	208.63	249.80	293.08	338.57	386.43
37	214.21	256.57	301.00	347.72	396.85
38	220.15	263.57	309.19	357.15	407.60
39	226.20	270.79	317.64	366.88	418.67
40	232.44	278.22	326.33	376.88	430.04
41	238.85	285.87	335.25	387.14	441.70
42	245.44	293.70	344.38	397.63	453.63
43	252.17	301.70	353.70	408.34	465.82
44	259.03	309.84	363.18	419.25	478.26
45	265.99	318.10	372.83	430.36	490.93
46	273.03	326.48	382.60	441.63	503.80
47	280.15	334.94	392.49	453.04	516.87
48	287.31	343.46	402.46	464.57	530.10
49	294.49	352.02	412.50	476.21	543.48
50	301.68	360.61	422.58	487.92	556.98
51	308.87	369.20	432.69	499.67	570.59
52	316.03	377.77	442.78	511.46	584.26
53	323.13	386.38	452.84	523.23	597.97
54	330.16	394.71	462.82	534.95	611.70
55	337.07	403.03	472.69	546.60	625.42
56	343.84	411.19	482.43	558.14	639.08
57	350.44	419.17	491.98	569.53	652.65
58	356.83	426.94	501.31	580.72	666.11
59	362.99	434.42	510.36	591.67	679.42
60	368.86	441.60	519.11	602.34	692.54

TABLE No. XXIII.

Net Value per $1.000 of a Ten-Year Endowment Policy, at the end of Various years, American Experience, 4½ per cent.

Age.	First year.	Second year.	Third year.	Fourth year.	Fifth year.
20	78.39	160.91	247.78	339.26	435.59
21	78.39	160.90	247.76	339.22	435.55
22	78.37	160.87	247.72	339.17	435.49
23	78.34	160.82	247.68	339.12	435.43
24	78.32	160.78	247.63	339.06	435.36
25	78.31	160.76	247.58	339.00	435.29
26	78.29	160.71	247.53	338.94	435.22
27	78.27	160.68	247.48	338.88	435.14
28	78.26	160.65	247.42	338.82	435.06
29	78.23	160.61	247.37	338.74	434.98
30	78.22	160.58	247.31	338.66	434.89
31	78.20	160.53	247.25	338.58	434.79
32	78.17	160.49	247.18	338.49	434.68
33	78.14	160.42	247.11	338.40	434.56
34	78.12	160.38	247.03	338.29	434.44
35	78.10	160.33	246.94	338.18	434.32
36	78.07	160.26	246.84	338.05	434.18
37	78.03	160.18	246.73	337.91	434.02
38	77.99	160.11	246.62	337.75	433.83
39	77.95	160.02	246.50	337.60	433.64
40	77.91	159.96	246.38	337.44	433.44
41	77.88	159.88	246.25	337.27	433.21
42	77.83	159.78	246.11	337.07	432.95
43	77.79	159.68	245.96	336.85	432.67
44	77.75	159.60	245.81	336.64	432.45
45	77.72	159.50	245.64	336.41	432.11
46	77.65	159 37	245.44	336 13	431.76
47	77.59	159.20	245.18	335.76	431.29
48	77.52	159.05	244.85	335.31	430.72
49	77.43	158.84	244.50	334.80	430.10
50	77.31	158.58	244.10	334.24	429.38
51	77.15	158.28	243.63	333.59	428.54
52	77.01	157.93	243.09	332.88	427.58
53	76.84	157.56	242.47	331.96	426.53
54	76.63	157.12	241.81	331.08	425.47
55	76.42	156.66	241.10	330.15	424.35
56	76.17	156 13.	240.30	329.07	423.00
57	75.90	155.56	239.39	327.83	421.53
58	75.60	154.92	238.36	326.42	419.79
59	75.28	154.23	237.24	324.93	417.92
60	74.92	153.46	236.08	323.35	415.99

TABLE No. XXIII—(Continued.)

Net Value per $1,000 of a Ten-Year Endowment Policy, at the
End of Various Years, American Experience, 4½ per cent.

Age.	Sixth year.	Seventh year.	Eighth year.	Ninth year.	Tenth year.
20	537.04	643.89	756.45	875.04	1,000.00
21	536.99	643.83	756.40	875.01	1,000.00
22	536.93	643.77	756.35	874.98	1,000.00
23	536.86	643.71	756.30	874.95	1,000.00
24	536.79	643.65	756.25	874.92	1,000.00
25	536.72	643.59	756.20	874.88	1,000.00
26	536.65	643.52	756.14	874.84	1,000.00
27	536.57	643.44	756.07	874.80	1,000.00
28	536.49	643.36	756.00	874.76	.1,000.00
29	536.40	643.27	755.92	874.71	1.000.00
30	536.29	643.17	755.84	874.66	1,000.00
31	536.18	643.06	755.75	874.60	1,000.00
32	536.06	642.94	755.65	874.54	1,000.00
33	535.94	642.82	755.54	874.47	1,000.00
34	535.81	642.69	755.42	874.40	1,000.00
35	535.66	642.54	755.29	874.31	1,000.00
36	535.49	642.37	755.14	874.21	1,000.00
37	535.31	642.18	754.98	874.10	1,000.00
38	535.11	641.97	754.80	873.99	1,000.00
39	534.90	641.76	754.62	873.87	1,000.00
40	534.69	641.55	754.42	873.74	1,000.00
41	534.44	641.30	754.18	873.59	1,000.00
42	534.15	641.01	753.90	873.41	1,000.00
43	533.88	640.67	753.58	873.20	1,000.00
44	533.53	640.31	753.25	872.97	1,000.00
45	533.13	639.90	752.90	872.72	1,000.00
46	532.68	639.42	752.46	872.43	1,000.00
47	532.13	638.85	752.03	872.09	1,000.00
48	531.44	638.17	751.41	871.68	1,000.00
49	530.77	637.44	750.70	871.25	1,000.00
50	529.99	636.64	749.98	870.79	1,000.00
51	529.12	635.72	749.15	870.27	1,000.00
52	528.10	634.66	748.20	869.64	1,000.00
53	526.94	633.46	747.07	868.98	1,000.00
54	525.71	632.18	745.94	868.19	1,000.00
55	524.33	630.83	744.81	867.39	1,000.00
56	522.79	629.27	743.44	866.50	1,000.00
57	520.96	627.46	741.82	865.45	1,000.00
58	518.95	625.38	739.96	864.24	1,000.00
59	516.91	623.29	738.06	862.98	1,000.00
60	514.86	621.09	736.09	861.64	1,000.00

TABLE No. XXIV.

NET VALUE PER $1,000 OF A FIFTEEN-YEAR ENDOWMENT POLICY,
AT THE END OF VARIOUS YEARS, AMERICAN EXPERIENCE, 4½ PER CENT.

Age.	First year.	Second year.	Third year.	Fourth year.	Fifth year.	Sixth year.	Seventh year.	Eighth year.
20	45.37	93.10	143.34	196.21	251.86	310.45	372.13	437.08
21	45.36	93.08	143.31	196.17	251.82	310.40	372.07	437.02
22	45.35	93.06	143.28	196.13	251.76	310.34	372.00	436.94
23	45.34	93.04	143.26	196.10	251.72	310.29	371.94	436.87
24	45.33	93.03	143.23	196.06	251.68	310.23	371.87	436.79
25	45.33	93.02	143.20	196.03	251.63	310.16	371.80	436.71
26	45.32	93.00	143.18	195.99	251.58	310.11	371.73	436.62
27	45.31	92.99	143.15	195.95	251.53	310.04	371.65	436.53
28	45.30	92.97	143.12	195.92	251.48	309.98	371.57	436.44
29	45.29	92.95	143.10	195.88	251.42	309.90	371.48	436.34
30	45.29	92.94	143.08	195.83	251.37	309.84	371.40	436.24
31	45.29	92.93	143.05	195.79	251.32	309.77	371.31	436.12
32	45.28	92.91	143.02	195.76	251.26	309.69	371.21	436.00
33	45.27	92.89	143.00	195.72	261.20	309.61	371.10	435.87
34	45.27	92.89	142.98	195.69	251.14	309.53	370.99	435.74
35	45.27	92.88	142.96	195.65	251.09	309.44	370.88	435.60
36	45.27	92.88	142.94	195.61	251.02	309.35	370.76	435.46
37	45.27	92.87	142.92	195.57	250.96	309.27	370.66	435.31
38	45.27	92.87	142.91	195.54	250.91	309.19	370.55	435.17
39	45.28	92.88	142.92	195.54	250.88	309.13	370.45	435.02
40	45.29	92.89	142.93	195.54	250.87	309.09	370.36	434.89
41	45.32	92.93	142.97	195.57	250.88	309.05	370.28	434.74
42	45.35	92.98	143.02	195.61	250.89	309.02	370.18	434.56
43	45.39	93.04	143.09	195.66	250.91	308.98	370.06	434.35
44	45.43	93.12	143.16	195.72	250.92	308.92	369.91	434.09
45	45.49	93.20	143.25	195.78	250.92	308.83	369.70	433.77
46	45.54	93.28	143.33	195.81	250.87	308.68	369.44	433.38
47	45.60	93.37	143.40	195.82	250.80	308.50	369.13	432.93
48	45.66	93.43	143.43	195.79	250.67	308.25	368.74	432.39
49	45.70	93.47	143.43	195.72	250.50	307.94	368.27	431.75
50	45.74	93.51	143.42	195.63	250.28	307.58	367.73	431.07
51	45.78	93.54	143.41	195.52	250.04	307.16	367.13	430.24
52	42.81	93.57	143.37	195.38	249.75	306.70	366.46	429.34
53	45.86	93.59	143.33	195.22	249.43	306.18	365.72	428.36
54	45.89	93.61	143.28	195.04	249.08	305.61	364.90	427.26
55	45.93	93.63	143.22	194.85	248.69	304.98	363.99	426.06
56	45.97	93.65	143.16	194.64	248.27	304.30	363.00	424.76
57	46.03	93.69	143.10	194.42	247.82	303.56	361.95	423.35
58	46.09	93.73	143.05	194.19	247.34	302.78	360.81	421.81
59	46.16	93.78	142.98	193.93	246.82	301.93	359.55	420.12
60	46.23	93.83	142.92	193.67	246.28	301.00	358.18	418.27

TABLE No. XXIV—(Continued.)

NET VALUE PER $1,000 OF A FIFTEEN-YEAR ENDOWMENT POLICY, AT THE END OF VARIOUS YEARS, AMERICAN EXPERIENCE, 4½ PER CENT.

Age.	Ninth year.	Tenth year.	Eleventh year.	Twelfth year.	Thirteenth year.	Fourteenth year.	Fifteenth year.
20	505 48	577.52	653.40	733.35	817.60	906.40	1,000
21	505.41	577.45	653.33	733.28	817.54	906.36	1,000
22	505.32	577.36	653.25	733.21	817.48	906.32	1.000
23	505.25	577.28	653.16	733.13	817.42	906.28	1,000
24	505.17	577.19	653.07	733.05	817.35	906.24	1,000
25	505.07	577.09	652.88	732.96	817.28	906.20	1,000
26	504.98	576 99	652.87	732.86	817.20	906.15	1,000
27	504.88	576.88	652.76	732.76	817.12	906.09	1,000
28	504.78	576.78	652.65	732.65	817.02	906.03	1,000
29	504.66	576.64	652.52	732.52	816.92	905.97	1,000
30	504.54	576.51	652.38	732.39	816.80	905.90	1,000
31	504.41	576.37	652.24	732.25	816.68	905.83	1,000
32	504.26	576.21	652.07	732.10	816.55	905.74	1,000
33	504.12	576.05	651.90	731.93	816.41	905.65	1,000
34	503.96	575.88	651.72	731.75	816.25	905.55	1,000
35	503.80	575.69	651.52	731.56	816.08	905.44	1,000
36	503.63	575 49	651.31	731.34	815.89	905.31	1,000
37	503.45	575.29	651.08	731.11	815.68	905.17	1,000
38	503.26	575.07	650.84	730.85	815.45	905.02	1,000
39	503.07	574.83	650.56	730.56	815 19	904.84	1,000
40	502.88	574.58	650.26	730 24	814.89	904.65	1,000
41	502.66	574.29	649.91	729 87	814 56	904.43	1.000
42	502.40	573.94	649.51	729.46	814.18	904.18	1,000
43	502.09	573.55	649.06	728 98	813 76	903 89	1,000
44	501.72	573.09	648.53	728.44	813.27	903 57	1,000
45	501.29	572.55	647.93	727.82	812 72	903.21	1,000
46	500.77	571 93	647.23	727.11	812.09	902.80	1,000
47	500.18	571.22	646.44	726.30	811 38	902.34	1,000
48	499.49	570.40	645.54	725 39	810.58	901.82	1,000
49	498.70	569.47	644.52	724.37	809.68	901.23	1,000
50	497.84	568.47	643.38	723.23	808.68	900.58	1,000
51	496.81	567.27	642.11	721.95	807.56	899.86	1,000
52	495.70	565.97	640.69	720.54	806.32	899.05	1.000
53	494.48	564.54	639.13	718.97	804.93	898.14	1,000
54	493.12	562.96	637.42	717.23	803.40	897.14	1,000
55	491.63	561.23	635.51	715.31	801.72	896.03	1,000
56	490.01	560.32	633.41	713.20	799.83	894.79	1,000
57	488.24	557.24	631.12	710.86	797.75	893.42	1,000
58	486.31	554.96	628.58	708.28	795 44	891.88	1,000
59	484.18	552.43	625.79	705.42	792.89	890.20	1,000
60	481.83	549.64	622.68	702.24	790.05	888.34	1,000

TABLE No. XXV.

NET VALUE PER $1,000, OF A TWENTY-YEAR ENDOWMENT POLICY, AT THE END OF VARIOUS YEARS, AMERICAN EXPERIENCE, 4 PER CENT

Age.	First year.	Second year.	Third year.	Fourth year.	Fifth year.	Sixth year.	Seventh year.	Eighth year.
20	29.45	60.41	92.98	127.23	163.27	201.20	241.10	283.10
21	29.44	60.40	92.97	127.22	163.26	201.18	241.07	283.06
22	29.44	60.40	92.96	127.22	163.25	201.16	241.06	283.03
23	29.44	60.40	92.97	127.22	163.25	201.16	241.04	283.01
24	29.44	60.41	92.97	127.22	163.25	201.15	241.02	282.99
25	29.45	60.42	92.98	127.23	163.26	201.15	241.02	282.98
26	29.45	60.42	92.99	127.24	163.26	201.15	241.01	282.95
27	29.46	60.44	93.01	127.25	163.27	201.16	241.01	282.94
28	29.47	60.45	93.02	127.28	163.30	201.17	241.02	282.94
29	29.48	60.47	93.05	127.31	163.32	201.20	241.04	282.95
30	29.50	60.50	93.09	127.34	163.36	201.24	241.07	282.96
31	29.52	60.54	93.13	127.39	163.42	201.29	241.12	283.00
32	29.54	60.57	93.18	127.46	163.48	201.36	241.17	283.04
33	29.56	60.61	93.25	127.53	163.57	201.43	241.24	283.10
34	29.59	60.68	93.33	127.64	163.68	201.55	241.35	283.20
35	29.64	60.76	93.44	127.76	163.81	201.68	241.49	283.33
36	39.68	60.84	93.55	127.90	163.96	201.85	241.65	283.49
37	29.74	60.94	93.69	128.06	164.15	202.06	241.87	283.69
38	29.79	61.05	93.84	128.26	164.39	202.32	242.14	283.96
39	29.87	61.19	94.05	128.52	164.69	202.64	242.47	284.27
40	29.95	61.36	94.29	128.82	165.03	203.01	242.84	284.64
41	30.06	61.56	94.58	129.17	165.44	203.44	243.29	285.06
42	30.18	61.80	94.90	129.58	165.89	203.93	243.77	285.50
43	30.33	62.06	95.28	130.03	166.41	204.47	244.29	285.96
44	30.48	62.36	95.69	130.54	166.97	205.04	244.83	286.45
45	30.66	62.69	96.15	131.09	167.56	205.63	245.40	286.95
46	30.85	63.04	96.63	131.65	168.16	206.24	245.97	287.45
47	31.06	63.43	97.14	132.25	168.80	206.88	246.57	287.97
48	31.29	63.83	97.67	132.86	169.46	207.54	247.18	288.50
49	31.51	64.23	98.21	133.49	170.15	208.23	247.83	289.04
50	31.74	64.66	98.79	134.18	170.88	208.96	248.51	289.62
51	32.00	65.12	99.41	134.91	171.67	209.75	249.24	290.25
52	32.27	65.63	100.09	135.71	172.52	210.61	250.05	290.94
53	32.58	66.17	100.83	136.57	173.45	211.55	250 93	291.69
54	32.89	66.76	101.62	137.50	174.47	212.58	251.89	292.51
55	33.25	67.40	102.48	138.53	175.59	213.70	252.94	293.41
56	33.62	68.09	103.42	139.65	176.79	214.91	254.08	294.39
57	34.03	68.84	104.44	140.85	178.09	216.22	255.31	295.46
58	34.48	69.66	105.54	142.14	179.48	217.63	256.64	296.58
59	34.95	70.52	106.70	143.51	180.97	219.13	258.03	297.75
60	35.45	71.44	107.94	144.98	182.57	220.71	259.48	298.96

TABLE No. XXV—(Continued.)

NET VALUE PER $1,000 OF A TWENTY-YEAR ENDOWMENT POLICY, AT THE
END OF VARIOUS YEARS, AMERICAN EXPERIENCE, 4½ PER CENT.

Age.	*Ninth year.*	*Tenth year.*	*Eleventh year.*	*Twelfth year.*	*Thirteenth year.*	*Fourteenth year.*	*Fifteenth year.*
20	327.29	373.82	422.80	474.37	528.68	585.88	646.14
21	327.24	373.75	422.74	474.30	528.60	585.79	646.05
22	327.21	373.72	422.68	474.23	528.52	585.70	645.96
23	327.18	373.67	422.62	474.16	528.44	585.61	645.86
24	327.15	373.63	422.56	474.09	528.35	585.52	645.76
25	327.12	373.59	422.51	474.02	528.27	585.42	645.65
26	327.08	373.54	422.45	473.95	528.18	585.32	645.53
27	327.07	373.51	422.40	473.87	528.09	585.20	645.41
28	327.05	373.48	422.35	473.80	527.99	585.11	645.28
29	327.05	373.45	422.29	473.72	527.89	584.97	645.14
30	327.03	373.42	422.25	473.65	527.80	584.86	645.01
31	327.06	373.42	422.22	473.59	527.72	584.74	644.86
32	327.08	373.42	422.19	473.54	527.63	584.63	644.72
33	327.12	373.44	422.19	473.51	527.56	584.52	644.58
34	327.20	373.50	422.22	473.50	527.51	584.42	644.43
35	327.32	373.59	422.27	473.50	527.46	584.32	644.27
36	327.47	373.71	422.34	473.53	527.42	584.20	644.09
37	327.65	373.85	422.45	473.57	527.39	584.09	643.88
38	327.88	374.05	422.58	473.62	527.34	583.94	643.65
39	328.17	374.29	422.73	473.67	527.29	583.78	643.40
40	328.50	374.54	422.89	473.72	527.21	583.59	643.10
41	328.86	374.81	423.05	473.76	527.13	583.37	642.75
42	329.23	375.08	423.21	473.79	527.00	583.10	642.35
43	329.61	375.35	423.36	473.78	526.84	582.78	641.89
44	330.01	375.64	423.49	473.75	526.63	582.40	641.35
45	330.41	375.91	423.60	473.68	526.37	581.95	640.74
46	330.80	376.15	423.67	473.56	527.05	581.43	640.04
47	331.20	376.39	423.73	473.40	525.67	580.83	639.23
48	331.60	376.62	423.75	473.20	525.22	580.14	638.33
49	332.00	376.84	423.76	472.95	524.71	579.36	637.32
50	332.43	377.08	423.74	472.67	524.13	578.50	636.20
51	332.89	377.32	423.73	472.35	523.52	577.56	634.97
52	333.40	377.59	423.71	472.02	522.83	576.53	633.62
53	333.95	377.89	423.74	471.67	522.21	575.41	632.15
54	334.57	378.24	423.72	471.29	521.40	574.18	630.52
55	335.25	378.63	423.74	470.88	520.42	572.82	628.72
56	335.99	379.03	423.74	470.41	519.42	571.30	626.70
57	336.78	379.46	423.72	469.85	518.29	569.57	624.43
58	337.60	379.87	423.62	469.17	516.97	567.60	621.88
59	338.43	380.24	423.43	468.34	515.43	565.39	619.09
60	339.26	380.57	423.13	467.34	513.71	563.00	616.13

TABLE No. XXVI.

NET VALUE PER $1,000. OF A TWENTY-FIVE YEAR ENDOWMENT POLICY, AT THE END OF VARIOUS YEARS, AMERICAN EXPERIENCE, 4½ PER CENT.

Age.	First year.	Second year.	Third year.	Fourth year.	Fifth year.	Sixth year.	Seventh year.	Eighth year.
20	20.36	41.75	64.24	87.87	112.72	138.85	166.33	195.22
21	20.37	41.77	64.26	87.90	112.76	138.89	166.37	195.27
22	20.37	41.78	64.29	87.94	112.81	138.95	166.43	195.32
23	20.39	41.81	64.33	87.99	112.86	139.01	166.49	195.39
24	20.41	41.85	64.38	88.05	112.94	139.09	166.58	195.48
25	20.43	41.89	64.43	88.13	113.02	139.18	166.68	195.59
26	20.45	41.93	64.50	88.21	113.12	139.30	166.81	195.71
27	20.48	41.99	64.58	88.31	113.24	139.43	166.95	195.87
28	20.51	42.05	64.67	88.43	113.38	139.59	167.12	196.06
29	20.55	42.12	64.78	88.57	113.54	139.77	167.33	196.28
30	20.59	42.21	64.91	88.73	113.74	140.01	167.58	196.55
31	20.65	42.32	65.05	88.91	113.97	140.27	167.88	196.86
32	20.71	42.43	65.22	89.14	114.23	140.57	168.21	197.22
33	20.77	42.56	65.42	89.39	114.55	140.93	168.61	197.64
34	20.85	42.73	65.65	89.70	114.91	141.35	169.07	198.15
35	20.95	42.91	65.93	90.05	115.33	141.83	169.61	198.74
36	21.06	43.12	66.23	90.44	115.80	142.38	170.23	199.42
37	21.18	43.36	66.58	90.89	116.36	143.03	170.96	200.22
38	21.31	43.62	66.97	91.41	116.99	143.77	171.79	201.12
39	21.47	43.93	67.43	92.01	117.73	144.62	172.74	202.15
40	21.65	44.29	67.95	92.70	118.56	145.58	173.81	203.30
41	21.86	44.70	68.56	93.48	119.51	146.67	175.02	204.59
42	22.09	45.16	69.23	94.36	120.55	147.87	176.34	205.99
43	22.36	45.68	69.99	95.33	121.72	149.20	177.78	207.50
44	22.65	46.25	70.82	96.39	122.99	150.62	179.31	209.11
45	22.98	46.88	71.73	97.55	124.35	152.15	180.97	210.85
46	23.32	47.56	72.71	98.79	125.80	153.77	182.73	212.17
47	23.71	48.30	73.76	100.10	127.35	155.51	184.62	214.69
48	24.12	49.08	74.87	101.50	129.00	157.37	186.63	216.82
49	24.55	49.89	76.03	102.98	130.75	159.35	188.79	212.08
50	25.00	50.77	77.29	104.58	132.64	161.48	191.10	221.53
51	25.49	51.71	78.64	106.30	134.67	163.76	193.59	224.17
52	26.02	52.72	80.09	108.14	134.85	166.22	196.27	227.00
53	26.58	53.80	81.65	110.11	139.18	168.86	199.14	230.03
54	27.18	54.95	83.30	112.21	141.67	171.67	202.20	233.25
55	27.82	56.18	85.06	114.46	144.33	174.67	205.46	236.69
56	28.50	57.49	86.95	116.85	147.16	177.85	208.92	240.35
57	29.23	58.89	88.96	119.39	150.14	181.23	212.60	244.24
58	30.01	60.38	91.09	122.19	153.34	184.82	216.50	248.34
59	30.82	61.95	93.33	124.92	156.70	188.61	220.60	252.64
60	31.68	63.59	95.69	127.92	160.25	192.59	224.91	257.17

TABLE No. XXVI—(CONTINUED.)

NET VALUE PER $1,000 OF A TWENTY-FIVE YEAR ENDOWMENT POLICY, AT THE END OF VARIOUS YEARS, AMERICAN EXPERIENCE, 4½ PER CENT.

Age.	Ninth year.	Tenth year.	Eleventh year.	Twelfth year.	Thirt'nth year.	Four'nth year.	Fifteenth year.	Twent'th year.
20	225.61	257.57	291.20	326.57	363.79	402.96	444.19	685.59
21	225.65	257.61	291.23	326.60	363.80	402.96	444.18	685.50
22	225.71	257.66	291.28	326.63	363.83	402.98	444.18	685.41
23	225.77	257.73	291.33	326.68	363.87	403.01	444.20	685.31
24	225.87	257.81	291.41	326.75	363.93	403.05	444.21	685.22
25	225.97	257.91	291.51	326.84	364.01	403.10	444.24	685.13
26	226.10	258.05	291.64	326.96	364.10	403.18	444.29	685.04
27	226.26	258.21	291.79	327.10	364.23	403.28	444.37	684.95
28	226.46	258.41	291.98	327.27	364.38	403.42	444.48	684.87
29	226.69	258.64	292.21	327.49	364.59	403.59	444.63	684.80
30	226.97	258.92	292.48	327.75	364.84	403.83	444.83	684.73
31	227.29	259.24	292.81	328.08	365.15	404.11	445.08	684.65
32	227.66	259.63	293.21	328.48	365.53	404.46	445.37	684.57
33	228.12	260.10	293.69	328.95	365.98	404.88	445.75	684.47
34	228.65	260.67	294.26	329.52	366.52	405.37	446.19	684.37
35	229.29	261.32	294.93	330.17	367.14	405.94	446.67	684.26
36	230.01	262.08	295.68	330.91	367.85	406.58	447.22	684.12
37	230.86	262.95	296.56	331.76	368.64	407.28	447.78	683.96
38	231.82	263.94	297.54	332.70	369.50	408.04	448.44	683.78
39	232.89	265.04	298.63	333.74	370.45	408.88	449.14	683.58
40	234.10	266.25	299.81	334.86	371.49	409.79	449.89	683.33
41	235.43	267.58	301.10	336.08	372.61	410.77	450.70	683.05
42	236.86	269.01	302.49	337.40	373.81	411.83	451.58	682.73
43	238.40	270.55	303.99	338.82	375.10	412.95	452.49	682.35
44	240.07	272.21	305.60	340.33	376.48	414.15	453.48	681.92
45	241.84	273.98	307.32	341.95	377.95	415.44	454.53	681.44
46	243.74	275.87	309.16	343.68	379.53	416.81	455.65	680.89
47	245.77	277.90	311.14	345.55	381.23	418.29	456.85	680.28
48	247.95	280.07	313.26	347.56	383.06	419.87	458.14	679.60
49	250.28	282.42	315.53	349.70	385.01	421.57	459.53	678.83
50	252.80	284.94	318.00	352.03	387.13	423.42	461.04	677.97
51	255.51	287.64	320.64	354.53	389.42	425.42	462.66	676.97
52	258.42	290.57	323.48	357.22	391.88	427.54	464.38	675.82
53	261.53	293.68	326.52	360.10	394.48	429.79	466.18	674.51
54	264.85	297.00	329.76	363.14	397.24	432.16	468.04	673.06
55	268.38	300.55	333.19	366.36	400.14	434.62	469.97	671.53
56	272.14	304.29	336.81	369.75	403.17	437.18	471.94	670.00
57	276.28	308.24	340.63	373.31	406.35	439.85	473.98	668.60
58	280.31	312.41	344.64	377.05	409.67	442.64	476.19	667.44
59	284.71	316.77	348.85	380.95	413.16	445.66	478.69	666.62
60	289.31	321.34	353.24	395.05	416.91	449.03	481.66	666.25

TABLE No. XXVII.

NET VALUE PER $1,000 OF A THIRTY-YEAR ENDOWMENT, AT THE END OF VARIOUS YEARS, AMERICAN EXPERIENCE, 4½ PER CENT.

Age.	First year.	Second year.	Third year.	Fourth year.	Fifth year.	Sixth year.	Seventh year.	Eighth year.
20	14.69	30.11	46.30	63.30	81.17	99.94	119.66	140.38
21	17.71	30.15	46.36	63.39	81.28	100.07	119.80	140.54
22	14.73	30.20	46.44	63.50	81.41	100.22	119.98	140.73
23	14.76	30.26	46.54	63.62	81.56	100.40	120.18	140.95
24	14.80	30.34	46.65	63.77	81.74	100.61	120.42	141.22
25	14.85	30.43	46.78	63.94	81.94	100.85	120.70	141.53
26	14.89	30.52	46.92	64.12	82.18	101.13	121.01	141.88
27	14.95	30.63	47 08	64.34	82.45	101.45	121.38	142.27
28	15.02	30.76	47.28	64.60	82.77	101.82	121.80	142.77
29	15.09	30.91	47.50	64.89	83.12	102.24	122.30	143.32
30	15.17	31.08	47.75	65.22	83.54	102.74	122.86	143.96
31	15.28	31.28	48.04	65.61	84.02	103.31	123.52	144.68
32	15.39	31.49	48.37	66.05	84.56	103.95	124.24	145.50
33	15.50	31.74	48.74	66.54	85.17	104.67	125.08	146.44
34	15.65	32.03	49.18	67.11	85.88	105.51	126.04	147.52
35	15.82	32.36	49.66	67.75	86.67	106.44	127.12	148.73
36	16.00	32.72	50.20	68.47	87.55	107.50	128.33	150.11
37	16.21	33.13	50.81	69.27	88.55	108.69	129.72	151.65
38	16.43	33.58	51.48	70.17	89.68	110.03	131.26	153.39
39	16.69	34.09	52.26	71.20	90.95	111.54	132.99	155.33
40	16.97	34.67	53.12	72.35	92.37	113.23	134.92	157.48
41	17.30	35.32	54.10	73.63	93.97	115.10	137.05	159.84
42	17.66	36.05	55.17	75.05	95.71	117.15	139.28	162.41
43	18.06	36.84	56.35	76.61	97.62	119.38	141.90	165.17
44	18.50	37.71	57.64	78.30	99.68	121.79	144.60	168.14
45	18.99	38.66	59.05	80.14	101.91	124.36	147.50	171.32
46	19.50	39.69	60.52	82.09	104.26	127.10	150.58	174.71
47	20.06	40.69	62.15	84.15	106.77	130.01	153.86	178.31
48	20.66	41.94	63.83	86.33	109.42	133.09	157.33	182.13
49	21.27	43.13	65.60	88.63	112.22	135.35	161.01	186.17
50	21.93	44.43	67.48	91.08	115.19	139.81	164.90	190.46
51	22.62	45.79	69.49	93.67	118.35	143.47	169.03	195.01
52	23.36	47.23	71.59	96.42	121.68	147.35	173.40	199.81
53	24.15	48.78	73.83	99.33	125.21	151.45	178.03	204.89
54	24.95	50.35	76.17	102.36	128.90	155.75	182.86	210.20
55	25.82	52.05	78.64	105.58	132.81	160.28	187.96	215.79

TABLE No. XXVII—(CONTINUED.)

NET VALUE PER $1,000 OF A THIRTY-YEAR ENDOWMENT POLICY, AT THE
END OF VARIOUS YEARS, AMERICAN EXPERIENCE, 4½ PER CENT.

Age.	Ninth year.	Tenth year.	Eleventh year.	Twelfth year.	Thirt'nth year.	Fourt'nth year.	Fifteenth year.	Twentieth year.
20	162.15	185.02	209.05	234.32	260.88	288.80	318.15	489.36
21	162.32	185.20	209.25	234.53	261.08	289.00	318.36	489.46
22	162.53	185.43	209.49	234.77	261.33	289.25	318.60	489.60
23	162.77	185.69	209.76	235.05	261.63	289.55	318.89	489.79
24	163.06	186.00	210.09	235.39	261.97	289.90	319.23	490.03
25	163.40	186.36	210.47	235.79	262.38	290.31	319.64	490.32
26	163.78	186.78	210.91	236.26	262.85	290.79	320.11	490.68
27	164.24	187.27	211.44	236.79	263.41	291.35	320.68	491.11
28	164.76	187.83	212.03	237.42	264.05	292.07	321.35	491.63
29	165.37	188.48	212.72	238.14	264.80	292.78	322.13	492.22
30	166.06	189.23	213.53	238.98	265.68	293.68	323.03	492.90
31	166.86	190.09	214.44	239.95	266.69	294.71	324.08	493.66
32	167.76	191.07	215.51	241.07	267.84	295.90	325.27	494.48
33	168.79	192.20	216.70	242.31	269.17	297.24	326.62	495.42
34	169.99	193.49	218.07	243.78	270.66	298.77	328.15	496.45
35	171.33	194.95	219.63	245.42	272.35	300.48	329.84	497.57
36	172.85	196.60	221.37	247.24	274.23	302.36	331.70	498.79
37	174.55	198.43	223.33	249.28	276.30	304.43	333.73	500.14
38	176.45	200.48	225.49	251.51	278.56	306.70	335.96	501.59
39	178.57	202.75	227.87	254.00	281.05	309.18	338.40	503.19
40	180.93	205.25	230.46	256.62	283.75	311.87	341.04	504.92
41	183.47	207.94	233.28	259.52	286.68	314.80	343.91	506.80
42	186.23	210.87	236.33	262.65	289.85	317.95	347.01	508.83
43	189.21	215.02	239.62	266.03	293.26	321.36	350.35	511.03
44	192.40	217.40	243.14	269.65	296.93	325.01	353.05	513.41
45	195.84	221.04	246.93	273.53	300.84	328.94	3 7.81	515.97
46	199.48	224.89	250.95	277.67	305.06	333.13	361.92	518.68
47	203.36	229.00	255.24	282.09	309.53	337.60	366.31	521.56
48	207.48	233.37	259.80	286.77	314.28	342.33	370.96	524.59
49	212.84	237.99	264.63	291.73	319.30	347.35	375.90	527.74
50	216.47	242.90	269.74	296.98	324.62	352.66	381.12	531.01
51	221.36	248.09	275.15	302.54	330.25	358.28	386.62	534.43
52	226.54	253 55	280.86	308.42	336.20	364.20	392.41	537.99
53	232.01	259.35	286.89	314.60	342.45	370.42	398.50	541.78
54	237.72	265.40	293.20	321.07	348.98	376.92	404.84	545.89
55	243.75	271.78	299.82	327.85	355.82	383.70	411.47	550.50

TABLE No. XXVIII.

NET VALUE PER $1,000 OF A THIRTY-FIVE YEAR ENDOWMENT POLICY, AT THE END OF VARIOUS YEARS, AMERICAN EXPERIENCE, 4½ PER CENT.

Age.	First year.	Second year.	Third year.	Fourth year.	Fifth year.	Sixth year.	Seventh year.	Eighth year.
20	10.97	22.48	34.55	47.21	60.50	74.45	89.08	104.44
21	11.01	22.56	34.67	47.38	60.72	74.71	89.38	104.79
22	11.06	22.65	34.82	47.58	60.96	75.00	89.73	105.18
23	11.11	22.77	34.99	47.81	61.23	75.34	90.12	105.63
24	11.18	22.90	35.19	48.07	61.58	75.73	90.59	106.16
25	11.26	23.05	35.41	48.37	61.95	76.18	91.11	106.75
26	11.34	23.21	35.66	48.70	62.37	76.69	91.69	107.41
27	11.43	23.41	35.95	49.08	62.85	77.27	92.36	108.18
28	11.54	23.62	36.27	49.52	63.39	77.91	93.12	109.05
29	11.66	23.86	36.64	50.01	64.00	78.65	93.99	110.03
30	11.79	24.14	37.05	50.56	64.70	79.49	94.97	111.15
31	11.95	24.45	37.52	51.19	65.49	80.44	96.07	112.40
32	12.12	24.79	38.04	51.89	66.36	81.49	97.29	113.80
33	12.31	25.18	38.63	52.68	67.35	82.67	98.67	115.37
34	12.53	25.62	39.29	53.56	68.45	84.00	100.21	117.13
35	12.78	26.11	40.03	54.54	69.68	85.47	101.93	119.10
36	13.04	26.65	40.83	55.62	71.04	87.11	103.85	121.29
37	13.34	27.24	41.74	56.83	72.56	88.93	105.99	123.72
38	13.66	27.90	42.73	58.17	74.23	90.96	108.34	126.41
39	14.03	28.63	43.84	59.65	76.11	93.20	110.95	129.36
40	14.43	29.44	45.06	61.29	78.15	95.65	113.79	132.58
41	14.88	30.34	46.42	63.09	80.41	98.33	116.90	136.06
42	15.36	31.32	47.88	65.06	82.84	101.24	120.25	139.84
43	15.90	32.39	49.48	67.17	85.47	104.36	123.83	143.85
44	16.47	33.54	51.20	69.45	88.29	107.68	127.63	148.10
45	17.10	34.78	53.04	71.88	91.28	111.20	131.65	152.60
46	17.75	36.09	54.99	74.44	94.42	114.90	135.88	157.34
47	18.46	37.49	57.05	77.14	97.72	118.80	140.34	162.32
48	19.20	38.94	59.19	79.95	101.17	122.88	149.88	167.54
49	19.96	40.44	61.42	82.88	104.81	127.14	145.00	172.98
50	20.76	42.03	63.77	85.97	108.59	131.61	154.98	178.69

TABLE No. XXVIII.—(Continued.)

Net Value per $1,000 of a Thirty-five Year Endowment Policy, at
the end of various years, American Experience, 4½ per cent.

Age.	Ninth year.	Tenth year.	Eleventh year.	Twelfth year.	Thirteenth year.	Fourteenth year.	Fifteenth year.	Twentieth year.
20	120.57	137.49	155.25	173.88	193.46	214.01	235.58	360.80
21	120.95	137.91	155.70	174.38	193.98	214.55	236.15	361.39
22	121.39	138.40	156.23	174.96	194.58	215.19	239.81	262.09
23	121.89	138.95	156.83	175.59	195.27	215.92	237.58	362.91
24	122.48	139.59	157.52	176.34	196.07	216.76	238.45	363.87
25	123.14	140.32	158.32	177.20	196.99	217.72	239.46	364.97
26	123.88	141.14	159.23	178.18	198.02	218.82	240.60	366.23
27	124.75	142.09	160.26	179.28	199.21	220.06	241.91	267.67
28	125.72	143.17	161.43	180.55	200.55	221.49	243.42	369.31
29	126.82	144.38	162.75	181.97	202.08	223.11	245.11	371.15
30	128.07	145.76	164.25	183.59	203.80	224.94	247.03	373.20
31	129.47	147.30	165.94	185.41	205.75	227.01	249.20	375.46
32	131.03	149.04	167.84	187.47	207.95	229.33	251.63	377.95
33	132.80	150.99	169.97	189.77	210.41	231.92	254.33	380.69
34	134.78	153.18	172.36	192.35	213.15	234.81	257.32	383.69
35	136.99	155.62	175.02	195.20	216.19	237.99	260.62	386.96
36	139.43	158.52	177.96	198.35	219.52	241.47	264.21	390.52
37	142.16	161.32	181.20	201.83	223.18	245.27	268.12	394.39
38	145.15	164.60	184.76	205.60	227.15	249.40	272.36	398.58
39	148.45	168.21	188.62	209.70	231.45	253.86	276.96	403.11
40	152.02	172.09	192.79	214.12	236.08	258.68	281.90	407.99
41	155.89	176.28	197.28	218.87	241.06	263.84	287.21	413.23
42	160.02	180.76	202.08	223.95	246.38	269.35	292.87	418.81
43	164.42	185.54	207.19	229.36	252.04	275.22	298.89	424.73
44	169.10	190.60	212.60	235.08	258.02	281.42	305.27	431.00
45	174.05	195.96	218.33	241.13	264.35	287.99	312.00	437.61
46	179.25	201.59	224.34	247.49	271.01	294.88	319.08	444.54
47	184.70	207.51	230.67	254.18	278.01	302.13	326.49	451.79
48	190.45	213.71	237.30	261.19	285.33	309.71	334.28	459.36
49	196.43	220.20	244.23	268.50	292.97	317.61	342.39	467.22
50	202.71	226.98	251.47	276.14	300.95	325.87	350.85	475.38

COMBINED EXPERIENCE TABLE OF MORTALITY.

This table of mortality, which was the result of the united efforts of the actuaries of seventeen life offices of England and Scotland, and for this reason is often termed the "Actuaries" table, is a far better criterion of mortality than any which preceded it. Heretofore, all tables of mortality were made from the average population of certain towns or countries, which included large numbers of persons who were not proper subjects for insurance, and consequently, the mortality record was much greater than was needed for the successful determination of the mortality of insured lives. But in this case, none but selected and insured lives were taken. It comprises the recorded experience of the *Amicable, Alliance, British Commercial, Crown, Economic, Equitable, Guardian, Imperial, Law Life, London Life, Norwich Union, Promoter, Scottish Widows' Fund, Sun, Universal,* and *University* offices. The data of these offices was collected under the superintendence of a committee of actuaries, who availed themselves of all the experience and research of those who had preceded them, in order to get a reliable table to measure the average mortality of assured lives. It was first published by Jenkin Jones, in 1843, and from that time till the present, it has been highly appreciated by the actuaries of England and America. The statistics upon which this table was founded have never yet been made public, only a few copies of them were printed, and they only for private circulation.

An objection has been raised against this table, that the average age of the policies was only $8\frac{1}{2}$ years, and that for lives which continue long in the company, this table would be found defective. The experience of many of the companies in this country is that this table gives results more nearly accurate than any other in use, and that it is far better adjusted. Another objection against it is, that some of the lives were assured in two or more different companies, and in the compilation of the table they would count as so many seperate lives. Neither of these objections appear to have had much practical influence. The fact still remains that for many years it was regarded as the best table of mortality in use, that it has done excellent s; vi e during the last thirty years and for some time to come will probably be the standard table in use in the New England states.

In compiling this table some curious and unexpected results were obtained. It was found that the mortality from town life taking all ages together, was more favorable than country life, and that the mortality among assured females was greater than among assured males. The first of these results does not appear to have been noticed in this country, and the latter may be attributed to defective medical examination, or that members of this class were induced to insure because they were conscious that they were relatively short-lived. The fact is clearly established by all writers on vital statistics that the average longevity of females is fully equal to that of males, and many companies make no distinction whatever in the risk.

TABLE No. XXX.

NET VALUE PER $1,000 OF AN ORDINARY LIFE POLICY, AT THE END OF VARIOUS YEARS, COMBINED EXPERIENCE, 4 PER CENT.

Age.	First year.	Second year.	Third year.	Fourth year.	Fifth year.	Sixth year.	Seventh year.	Eighth year.
20	6.22	12.66	19.31	26.19	33.30	40 64	48.23	56.07
21	6.47	13.17	20.09	27.24	34.64	42.27	50.16	58.31
22	6.74	13.71	20.90	28.34	36.03	43.97	52.17	60.64
23	7.01	14.26	21.75	29.49	37.48	45.74	54.26	63.07
24	7.30	14.84	22.64	30.69	39.00	47.59	56.45	65.60
25	7.60	15.45	23.56	31.94	40.58	49.51	58.73	68.24
26	7.91	16.09	24.52	33.24	42.24	51.52	61.11	71.00
27	8.24	16.75	25.53	34.60	43.96	53.62	63.59	73.89
28	8.58	17.43	26.58	36.02	45.76	55.81	66.20	76.92
29	8.93	18.16	27.68	37.50	47.64	58.12	68.93	80.09
30	9.31	18.91	28.83	39.06	49.63	60.54	71.80	83.45
31	9.70	19.70	30.03	40.70	51.71	63 08	74.84	86.98
32	10.11	20.54	31.31	42.43	53.91	65.78	78.04	90.72
33	10.54	21.42	32.65	44.25	56.25	68.63	81.43	94.67
34	11.00	22.35	34.07	46.20	58.71	71.65	85.03	98.86
35	11.48	23.33	35.59	48.25	61.34	74.86	88.84	103.29
36	11.99	24.39	37.19	50.43	64.11	78.26	92.87	107.92
37	12.55	25.51	38.90	52.75	67.08	81.87	97.09	112.71
38	13.12	26.69	40.72	55.22	70.20	85.62	101.43	117.61
39	13.74	27.96	42.65	57.83	73.46	89.48	105.88	122.59
40	14.41	29.31	44.70	60.55	76.79	93.42	110.36	127.60
41	15.12	30.73	46.81	63.29	80.16	97.35	114.85	132.64
42	15.85	32.18	48.91	66.04	83.49	101.26	119.32	137.69
43	16.59	33.59	51.00	68 73	86.78	105.11	123.80	142.74
44	17.30	34 99	53.02	71.38	90.04	109.02	128.28	147.80
45	18.01	36.36	55.04	74.03	93.34	112.94	132.80	152.91
46	18.69	37.71	57.05	76.72	96.67	116.90	137.38	158.08
47	19.39	39.10	59.14	79.47	100.09	120.95	142.05	163.37
48	20.10	40.54	61.28	82.30	103.57	125.09	146.83	168.78
49	20.86	42.02	63.47	85.19	107.14	129.34	151.73	174.30
50	21.62	43.52	65.70	88.13	110.79	133.67	156.72	179.95
51	22.39	45.06	67.98	91.14	114.53	138.09	161.84	185.74
52	23.19	46 63	70.33	94.24	118.34	142.64	167.09	191.66
53	24.00	48.26	72.74	97.42	122.29	147.32	172.47	197.66
54	24.85	49.94	75.22	100.70	126.35	152.12	177.93	203.75
55	25.72	51.65	77.78	104.08	130.51	156.98	183.46	209.87
56	26.61	53.43	80.42	107.55	134.72	161.90	189.01	216.02
57	27.56	55.29	83.15	111.07	138.99	166.84	194.59	222.18
58	28.52	57.18	85.88	114.59	142.23	171.76	200.14	228.28
59	29.50	59.05	88.60	118.08	147.46	176.66	205.63	234.30
60	30.45	60.90	91.28	121.54	151.63	181.49	211.02	240.21

TABLE No. XXX—(Continued.)

NET VALUE PER $1,000 OF AN ORDINARY LIFE POLICY, AT THE END OF
VARIOUS YEARS, COMBINED EXPERIENCE, 4 PER CENT.

Age.	Ninth year.	Tenth year.	Eleventh year.	Twelfth year.	Thirteenth year.	Fourteenth year.	Fifteenth year.	Twentieth year.
20	64.17	72.53	81.16	90.07	99.27	108.75	118.56	172.61
21	66.72	75.41	84.37	93.62	103.17	113.04	123.22	179.43
22	69.38	78.41	87.72	97.33	107.26	117.51	128.09	186.57
23	72.15	81.53	91.20	101.20	111.52	122.17	133.19	194.03
24	75.04	84.78	94.85	105.24	115.97	127.07	138.52	201.80
25	78.06	88.20	98.67	109.47	120.65	132.19	144.12	209.84
26	81.22	91.76	102.65	113.92	125.54	137.56	149.99	218.13
27	84.52	95.50	106.85	118.57	130.69	143.22	156.17	226.62
28	87.99	99.43	111.25	123.46	136.10	149.16	162.65	235.31
29	91.64	103.56	115.88	128.62	141.80	155.40	169.41	244.20
30	95.48	107.91	120.77	134.06	147.79	161.93	176.42	253.29
31	99.53	112.51	125.93	139.79	154.05	168.68	183.65	262.57
32	103.82	117.37	131.36	145.77	160.54	175.66	191.06	272.02
33	108.36	122.50	137.05	151.97	167.24	182.80	198.65	281.65
34	113.15	127.86	142.94	158.38	174.10	190.11	206.39	291.42
35	118.16	133.41	149.02	164.92	181.11	197.57	214.30	301.35
36	123.35	139.13	155.22	171.60	188.25	205.13	222.36	311.42
37	128.69	144.97	161.54	178.39	195.53	212.92	230.54	321.60
38	134.10	150.89	167.95	185.31	202.92	220.76	238.83	331.91
39	139.60	156.89	174.47	192.32	210.40	228.71	247.22	342.33
40	145.14	162.97	181.06	199.40	217.96	236.73	255.70	352.84
41	150.73	169.09	187.69	206.53	225.57	244.82	264.25	363.37
42	156.33	175.22	194.35	213.68	233.23	252.95	272.83	373.90
43	161.94	181.37	201.02	220.87	240.92	261.11	281.47	384.39
44	167.56	187.54	207.73	228.11	248.65	269.36	290.19	394.86
45	173.24	193.79	214.53	235.43	256.50	277.70	299.01	405.30
46	179.12	200.13	221.41	242.86	264.45	286.15	307.87	415.71
47	184.90	206.59	228.45	250.45	272.56	294.71	316.86	426.07
48	190.90	213.19	235.63	258.18	280.76	303.35	325.89	436.37
49	197.06	219.95	242.96	266.01	289.07	312.06	334.98	446.62
50	203.34	226.84	250.38	273.92	297.41	320.81	344.07	456.79
51	209.76	223.82	257.88	281.89	305.81	329.58	353.18	466.88
52	216.27	240.88	265.44	289.91	314.23	338.36	362.24	476.87
53	222.86	248.00	273.05	297.95	322.65	347.19	371.25	486.76
54	229.51	255.18	280.68	306.00	331.04	355.70	380.21	496.55
55	236.19	262.35	288.31	313.99	339.37	364.42	389.11	506.21
56	242.87	269.52	295.88	321.93	347.63	372.98	397.92	515.79
57	249.54	276.63	303.39	329.80	355.84	381.47	406.65	525.16
58	256.13	283.65	310.81	337.59	363.94	389.84	415.26	534.43
59	262.63	290.58	318.14	345.27	371.93	398.09	423.74	534.53
60	269.02	297.42	325.37	352.84	379.80	406.22	432.09	552.49

TABLE No. XXXI.

NET VALUE PER $1,000 OF A TEN-PAYMENT LIFE POLICY, AT THE END
OF VARIOUS YEARS, COMBINED EXPERIENCE, 4 PER CENT.

Age.	First year.	Second year.	Third year.	Fourth year.	Fifth year.
20	24.94	50.98	78.19	106.61	136.30
21	25.46	52.06	79.84	108.85	139.17
22	26.01	53.17	81.54	111.17	142.13
23	26.57	54.31	83.29	113.56	145.19
24	27.14	55.49	85.10	116.03	148.34
25	27.74	56.71	86.97	118.57	151.59
26	28.35	57.96	88.89	121.19	154.94
27	28.99	59.26	90.87	123.90	158.40
28	29.64	60.59	92.91	126.68	161.95
29	30.31	61.96	95.01	129.54	165.61
30	31.00	63.37	97.17	132.49	169.40
31	31.71	64.82	99.40	135.53	173.30
32	32.44	66.32	101.70	138.68	177.32
33	33.20	67.87	104.08	141.92	181.48
34	33.98	69.46	106.53	145.27	185.79
35	34.78	71.11	109.06	148.74	190.23
36	35.61	72.81	111.69	152.33	194.84
37	36.48	74.58	114.41	156.05	199.61
38	37.37	76.42	117.23	159.91	204.55
39	38.30	78.32	120.16	163.90	209.61
40	39.27	80.31	123.20	167.99	214.75
41	40.28	82.36	126.30	172.13	219.96
42	41.32	84.44	129.39	176.27	225.14
43	42.35	86.48	132.46	180.36	230.29
44	43.35	88.49	135.47	184.40	235.41
45	44.34	90.45	138.44	188.41	240.52
46	45.29	92.37	141.37	192.40	245.62
47	46.25	94.31	144.31	196.41	250.73
48	47.18	96.22	147.24	200.35	255.80
49	48.11	98.12	150.15	204.33	260.84
50	49.06	100.02	153.03	208.25	265.87
51	49.97	101.88	155.86	212.12	270.83
52	50.87	103 70	158 67	215.94	275.74
53	51.75	105.51	161.42	219.70	280.60
54	52.63	107.28	164.13	223.43	285.37
55	53.49	109.01	166.81	227.05	290.07
56	54.31	110.73	169.40	230.62	294.62
57	55.16	112.39	171.96	234 06	299.02
58	55.92	113.98	174.35	237.30	303.18
59	56.71	115.51	176.63	240.38	307.13
60	57.39	116.88	178.70	243.20	310.78

TABLE No. XXXI—(Continued.)

NET VALUE PER $1.000 OF A TEN-PAYMENT LIFE POLICY, AT THE
END OF VARIOUS YEARS, COMBINED EXPERIENCE, 4 PER CENT.

Age.	*Sixth year.*	*Seventh year.*	*Eighth year.*	*Ninth year.*	*Tenth year.*
20	167.33	199.75	233.65	269.10	306.17
21	170.85	203.96	238.58	274.77	312.62
22	174.49	208.30	243.66	280.62	319.29
23	178.24	212.78	248.90	286.66	326.17
24	182.12	217.40	254.31	292.90	333.27
25	186.10	222.17	259.88	299.33	340.60
26	190.21	227.08	265.63	305.97	348.17
27	194.45	232.15	271.57	312.82	355.99
28	198.82	237.37	277.70	319.90	364.07
29	203 33	242.77	284.02	327.20	372.42
30	207.98	248 33	290.56	334.76	381.04
31	212.78	254 08	297.31	342.56	389.96
32	217.74	260.03	304.28	350.63	399.18
33	222.87	266.17	311.50	358.97	408.71
34	228.16	272.52	318.96	367.59	418 52
35	233.64	279.08	326.66	376.45	428.57
36	239.32	285.87	334.58	385.53	438.86
37	245.18	292.85	342.68	394.81	449.35
38	251.21	299.97	350.95	404.25	460.02
39	257.35	307.23	359.33	413.83	470.88
40	263.59	314.56	367.82	423.54	481.91
41	269.85	321.94	376.40	433.38	493.11
42	276.12	329.37	385.04	443.34	504.46
43	282.39	336.81	393.75	453.38	515.95
44	288.65	344.29	402.50	463.51	527.57
45	294.92	351.78	411.29	473.71	539.31
46	301.18	359.28	420.12	483.98	551.16
47	307.45	366.78	428.98	494.31	563.10
48	313.70	374.29	437.85	504.66	574.14
49	319.92	381.78	446.71	515.09	587.26
50	326.12	389.25	455.62	525.52	599.43
51	332.26	396.71	464.45	535.95	611.63
52	338 36	404 08	473.26	546.33	623.83
53	344.37	411.38	481.97	556.65	636.00
54	350.32	418.57	490.58	566.88	648.12
55	356.12	425.62	499.05	576.98	660.17
56	361.77	432.49	507.32	586.92	672.13
57	367.22	439.14	515.39	596.68	683.96
58	372.41	445.53	523.18	606.22	695.66
59	377.35	451.63	530.72	615.50	707.19
60	381 96	457.40	537.89	624.51	718.57

TABLE No. XXXII.

NET VALUE OF A TEN-YEAR ENDOWMENT POLICY, AT THE END OF VARIOUS YEARS, COMBINED EXPERIENCE, 4 PER CENT.

Age.	First year.	Second year.	Third year.	Fourth year.	Fifth year.
20	80.51	164.79	253.02	345.41	442.17
21	80.49	164.74	252.95	345.32	442.07
22	80.46	164.69	252.87	345.23	441.97
23	80.43	164.63	252.79	345.13	441.85
24	80.40	164.57	252.71	345.02	441.73
25	80.37	164.51	252.62	344.91	441.60
26	80.33	164.44	252.53	344.79	441.47
27	80.30	164.37	252.43	344.66	441.32
28	80.27	164.30	252.31	344.53	441.16
29	80.22	164.21	252.20	344.38	440.99
30	80.17	164.12	252.06	344.21	440.81
31	80.12	164.03	251.93	344.05	440.63
32	80.06	163.92	251.78	343.87	440.43
33	80.01	163.82	251.63	343.68	440.22
34	79.95	163.70	251.47	343.49	440.00
35	78.89	163.61	251.31	343.29	439.79
36	79.83	163.48	251.15	343.11	439.57
37	79.76	163 36	251.00	342.92	439.37
38	79.72	163.27	250.88	342.77	439.21
39	79.68	163.20	250.78	342.65	439.05
40	79.65	163.16	250.71	342.54	438.87
41	79.65	163.13	250.64	342.39	438.65
42	79.65	163.09	250.51	342.17	438.33
43	79.62	162.98	250.32	341.85	437.90
44	79.55	162.82	250.02	341.43	437.38
45	79.45	162.58	249.63	340.92	436.77
46	79.30	162.27	249 17	340.33	436.07
47	79.14	161.94	248.68	339.69	435.32
48	78.96	161.58	248.14	338.99	434.49
49	78.77	161.19	247.56	338.23	433.58
50	78.56	160.80	246.92	337.39	432.60
51	78.33	160.29	246.21	336.48	431.52
52	78.07	159.77	245.45	335.49	430.35
53	77.79	159.22	244.62	334.42	429.10
54	77.51	158.64	243.75	333.29	427.78
55	77.20	158.00	242.82	332.10	426.36
56	76.86	157.35	241.86	330.84	424.84
57	76.55	156.69	240.85	329.48	423.19
58	76.20	155.98	239.74	327.99	421.36
59	75.84	155.19	238.50	326.33	419.35
60	75.40	154.29	237.12	324.50	417.14

TABLE No. XXXII—(Continued.)

NET VALUE PER $1,000 OF A TEN-YEAR ENDOWMENT POLICY, AT THE END OF VARIOUS YEARS, COMBINED EXPERIENCE, 4 PER CENT.

Age.	*Sixth year.*	*Seventh year.*	*Eighth year.*	*Ninth year.*	*Tenth year.*
20	543.53	649.72	761.01	877.67	1,000.00
21	543.42	649.62	760.92	877.62	1,000.00
22	543.32	649.51	760.84	877.57	1,000.00
23	543.19	649.42	760.77	877.53	1,000.00
24	543.07	649.30	760.67	877.47	1,000.00
25	542.93	649.21	760.55	877.40	1,000.00
26	542.79	649.11	760.42	877.31	1,000.00
27	542.64	648.87	760.30	877.24	1,000.00
28	542.47	648.71	760.18	877.16	1,000.00
29	542.30	648.55	760.04	877.08	1,000.00
30	542.11	648.38	759.90	876.99	1,000.00
31	541.92	648.24	759.80	876.90	1,000.00
32	541.71	648.00	759.59	876.81	1,000.00
33	541.50	647.80	759.43	876.71	1,000.00
34	541.28	647.59	759.25	876.60	1,000.00
35	541.06	647.38	759.09	876.49	1,000.00
36	540.84	647.18	758.91	876.38	1,000.00
37	540.64	646.98	758.73	876.25	1,000.00
38	540.45	646.77	758.53	876.11	1,000.00
39	540.24	646.53	758.30	875.95	1,000.00
40	540.00	646.24	758.02	875.76	1,000.00
41	539.70	645.92	757.71	875.56	1,000.00
42	539.31	645.48	757.32	875.30	1,000.00
43	538.82	644.98	756.87	875.01	1,000.00
44	538.23	644.40	756.37	874.69	1,000.00
45	537.56	643.73	755.79	874.32	1,000.00
46	536.81	642.99	755.15	873.92	1,000.00
47	535.98	642.15	754.43	873.44	1,000.00
48	535.08	641.29	753.69	872.99	1,000.00
49	534.10	640.31	752.84	872.45	1,000.00
50	533.03	639.23	751.92	871.86	1,000.00
51	531.85	638.08	750.94	871.25	1,000.00
52	530.59	636.85	749.87	870.56	1,000.00
53	529.24	635.50	748.70	869.80	1,000.00
54	527.80	634.06	747.44	868.99	1,000.00
55	526.23	632.54	746.11	868.15	1,000.00
56	524.54	630.76	744.53	867.10	1,000.00
57	522.68	628.88	742.88	866.02	1,000.00
58	520.65	626.80	741.03	864.81	1,000.00
59	518.41	624.54	739.04	863.51	1,000.00
60	515.94	622.02	736.80	862.05	1,000.00

TABLE No. XXXIII.

NET VALUE PER $1,000 OF A FIFTEEN-YEAR ENDOWMENT POLICY, AT THE
END OF VARIOUS YEARS, COMBINED EXPERIENCE, 4 PER CENT.

Age.	First year.	Second year.	Third year.	Fourth year.	Fifth year.	Sixth year.	Seventh year.	Eighth year.
20	47.42	97.01	148.90	203.19	260.01	319.48	381.75	446.95
21	47.40	96.98	148.85	203.12	259.91	319.37	381.62	446.80
22	47.38	96.94	148.79	203.04	259.82	319.26	381.49	446.66
23	47.36	96.90	148.73	202.96	259.71	319.13	381.34	446.50
24	47.34	96.86	148.66	202.87	259.61	319.00	381.19	446.33
25	47.32	96.82	148.60	202.78	259.49	318.85	381.03	446.15
26	47.30	96.77	148.52	202.68	259.35	318.69	380.84	445.95
27	47.27	96.72	148.44	202.56	259.21	318.52	380.74	445.72
28	47.25	96.66	148.35	202.44	259.05	318.34	380.43	445.50
29	47.22	96.59	148.25	202.30	258.89	318.14	380.30	445.25
30	47.18	96.52	148.14	202.16	258.71	317.94	379.96	444.99
31	47.15	96.45	148.03	202.01	258.53	317.72	379.75	444.74
32	47.11	96.37	147.92	201.87	258.36	317.52	379.51	444.50
33	47.07	96.31	147.82	201.73	258.19	317.31	379.30	444.28
34	47.05	96.25	147.73	201.62	258.05	317.17	379.13	444.10
35	47.02	96.20	147.66	201.52	257.94	317.05	378.99	443.96
36	47.00	96.17	147.61	201.47	257.88	316.99	378.94	443.88
37	47.00	96.16	147.61	201.46	257.88	316.99	378.91	443.79
38	47.01	96.18	147.64	201.52	257.94	317.02	378.88	443.69
39	47.04	96.24	147.73	201.63	258.04	317.06	378.85	443.35
40	47.08	96.34	147.87	201.76	258.12	317.06	378.72	443.31
41	47.16	96.47	148.02	201.87	258.16	316.99	378.54	443.01
42	47.24	96.59	148.11	201.92	258.09	316.80	378.23	442.58
45	47.30	96.65	148.14	201.84	257.90	316.50	377.80	442.04
44	47.33	96.66	148.06	201.66	257.61	316.09	377.27	441.39
45	47.33	96.60	147.91	201.41	257.24	315.59	376.64	440.63
46	47.28	96.48	147.70	201.09	256.80	315.01	375.92	439.77
47	47.23	96.35	147.48	200.75	256.32	315.38	375.13	438.84
48	47.18	96.22	147.24	200.38	255.80	313.69	374.21	437.75
49	47.12	96.08	146.98	199.98	255.23	312.98	373.36	436.74
50	47.07	95.93	146.70	199.54	254.64	312.18	372.39	435.62
51	47.00	95.76	146.40	199.09	254.00	311.34	371.38	434.41
52	46.93	95.58	146.10	198.62	253.33	310.48	370.32	433.16
53	46.86	95.42	145.78	198.13	252.67	309.61	369.24	431.83
54	46.81	95.25	145.43	197.66	252.01	308.73	368.08	430.40
55	46.75	95.08	145.19	197.21	251.35	307.80	366.86	428.87
56	46.69	94.96	144.93	196.78	250.65	306.81	365.54	427.22
57	46.68	94.87	144.71	196.33	249.92	305.74	364.12	425.43
58	46.67	94.79	144.45	195.82	249.10	304.58	362.56	423.47
59	46.67	94.67	144.14	195.24	248.20	303.28	360.83	421.31
60	46.63	94.51	143.76	194.58	247.18	301.84	358.93	418.93

TABLE No. XXXIII—(Continued.)

Net Value per $1,000 of a Fifteen-Year Endowment Policy, at the End of various Years, Combined Experience, 4 per cent.

Age.	Ninth year.	Tenth year.	Eleventh year.	Twelfth year.	Thir'nth year.	Four'nth year.	Fifteenth year.
20	515.24	586.80	661.78	740.39	822.81	909.28	1,000.00
21	515.09	586.64	661.62	740.21	822.70	909.20	1,000.00
22	514.93	586.48	661.47	740.11	822.59	909.14	1,000.00
23	514.76	586.30	661.30	739.95	822.47	909.07	1,000.00
24	514.58	586.12	661.12	739.80	822.35	909.00	1,000.00
25	514.39	585.92	660.93	739.62	822.19	908.90	1,000.00
26	514.18	585.71	660.73	739.44	822.07	908.80	1,000.00
27	513.94	585.46	660.49	739.23	821.90	908.73	1,000.00
28	513.70	585.22	660.27	739.03	821.74	908.64	1,000.00
29	513.44	584.97	660.02	738.80	821.59	908.56	1,000.00
30	513.17	584.70	659.77	738.59	821.39	908.43	1,000.00
31	512.91	584.44	659.52	738.37	821.22	908.31	1,000.00
32	512.68	584.21	659.31	738.18	821.06	908.23	1,000.00
33	512.45	583.99	659.09	737.96	820.86	908.09	1,000.00
34	512.27	583.79	658.87	737.73	820.66	907.95	1,000.00
35	512.10	583.58	658.63	737.47	820.42	907.79	1,000.00
36	511.97	583.41	658.40	737.22	820.19	907.65	1,000.00
37	511.81	583.16	658.10	736.91	819.90	907.46	1,000.00
38	511.61	582.88	657.76	736.55	819.59	907.25	1,000.00
39	511.37	582.56	657.40	736.17	819.26	907.01	1,000.00
40	511.03	582.23	656.91	735.68	818.82	906.75	1,000.00
41	510.63	582.66	656.39	735.16	818.37	906.48	1,000.00
42	510.10	582.05	655.73	734.51	817.81	906.12	1,000.00
43	509.46	580.33	654.98	733.79	817.20	905.74	1,000.00
44	508.70	579.49	654.11	732.96	816.50	905.30	1,000.00
45	507.82	578.54	653.14	732.03	815.73	904.81	1,000.00
46	506.86	577.50	652.06	731.02	814.89	904.30	1,000.00
47	505.80	576.35	650.89	729.91	813.97	903.72	1,000.00
48	504.56	575.01	649.51	728.58	812.90	903.11	1,000.00
49	503.43	573.80	648.32	727.46	811.88	902.40	1,000.00
50	502.16	572.42	646.86	727.05	810.70	901.66	1,000.00
51	500.80	570.91	645.29	724.53	809.41	900.84	1,000.00
52	499.33	569.30	643.59	722.89	808.00	899.95	1,000.00
53	497.78	567.56	641.77	721.11	806.48	898.99	1,000.00
54	496.10	565.68	639.77	719.15	804.80	897.91	1,000.00
55	494.29	563.64	637.61	717.03	802.97	896.74	1,000.00
56	492.32	561.41	635.24	714.70	800.95	895.45	1,000.00
57	490.19	559.00	632.66	712.16	798.76	894.03	1,000.00
58	487.84	556.34	629.82	709.37	796.35	892.48	1,000.00
59	485.26	553.43	626.73	706.33	793.70	890.77	1,000.00
60	482.44	550.26	626.36	703.01	790.82	888.87	1,000.00

TABLE No. XXXIV.

NET VALUE PER $1,000 OF A TWENTY-YEAR ENDOWMENT POLICY, AT THE END OF VARIOUS YEARS, COMBINED EXPERIENCE, 4 PER CENT.

Age.	First year.	Second year	Third year.	Fourth year.	Fifth year.	Sixth year.	Seventh year.
20	31.39	64.19	98.48	134.32	171.80	210.99	251.98
21	31.38	64.18	98.46	134.28	171.75	210.92	251.89
22	31.38	64.16	98.43	134.25	171.69	210.85	251.80
23	31.37	64.14	98.40	134.20	171.63	210.76	251.69
24	31.36	64.13	98.37	134.15	171.56	210.68	251.58
25	31.35	64.11	98.34	134.10	171.49	210.58	251.45
26	31.34	64.09	98.30	134.04	171.40	210.47	251.32
27	31.34	64.06	98.25	133.98	171.32	210.36	251.18
28	31.32	64.04	98.21	133.92	171.23	210.25	251.05
29	31.32	64.02	98.17	133.86	171.15	210.15	250.94
30	31.31	64.00	98.14	133.80	171.09	210.06	250.82
31	31.31	63.98	98.12	133.78	171.04	210.00	250.75
32	31.30	63.98	98.11	133.76	171.03	209.99	250.73
33	31.31	64.00	98.13	133.79	171.06	210.02	250.78
34	31.33	64.03	98.18	133.86	171.14	210.13	250.90
35	31.36	64.09	98.27	133.97	171.29	210.31	251.11
36	31.40	64.18	98.40	134.15	171.52	210.59	251.40
37	31.47	64.30	98.59	134.41	171.84	210.97	251.85
38	31.54	64.47	98.84	134.75	172.26	211.43	252.24
39	31.65	64.69	99.17	135.18	172.74	211.89	252.80
40	31.79	64.96	99.57	135.65	173.23	212.36	253.09
41	31.96	65.28	99.99	136.12	173.79	212.77	253.42
42	32.14	65.60	100.98	136.54	174.08	213.09	253.65
43	32.31	65.87	100.71	136.85	174.36	213.31	253.81
44	32.44	66.10	100.96	137.10	174.57	213.47	253.87
45	32.57	66.27	101.16	137.29	174.74	213.58	253.90
46	32.61	66.37	101.33	137.47	174.89	213.67	253.90
47	32.75	66.58	101.53	137.67	175.06	213.78	253.90
48	32.85	66.76	101 76	137.90	175.26	213.91	253.95
49	32.98	66.96	102.01	138.16	175.49	214.08	254.01
50	33.11	67.19	102.29	138.45	175.76	214.29	254.13
51	33.25	67.44	102.59	138.77	176 08	214.55	254.32
52	33.44	67.71	102.95	139.18	176.46	214.90	254.59
53	33.58	68.03	103.36	139.64	176.94	215.36	254.96
54	33.80	68.40	103.84	140.20	177.54	215.92	255.40
55	34.03	68.80	104.40	140.86	178.24	216.55	255.90
56	34.28	69.30	105.07	141.64	179.02	217.26	256.46
57	34.60	69.87	105.84	142.49	179.87	218.03	257.07
58	34.95	70.51	106.64	143.40	180.76	218.84	257.70
59	35.33	71.15	107.47	144.30	181.68	219.67	258.35
60	35.70	71.80	108.30	145.24	182.62	220.52	259.01

TABLE No. XXXIV—(Continued.)

Net Value per $1,000 of a Twenty-Year Endowment Policy, at the end of various years, Combined Experience, 4 per cent.

Age.	Eighth year.	Ninth year.	Tenth year.	Eleventh year.	Twelfth year.	Thirt'nth year.	Four'nth year.	Fift'enth year.
20	294.86	339.73	386.71	435.87	487.36	541.29	597.82	657.05
21	294.75	339.61	386.55	435.70	487.17	541.09	597.60	656.84
22	294.64	339.47	386.40	435.52	486.98	540.89	597.39	656.64
23	294.51	339.31	386.21	435.32	486.75	540.65	597.15	656.39
24	294.38	339.16	386.03	435.12	486.54	540.45	596.92	656.18
25	294.21	338.97	385.82	434.88	486.28	540.15	596.64	655.90
26	294.06	338.79	385.62	434.66	486.05	539.92	596.41	655.68
27	293.89	338.60	385.40	434.42	485.80	539.65	596.15	655.43
28	293.73	338.41	385.20	434.21	485.57	539.43	565.93	655.21
29	293.61	338.27	385.04	434.04	485.40	539.26	595.76	655.04
30	293.43	338.13	384.89	433.89	485.24	539.09	595.59	654.86
31	293 39	338.04	384.76	433.80	485.15	538.98	595.43	654.64
32	293.37	338.02	384.79	433.79	485.12	538.90	595.29	654.44
33	293.43	338.10	384.87	433.84	485.12	538.84	595.15	654.23
34	293.58	338.25	385.01	433.93	485.14	538.76	594.98	653.98
35	293.81	338.47	385.17	434.02	485.12	538.64	594.75	653.68
36	294.21	338.83	385.37	434.14	485.10	538.52	594.56	653.41
37	294.50	339.07	385.58	434.20	485.06	538.37	594.28	653.04
38	294.86	339.20	385.72	434.22	484.97	538.14	593.94	653.60
39	295.22	339 68	385.97	434.34	484.85	537.89	593.59	652.14
40	295.51	339.74	385.90	434.14	484.62	537.52	593.07	651.54
41	295.75	339.86	385.90	434.00	484.34	537.10	592.54	651.90
42	295.88	339.87	385.77	433.72	483.90	536.53	591.83	650.09
43	295.93	339.80	385.56	433.36	483.40	535.87	591.05	649.22
44	295.89	339.63	385.24	432.89	482.76	535.07	590.12	648.21
45	295.79	339.40	384.86	432.34	482.04	534.21	589.13	647.11
46	295.68	339.16	384.47	431.78	481.32	533.33	588.11	645.97
47	295.57	338.90	384.03	431.18	480.54	532.38	586.97	644.69
48	295.49	338.66	383.53	430.60	479.78	531.40	585.79	643.34
49	295.42	338.45	383.23	430.02	478.95	530.34	584.50	641.86
50	295.42	338.30	382.92	429.45	478.13	529.24	583.15	640.32
51	295.49	338.21	382.60	428.87	477.25	528.08	581.71	638.64
52	295.68	338.14	382.28	428.25	476.33	526.82	580.15	636.82
53	295.83	338.12	381.97	427.63	475.35	525.48	578.46	634 84
54	296.09	338.12	381.67	426.98	474.31	524.05	576.65	632.71
55	296.38	338.14	381.36	426.28	473.20	522.50	574.69	630.42
56	296.72	338.18	381.04	425.54	472.00	520.85	572.60	627.96
57	297.09	338.23	380.70	424.74	470.72	519.08	570.38	625.33
58	297.46	338.26	380.30	423.88	469 36	517.20	567.99	622.51
59	297.83	338.26	379.87	422.98	467.93	515.22	565.47	619.42
60	298.19	338.25	379.44	422.04	466.43	513.13	562.80	616.32

TABLE No. XXXV.

NET VALUE PER $1,000 OF A TWENTY-FIVE YEAR ENDOWMENT POLICY,
AT THE END OF VARIOUS YEARS, COMBINED EXPERIENCE, 4 PER CENT.

Age.	First year.	Second year.	Third year.	Fourth year.	Fifth year.	Sixth year.	Seventh year.	Eighth year.
20	22.19	45.36	69.55	94 81	121.18	148.74	177.52	207.60
21	22.20	45.37	69.56	94.81	121.18	148.73	177.50	207.56
22	22.21	45.38	69.57	94.82	121.19	148.72	177.48	207.53
23	22.21	45.39	69.58	94.84	121.20	148.73	177.48	207.51
24	22.22	45.41	69.61	94.86	121.22	148.74	177.48	207.50
25	22.23	45.43	69.63	94.88	121.23	148.74	177.47	207.47
26	22.25	45.46	69.66	94.92	121.27	148.78	177.50	207.49
27	22.27	45.48	69.70	94.96	121.32	148.82	177.54	207.52
28	22.29	45.52	69.74	95.03	121.39	148.90	177.61	207.60
29	22.32	45.57	69.82	95.10	121.47	149.00	177.72	207.72
30	22.34	45.63	69.90	95.21	121.61	149.15	177.89	207.92
31	22.39	45.71	70.01	95.36	121.79	149.36	178.14	208.20
32	22.43	45.80	70.15	95.54	122.01	149.63	178.46	208.56
33	22.49	45.93	70.34	95.84	122.39	150.08	178.99	209.16
34	22.58	46.09	70.58	96.12	122.64	150.51	179.49	209.76
35	22.67	46.27	70.86	96.49	123.21	151.08	180.17	210.52
36	22.78	46.50	71.20	96.95	123.79	151.79	180.99	211.41
37	22.92	46.78	71.63	97.53	124.53	152.66	181.95	212.41
38	23.08	47.12	72.15	98.23	125.40	153.65	183.01	213.49
39	23.28	47.52	72.76	99.03	126.34	154.69	184.09	214.55
40	23.52	48.00	73.47	99.92	127.36	155.79	185.20	215.65
41	23.79	48.53	74.20	100.80	128.34	156.80	186.23	216.66
42	24.08	49.07	74.94	101.67	129.31	157.74	187.18	217.60
43	29.39	49.61	75.67	102.54	130.25	158.72	188.30	218.73
44	24.65	50.10	76.31	103.30	131.10	159.75	189.28	219.72
45	24.93	50.57	76.96	104.09	132.02	160.76	190.34	220.81
46	25.16	51.02	77.69	104.93	132.95	161.78	191.42	221.90
47	25.43	51.52	78.30	105.78	133.97	162.91	192.61	223.13
48	25.71	52.06	79.07	106.74	135.09	164.14	193.93	224.49
49	26.03	52.66	79.91	107.79	136.31	165.50	195.39	225.99
50	26.36	53.30	80.82	108.92	137.64	166.99	196.98	227.68
51	26.73	54.00	81.80	110.17	139.10	168.61	198.76	229.56
52	27.12	54.74	82.88	112.53	140.69	170.43	200.74	231.65
53	27.54	55.56	84.05	113.00	142.47	172.44	202.93	233.92
54	28.02	56.46	85.33	114.66	144.44	174.67	205.29	236.38
55	28 52	57.42	86.75	116.46	146.58	177.05	207.86	239.01
56	29.06	58.50	88.30	118.45	148.89	179.60	210.58	241.83
57	29.69	59.71	90.01	120.56	151.34	182.31	213.47	244.81
58	30.34	60.96	91.77	122.76	153.88	185.13	216.49	247.91
59	31.05	62.25	93.60	125.03	156.53	188.05	219.59	251.13
60	31.73	63.57	95.46	127.36	159.24	191.06	222.80	254.44

TABLE No. XXXV—(Continued.)

NET VALUE PER $1,000 OF A TWENTY-FIVE YEAR ENDOWMENT POLICY, AT THE 2ND OF VARIOUS YEARS, COMBINED EXPERIENCE, 4 PER CENT.

Age.	Ninth year.	Tenth year.	Eleventh year.	Twelfth year.	Thirteenth year.	Fourteenth year.	Fifteenth year.	Twentieth year.
20	239.04	271.90	306.25	342.18	379.76	419.09	460.27	697.64
21	238.97	271.81	306.14	342.04	379.60	418.91	460.06	697.38
22	238.92	271.73	306.04	341.91	379.45	418.74	459.87	697.17
23	238.89	271.68	305.97	341.83	379.35	418.63	459.74	697.03
24	238.86	271.62	305.88	341.71	379.23	418.48	459.59	696.84
25	238.81	271.57	305.84	341.66	379.17	418.37	459.41	696.70
26	238.82	271.57	305.80	341.62	379.10	418.32	459.42	696.54
27	238.85	271.59	305.82	341.63	379.10	418.34	459.43	696.39
28	238.93	271.68	305.91	341.71	379.21	418.46	459.55	696.21
29	239.06	271.81	306.06	341.89	379.39	418.63	459.71	696.01
30	239.27	272.05	306.32	342.18	379.69	418.92	459.94	695.80
31	239.59	271.41	306.72	342.60	380.10	419.29	460.24	695.59
32	240.01	272.87	307.22	343.10	380.56	419.68	460.52	695.36
33	240.69	273.62	307.89	343.73	381.15	420.15	460.88	695.12
34	241.35	274.30	308.66	344.47	381.78	420.69	461.30	694.84
35	242.15	275.11	309.42	345.13	382.33	421.10	461.58	694.51
36	243.07	276.00	310.21	345.82	382.90	421.54	461.88	694.05
37	244.05	276.93	311.07	346.58	383.54	422.05	462.24	693.63
38	245.10	277.91	311.97	347.39	384.23	422.60	462.63	693.24
39	246.13	278.87	312.82	348.12	384.83	423.04	462.88	692.67
40	247.17	279.84	313.75	348.94	385.48	423.54	463.21	692.08
41	248.15	280.76	314.56	349.62	386.03	423.92	463.41	691.31
42	249.06	281.62	315.46	350.26	386.63	424.35	463.67	690.63
43	250.17	282.65	316.26	351.08	387.21	424.76	463.88	689.77
44	251.14	283.58	317.11	351.82	387.81	425.21	464.15	688.89
45	252.19	284.58	318.01	352.58	388.42	425.64	464.36	687.77
46	253.29	285.62	318.97	353.46	389.16	426.19	464.68	686.68
47	254.51	286.79	320.09	354.46	390.00	426.81	465.04	685.48
48	255.86	288.13	321.35	355.61	390.96	427.53	465.46	684.17
49	257.40	289.65	322.80	356.89	392.04	428.34	465.96	682.78
50	259.12	291.35	324.39	358.32	393.23	429.24	466.51	681.29
51	261.04	293.22	326.14	359.88	394.54	430.24	467.14	679.71
52	263.14	295.26	328.05	361.60	395.98	431.34	467.83	678.05
53	265.42	297.48	330.13	363.46	397.55	432.54	468.59	676.29
54	267.89	299.88	332.38	365.47	399.25	433.84	469.44	674.47
55	270.54	302.44	334.78	367.62	401.06	435.38	470.41	672.56
56	273.35	305.17	337.34	369.92	403.02	436.82	471.49	670.60
57	276.33	308.07	340.06	372.37	405.16	438.54	472.72	668.61
58	279.44	311.09	342.90	374.99	407.44	440.40	474.08	666.56
59	282.66	314.24	345.92	377.77	409.89	442.43	475.61	664.46
60	286.00	317.55	349.09	380.71	412.52	444.65	477.30	662.31

TABLE No. XXXVI.

NET VALUE PER $1,000 OF A THIRTY-YEAR ENDOWMENT POLICY, AT THE
END OF VARIOUS YEARS, COMBINED EXPERIENCE, 4 PER CENT.

Age.	First year.	Second year.	Third Year.	Fourth year.	Fifth year.	Sixth year.	Seventh year.	Eighth year.
20	16.42	33.54	51.39	70.00	89.41	109.66	130.78	152.81
21	16.45	33.60	51.48	70.11	89.55	109.87	130.90	152.95
22	16.47	33.64	51.53	70.18	89.62	109.88	131.03	153.08
23	16.50	33.69	51.61	70.28	89.75	110.03	131.19	153.24
24	16.54	33.77	51.71	70.41	89.90	110.21	131.37	153.44
25	16.58	33.85	51.83	70.56	90.08	110.41	131.60	153.68
26	16.63	33.94	51.97	70.74	90.29	110.65	131.87	153.98
27	16.68	34.04	52.12	70.93	90.52	110.92	132.19	154.33
28	16.74	34.15	52.28	71.14	90.77	111.21	132.51	154.70
29	16.82	34.31	52.51	71.45	91.16	111.66	133.03	155.27
30	16.89	34.46	52.73	71.73	91.51	112.10	133.54	155.87
31	16.99	34.65	53.01	72.11	91.98	112.67	133.21	156.64
32	17.09	34.86	53.33	72.54	92.52	113.32	134.97	157.52
33	17.22	35.11	53.71	73.05	93.17	114.10	135.89	158.59
34	17.37	35.41	54.16	73.66	93.93	115.03	136.99	159.86
35	17.53	35.74	54.67	73.34	94.80	116.09	138.24	161.29
36	17.73	36.15	55.28	75.17	95.85	117.39	139.83	162.95
37	17.96	36.61	55.98	76.11	97.05	118.80	141.36	164.72
38	18.22	37.13	56.78	77.20	98.41	120.37	143.11	166.61
39	18.52	37.75	57.73	78.46	99.93	122.06	144.96	168.54
40	18.87	38.45	58.77	79.80	101.52	123.91	146.95	170.65
41	19.26	39.23	59.89	81.20	103.16	125.73	148.92	172.75
42	19.68	40.03	61.02	82.61	104.79	127.55	150.91	174.84
43	20.11	40.82	62.14	83.99	106.41	129.38	152.93	177.07
44	20.52	41.61	63.22	85.37	108.04	131.25	155.01	179.31
45	20.94	42.38	64.33	86.77	109.73	133.21	157.19	181.69
46	21.34	43.16	65.45	88.24	111.51	135.26	159.48	184.19
47	21.76	43.99	66.68	89.83	113.43	137.47	162.01	186.90
48	22.22	44.88	67.99	91.52	115.48	139.84	164.62	189.82
49	22.72	45.85	69.40	93.36	117.67	142.39	167.49	192.96
50	23.25	46.88	70.90	95.28	120.02	145.12	170.56	196.36
51	23.81	47.97	73.49	97.35	122.54	148.04	173.87	200.02
52	24.40	49.13	74.19	99.56	125.22	151.19	177.45	203.95
53	25.03	50.37	76.01	101.91	128.11	154.57	181.26	208.13
54	25.71	51.70	77.94	104.46	131.21	158.18	185.30	212.53
55	26.42	53.08	80.01	107.16	134.51	161.97	189.53	217.12

TABLE No. XXXVI.—(CONTINUED.)

NET VALUE PER $1,000 OF A THIRTY-YEAR ENDOWMENT POLICY, AT THE END OF VARIOUS YEARS, COMBINED EXPERIENCE, 4 PER CENT.

Age.	Ninth year.	Tenth year.	Eleventh year.	Twelfth year.	Thirteenth year.	Fourteenth year.	Fifteenth year.	Twentieth year.
20	175.81	199.81	224.87	251.03	278.34	306.89	336.72	507.81
21	175.93	199.92	224.97	251.11	278.42	306.95	336.77	507.80
22	176.08	200.07	225.12	251.26	278.56	307.08	336.89	507.90
23	176.24	200.24	225.28	251.42	278.72	307.23	337.04	508.03
24	176.45	200.45	225.50	251.64	278.94	307.46	337.27	508.26
25	176.71	200.73	225.79	251.94	279.26	307.79	337.61	508.57
26	177.04	201.08	226.18	252.36	279.72	308.29	338.15	509.08
27	177.42	201.49	226.51	252.82	280.20	308.80	339.02	509.35
28	177.89	202.03	227.14	253.47	280.90	309.55	339.49	509.84
29	178.47	202.66	227.89	254.22	281.72	310.43	340.35	510.31
30	179.13	203.42	228.64	255.16	282.72	311.46	341.39	510.86
31	180.02	204.40	229.82	256.34	283.95	312.70	342.60	511.42
32	181.03	205.52	231.06	257.63	285.27	313.99	343.81	511.99
33	182.24	206.87	232.49	259.11	286.74	315.40	345.15	512.65
34	183.67	208.42	234.10	260.75	288.34	316.95	346.61	513.40
35	185.24	210.06	235.79	262.41	289.97	318.50	348.08	514.11
36	187.01	211.91	237.65	264.26	291.78	320.26	349.75	514.91
37	188.88	213.81	239.56	266.15	293.63	322.04	351.43	515.70
38	190.86	215.84	241.60	268.19	295.63	323.98	353.27	516.68
39	192.91	217.94	243.73	270.31	297.72	326.00	355.18	517.68
40	195.03	220.12	245.94	272.52	299.89	328.04	357.19	518.75
41	197.23	222.39	248.25	274.83	302.17	333.32	359.32	519.90
42	199.48	224.72	250.63	277.22	304.54	332.63	361.27	521.10
43	201.79	227.12	253.08	279.70	307.01	335.04	393.44	522.34
44	204.18	229.62	255.66	282.31	309.62	337.67	366.39	523.65
45	206.70	232.27	258.40	285.10	312.42	340.42	369.20	525.05
46	209.40	235.10	261.32	288.11	315.47	343.44	372.03	526.56
47	212.30	238.16	264.51	291.40	318.80	346.72	375.20	528.19
48	215.43	241.50	268.01	294.97	322.38	350.25	378.60	529.96
49	218.84	245.11	271.78	298.82	326.24	354.04	382.26	531.87
50	222.51	249.02	275.81	302.94	330.35	358.09	386.17	533.97
51	226.47	253.18	280.13	307.31	334.73	362.39	370.31	536.25
52	230.68	257.61	284.70	311.96	339.37	366.95	394.71	538.74
53	235.14	262.28	289.45	316.85	344.26	371.75	399.34	541.46
54	239.84	267.20	294.59	321.99	349.39	376.78	404.22	544.41
55	244.74	272.32	299.86	327.34	354.72	382.04	409.34	547.61

TABLE No. XXXVII.

Net Annual Premiums per $1,000 for Joint Life Policies, Combined Experience, 4 per cent.

Younger Age.	Equal ages.	Difference in ages. 5 years.	Difference in ages. 10 years.	Difference in ages. 15 years.	Difference in ages. 20 years.	Difference in ages. 25 years.	Difference in ages. 30 years.
15	19.17	20.20	21.61	23.51	26.09	29.62	34.55
16	19.52	20.61	22.09	24.09	26.82	30.58	35.82
17	19.90	21.04	22.59	24.71	27.59	31.59	37.18
18	20.30	21.48	23.12	25.35	28.41	32.68	38.61
19	20.71	21.96	23.68	26.03	29.27	33.83	40.13
20	21.14	22.45	24.26	26.75	30.20	35.06	41.73
21	21.60	22.97	24.88	27.51	31.17	36.36	43.43
22	22.07	23.52	25.53	28.31	32.22	37.73	45.24
23	22.57	24.10	26.21	29.16	33.33	39.19	47.15
24	23.10	24.70	26.93	30.06	34.52	40.73	49.18
25	23.65	25.34	27.69	31.02	35.78	42.36	51.33
26	24.23	26.01	28.50	32.04	37.11	44.10	53.62
27	24.84	26.71	29.35	33.13	38.53	45.93	56.05
28	25.48	27.46	30.25	34.29	40.02	47.88	58.64
29	26.16	28.24	31.21	35.52	41.61	49.94	61.40
30	26.87	29.07	32.23	36.83	43.29	52.13	64.34
31	27.63	29.95	33.32	38.23	45.06	54.46	67.47
32	28.42	30.88	34.47	39.70	46.95	56.94	70.78
33	29.25	31.86	35.70	41.26	48.95	59.58	74.35
34	30.14	32.91	37.02	42.91	51.08	62.39	78.13
35	31.08	34.03	38.42	44.67	53.33	65.38	82.15
36	32.07	35.22	39.90	46.53	55.74	68.58	....
37	33.13	36.49	41.48	48.50	58.30	71.98	....
38	34.25	37.85	43.16	50.62	61.02	75.61	....
39	35.45	39.31	44.94	52.86	63.94	79.48	....
40	36.73	40.86	46.84	55.25	67.06	83.61	....
41	38.11	42.52	48.87	57.80	70.39	....	....
42	39.58	44.29	51.03	60.53	73.95	....	....
43	41.17	46.18	53.34	63.45	77.75	....	....
44	42.87	48.20	55.80	66.57	81.83	....	....
45	44.69	50.35	58.43	69.92	86.17	....	....
46	46.62	52.63	61.23	73.48	....	....	....
47	48.68	55.06	64.21	77.29	....	....	....
48	50.86	57.65	67.39	81.34	....	....	....
49	53.18	60.40	70.78	85.67	....	....	....
50	55.64	63.32	74.41	90.28	....	....	....
51	58.26	66.44	78.27	....	....	....	....
52	61.05	69.76	82.40	....	....	....	....
53	64.02	73.30	86.79	....	....	....	....
54	67.17	77.08	91.48	....	....	....	....
55	70.54	81.13	96.48	....	....	....	....
56	74.13	85.44	....	....	....	....	....
57	77.96	90.05	....	....	....	....	....
58	82.05	94.97	....	....	....	....	....
59	86.44	100.23	....	....	....	....	....
60	91.13	105.85	....	....	....	....	....
61	96.14	....	....	....	....	....	....
62	101.50	....	....	....	....	....	....
63	107.22	....	....	....	....	....	....
64	113.33	....	....	....	....	....	....
65	119.85	....	....	....	....	....	....

TABLE No. XXXVIII.

NET VALUE PER $1,000 OF AN ORDINARY JOINT-LIFE POLICY, (EQUAL
AGES,) COMBINED EXPERIENCE, 4 PER CENT.

Age.	First year.	Second year.	Third year.	Fourth year.	Fifth year.	Sixth year.	Seventh year.	Eighth year.
20	7.57	15.39	23.47	31.80	40.40	49.29	58.46	67.92
21	7.88	16.02	24.42	33.09	42.04	51.28	60.81	70.64
22	8.21	16.67	25.41	34.44	43.74	53.35	63.26	73.48
23	8.53	17.34	26.45	35.83	45.52	55.51	65.81	76.44
24	8.87	18.07	27.53	37.31	47.38	57.77	68.47	79.51
25	9.26	18.81	28.67	38.84	49.32	60.12	71.26	82.73
26	9.64	19.59	29.85	40.43	51.34	62.58	74.15	86.09
26	10.05	20.41	31.09	42.10	54.45	65.14	77.20	89.63
28	10.46	21.25	32.37	43.84	55.65	67.83	80.39	93.35
29	10.90	22.14	33.73	45.67	57.97	70.67	83.76	97.28
30	11.36	23.08	35.14	47.58	60.42	73.66	87.33	101.44
31	11.85	24.05	36.64	49.63	63.02	76.84	91.12	105.86
32	12.35	25.09	38.23	51.78	65.77	80.22	95.14	110.57
33	12.89	26.20	39.92	54.09	68.72	83.83	99.45	115.62
34	13.48	27.38	41.73	56.55	71.86	87.68	104.07	121.02
35	14.09	28.63	43.66	59.18	75.22	91.82	109.01	126.76
36	14.75	29.99	45.73	62.00	78.84	96.27	114.28	132.80
38	15.47	31.44	47.96	65.05	82.74	101.02	119.82	139.04
38	16.23	33.00	50.36	68.33	86.90	105.99	125.51	145.40
39	17.05	34.70	52.96	71.84	91.24	111.09	131.31	151.79
40	17.95	36.53	55.73	75.48	95.67	116.24	137.08	158.16
41	18.92	38.47	58.57	79.13	100.08	121.30	142.77	164.45
42	19.93	40.42	61.37	82.73	104.35	126.23	148.34	170.64
43	20.91	42.29	64.08	86.14	108.41	131.02	153.78	176.71
44	21.83	44.09	66.62	89.43	112.46	135.71	159.13	182.69
45	22.75	45.79	69.10	92.65	116.41	140.36	164.44	188.63
46	23.58	47.43	71.52	95.84	120.33	144.99	169.74	194.56
47	24.43	49.11	74.01	99.10	124.35	149.70	175.11	200.59
48	25.29	50.82	76.54	102.42	128.41	154.46	180.57	206.69
49	26.19	52.58	79.13	105.79	132.51	159.31	186.10	212.86
50	27.10	54.36	81.74	109.18	136.71	164.21	191.69	219.16
51	28.02	56.16	84.37	112.65	140.93	169.18	197.41	225.57
52	28.95	57.97	87.07	116.17	145.23	174.28	203.25	232.10
53	29.89	59.86	89.82	119.74	149.66	179.49	209.21	238.66
54	30.89	61.77	92.62	123.46	154.22	184.84	215.21	245.25
55	31.87	63.70	95.52	127.26	158.86	190.27	221.20	251.77
56	32.88	65.75	98.53	131.18	163.53	195.56	227.14	258.25
57	33.98	67.88	101.63	135.13	168.21	200.87	233.03	264.61
58	35.09	70.02	104.67	138.95	172.76	206.05	238.74	270.75
59	36.22	72.11	107.64	142.67	177.16	211.06	244.23	276.65
60	37.25	74.11	110.46	146.26	181.41	215.69	249.47	282.23

TABLE No. XXXIX.

NET VALUE PER $1,000 OF AN ORDINARY JOINT-LIFE POLICY (DIFFER-
ENCE IN AGES, FIVE YEARS), COMBINED EXPERIENCE, 4 PER CENT.

Older Age.	First year.	Second year.	Third year.	Fourth year.	Fifth year.	Sixth year.	Seventh year.	Eighth year.
20	6.92	14.08	21.48	29.13	37.03	45.19	53.62	62.32
21	7.21	14.66	22.37	30.32	38.54	47.02	55.78	64.82
22	7.51	15.27	23.28	31.56	40.11	48.93	58.03	67.42
23	7.82	15.89	24.23	32.86	41.73	50.90	60.36	70.13
24	8.14	16.55	25.22	34.18	43.43	52.96	62.80	72.95
25	8.48	17.22	26.26	35.58	45.19	55.11	65.34	75.89
26	8.82	17.93	27.33	37.03	47.04	57.35	67.99	78.96
27	9.19	18.67	28.46	38.55	48.96	59.19	70.76	82.18
28	9.57	19.44	29.63	40.14	50.97	62.14	73.66	85.54
29	9.97	20.26	30.86	41.80	53.08	64.71	76.71	89.09
30	10.39	21.10	32.15	43.54	55.30	67.41	79.91	92.81
31	10.83	21.98	33.50	45.38	57.62	70.25	83.29	96.75
32	11.29	22.92	34.93	47.31	60.08	73.26	86.86	100.91
33	11.77	23.91	36.43	49.35	62.68	76.44	90.65	105.33
34	12.29	24.96	38.03	51.52	65.44	79.82	94.68	110.04
35	12.83	26.06	39.72	53.81	68.37	83.42	98.97	115.04
36	13.41	27.24	41.52	56.27	71.51	87.26	103.54	120.32
37	14.02	28.49	43.44	58.89	74.86	91.36	108.34	125.83
38	14.68	29.84	45.51	61.70	78.40	95.69	114.40	131.58
39	15.39	31.29	47.73	64.71	82.22	100.20	118.65	137.51
40	16.15	32.85	50.10	67.87	86.14	104.88	124.03	143.61
41	16.97	34.50	52.57	71.13	90.18	109.66	129.55	149.80
42	17.84	36.22	55.10	74.48	94.29	114.52	135.13	156.05
43	18.71	37.94	57.67	77.84	98.44	119.42	140.72	162.29
44	19.59	39.70	60.25	81.25	102.63	124.33	146.32	168.50
45	20.51	41.47	62.89	84.69	106.83	129.26	151.89	174.69
46	21.40	43.27	65.53	88.13	111.03	134.13	157.41	180.83
47	22.34	45.09	68.19	91.58	115.19	138.98	162.91	186.98
48	23.27	46.89	70.82	94.97	119.30	143.78	168.40	193.10
49	24.19	48.69	73.41	98.32	123.38	148.59	173.88	199.22
50	25.11	50.44	75.97	101.65	127.48	153.40	179.37	205.39
51	25.99	52.17	78.52	105.01	131.60	158.24	184.92	211.60
52	26.89	53.93	81.13	108.43	135.78	163.18	190.57	217.94
53	27.79	55.75	83.80	111.90	140.06	168.20	196.32	224.30
54	28.75	57.60	86.51	115.47	144.42	173.35	202.13	230.73
55	29.71	59.47	89.29	119.19	148.87	178.51	207.95	237.64
56	30.68	61.41	92.13	122.82	153.36	183.71	213.82	243.64
57	31.70	63.40	95.06	126.56	157.87	188.94	219.71	250.11
58	32.73	65.43	97.97	130.30	162.38	194.16	225.56	256.48
59	33.80	67.44	100.87	134.04	166.89	199.35	231.32	262.74
60	34.82	69.41	103.74	137.74	171.34	204.43	236.94	268.79

TABLE No. XL.

NET VALUE PER $1,000 OF AN ORDINARY JOINT-LIFE POLICY, (DIFFER-
ENCE IN AGES, TEN YEARS,) COMBINED EXPERIENCE, 4 PER CENT.

Older Age.	First year.	Second year.	Third year.	Fourth year.	Fifth year.	Sixth year.	Seventh year.	Eighth year.
25	7.93	16.14	24.59	33.34	42.35	51.69	61.31	71.24
26	8.26	16.80	25.61	34.70	44.11	53.81	63.82	74.14
27	8.61	17.50	26.66	36.16	45.93	56.02	66.43	77.18
28	8.97	18.21	27.78	37.65	47.82	58.32	69.16	80.35
29	9.32	18.99	28.94	39.21	49.80	60.72	72.03	83.69
30	9.76	19.80	30.17	40.86	51.90	63.30	75.07	87.22
31	10.14	20.61	31.41	42.56	54.07	65.95	78.23	90.90
32	10.58	21.49	32.75	44.38	56.38	68.78	81.58	94.82
33	11.03	22.41	34.16	46.30	58.81	71.77	85.14	98.96
34	11.51	23.40	35.66	48.34	61.42	74.94	88.91	103.35
35	12.02	24.43	37.25	50.49	64.17	78.30	92.91	108.00
36	12.56	25.54	38.94	52.78	67.07	81.87	97.14	112.88
37	13.14	26.71	40.73	55.22	70.19	85.68	101.58	117.92
38	13.75	27.95	42.64	57.81	73.50	89.61	106.18	123.14
39	14.40	29.29	44.68	60.59	76.92	93.72	110.91	128.46
40	15.10	30.72	46.84	63.43	80.47	97.92	115.72	133.89
41	15.85	32.22	49.07	66.37	84.08	102.16	120.61	139.41
42	16.63	33.75	51.33	69.33	87.70	106.44	125.54	145.01
43	17.41	35.29	53.59	72.27	91.33	110.75	130.55	150.71
44	18.19	36.82	55.83	75.23	95.00	115.14	135.66	156.53
45	18.98	38.34	58.10	78.22	98.75	119.64	140.90	162.50
46	19.74	39.88	60.40	81.32	102.61	124.29	146.31	168.61
47	20.55	41.48	62.82	84.55	106.65	129.12	151.87	174.87
48	21.37	43.16	65.34	87.92	110.85	134.08	157.56	181.23
49	22.26	44.98	67.99	91.43	115.17	139.16·	163.35	187 65
50	23.19	46.78	70.74	95.02	119.57	144.30	169.15	194.13
51	24.15	48.69	73.54	98.67	123.99	149.43	175.00	200.63
52	25.14	50.61	76.36	102.31	128.38	154.58	180.84	207.15
53	26.13	52.54	79.16	105.90	132.77	159.72	186.70	213.63
54	27.12	54.45	81.92	109.51	137.17	164.88	192.53	220.08
55	28.10	56.32	84.46	113.12	141.60	170.02	198.34	226.47
56	29.04	58.22	87.48	116.78	146.03	175.16	204.11	232.83
57	30.05	60.19	90.37	120.48	150.49	180.30	209.88	239.17
58	31.07	62.18	93.23	124.17	154.91	185.40	215.59	245.41
59	32.11	64.16	96.08	127.81	159.28	190.46	221.22	251.36
60	33.11	66.10	98.87	131.39	163.59	195.38	226.73	257.59

TABLE No. XLI.

NET VALUE PER $1,000 OF AN ORDINARY JOINT-LIFE POLICY, (DIFFERENCE IN AGES, FIFTEEN YEARS,) COMBINED EXPERIENCE, 4 PER CENT.

Older age.	First year.	Second year.	Third year.	Fourth year.	Fifth year.	Sixth year.	Seventh year.	Eighth year.
30	9.28	18.88	28.80	39.04	49.62	60.55	71.85	83.52
31	9.69	19.70	30.03	40.72	51.75	63.15	74.93	87.10
32	10.11	20.54	31.33	42.47	53.98	65.88	79.17	90.88
33	10.54	21.44	32.70	44.32	56.34	68.76	81.60	94.89
34	11.02	22.39	34.14	47.29	59.84	71.82	85.25	99.14
35	11.50	23.38	35.66	48.35	61.48	75.06	89.11	103.63
36	12.02	24.45	37.29	50.56	64.30	78.51	93.20	108.33
37	12.58	25.54	39.01	52.92	67.30	82.17	97.48	113.20
38	13.16	26.77	40.85	55.42	70.48	85.99	101.90	118.20
39	13.79	28.06	42.82	58.08	73.80	89.92	106.44	123.28
40	14.47	29.44	44.91	60.85	77.20	93.94	111.02	128.43
41	15.19	30.89	47.05	63.65	80.64	97.97	115.72	133.60
42	15.94	32.36	49.21	66.46	84.06	101.99	120.24	138.82
43	16.68	33.81	51.34	69.22	87.44	105.99	124.87	144.06
44	17.41	35.24	53.43	71.96	90.82	110.03	129.54	149.35
45	18.15	36.65	55.51	74.71	94.25	114.11	134.28	154.75
46	18.85	38.06	57.61	77.51	97.74	118.28	139.12	160.25
47	19.58	39.50	59.79	80.40	101.34	122.59	144.12	165.95
48	20.33	41.01	62.04	83.40	105.07	127.03	149.30	171.84
49	21.12	42.58	64.38	86.50	108.92	131.65	154.66	177.94
50	21.93	44.20	66.80	89.69	112.91	136.42	160.21	184.27
51	22.77	45.87	69.29	93.03	117.06	141.38	165.98	190.80
52	23.64	47.60	71.89	96.49	121.38	146.55	171.95	197.49
53	24.54	49.42	74.61	100.10	125.89	151.90	178.09	204.26
54	25.51	51.33	77.46	103.90	130.56	157.38	184.24	211.06
55	26.50	53.31	80.44	107.80	135.32	162.89	190.41	217.81
56	27.54	55.41	83.52	111.79	140.10	168.37	196.52	224.51
57	28.66	57.56	86.63	115.75	144.81	173.76	202.54	232.10
58	29.76	59.68	89.66	119.59	149.39	179.02	208.41	237.51
59	30.84	61.74	92.59	123.30	153.84	184.14	214.12	243.74
60	31.88	63.70	95.40	126.91	158.17	189.11	219.67	249.78
61	32.87	65.61	98.16	130.45	162.41	193.98	225.08	255.68
62	33.85	67.51	100.89	133.94	166.58	198.74	230.38	261.50
63	34.84	69.39	103.59	137.30	170.67	203.42	235.63	267.23
64	35.80	71.24	106.25	140.73	174.67	208.04	240.78	272.86
65	36.75	73.06	108.83	144.02	178.63	212.59	245.68	278.42

COST OF INSURANCE.

COST OF INSURANCE.

These tables for the cost of insurance, give the tabular value of carrying the risk of a policy of $1.000 for various ages and conditions, and during the first eight years it is in force, and they are computed on the American Experience Table of Mortality, 4½ per cent interest, and on the Combined Experience 4 per cent.

Since the Contribution Plan for dividing the surplus has been generally adopted, the cost of insurance has become one of the most important subjects of computation. It shows the tabular expense a company incurs in carrying a policy a year, and is an important aid in finding what should be the surrender charge. By comparing the cost of insurance for a given age in different classes of policies for a series of years, one is enabled to judge pretty correctly of their relative insurance value.

By running the eye over these tables, it will be noticed that the cost of insurance in a whole life policy increases from year to year, while that of a ten payment life and short term endowment decreases until we get among the older ages. The reason of this that the tabular cost of insurance depends upon two variable quantities which are multiplied into each other, the probability of dying which is continually increasing and the amount at risk which is continually decreasing. If the amount at risk decreases with sufficient rapidity, as in a ten year endowment, the cost of insurance is annually lessened, until the last year it is nothing. In a twenty year endowment, the cost of insurance increases or decreases each successive year, according to the age of the policy-holder at the time he was insured.

TABLE No. XLII.

COST OF INSURANCE PER $1,000 OF AN ORDINARY LIFE SINGLE-PREMIUM POLICY, AMERICAN EXPERIENCE, 4½ PER CENT.

Age.	Cost of Insurance.	Age.	Cost of Insurance.	Age.	Cost of Insurance.
20	6.11	40	6.55	60	11.83
21	6.12	41	6.61	61	12.40
22	6.13	42	6.68	62	13.01
23	6.14	43	6.76	63	13.65
24	6.14	44	6.86	64	14.32
25	6.15	45	6.96	65	15.03
26	6.16	46	7.09	66	15.78
27	6.17	47	7.24	67	16.55
28	6.18	48	7.41	68	17.36
29	6.20	49	7.62	69	18.20
30	6.21	50	7.86	70	19.06
31	6.23	51	8.12	71	19.93
32	6.25	52	8.41	72	20.78
33	6.27	53	8.73	73	21.60
34	6.30	54	9.08	74	22.39
35	6.32	55	9.45	75	23.13
36	6.36	56	9.87		
37	6.40	57	10.31		
38	6.44	58	10.78		
39	6.49	59	11.29		

TABLE No. XLII—(CONTINUED.)

COST OF INSURANCE PER $1,000 OF AN ORDINARY LIFE SINGLE-PREMIUM POLICY, COMBINED EXPERIENCE, 4 PER CENT.

Age.	Cost of Insurance.	Age.	Cost of Insurance.	Age.	Cost of Insurance.
20	5.42	40	6.32	60	11.78
21	5.45	41	6.38	61	12.27
22	5.48	42	6.44	62	12.78
23	5.51	43	6.54	63	13.32
24	5.54	44	6.68	64	13.87
25	5.58	45	6.85	65	14.45
26	5.62	46	7.07	66	15.05
27	5.65	47	7.30	67	15.67
28	5.70	48	7.54	68	16.29
29	5.74	49	7.80	69	16.91
30	5.79	50	8.08	70	17.55
31	5.84	51	8.37	71	18.19
32	5.89	52	8.69	72	18.83
33	5.95	53	9.02	73	19.48
34	6.00	54	9.36	74	20.13
35	6.05	55	9.72	75	20.77
36	6.11	56	10.11		
37	6.16	57	10.49		
38	6.22	58	10.89		
39	6.27	59	11.32		

For net value of an Ordinary Life Single-Premium Policy, see Tables No. XVIII and XIX.

TABLE No. XLIII.

COST OF INSURANCE PER $1,000 OF AN ORDINARY LIFE POLICY, DURING VARIOUS YEARS, AMERICAN EXPERIENCE, 4½ PER CENT.

Age.	First year.	Second year.	Third year.	Fourth year.	Fifth year.	Sixth year.	Seventh year.	Eighth year.
20	7.77	7.78	7.79	7.80	7.80	7.81	7.82	7.84
21	7.82	7.83	7.84	7.84	7.85	7.86	7.87	7.88
22	7.87	7.87	7.88	7.89	7.90	7.91	7.92	7.94
23	7.92	7.92	7.93	7.94	7.95	7.96	7.98	8.00
24	7.97	7.97	7.98	8.00	8.01	8.03	8.04	8.06
25	8.02	8.03	8.04	8.05	8.07	8.09	8.10	8.13
26	8.08	8.09	8.10	8.12	8.14	8.15	8.18	8.21
27	8.14	8.15	8.17	8.19	8.20	8.23	8.26	8.29
28	8.21	8.23	8.24	8.26	8.28	8.31	8.34	8.37
29	8.28	8.30	8.32	8.34	8.37	8.40	8.43	8.47
30	8.36	8.38	8.40	8.43	8.46	8.49	8.54	8.58
31	8.44	8.48	8.50	8.53	8.56	8.60	8.64	8.71
32	8.53	8.56	8.60	8.62	8.67	8.71	8.78	8.84
33	8.64	8.67	8.70	8.75	8.79	8.85	8.91	8.99
34	8.75	8.78	8.82	8.87	8.92	8.99	9.07	9.15
35	8.86	8.91	8.95	9.02	9.08	9.16	9.23	9.33
36	9.00	9.04	9.11	9.17	9.25	9.32	9.42	9.52
37	9.13	9.20	9.26	9.34	9.42	9.52	9.62	9.75
38	9.30	9.36	9.45	9.52	9.62	9.73	9.86	10.00
39	9.47	9.56	9.63	9.73	9.84	9.97	10.12	10.30
40	9.67	9.75	9.85	9.96	10.09	10.24	10.42	10.63
41	9.88	9.98	10.08	10.22	10.37	10.56	10.76	11.01
42	10.11	10.22	10.36	10.51	10.70	10.91	11.16	11.46
43	10.36	10.51	10.66	10.85	11.06	11.31	11.62	11.97
44	10.66	10.81	11.01	11.22	11.48	11.79	12.15	12.54
45	10.98	11.18	11.40	11.66	11.98	12.34	12.74	13.18
46	11.37	11.59	11.85	12.18	12.54	12.95	13.40	13.89
47	11.79	12.06	12.39	12.76	13.17	13.63	14.13	14.68
48	12.28	12.61	12.99	13.41	13.88	14.39	14.95	15.56
49	12.85	13.24	13.67	14.14	14.66	15.23	15.85	16.53
50	13.50	13.94	14.42	14.95	15.54	16.17	16.86	17.59
51	14.23	14.72	15.26	15.86	16.54	17.21	17.96	18.75
52	15.05	15.60	16.21	16.87	17.58	18.35	19.16	20.04
53	15.95	16.58	17.25	17.99	18.77	19.60	20.50	21.46
54	16.97	17.66	18.41	19.22	20.07	20.99	21.97	23.01
55	18.10	18.87	19.69	20.57	21.51	22.52	23.59	24.71
56	19.36	20.20	21.10	22.07	23.10	24.20	25.35	26.56
57	20.75	21.67	22.67	23.73	24.85	26.04	27.28	28.59
58	22.28	23.31	24.39	25.55	26.77	28.05	29.39	30.82
59	23.99	25.11	26.30	27.56	28.87	30.26	31.73	33.26
60	25.87	27.10	28.40	29.75	31.18	32.69	34.27	35.91

TABLE No. XLIV.

COST OF INSURANCE PER $1,000 OF A TEN-PAYMENT LIFE POLICY, DURING VARIOUS YEARS, AMERICAN EXPERIENCE, 4½ PER CENT.

Age.	First year.	Second year.	Third year.	Fourth year.	Fifth year.	Sixth year.	Seventh year.	Eighth year.
20	7.64	7.52	7.39	7.25	7.09	6.92	6.75	6.57
21	7.70	7.56	7.43	7.28	7.12	6.95	6.78	6.58
22	7.74	7.60	7.46	7.31	7.16	6.99	6.80	6.61
23	7.78	7.65	7.50	7.35	7.19	7.02	6.83	6.64
24	7.83	7.69	7.55	7.40	7.23	7.06	6.87	6.66
25	7.88	7.74	7.60	7.44	7.27	7.09	6.90	6.69
26	7.94	7.80	7.65	7.49	7.32	7.13	6.94	6.73
27	8.00	7.85	7.71	7.54	7.37	7.18	6.99	6.77
28	8.06	7.92	7.76	7.60	7.42	7.24	7.03	6.81
29	8.13	7.99	7.83	7.66	7.48	7.29	7.08	6.86
30	8.21	8.05	7.90	7.73	7.55	7.35	7.15	6.92
31	8.28	8.13	7.98	7.81	7.62	7.42	7.21	6.99
32	8.37	8.23	8.06	7.88	7.70	7.50	7.29	7.06
33	8.47	8.32	8.15	7.98	7.79	7.60	7.37	7.14
34	8.57	8.41	8.26	8.08	7.90	7.69	7.47	7.23
35	8.68	8.53	8.37	8.20	8.01	7.81	7.57	7.33
36	8.81	8.65	8.50	8.32	8.14	7.92	7.69	7.44
37	8.94	8.80	8.63	8.47	8.27	8.06	7.82	7.57
38	9.10	8.95	8.80	8.61	8.42	8.20	7.98	7.71
39	9.27	9.13	8.96	8.78	8.59	8.38	8.14	7.89
40	9.46	9.31	9.15	8.97	8.78	8.57	8.35	8.09
41	9.66	9.51	9.35	9.19	9.00	8.80	8.57	8.32
42	9.88	9.74	9.60	9.43	9.26	9.06	8.84	8.59
43	10.13	10.00	10.17	9.71	9.54	9.36	9.15	8.91
44	10.42	10.29	10.17	10.03	9.88	9.71	9.51	9.26
45	10.72	10.63	10.52	10.40	10.27	10.12	9.92	9.65
46	11.09	11.00	10.92	10.83	10.70	10.57	10.37	10.09
47	11.50	11.45	11.40	11.33	11.23	11.08	10.86	10.57
48	11.98	11.96	11.94	11.88	11.79	11.64	11.42	11.10
49	12.53	12.52	12.54	12.51	12.42	12.27	12.03	11.68
50	13.16	13.21	13.22	13.20	13.13	12.97	12.71	12.32
51	13.87	13.94	13.98	13.98	13.90	13.74	13.46	13.01
52	14.66	14.76	14.83	14.83	14.74	14.59	14.27	13.77
53	15.55	15.68	15.77	15.79	15.72	15.53	15.17	14.61
54	16.54	16.70	16.82	16.85	16.77	16.56	16.16	15.51
55	17.64	17.84	17.97	17.94	17.94	17.70	17.24	16.50
56	18.86	19.10	19.25	19.31	19.22	18.95	18.43	17.57
57	20.22	20.48	20.67	20.74	20.69	20.33	19.72	18.73
58	21.71	22.03	22.24	22.32	22.20	21.83	21.13	20.01
59	23.38	23.73	23.92	24.06	23.92	23.49	22.70	21.40
60	25.22	25.62	25.90	25.97	25.81	25.33	24.41	22.91

TABLE No. XLV.

COST OF INSURANCE PER $1,000 OF A TEN-YEAR ENDOWMENT POLICY, DURING VARIOUS YEARS, AMERICAN EXPERIENCE, 4½ PER CENT.

Age.	First year.	Second year.	Third year.	Fourth year.	Fifth year.	Sixth year.	Seventh year.	Eighth year.	Ninth year.
20	7.19	6.59	5.95	5.26	4.52	3.73	2.90	2.00	1.03
21	7.24	6.63	5.99	5.29	4.55	3.76	2.92	2.01	1.04
22	7.29	6.68	6.03	5.33	4.59	3.80	2.94	2.03	1.05
23	7.34	6.72	6.07	5.37	4.63	3.83	2.97	2.05	1.06
24	7.38	6.77	6.12	5.42	4.67	3.87	3.00	2.07	1.08
25	7.43	6.82	6.17	5.46	4.71	3.90	3.03	2.10	1.09
26	7.49	6.88	6.22	5.52	4.76	3.94	3.07	2.13	1.11
27	7.56	6.94	6.28	5.57	4.81	3.99	3.11	2.15	1.12
28	7.62	7.00	6.34	5.63	4.86	4.04	3.15	2.18	1.14
29	7.69	7.07	6.41	5.69	4.93	4.09	3.19	2.22	1.16
30	7.77	7.14	6.48	5.77	4.99	4.15	3.24	2.26	1.18
31	7.85	7.23	6.56	5.84	5.06	4.22	3.30	2.30	1.20
32	7.93	7.32	6.65	5.92	5.14	4.28	3.36	2.34	1.23
33	8.04	7.41	6.74	6.01	5.22	4.37	3.42	2.39	1.26
34	8.14	7.51	6.84	6.11	5.32	4.45	3.50	2.45	1.29
35	8.25	7.63	6.95	6.23	5.42	4.55	3.58	2.51	1.32
36	8.38	7.75	7.09	6.35	5.54	4.65	3.67	2.58	1.36
37	8.51	7.90	7.22	6.49	5.66	4.76	3.76	2.65	1.41
38	8.68	8.05	7.38	6.63	5.81	4.89	3.88	2.74	1.46
39	8.84	8.23	7.54	6.79	5.96	5.04	4.00	2.84	1.51
40	9.04	8.41	7.73	6.97	6.14	5.19	4.14	2.95	1.58
41	9.23	8.61	7.93	7.18	6.33	5.38	4.31	3.08	1.66
42	9.45	8.84	8.16	7.40	6.56	5.59	4.49	3.23	1.75
43	9.70	9.10	8.42	7.67	6.81	5.83	4.71	3.40	1.84
44	9.99	9.38	8.72	7.96	7.10	6.11	4.96	3.59	1.96
45	10.30	9.72	9.05	8.30	7.44	6.43	5.24	3.80	2.08
46	10.66	10.09	9.44	8.70	7.83	6.80	5.55	4.04	2.22
47	11.07	10.52	9.89	9.16	8.27	7.20	5.91	4.32	2.38
48	11.54	11.02	10.41	9.67	8.76	7.65	6.29	4.62	2.55
49	12.09	11.59	10.99	10.24	9.31	8.16	6.73	4.96	2.75
50	12.72	12.24	11.63	10.87	9.93	8.73	7.23	5.33	2.96
51	13.42	12.95	12.35	11.59	10.61	9.36	7.77	5.75	3.20
52	14.20	13.75	13.17	12.39	11.38	10.07	8.38	6.22	3.48
53	15.08	14.66	14.07	13.28	12.23	10.85	9.06	6.75	3.78
54	16.06	15.65	15.08	14.27	13.18	11.73	9.82	7.33	4.12
55	17.15	16.77	16.19	15.36	14.23	12.70	10.66	7.99	4.50
56	18.37	18.00	17.42	16.59	15.40	13.78	11.60	8.71	4.92
57	19.72	19.37	18.80	17.94	16.71	14.99	12.64	9.52	5.40
58	21.20	20.89	20.33	19.45	18.16	16.32	13.80	10.43	5.93
59	22.86	22.58	22.03	21.12	19.76	17.80	15.11	11.44	6.53
60	24.69	24.45	23.90	22.97	21.53	19.47	16.56	12.58	7.20

TABLE No. XLVI.

COST OF INSURANCE PER $1,000 OF A FIFTEEN-YEAR ENDOWMENT POLICY, DURING VARIOUS YEARS, AMERICAN EXPERIENCE, 4½ PER CENT.

Age.	*First year.*	*Second year.*	*Third year.*	*Fourth year.*	*Fifth year.*	*Sixth year.*	*Seventh year.*	*Eighth year.*
20	7.45	7.12	6.77	6.40	5.99	5.56	5.10	4.61
21	7.50	7.17	6.82	6.44	6.03	5.61	5.15	4.65
22	7.55	7.22	6.86	6.48	6.08	5.65	5.19	4.70
23	7.60	7.27	6.91	6.54	6.13	5.70	5.24	4.75
24	7.65	7.31	6.97	6.59	6.19	5.76	5.29	4.79
25	7.70	7.37	7.02	6.65	6.25	5.81	5.35	4.85
26	7.76	7.43	7.08	6.71	6.31	5.87	5.41	4.91
27	7.83	7.50	7.15	6.77	6.37	5.94	5.48	4.98
28	7.89	7.57	7.22	6.84	6.44	6.02	5.55	5.04
29	7.97	7.64	7.29	6.92	6.53	6.09	5.62	5.12
30	8.05	7.72	7.38	7.01	6.61	6.17	5.71	5.21
31	8.13	7.81	7.47	7.10	6.70	6.27	5.81	5.31
32	8.22	7.91	7.57	7.20	6.81	6.38	5.92	5.41
33	8.32	8.01	7.67	7.31	6.92	6.50	6.03	5.53
34	8.43	8.12	7.79	7.43	7.05	6.62	6.16	5.65
35	8.54	8.25	7.91	7.57	7.18	6.76	6.30	5.79
36	8.68	8.38	8.06	7.71	7.34	6.91	6.45	5.94
37	8.82	8.54	8.22	7.88	7.50	7.08	6.62	6.12
38	8.98	8.70	8.40	8.05	7.68	7.27	6.82	6.31
39	9.15	8.89	8.58	8.25	7.88	7.48	7.03	6.53
40	9.35	9.08	8.79	8.46	8.11	7.71	7.28	6.78
41	9.55	9.30	9.01	8.71	8.36	7.99	7.56	7.07
42	9.79	9.54	9.28	8.98	8.66	8.29	7.88	7.41
43	10.04	9.82	9.57	9.30	8.99	8.64	8.26	7.80
44	10.34	10.12	9.91	9.65	9.37	9.06	8.68	8.23
45	10.66	10.48	10.28	10.06	9.82	9.53	9.17	8.71
46	11.04	10.88	10.72	10.54	10.35	10.05	9.70	9.26
47	11.45	11.34	11.23	11.08	10.89	10.64	10.30	9.87
48	11.94	11.88	11.81	11.69	11.53	11.30	10.98	10.54
49	12.51	12.49	12.46	12.38	12.24	12.04	11.73	11.30
50	13.15	13.18	13.18	13.14	13.04	12.86	12.57	12.14
51	13.88	13.95	13.99	13.99	13.93	13.78	13.50	13.07
52	14.68	14.81	14.90	14.94	14.92	14.79	14.53	14.11
53	15.58	15.77	15.91	16.00	16.01	15.91	15.68	15.26
54	16.60	16.83	17.04	17.17	17.22	17.17	16.95	16.54
55	17.72	18.02	18.28	18.47	18.57	18.55	18.37	17.96
56	18.97	19.34	19.65	19.91	20.07	20.09	19.93	19.53
57	20.35	20.79	21.18	21.50	21.72	21.79	21.66	21.26
58	21.88	22.40	22.88	23.27	23.55	23.67	23.57	23.30
59	23.58	24.19	24.75	25.23	25.57	25.74	25.70	25.35
60	25.46	26.17	26.82	27.37	27.79	28.05	28.05	27.72

TABLE No. XLVII.

COST OF INSURANCE PER $1,000 OF A TWENTY-YEAR ENDOWMENT POLICY, DURING VARIOUS YEARS, AMERICAN EXPERIENCE, 4½ PER CENT.

Age.	First year.	Second year.	Third year.	Fourth year.	Fifth year.	Sixth year.	Seventh year.	Eighth year.
20	7.58	7.38	7.17	6.95	6.70	6.44	6 17	5.88
21	7.62	7.43	7.22	6.99	6.75	6.50	6.22	5.93
22	7.67	7.48	7.27	7.04	6.80	6.55	6.27	5.98
23	7.72	7.53	7.32	7.10	6.86	6.60	6.33	6.04
24	7.78	7.58	7.37	7.15	6.92	6.67	6.40	6.10
25	7.83	7.64	7.44	7.21	6.98	6.73	6.46	6.17
26	7.89	7.70	7.50	7.28	7.05	6.80	6.53	6.25
27	7.96	7.77	7.57	7.36	7.12	6.88	6.62	6.33
28	8.02	7.84	7.64	7.43	7.20	6.96	6.70	6.42
29	8.10	7.92	7.72	7.51	7.29	7.05	6.79	6.52
30	8.18	8.00	7.81	7.61	7.39	7.15	6.90	6.62
31	8.26	8.09	7.91	7.71	7.48	7.26	7.01	6.75
32	8.35	8.19	8.01	7.81	7.60	7.38	7.14	6.87
33	8.46	8.30	8.11	7.93	7.72	7.51	7.27	7.02
34	8.57	8.40	8.24	8.06	7.87	7.65	7.43	7.17
35	8.68	8.54	8.37	8.21	8.02	7.82	7.59	7.35
36	8.82	8.67	8.53	8.36	8.19	7.99	7.78	7.54
37	8.96	8.84	8.69	8.54	8.37	8.18	7.97	7.76
38	9.13	9.00	8.88	8.72	8.57	8.39	8.21	7.99
39	9.30	9.20	9.07	8.94	8.79	8.64	8.46	8.28
40	9.50	9.39	9.29	9.16	9.04	8.90	8.75	8.56
41	9.71	9.62	9.52	9.43	9.32	9.21	9.08	8.94
42	9.94	9.87	9.80	9.72	9.64	9.55	9.46	9.36
43	10.20	10.16	10.10	10.06	10.00	9.95	9.90	9.84
44	10.50	10.47	10.46	10.42	10.42	10.42	10.41	10.38
45	10.82	10.84	10.85	10.87	10.91	10.95	10.97	10.97
46	11.21	11.24	11.30	11.38	11.46	11.54	11.60	11.64
47	11.63	11.72	11.83	11.96	12.09	12.21	12.31	12.39
48	12.12	12.27	12.44	12.61	12.78	12.94	13.10	13.21
49	12.69	12.90	13.11	13.34	13.55	13.77	13.97	14.14
50	13.34	13.60	13.87	14.14	14.42	14.69	14.94	15.16
51	14.08	14.39	14.71	15.05	15.38	15.71	16.02	16.26
52	14.89	15.26	15.66	16.05	16.45	16.84	17.20	17.53
53	15.80	16.25	16.70	17.17	17.64	18.08	18.52	18.91
54	16.82	17.33	17.86	18.40	18.93	19.47	19.97	20.43
55	17.95	18.55	19.15	19.16	20.38	20.99	21.58	22.11
56	19.22	19.88	20.56	21.27	21.97	22.67	23.34	23.95
57	20.61	21.36	22.14	22.93	23.74	24.53	25.28	25.98
58	22.15	23.00	23.88	24.78	25.68	26.56	27.41	28.23
59	23.86	24.81	25.80	26.80	27.80	28.79	29.78	30.69
60	25.75	26.82	27.91	29.02	30.14	31.27	32.37	33.40

TABLE No. XLVIII.

Cost of Insurance per \$1,000 of a Twenty-five Year Endowment Policy, during various years, American Experience, 4½ per cent.

Age.	First year.	Second year.	Third year.	Fourth year.	Fifth year.	Sixth year.	Seventh year.	Eighth year.
20	7.65	7.53	7.40	7.26	7.11	6.95	6.78	6.60
21	7.70	7.58	7.45	7.31	7.16	7.00	6.84	6.65
22	7.75	7.63	7.50	7.36	7.21	7.06	6.89	6.72
23	7.80	7.68	7.55	7.42	7.27	7.12	6.96	6.78
24	7.85	7.73	7.61	7.48	7.33	7.18	7.02	6.85
25	7.90	7.79	7.67	7.54	7.40	7.25	7.09	6.92
26	7.96	7.85	7.73	7.61	7.47	7.33	7.17	7.01
27	8.03	7.92	7.81	7.68	7.55	7.41	7.26	7.10
28	8.10	7.99	7.88	7.76	7.63	7.50	7.36	7.19
29	8.17	8.07	7.96	7.85	7.73	7.60	7.45	7.31
30	8.25	8.15	8.05	7.94	7.83	7.69	7.57	7.42
31	8.34	8.24	8.15	8.05	7.93	7.81	7.68	7.56
32	8.43	8.35	8.26	8.15	8.05	7.94	7.83	7.70
33	8.54	8.46	8.36	8.28	8.18	8.08	7.97	7.86
34	8.65	8.56	8.49	8.41	8.33	8.23	8.14	8.03
35	8.76	8.70	8.63	8.56	8.48	8.41	8.31	8.22
36	8.90	8.84	8.79	8.72	8.66	8.58	8.51	8.42
37	9.04	9.00	8.95	8.90	8.84	8.79	8.72	8.66
38	9.21	9.17	9.14	9.09	9.05	9.01	8.96	8.92
39	9.38	9.36	9.33	9.31	9.28	9.26	9.24	9.23
40	9.58	9.56	9.56	9.54	9.55	9.54	9.55	9.56
41	9.79	9.79	9.80	9.82	9 83	9.87	9.90	9.95
42	10.03	10.04	10.08	10.11	10.17	10.23	10.30	10.41
43	10.28	10.33	10.38	10.46	10.54	10.64	10.78	10.92
44	10.58	10.65	10.74	10.84	10.97	11.13	11.31	11.50
45	10.91	11.02	11.14	11.29	11.48	11.69	11.91	12.14
46	11.29	11.43	11.60	11.81	12.05	12.31	12.58	12.89
47	11.72	11.91	12.14	12.40	12.69	13.00	13.32	13.66
48	12.24	12.46	12.75	13.07	13.40	13.76	14.18	14.54
49	12.78	13.13	13.44	13.80	14.20	14.62	15.09	15.53
50	13.44	13.80	14.20	14.63	15.09	15.57	16.09	16.61
51	14.17	14.59	15.05	15.55	16.07	16.63	17.21	17.79
52	14.99	15.47	16.00	16.56	17.16	17.79	18.43	19.11
53	15.90	16.46	17.06	17.70	18.37	19.06	19.80	20.55
54	16.92	17.55	18.23	18.94	19.69	20.48	21.30	22.14
55	18.05	18.77	19.52	20.30	21.15	22.03	22.95	23.89
56	19.32	20.11	20.94	21.83	22.77	23.74	24.75	25.79
57	20.71	21.59	22.52	23.51	24.54	25.62	26.73	27.87
58	22.25	23.23	24.26	25.35	26.49	27.67	28.89	30.16
59	23.96	25.04	26.19	27.38	28.62	29.92	31.28	32.66
60	25.85	27.04	28.30	29.60	30.96	32.40	33.88	35.39

TABLE No. XLIX.

COST OF INSURANCE PER $1,000 OF A THIRTY-YEAR ENDOWMENT POLICY, DURING VARIOUS YEARS, AMERICAN EXPERIENCE, 4½ PER CENT.

Age.	First year.	Second year.	Third year.	Fourth year.	Fifth year.	Sixth year.	Seventh year.	Eighth year.
20	7.69	7.62	7.54	7.46	7.36	7.26	7.16	7.05
21	7.74	7.67	7.59	7.50	7.41	7.32	7.22	7.10
22	7.79	7.72	7.64	7.55	7.47	7.37	7.27	7.17
23	7.84	7.77	7.69	7.61	7.53	7.44	7.34	7.24
24	7.89	7.82	7.75	7.67	7.59	7.51	7.41	7.31
25	7.95	7.88	7.81	7.74	7.66	7.58	7.48	7.39
26	8.01	7.95	7.88	7.81	7.73	7.65	7.57	7.48
27	8.07	8.01	7.95	7.89	7.81	7.73	7.66	7.57
28	8.14	8.09	8.03	7.96	7.90	7.83	7.76	7.67
29	8.22	8.17	8.11	8.05	7.99	7.93	7.85	7.79
30	8.30	8.25	8.20	8.15	8.09	8.02	7.97	7.91
31	8.38	8.34	8.30	8.25	8.20	8.15	8.09	8.05
32	8.48	8.44	8.40	8.36	8.32	8.27	8.24	8.19
33	8.58	8.55	8.51	8.48	8.45	8.42	8.39	8.36
34	8.69	8.66	8.64	8.62	8.60	8.58	8.56	8.53
35	8.81	8.80	8.78	8.77	8.76	8.75	8.74	8.73
36	8.94	8.93	8.94	8.93	8.94	8.93	8.94	8.94
37	9.09	9.10	9.10	9.12	9.12	9.14	9.15	9.19
38	9.25	9.27	9.29	9.31	9.33	9.37	9.41	9.45
39	9.43	9.46	9.49	9.52	9.56	9.62	9.68	9.77
40	9.63	9.66	9.71	9.76	9.83	9.90	10.00	10.11
41	9.84	9.89	9.95	10.03	10.11	10.23	10.36	10.51
42	10.07	10.14	10.23	10.33	10.46	10.60	10.77	10.98
43	10.33	10.43	10.53	10.63	10.83	11.02	11.25	11.51
44	10.63	10.74	10.90	11.06	11.26	11.51	11.79	12.10
45	10.95	11.12	11.29	11.51	11.77	12.10	12.40	12.75
46	11.34	11.52	11.75	12.03	12.35	12.69	13.07	13.48
47	11.76	12.00	12.29	12.62	12.99	13.39	13.82	14.29
48	12.25	12.56	12.90	13.29	13.71	14.16	14.66	15.19
49	12.83	13.19	13.59	14.03	14.50	15.02	15.58	16.18
50	13.48	13.90	14.35	14.85	15.39	15.98	16.61	17.27
51	14.21	14.68	15.20	15.77	16.37	17.03	17.73	18.46
52	15.03	15.56	16.15	16.78	17.47	18.19	18.96	19.78
53	15.94	16.55	17.20	17.91	18.66	19.46	20.32	21.22
54	16.96	17.64	18.37	19.15	19.98	20.87	21.81	22.81
55	18.09	18.85	19.66	20.51	21.44	22.42	23.45	24.54

TABLE No. L.

Cost of Insurance per $1,000 of an Ordinary Life Policy, during various years, Combined Experience, 4 per cent.

Age.	First year.	Second year.	Third year.	Fourth year.	Fifth year.	Sixth year.	Seventh year.	Eighth year.
20	7.25	7.28	7.32	7.37	7.41	7.46	7.51	7.56
21	7.33	7.37	7.41	7.46	7.50	7.55	7.60	7.66
22	7.41	7.46	7.51	7.55	7.60	7.65	7.71	7.77
23	7.51	7.56	7.60	7.65	7.71	7.77	7.83	7.89
24	7.61	7.66	7.71	7.76	7.82	7.88	7.95	8.02
25	7.71	7.76	7.82	7.88	7.94	8.01	8.08	8.15
26	7.82	7.88	7.94	8.00	8.07	8.14	8.21	8.29
27	7.94	8.00	8.06	8.13	8.20	8.28	8.35	8.42
28	8.07	8.13	8.20	8.27	8.35	8.42	8.49	8.57
29	8.20	8.27	8.34	8.42	8.49	8.57	8.65	8.73
30	8.35	8.41	8.49	8.57	8.64	8.72	8.80	8.88
31	8.50	8.57	8.65	8.73	8.81	8.89	8.96	9.04
32	8.66	8.74	8.81	8.89	8.97	9.05	9.13	9.21
33	8.83	8.90	8.98	9.07	9.14	9.23	9.31	9.38
34	9.00	9.08	9.16	9.24	9.33	9.40	9.48	9.56
35	9.18	9.26	9.34	9.43	9.51	9.58	9.67	9.77
36	9.37	9.45	9.54	9.62	9.70	9.78	9.88	10.04
37	9.56	9.65	9.74	9.81	9.90	10.00	10.16	10.38
38	9.78	9.86	9.94	10.03	10.13	10.29	10.51	10.78
39	9.99	10.07	10.16	10.27	10.43	10.65	10.92	11.27
40	10.21	10.30	10.41	10.57	10.80	11.07	11.42	11.79
41	10.45	10.56	10.72	10.96	11.23	11.59	11.97	12.37
42	10.72	10.89	11.13	11.41	11.77	12.15	12.56	12.99
43	11.07	11.30	11.59	11.96	12.34	12.76	13.20	13.66
44	11.50	11.79	12.16	12.55	12.97	13.42	13.90	14.40
45	11.99	12.37	12.77	13.20	13.65	14.14	14.65	15.20
46	12.60	13.01	13.44	13.90	14.40	14.92	15.48	16.08
47	13.26	13.70	14.17	14.67	15.21	15.78	16.38	17.00
48	13.97	14.45	14.96	15.51	16.09	16.71	17.33	18.01
49	14.75	15.27	15.83	16.42	17.05	17.69	18.38	19.10
50	15.59	16.16	16.77	17.41	18.06	18.77	19.50	20.24
51	16.52	17.14	17.80	18.46	19.18	19.93	20.69	21.49
52	17.53	18.20	18.88	19.62	20.40	21.16	21.98	22.83
53	18.64	19.33	20.09	20.87	21.66	22.50	23.38	24.34
54	19.81	20.60	21.39	22.19	23.06	23.95	24.94	25.97
55	21.11	21.93	22.76	23.54	24.56	25.58	26.63	27.75
56	22.51	23.36	24.26	25.21	26.25	27.33	28.48	29.67
57	24.00	24.93	25.90	26.97	28.08	29.26	30.48	31.75
58	25.64	26.63	27.73	28.88	30.09	31.34	32.65	34.02
59	27.42	28.55	29.72	30.99	32.26	33.61	35.02	36.46
60	29.41	30.62	31.92	33.24	34.63	36.08	37.57	39.11
61	31.58	32.92	34.28	35.72	37.22	38.75	40.34	41.94
62	33.98	35.39	36.88	38.42	40.00	41.65	43.40	44.95
63	36.58	38.11	39.71	41.34	43.04	44.75	46.46	48.21
64	39.43	41.08	42.76	44.52	46.29	48.06	49.87	51.69
65	42.53	44.28	46.10	47.93	49.76	51.64	53.52	55.42

TABLE No. LI.

COST OF INSURANCE PER $1,000 OF A TEN-PAYMENT LIFE POLICY, DURING VARIOUS YEARS, COMBINED EXPERIENCE, 4 PER CENT.

Age.	First year.	Second year.	Third year.	Fourth year.	Fifth year.	Sixth year.	Seventh year.	Eighth year.
20	7.11	7.00	6.88	6.76	6.62	6.47	6.31	6.14
21	7.19	7.08	6.96	6.83	6.69	6.54	6.37	6.20
22	7.27	7.16	7.04	6.91	6.77	6.61	6.44	6.26
23	7.36	7.25	7.12	6.99	6.84	6.69	6.51	6.33
24	7.46	7.34	7.22	7.08	6.94	6.77	6.59	6.40
25	7.56	7.44	7.31	7.17	7.02	6.86	6.67	6.47
26	7.66	7.54	7.42	7.27	7.12	6.95	6.76	6.55
27	7.77	7.66	7.52	7.38	7.22	7.05	6.85	6 63
28	7.90	7.77	7.64	7.49	7.33	7.15	6.94	6.71
29	8.03	7.90	7.76	7.61	7.44	7.25	7.03	6.79
30	8.16	8.04	7.90	7.74	7.55	7.36	7.13	6.87
31	8.31	8.18	8.03	7.86	7.68	7.47	7.23	6.96
32	8.46	8.33	8.17	8.00	7.80	7.58	7.33	7.05
33	8.62	8.48	8.32	8.14	7.93	7.70	7.43	7.13
34	8.79	8.64	8.47	8.28	8.07	7.82	7.54	7.23
35	8.96	8.81	8.63	8.43	8.20	7.94	7.65	7.34
36	9.15	8.98	8.80	8.59	8.34	8.07	7.78	7.49
37	9.38	9.17	8.97	8 74	8.49	8.22	7.96	7.69
38	9.54	9.36	9.15	8.92	8.67	8.43	8.19	7.93
39	9.74	9.55	9.34	9.11	8.90	8.69	8.46	8.23
40	9.95	9.76	9.55	9.36	9.19	8.99	8.81	8.55
41	10.19	10.00	9.83	9.68	9.53	9.38	9.17	8.89
42	10.45	10.30	10.19	10.06	9.95	9.79	9.56	9.26
43	10.78	10.69	10.60	10.52	10.41	10.23	9.99	9.67
44	11.19	11.13	11.10	11.03	10.90	10.72	10.45	10.10
45	11.67	11.68	11.65	11.57	11.44	11.24	10.95	10.57
46	12.27	12.27	12.24	12.16	12.02	11.81	11.50	11.07
47	12.90	12.91	12.89	12.81	12.66	12.43	12.09	11.60
48	13.59	13.61	13.59	13.51	13.36	13.10	12.71	12.18
49	14.34	14.38	14.36	14.28	14.11	13.82	13.39	12.80
50	15.16	15.21	15.20	15.12	14.91	14.60	14.12	13.44
51	16.05	16.12	16.12	16.01	15.80	15.44	14.89	14.13
52	17.04	17.11	17.09	16.99	16.75	16.33	15.72	14.88
53	18.11	18.17	18.17	18.05	17.76	17.30	16.63	15.72
54	19.25	19.34	19.33	19.17	18.86	18.35	17.64	16.61
55	20.51	20.61	20.56	20.40	20.05	19.53	18.73	17.59
56	21.87	21.95	21.92	21.73	21.40	20.81	19.93	18.64
57	23.32	23.42	23.39	23.24	22.86	22.22	21.22	19.79
58	24.91	25.03	25.05	24.87	24.47	23.75	22.64	21.02
59	26.65	26.83	26.85	26.68	26.22	25.42	24.17	22.34
60	28.60	28.80	28.84	28.64	28.14	27.24	25.84	23.79

TABLE No. LII.

COST OF INSURANCE PER $1,000 OF A TEN-YEAR ENDOWMENT POLICY, DURING VARIOUS YEARS, COMBINED EXPERIENCE, 4 PER CENT.

Age.	First year.	Second year.	Third year.	Fourth year.	Fifth year.	Sixth year.	Seventh year.	Eighth year.
20	6.70	6.16	5.58	4.95	4.28	3.55	2.76	1.91
21	6.78	6.24	5.65	5.02	4.34	3.60	2.80	1.94
22	6.86	6.32	5.73	5.08	4.40	3.66	2.85	1.98
23	6.96	6.40	5.81	5.16	4.47	3.72	2.90	2.02
24	7.05	6.49	5.89	5.24	4.54	3.78	2.96	2.05
25	7.14	6.59	5.98	5.33	4.62	3.85	3.01	2.09
26	7.25	6.69	6.08	5.42	4.71	3.92	3.07	2.14
27	7.36	6.80	6.19	5.52	4.79	4.00	3.13	2.18
28	7.49	6.92	6.30	5.62	4.89	4.08	3.19	2.22
29	7.61	7.04	6.41	5.73	4.99	4.16	3.26	2.28
30	7.75	7.17	6.54	5.85	5.09	4.25	3.34	2.33
31	7.89	7.31	6.67	5.97	5.20	4.35	3.41	2.38
32	8.05	7.46	6.80	6.09	5.31	4.40	3.49	2.44
33	8.21	7.60	6.95	6.22	5.42	4.54	3.57	2.49
34	8.37	7.77	7.10	6.36	5.55	4.65	3.65	2.55
35	8.55	7.93	7.25	6.51	5.68	4.76	3.74	2.63
36	8.73	8.10	7.42	6.65	5.81	4.87	3.84	2.71
37	8.91	8.29	7.59	6.81	5.95	5.00	3.96	2.82
38	9.12	8.48	7.76	6.97	6.11	5.17	4.13	2.95
39	9.32	8.67	7.95	7.16	6.31	5.38	4.31	3.10
40	9.54	8.88	8.16	7.40	6.56	5.62	4.55	3.27
41	9.77	9.12	8.43	7.69	6.85	5.91	4.79	3.45
42	10.03	9.42	8.77	8.03	7.21	6.23	5.05	3.66
43	10.36	9.79	9.15	8.45	7.60	6.58	5.34	3.88
44	10.77	10.22	9.63	8.90	8.02	6.95	5.67	4.12
45	11.24	10.75	10.14	9.40	8.48	7.37	6.02	4.38
46	11.82	11.32	10.71	9.94	8.99	7.83	6.41	4.67
47	12.24	11.95	11.32	10.52	9.54	8.33	6.83	4.99
48	13.13	12.63	11.98	11.17	10.15	8.88	7.28	5.33
49	13.87	13.37	12.71	11.88	10.81	9.46	7.80	5.71
50	14.69	14.18	13.52	12.65	11.53	10.12	8.36	6.12
51	15.57	15.07	14.39	13.48	12.32	10.83	8.94	6.57
52	16.55	16.04	15.33	14.40	13.17	11.58	9.58	7.06
53	17.61	17.08	16.36	15.39	14.09	12.42	10.29	7.62
54	18.74	18.23	17.49	16.45	15.10	13.34	11.10	8.23
55	19.99	19.47	18.69	17.62	16.20	14.37	11.98	8.92
56	21.34	20.80	20.00	18.90	17.45	15.51	12.97	9.67
57	22.79	22.25	21.44	20.34	18.88	16.76	14.04	10.50
58	24.38	23.84	23.06	21.92	20.32	18.14	15.23	11.42
59	26.10	25.63	24.83	23.66	21.97	19.66	16.55	12.42
60	28.15	27.58	26.79	25.56	23.80	21.34	17.99	13.55

TABLE No. LIII.

COST OF INSURANCE PER $1,000 OF A FIFTEEN-YEAR ENDOWMENT POLICY,
DURING VARIOUS YEARS, COMBINED EXPERIENCE, 4 PER CENT.

Age.	First year.	Second year.	Third year.	Fourth year.	Fifth year.	Sixth year.	Seventh year.	Eighth year.
20	6.94	6.66	6.35	·6.03	5.67	5.29	4.88	4.43
21	7.03	6.74	6.44	6.11	5.75	5.37	4.95	4.50
22	7.11	6.83	6.52	6.19	5.84	5.45	5.03	4.57
23	7.21	6.92	6.61	6.29	5.93	5.54	5.11	4.66
24	7.30	7.02	6.71	6.38	6.03	5.63	5.21	4.75
25	7.40	7.12	6.82	6.49	6.13	5.74	5.31	4.84
26	7.51	7.23	6.93	6.60	6.24	5.84	5.42	4.94
27	7.63	7.35	7.05	6.72	6.35	5.96	5.53	5.03
28	7.75	7.48	7.17	6.84	6.48	6.08	5.64	5.14
29	7.88	7.61	7.31	6.98	6.61	6.20	5.75	5.27
30	8.03	7.75	7.45	7.12	6.74	6.33	5.88	5.38
31	8.17	7.90	7.60	7.25	6.89	6.47	5.99	5.50
32	8.33	8.06	7.75	7.41	7.03	6.61	6.14	5.63
33	8.50	8.22	7.91	7.57	7.19	6.76	6.29	5.76
34	8.67	8.39	8.08	7.73	7.35	6.92	6.43	5.90
35	8.85	8.57	8.26	7.91	7.52	7.08	6.59	6.06
36	9.04	8.75	8.44	8.09	7.69	7.25	6.76	6.25
37	9.23	8.95	8.64	8.27	7.87	7.44	6.98	6.51
38	9.44	9.16	8.83	8.47	8.08	7.68	7.26	6.80
39	9.65	9.36	9.04	8.70	8.35	7.99	7.58	7.14
40	9.87	9.59	9.28	8.98	8.68	8.34	7.97	7.52
41	10.11	9.82	9.59	9.34	9.06	8.77	8.40	7.94
42	10.38	10.16	9.96	9.75	9.52	9.23	8.87	8.39
43	10.72	10.57	10.40	10.25	10.03	9.45	9.37	8.89
44	11.15	11.03	10.94	10.79	10.59	10.30	9.92	9.44
45	11.63	11.60	11.52	11.39	11.19	10.91	10.53	10.04
46	12.23	12.21	12.15	12.03	11.85	11.58	11.20	10.70
47	12.88	12.89	12.84	12.74	12.57	12.30	11.93	11.40
48	13.59	13.61	13.59	13.51	13.36	13.10	12.71	12.18
49	14.35	14.41	14.41	14.36	14.22	13.96	13.57	13.03
50	15.19	15.28	15.31	15.28	15.14	14.90	14.51	13.94
51	16.10	16.23	16.30	16.27	16.16	15.93	15.51	14.92
52	17.11	17.27	17.35	17.36	17.27	17.02	16.61	16.00
53	18.20	18.37	18.51	18.54	18.44	18.22	17.82	17.23
54	19.36	19.60	19.76	19.80	19.74	19.53	19.18	18.58
55	20.65	20.93	21.10	21.18	21.15	21.00	20.64	20.05
56	22.05	22.34	22.56	22.69	22.73	22.61	22.28	21.67
57	23.53	23.88	24.16	24.38	24.46	24.38	24.06	23.46
58	25.15	25.57	25.95	26.23	26.37	26.31	26.02	25.42
59	26.93	27.46	27.89	28.26	28.45	28.44	28.18	27.55
60	28.99	29.53	30.07	30.48	30.73	30.78	30.52	29.91

TABLE No. LIV.

COST OF INSURANCE PER $1,000 OF A TWENTY-YEAR ENDOWMENT POLICY, DURING VARIOUS YEARS, COMBINED EXPERIENCE, 4 PER CENT.

Age.	First year.	Second year.	Third year.	Fourth year.	Fifth year.	Sixth year.	Seventh year.	Eighth year.
20	7.06	6.90	6.73	6.55	6.35	6.13	5.80	5.65
21	7.14	6.98	6.82	6.64	6.43	6.22	5.99	5.74
22	7.23	7.08	6.91	6.73	6.53	6.32	6.09	5.84
23	7.33	7.17	7.00	6.83	6.63	6.42	6.19	5.95
24	7.43	7.27	7.11	6.93	6.74	6.53	6.31	6.05
25	7.53	7.38	7.22	7.05	6.86	6.65	6.42	6.17
26	7.64	7.49	7.34	7.17	6.98	6.77	6.55	6.29
27	7.75	7.62	7.46	7.30	7.11	6.91	6.68	6.42
28	7.88	7.74	7.60	7.43	7.25	7.04	6.81	6.56
29	8.02	7.89	7.74	7.57	7.39	7.18	6.96	6.70
30	8.16	8.03	7.89	7.73	7.54	7.34	7.11	6.84
31	8.31	8.19	8.04	7.88	7.70	7.49	7.26	7.00
32	8.47	8.35	8.20	8.05	7.86	7.65	7.42	7.16
33	8.64	8.51	8.38	8.22	8.03	7.83	7.59	7.32
34	8.81	8.69	8.55	8.39	8.21	8.00	7.77	7.50
35	9.00	8.88	8.73	8.58	8.40	8.18	7.94	7.69
36	9.19	9.06	8.93	8.77	8.58	8.38	8.18	7.92
37	9.38	9.27	9.13	8.97	8.79	8.60	8.42	8.25
38	9.59	9.48	9.34	9.18	9.02	8.87	8.75	8.61
39	9.81	9.69	9.56	9.42	9.31	9.22	9.12	9.04
40	10.03	9.92	9.81	9.72	9.67	9.62	9.60	9.52
41	10.27	10.18	10.13	10.10	10.09	10.11	10.08	10.04
42	10.54	10.51	10.52	10.54	10.60	10.64	10.64	10.60
43	10.89	10.93	10.98	11.08	11.16	11.22	11.23	11.22
44	11.32	11.40	10.54	11.66	11.77	11.85	11.89	11.89
45	11.81	11.99	12.15	12.30	12.43	12.54	12.61	12.64
46	12.42	12.62	12.81	12.99	13.15	13.29	13.39	13.45
47	13.07	13.31	13.53	13.74	13.94	14.11	14.24	14.31
48	13.79	14.05	14.32	14.57	14.80	15.01	15.15	15.26
49	14.56	14.87	15.17	15.47	15.74	15.97	16.16	16.30
50	15.41	15.76	16.11	16.45	16.74	17.02	17.24	17.39
51	16.34	16.74	17.13	17.49	17.85	18.16	18.40	18.59
52	17.35	17.80	18.22	18.65	19.04	19.38	19.67	19.90
53	18.45	18.93	19.42	19.90	20.31	20.70	21.04	21.36
54	19.63	20.18	20.72	21.22	21.70	22.15	22.59	22.96
55	20.93	21.53	22.10	22.67	23.21	23.77	24.27	24.71
56	22.33	22.97	23.61	24.25	24.90	25.53	26.12	26.61
57	23.83	24.54	25.26	26.01	26.75	27.46	28.11	28.70
58	25.46	26.26	27.10	27.94	28.77	29.56	30.31	30.97
59	27.25	28.18	29.11	30.05	30.97	31.86	32.69	33.43
60	29.25	30.27	31.32	32.34	33.37	34.36	35.28	36.13

TABLE No. LV.

COST OF INSURANCE PER $1,000 OF A TWENTY-FIVE YEAR ENDOWMENT POLICY, DURING VARIOUS YEARS, COMBINED EXPERIENCE, 4 PER CENT.

Age.	First year.	Second year.	Third year.	Fourth year.	Fifth year.	Sixth year.	Seventh year.	Eighth year.
20	7.13	7.04	6.94	6.85	6.74	6.61	6.49	6.34
21	7.21	7.13	7.04	6.94	6.83	6.71	6.59	6.45
22	7.30	7.22	7.13	7.03	6.93	6.81	6.69	6.55
23	7.40	7.32	7.23	7.14	7.04	6.93	6.81	6.68
24	7.50	7.42	7.34	7.25	7.15	7.04	6.93	6.80
25	7.60	7.53	7.45	7.37	7.27	7.17	7.06	6.94
26	7.71	7.64	7.57	7.49	7.40	7.30	7.19	7.07
27	7.83	7.77	7.70	7.62	7.54	7.44	7.34	7.21
28	7.96	7.90	7.84	7.76	7.68	7.59	7.48	7.36
29	8.08	8.04	7.98	7.91	7.84	7.74	7.64	7.52
30	8.24	8.19	8.14	8.07	7.99	7.90	7.80	7.67
31	8.39	8.35	8.30	8.23	8.16	8.07	7.96	7.85
32	8.55	8.51	8.46	8.40	8.33	8.24	8.14	8.02
33	8.72	8.68	8.63	8.58	8.50	8.42	8.32	8.20
34	8.89	8.86	8.82	8.76	8.69	8.61	8.50	8.38
35	9.08	9.05	9.00	8.95	8.88	8.80	8.69	8.59
36	9.27	9.24	9.20	9.15	9.08	9.00	8.92	8.87
37	9.47	9.44	9.40	9.35	9.29	9.23	9.20	9.21
38	9.68	9.65	9.61	9.57	9.53	9.52	9.56	9.60
39	9.90	9.87	9.84	9.82	9.83	9.89	9.96	10.08
40	10.12	10.10	10.09	10.13	10.21	10.31	10.47	10.60
41	10.36	10.37	10.42	10.52	10.64	10.83	10.99	11.17
42	10.63	10.70	10.82	10.97	11.18	11.38	11.48	11.78
43	10.98	11.12	11.29	11.52	11.76	12.00	12.22	12.45
44	11.41	11.60	11.86	12.12	12.39	12.66	12.93	13.18
45	11.91	12.19	12.48	12.77	13.07	13.38	13.68	13.99
46	12.51	12.83	13.15	13.48	13.82	14.17	14.51	14.86
47	13.17	13.53	13.88	14.25	14.63	15.02	15.42	15.78
48	13.89	14.28	14.68	15.10	15.52	15.96	16.37	16.80
49	14.67	15.10	15.55	16.01	16.49	16.95	17.43	17.90
50	15.52	16.00	16.50	17.01	17.52	18.05	18.57	19.06
51	16.45	16.98	17.51	18.08	18.65	19.23	19.77	20.33
52	17.46	18.05	18.63	19.25	19.87	20.47	21.09	21.70
53	18.57	19.19	19.84	20.51	21.16	21.84	22.51	23.24
54	19.74	20.44	21.15	21.85	.22.57	23.31	24.11	24.90
55	21.05	21.80	22.54	23.31	24.11	24.97	25.83	26.73
56	22.45	23.24	24.06	24.90	25.82	26.75	27.72	28.69
57	23.95	24.81	25.70	26.68	27.68	28.72	29.76	30.83
58	25.59	26.53	27.55	28.61	29.72	30.84	31.99	33.15
59	27.37	28.45	29.56	30.73	31.92	33.15	34.40	35.66
60	29.37	30.54	31.77	33.02	34.33	35.66	37.01	38.38

TABLE No. LVI.

COST OF INSURANCE PER $1,000 OF A THIRTY-YEAR ENDOWMENT POLICY, DURING VARIOUS YEARS, COMBINED EXPERIENCE, 4 PER CENT.

Age.	First year.	Second year.	Third year.	Fourth year.	Fifth year.	Sixth year.	Seventh year.	Eighth year.
20	7.17	7.13	7.08	7.03	6.98	6.92	6.85	6.80
21	7.26	7.21	7.17	7.13	7.07	7.02	6.95	6.89
22	7.34	7.31	7.27	7.22	7.18	7.13	7.07	7.01
23	7.44	7.41	7.37	7.33	7.29	7.24	7.19	7.13
24	7.54	7.51	7.47	7.44	7.41	7.36	7.31	7.26
25	7.64	7.62	7.59	7.56	7.53	7.49	7.45	7.40
26	7.76	7.73	7.72	7.69	7.66	7.63	7.59	7.54
27	7.87	7.86	7.84	7.83	7.80	7.78	7.73	7.69
28	8.00	7.99	7.98	7.97	7.95	7.93	7.89	7.85
29	8.14	8.14	8.13	8.12	8.11	8.08	8.05	8.01
30	8.28	8.28	8.29	8.28	8.26	8.25	8.22	8.18
31	8.43	8.44	8.45	8.44	8.43	8.42	8.38	8.35
32	8.60	8.61	8.61	8.61	8.61	8.59	8.57	8.54
33	8.77	8.78	8.79	8.79	8.78	8.78	8.75	8.71
34	8.94	8.96	8.97	8.97	8.97	8.97	8.94	8.91
35	9.12	9.15	9.16	9.17	9.17	9.16	9.15	9.13
36	9.32	9.34	9.36	9.37	9.37	9.37	9.37	9.42
37	9.51	9.54	9.56	9 57	9.58	9.60	9.66	9.77
38	9.73	9.75	9.77	9.79	9.82	9.90	10.02	10.18
39	9.94	9.97	10.00	10.04	10.13	10.27	10.44	10.67
40	10.17	10.20	10.25	10.35	10.51	10.70	10.95	11.21
41	10.41	10.47	10.58	10.75	10.95	11.23	11.48	11.80
42	10.68	10.80	10.98	11.20	11.49	11.79	12.11	12.43
43	11.02	11.22	11.45	11.76	12.08	12.42	12.76	13.12
44	11.46	11.70	12.03	12.36	12.72	13.08	13.47	13.87
45	11.96	12.30	12.65	13.01	13.41	13.82	14.24	14.69
46	12.57	12.93	13.33	13.73	14.16	14.61	15.09	15.58
47	13.22	12.63	14.06	14.51	14.98	15.48	16.00	16.52
48	13.94	14.39	14.86	15.35	15.88	16.42	16.97	17.55
49	14.72	15.21	15.73	16.27	16.85	17.42	18.04	18.66
50	15.57	16.11	16.68	17.27	17.87	18.52	19.18	19.83
51	16.50	17.09	17.71	18.34	19.01	19.70	20.39	21.11
52	17.51	18.16	18.81	19.51	20.23	20.95	21.70	22.49
53	18.62	19.29	20.02	20.77	21.52	22.31	23.13	24.02
54	19.79	20.54	21.32	22.10	22.92	23.78	24.72	25.68
55	21.09	21.90	22.70	23.56	24.45	25.42	26.43	27.50

TABLE No. LVII.

NET SINGLE PREMIUMS PER $1,000 FOR A TEMPORARY INSURANCE FROM ONE TO FIFTEEN YEARS (MASSACHUSETTS NON-FORFEITURE LAW,) COMBINED EXPERIENCE, 4 PER CENT.

Ages.	20	21	22	23	24	25	26	27
Years.								
1	7.01	7.09	7.17	7.27	7.37	7.47	7.58	7.70
2	13.78	13.94	14.12	14.31	14.50	14.71	14.93	15.16
3	20.32	20.57	20.83	21.11	21.40	21.72	22.05	22.40
4	26.64	26.98	27.32	27.70	28.09	28.51	28.95	29.43
5	32.76	33.17	33.61	34.08	34.57	58.10	35.66	36.25
6	38.67	39.17	39.70	40.26	40.86	41.49	42.17	42.88
7	44.40	44.98	45.60	46.26	46.96	47.70	48.49	49.33
8	49.95	50.62	51.33	52.08	52.88	53.74	54.64	55.59
9	55.33	56.08	56.88	57.74	58.64	59.60	60.61	61.68
10	60.54	61.39	62.28	63.23	64.24	65.30	66.43	67.61
11	65.61	66.54	67.52	68.57	69.68	70.85	72.08	73.38
12	70.52	71.54	72.62	73.76	74.97	76.25	77.58	78.99
13	75.30	76.41	77.57	78.81	80.12	81.49	82.94	84.46
14	79.94	81.14	82.29	83.73	85.13	86.60	88.16	89.79
15	84.46	85.74	87.08	85.50	90.00	91.58	93.23	94.98

Ages.	28	29	30	31	32	33	34	35
Years.								
1	7.83	7.96	8.10	8.25	8.41	8.58	8.75	8.93
2	15.41	15.68	15.97	16.27	16.58	16.91	17.26	17.62
3	22.78	23.18	23.61	24.06	24.53	25.02	25.53	26.06
4	29.93	30.47	31.04	31.63	32.26	32.91	35.59	34.30
5	36.89	37.55	38.26	39.00	39.78	40.58	41.43	42.31
6	43.64	44.44	45.28	46.17	47.09	48.05	49.06	50.11
7	50.21	51.14	52.12	53.14	54.21	55.33	56.49	57.71
8	56.60	57.66	58.76	59.93	61.14	62.41	63.73	65.14
9	62.81	63.99	65.24	66.54	67.89	69.31	70.81	72.43
10	68.86	70.17	71.54	72.97	74.47	76.05	77.75	79.63
11	74.74	76.18	77.67	79.24	80.90	82.67	84.62	86.78
12	80.48	82.03	83.65	85.37	87.21	89.22	91.43	93.92
13	86.06	87.73	89.49	91.38	93.44	95.71	98.24	101.06
14	91.49	93.30	95.23	97.33	99.63	102.19	105.03	108.20
15	96.79	98.76	100.90	103.23	105.81	108.67	111.84	115.34

Ages.	36	37	38	39	40	41	42	43
Years.								
1	9.12	9.31	9.53	9.74	9.96	10.24	10.48	10.82
2	17.99	18.38	18.80	19.22	19.67	20.17	20.77	21.51
3	26.63	27.22	27.83	28.47	29.16	29.96	30.94	32.12
4	35.04	35.82	36.63	37.49	38.47	39.63	41.03	42.69
5	43.23	44.20	45.22	46.36	47.68	49.23	51.10	53.27
6	51.21	52.38	53.66	55.12	56.81	58.82	61.17	63.87
7	59.00	60.42	61.99	63.81	65.93	68.39	71.24	74.47
8	66.66	68.36	70.27	72.50	75.05	77.98	81.33	85.10
9	74.22	76.25	78.53	81.17	84.17	87.57	91.44	95.72
10	81.73	84.12	86.79	89.85	93.30	97.19	101.58	106.43
11	89.22	91.98	95.05	98.54	102.45	106.84	111.76	117.18
12	96.71	99.85	103.33	107.25	111.63	116.52	121.99	127.97
13	104.21	107.74	111.63	115.99	120.84	126.25	132.25	138.81
14	111.71	115.63	119.95	124.76	130.10	136.01	142.56	149.70
15	119.23	123.55	128.30	133.57	139.39	145.82	152.91	160.61

TABLE No. LVII—(CONTINUED.)

NET SINGLE PREMIUMS, PER $1,000, FOR A TEMPORARY INSURANCE FROM ONE TO FIFTEEN YEARS (MASSACHUSETTS NON-FORFEITURE LAW) COMBINED EXPERIENCE, 4 PER CENT.

Ages.	44	45	46	47	48	49	50	51
Years.								
1	11.25	11.74	12.35	13.00	13.71	14.48	15.33	16.25
2	22.41	23.47	24.68	26.00	27.44	29.00	30.70	32.56
3	33.55	35.18	37.03	39.02	41.19	43.56	46.14	48.95
4	44.68	46.91	49.38	52.07	55.00	58.17	61.64	65.39
5	55.83	58.65	61.77	65.16	68.85	72.86	77.21	81.91
6	66.98	70.41	74.20	78.31	82.77	87.59	92.83	98.50
7	78.16	82.21	86.67	91.51	96.74	102.40	108.53	115.13
8	89.37	94.06	99.20	104.76	110.77	117.26	124.27	131.80
9	100.63	105.94	111.78	118.07	124.86	132.17	140.04	148.51
10	111.94	117.88	124.41	131.43	138.98	147.11	155.85	165.28
11	123.29	129.88	137.10	144.83	153.15	162.08	171.72	182.09
12	134.70	141.93	149.82	158.26	167.34	177.11	187.62	198.93
13	146.15	154.01	162.57	171.73	181.58	192.17	203.56	215.76
14	157.63	166.12	175.34	185.24	195.86	207.26	219.48	232.55
15	169.13	178.25	188.17	198.78	210.16	222.34	235.37	249.28

Ages.	52	53	54	55	56	57	58	59
Years.								
1	17.26	18.36	19.53	20.83	22.24	23.73	25.37	27.16
2	34.60	36.78	39.16	41.75	44.53	47.52	50.80	54.42
3	51.99	55.29	58.86	62.72	66.88	71.37	76.31	81.73
4	69.47	73.87	78.61	83.74	89.27	95.30	101.89	109.10
5	87.02	92.50	98.42	104.81	111.75	119.28	127.51	136.45
6	104.61	111.18	118.26	125.95	134.28	143.31	153.11	163.76
7	122.25	129.90	138.18	147.15	156.85	167.32	178.68	190.95
8	139.93	148.69	158.14	168.38	179.40	191.29	204.13	217.94
9	157.67	167.52	178.14	189.60	200.92	215.17	229.40	244.67
10	175.45	186.38	198.13	210.78	224.34	238.87	254.42	271.01
11	193.26	205.23	218.09	231.87	246.61	262.33	279.08	296.85
12	211.06	224.05	237.96	252.81	268.64	285.46	303.27	322.08
13	228.83	242.79	257.68	273.55	290.37	308.14	326.89	346.59
14	246.53	261.40	277.21	293.98	311.67	330.29	349.84	370.27
15	264.10	279.82	296.46	314.02	332.48	351.81	372.01	393.01

Ages.	60	61	62	63	64	65	66	67
Years.								
1	29.17	31.36	33.77	36.38	39.25	42.39	45.78	49.49
2	58.41	62.77	67.53	72.70	78.35	84.47	91.10	98.28
3	87.69	94.17	101.22	108.87	117.16	126.13	135.78	146.13
4	116.97	125.51	134.77	144.77	155.58	167.19	179.60	192.86
5	146.19	156.72	168.09	180.32	193.45	207.47	222.40	238.26
6	175.29	187.71	201.07	215.36	230.60	246.80	263.97	282.12
7	204.18	218.39	233.57	249.72	266.88	285.01	304.13	324.21
8	232.79	248.63	265.45	283.26	302.12	321.93	342.68	364.37
9	260.98	278.28	296.59	315.89	336.16	357.36	379.45	402.38
10	288.63	307.24	326.84	347.31	368.84	391.16	414.26	438.08
11	315.63	335.38	356.07	377.55	400.01	423.16	446.95	471.33
12	341.87	362.56	384.12	406.39	429.52	453.20	477.40	502.03
13	367.21	388.66	410.87	433.69	457.23	481.19	505.51	530.06
14	391.54	413.54	436.20	459.32	483.05	507.03	531.19	555.38
15	414.74	437.10	459.98	483.21	506.88	530.63	554.37	577.95

PRINCIPLES AND PRACTICE

TABLE No. LVIII.

SHOWING INSURANCE DUE ON WHOLE LIFE POLICIES, ACCORDING TO THE MASSACHUSETTS NON-FORFEITURE LAW.

No. of Premiums paid.	Age 20.		Age 21.		Age 22.		Age 23.		Age 24.	
	Years.	Days.	Years.	Days.	Years.	Days.	Years.	Days.	Years.	Days.
1	..	256	..	263	..	271	..	278	..	285
2	1	155	1	169	1	184	1	199	1	213
3	2	61	2	83	2	105	2	127	2	149
4	2	341	3	4	3	33	3	62	3	90
5	3	264	3	299	3	334	4	3	4	38
6	4	194	4	235	4	275	4	316	4	355
7	5	128	5	175	5	222	5	268	5	314
8	6	68	6	121	6	172	6	224	6	276
9	7	11	7	69	7	127	7	185	7	243
10	7	324	8	22	8	85	8	149	8	211
11	8	276	8	344	9	47	9	113	9	175
12	9	231	9	303	10	6	10	68	10	120
13	10	185	10	254	10	315	10	364	11	37
14	11	128	11	186	11	233	11	267	11	291
15	12	47	12	91	12	121	12	142	12	149

No. of Premiums paid.	Age 25.		Age 26.		Age 27.		Age 28.		Age 29.	
	Years.	Days.	Years.	Days.	Years.	Days.	Years.	Days.	Years.	Days.
1	..	293	..	300	..	307	..	315	..	322
2	1	228	1	242	1	257	1	271	1	286
3	2	170	2	192	2	213	2	234	2	255
4	3	119	3	146	3	174	3	202	3	230
5	4	72	4	107	4	141	4	176	4	211
6	5	31	5	72	5	113	5	154	5	196
7	5	360	6	42	6	89	6	137	6	184
8	6	328	7	15	7	69	7	121	7	168
9	7	300	7	357	8	46	8	94	8	134
10	8	272	8	326	9	7	9	44	9	71
11	9	229	9	273	9	307	9	329	9	341
12	10	161	10	191	10	210	10	218	10	216
13	11	64	11	79	11	84	11	77	11	60
14	11	302	11	302	11	292	11	270	11	242
15	12	145	12	130	12	105	12	72	12	26

No. of Premiums paid.	Age 30.		Age 31.		Age 32.		Age 33.		Age 34.	
	Years.	Days.	Years.	Days.	Years.	Days.	Years.	Days.	Years.	Days.
1	..	329	..	337	..	344	..	352	..	362
2	1	300	1	315	1	330	1	345	1	360
3	2	277	2	299	2	321	2	343	3	2
4	3	259	3	288	3	317	3	347	4	14
5	4	246	4	282	4	318	4	356	5	26
6	5	238	5	279	5	320	5	356	6	20
7	6	229	6	272	6	307	6	334	6	351
8	7	210	7	243	7	266	7	280	7	284
9	8	164	8	183	8	193	8	193	8	186
10	9	87	9	92	9	88	9	78	9	53
11	9	343	9	335	9	319	9	291	9	257
12	10	203	10	183	10	150	10	112	10	72
13	11	36	10	363	10	321	10	270	10	214
14	11	200	11	153	11	98	11	38	10	338
15	11	341	11	282	11	218	11	148	11	74

TABLE No. LVIII.—(CONTINUED.)

SHOWING INSURANCE DUE ON WHOLE LIFE POLICIES, ACCORDING TO THE MASSACHUSETTS NON-FORFEITURE LAW.

No. of Premiums paid.	Age 35.		Age 36.		Age 37.		Age 38.		Age 39.	
	Years.	Days.	Years.	Days.	Years.	Days.	Years.	Days.	Years.	Days.
1	1	3	1	11	1	20	1	29	1	39
2	2	12	2	29	2	47	2	65	2	82
3	3	27	3	52	3	69	3	99	3	115
4	4	46	4	74	4	98	4	114	4	123
5	5	56	5	78	5	93	5	99	5	96
6	6	41	6	52	6	56	6	49	6	36
7	6	359	6	359	6	349	6	332	6	307
8	7	280	7	266	7	245	7	216	7	181
9	8	167	8	142	8	109	8	69	8	24
10	9	24	8	351	8	308	8	258	8	202
11	9	215	9	167	9	113	9	59	8	354
12	10	14	9	321	9	258	9	193	9	116
13	10	152	10	85	10	13	9	301	9	219
14	10	267	10	191	10	114	10	24	9	299
15	10	359	10	274	10	184	10	91	9	359

No. of Premiums paid.	Age 40.		Age 41.		Age 42.		Age 43.		Age 44.	
	Years.	Days.	Years.	Days.	Years.	Days.	Years.	Days.	Years.	Days.
1	1	49	1	57	1	64	1	66	1	65
2	2	96	2	106	2	109	2	106	2	98
3	3	125	3	128	3	123	3	111	3	95
4	4	123	4	116	4	102	4	81	4	56
5	5	86	5	69	5	45	5	15	4	344
6	6	16	5	353	5	318	5	279	5	234
7	6	276	6	238	6	194	6	144	6	88
8	7	139	7	91	7	38	6	344	6	282
9	7	337	7	280	7	217	7	151	7	81
10	8	141	8	76	8	5	7	295	7	217
11	8	285	8	210	8	132	8	49	7	327
12	9	38	8	320	8	234	8	143	8	50
13	9	133	9	42	8	313	8	216	8	117
14	9	205	9	108	9	7	8	269	8	164
15	9	258	9	154	9	48	8	304	8	194

No. of Premiums paid.	Age 45.		Age 46.		Age 47.		Age 48.		Age 49.	
	Years.	Days.	Years.	Days.	Years.	Days.	Years.	Days.	Years.	Days.
1	1	61	1	55	1	48	1	40	1	32
2	2	86	2	72	2	57	2	41	2	24
3	3	75	3	52	3	28	3	16	2	340
4	4	26	3	359	3	325	3	289	3	253
5	4	306	4	262	4	220	4	176	4	131
6	5	184	5	135	5	80	5	30	4	342
7	6	34	6	14	5	280	5	218	5	156
8	6	217	6	150	6	82	6	12	5	306
9	7	75	6	333	6	221	6	143	6	65
10	7	136	7	53	6	334	6	249	6	164
11	7	239	7	149	7	59	6	332	6	241
12	7	320	7	224	7	127	7	30	6	299
13	8	15	7	279	7	177	7	75	6	339
14	8	58	7	316	7	210	7	104	6	364
15	8	83	7	338	7	228	7	120	7	11

TABLE No. LIX

DECIMAL PART OF A YEAR FROM ANY DATE TO JANUARY 1, FOLLOWING.

Day.	Jan.	Feb.	March.	April.	May.	June.
1	.0000	.9151	.8384	.7534	.6712	.5863
2	.9973	.9123	.8356	.7507	.6685	.5836
3	.9945	.9096	.8329	.7479	.6658	.5808
4	.9918	.9068	.8301	.7452	.6630	.5781
5	.9890	.9041	.8274	.7425	.6603	.5753
6	.9863	.9014	.8247	.7397	.6575	.5726
7	.9836	.8986	.8219	.7370	.6548	.5699
8	.9808	.8959	.8192	.7342	.6521	.5671
9	.9781	.8932	.8164	.7315	.6493	.5644
10	.9753	.8905	.8137	.7288	.6466	.5616
11	.9726	.8877	.8110	.7260	.6438	.5589
12	.9699	.8849	.8082	.7233	.6411	.5562
13	.9671	.8822	.8055	.7205	.6384	.5534
14	.9644	.8795	.8027	.7178	.6356	.5507
15	.9616	.8767	.8000	.7151	.6329	.5479
16	.9589	.8740	.7973	.7123	.6301	.5452
17	.9562	.8712	.7945	.7096	.6274	.5425
18	.9534	.8685	.7918	.7068	.6247	.5397
19	.9507	.8658	.7890	.7041	.6219	.5370
20	.9479	.8630	.7863	.7014	.6192	.5342
21	.9452	.8603	.7836	.6986	.6164	.5315
22	.9425	.8575	.7808	.6959	.6137	.5288
23	.9397	.8548	.7781	.6932	.6110	.5260
24	.9370	.8521	.7753	.6904	.6082	.5233
25	.9342	.8493	.7726	.6877	.6055	.5205
26	.9315	.8466	.7699	.6849	.6027	.5178
27	.9288	.8438	.7671	.6822	.6000	.5151
28	.9260	.8411	.7644	.6795	.5973	.5123
29	.9233	.8411	.7616	.6767	.5945	.5096
30	.9205		.7589	.6740	.5918	.5068
31	.9178		.7562		.5890	
	1st Mo.	2d Mo.	3d Mo.	4th Mo.	5th Mo.	6th Mo.

TABLE No. LIX (CONTINUED.)

DECIMAL PART OF A YEAR FROM ANY DATE TO JANUARY 1, FOLLOWING.

July.	*Aug.*	*Sept.*	*Oct.*	*Nov.*	*Dec.*	*Day.*
.5041	.4192	.3342	.2521	.1671	.0849	1
.5014	.4164	.3315	.2493	.1644	.0822	2
.4986	.4137	.3288	.2466	.1616	.0795	3
.4959	.4110	.3260	.2438	.1589	.0767	4
.4932	.4082	.3233	.2411	.1562	.0740	5
.4904	.4055	.3205	.2384	.1534	.0712	6
.4877	.4027	.3178	.2356	.1507	.0685	7
.4849	.4000	.3151	.2329	.1479	.0658	8
.4822	.3973	.3123	.2301	.1452	.0630	9
.4795	.3945	.3096	.2274	.1425	.0603	10
.4767	.3918	.3068	.2247	.1397	.0575	11
.4740	.3890	.3041	.2219	.1370	.0548	12
.4712	.3863	.3014	.2192	.1342	.0521	13
.4685	.3836	.2986	.2164	.1315	.0493	14
.4658	.3808	.2959	.2137	.1288	.0466	15
.4630	.3781	.2932	.2110	.1260	.0438	16
.4603	.3753	.2904	.2082	.1233	.0411	17
.4575	.3726	.2877	.2055	.1205	.0384	18
.4548	.3699	.2849	.2027	.1178	.0356	19
.4521	.3671	.2822	.2000	.1151	.0329	20
.4493	.3644	.2795	.1973	.1123	.0301	21
.4466	.3616	.2767	.1945	.1096	.0274	22
.4438	.3589	.2740	.1918	.1068	.0247	23
.4411	.3562	.2712	.1890	.1041	.0219	24
.4384	.3534	.2685	.1863	.1014	.0192	25
.4356	.3507	.2658	.1836	.0986	.0164	26
.4329	.3479	.2630	.1808	.0959	.0137	27
.4301	.3452	.2603	.1781	.0932	.0110	28
.4274	.3425	.2575	.1753	.0904	.0082	29
.4247	.3397	.2547	.1726	.0877	.0055	30
.4219	.3370		.1699		.0027	31
7th Mo.	8th Mo.	9th Mo.	10th Mo.	11th Mo.	12th Mo.	

LIFE INSURANCE FORMULÆ.*

In the American Table of Mortality we have at the age 10 100,000 persons living at the beginning of the year, and during that year 749 die before the survivors reach the age 11. In the application of algebraic notation to life insurance, we designate the living at any age in the table of mortality by l_x, or by l with the number denoting the age, as l_{10}, l_{11}, etc. If we make $x=10$, the number living at the age 11 is denoted by l_{x+1}, and at 12 by l_{x+2}; and hence we have a series of living at all ages, $l_{10}+l_{11}+l_{12}\ldots . l_{95}=l_x+l_{x+1}+l_{x+2}\ldots . l\omega$, the oldest age in the mortality table expressed by $l\omega$. The same formula will apply if we make any other number in the table $=x$, as $l_{40}+l_{41}+l_{42}$, etc. $=l_x+l_{x+1}+l_{x+2}$, etc. But since l_x is the number living at the beginning of the year, and l_{x+1} the number living at the end, the probability of a person aged x surviving during the year is $\frac{l_{x+1}}{l_x}$, and at the end of each of two years is $\frac{l_{x+1}}{l_x}+\frac{l_{x+2}}{l_x}$, and consequently the probability of his surviving each year till he reaches the age 95 is expressed by the formula, $\frac{l_{x+1}}{l_x}+\frac{l_{x+2}}{l_x}+\frac{l_{x+3}}{l_x}\ldots . \frac{l\omega}{l_x}$. If each person in the number l should pay \$1 at the beginning of each year during life into a common fund, the total amount paid would be $l_x+l_{x+1}+l_{x+2}\ldots . l\omega$ dollars, and the average amount which each person living at the age x would pay would be $\frac{l_x}{l_x}+\frac{l_{x+1}}{l_x}+\frac{l_{x+2}}{l_x}\ldots . \frac{l\omega}{l_x}$. But payments to be made in the future have a present value depending upon the rate of discount assumed, as well as the probability of living ; and, if we discount each term in the series after the first by 4 1-2 per cent, or multiply each term after the first by $\frac{1}{1.045}$, $\left(\frac{1}{1.045}\right)^2$, $\left(\frac{1}{1.045}\right)^3$, etc., and make $\frac{1}{1.045}=v$,

* In these formulæ the life insurance symbols of Dr. William Farr, as published in Circular No. 39 of the New York Insurance Department, have been adopted.

we have the series $\frac{l_z}{l_z} + \frac{v.\,l_{z+1}}{l_z} + \frac{v^2 l_{z+2}}{l_z} + \frac{v^3.\,l_{z+3}}{l_z} \cdots \frac{vw^z.\,l\omega}{l_z}$. If we multiply the numerators and denominators of this series by v raised to the xth power, which does not alter the value of the fractions, we have $\frac{v^z.\,l_z}{v^z.\,l_z} + \frac{v^{z+1}.\,l_{z+1}}{v^z.\,l_z} + \frac{v^{z+2}.\,l_{z+2}}{v^z.\,l_z} + \frac{v^{z+3}.\,lx+3}{v^z.\,l_z} \cdots$ $\frac{v^\omega.\,l\omega}{v^z.\,l_z}$. Making $v^z.l_z = D_z$, we have the series $\frac{D_z}{D_z} + \frac{D_{z+1}}{D_z} + \frac{D_{z+2}}{D_z}$

$\therefore \frac{D\omega}{D_z} = \frac{D_z + D_{z+1} + D_{z+2} + D_{z+3}}{D_z}$, etc.; and, substituting N_z for all the terms in the numerator up to and including the oldest age in the mortality table, we have the last fraction $= \frac{N_z}{D_z}$, a formula which is applied to a life annuity, the first payment to be made at the beginning of the year at age x, and which is also represented by A_z.

Since $A_z = \frac{D_z}{D_z} + \frac{D_{z+1}}{D_z} + \frac{D_{z+2}}{D_z}$, etc., the temporary annuity of \$1 for one year is $\frac{D_z}{D_z} = \frac{N_z - N_{z-1}}{D_z} = A_{z1} = 1$, and for two years is $\frac{D_z}{D_z} + \frac{D_{z+1}}{D_z} = \frac{N_z - N_{z+2}}{D_n} = A_{z2}$, and for n years is $\frac{N_z - N_{z+n}}{D_z} = A_{zn}$.

The present value of an annuity deferred for three years is $\frac{N_z}{D_z} - \frac{D_z + D_{z+1} + D_{z+2}}{D_z} = \frac{D_{z+3} + D_{z+4} + D_{z+5}, \text{etc.},}{D_z} = \frac{N_{z+3}}{D_z}$, and, in general, the expression for a deferred life annuity is $\frac{N_{z+n}}{D_z} = A_{z|n}$.

The formula for a deferred temporary annuity to commence after n years and to continue m years, is

$$\frac{N_{z+n} - N_{n+n+m}}{D_z} = A_{z|n} - A_{z|n+m}.$$

The number of deaths at any given age x is expressed by d_z. At age 10 the number dying during the year is, by the American Table of Mortality, 749, and hence the probability that a person aged 10 years will die during the year is $\frac{749}{100,000} = \frac{d_z}{l_z}$. The probability of dying during each of the first two years is $\frac{d_z}{l_z} + \frac{d_{z+1}}{l_z}$, and we have the following series representing the probability of a life aged x dying each year: $\frac{d_z}{l_z} + \frac{d_{z+1}}{l_z} + \frac{d_{z+2}}{l_z} + \frac{d_{z+3}}{l_z}$, etc. Since $\frac{d_z}{l_z}$ is the probability of dying during the first year, it is the undiscounted sum required to insure the life x for $1 one year, or payable at the end of the year. The premium required payable at the beginning of the year is $\frac{d_x}{l_x}$ multiplied by the present worth of $1, or $\frac{v \cdot d_x}{l_x}$ and for two years is $1 multiplied by $\frac{v \cdot d_x}{l_x} + \frac{v^2 \cdot d_{x+1}}{l_x}$, and, generally, the single premium to insure a life aged x is $\frac{v \cdot d_x}{l_x} + \frac{v^2 d_{x+1}}{l_x} + \frac{v^3 d_{x+2}}{l_x}$, etc., $=$

$$\frac{v \cdot d_x + v^2 d_{x+1} + v^3 d_{x+2}}{l_x} \ldots \text{. etc.}$$

Multiplying both numerator and denominator by v^x, we have $\frac{v^{x+1} \cdot d_x \times v^{x+2} \cdot d_{x+1} \times v^{x+3} \cdot d_{x+2}, \text{ etc.}}{v^x \cdot l_x}$. Putting $v^{x+1} \cdot d_x = C_x$, we have the single premium $= \frac{C_x + C_{x+1} + C_{x+2}, \text{ etc.}}{D_x}$, and, making the numerator or the sum of all the C's $= M_x$, we have the single premium $= \frac{M_x}{D_x}$, which we represent by Π_x.

If π_x represents the annual premium on a life aged x, it is evident Π_x, the single premium, is the present value of the annuity π_x, or the annual premiums during life. Hence, $\pi_x \cdot A_x = \Pi_x$, and $\pi_x = \frac{\Pi_x}{A_x}$. Since $\Pi_x = \frac{M_x}{D_x}$, and $A_x = \frac{N_x}{D_x}$, $\frac{\Pi_x}{A_x} = \frac{M_x}{D_x} \div \frac{N_x}{D_x} = \frac{M_x}{N_x}$, the net annual premium.

The annual premium on a limited payment life policy is found by dividing the single life premium by the temporary annuity for the number of years in which the payments are made:

$$\pi_x = \frac{\Pi_x}{A_{xn}} = \frac{M_x}{D_x} + \frac{N_x - N_{x+n}}{D_x} = \frac{M_x}{N_x - N_{x+n}}.$$

Term Insurance.—We have seen that the cost of insuring a person for a single year is $\frac{v^{x+1} \cdot d_x}{v^x \cdot l_x} = \frac{C_x}{D_x} = \frac{M_x - M_{x+1}}{D_x}$, and for two years is $\frac{C_x}{D_x} + \frac{C_{x+1}}{D_x} = \frac{M_x - M_{x+2}}{D_x}$, and therefore the single premium to insure a life for n years is $\frac{M_x - M_{x+n}}{D_x}$. To find the annual premium, we divide this by the temporary annuity for n years,

$$\frac{M_x - M_{x+n}}{D_x} + \frac{N_x - N_{x+n}}{. \ D_x} = \frac{M_x - M_{x+n}}{N_x - N_{x+n}}.$$

Endowment.—The single premium required to purchase the simple endowment of $1 payable n years hence, if the insured lives, is the discounted number of the living at the age $x+n$

divided by the discounted number of living at age x, $\dfrac{v^{x+n}.\, l_{x+n}}{v^x.\, l_x} =$

$\dfrac{D_{x+n}}{D_x}$, and the annual premium is found by dividing the single pre-

mium by the temporary annuity for n years, $\dfrac{D_{x+n}}{D_x} \div \dfrac{N_x - N_{x+n}}{D_x} =$

$\dfrac{D_{x+n}}{N_x - N_{x+n}}$

Endowment insurance.—This is a combination of term insurance and simple endowment. The single premium on an endowment assurance policy payable in n years or at death, if prior, is the sum of the single premiums of a term and a simple endowment policy for n years $= \dfrac{M_x - M_{x+n}}{D_x} + \dfrac{D_{x+n}}{D_x} = \dfrac{M_x - M_{x+n} + D_{x+n}}{D_x}$

and, dividing by the temporary annuity $\dfrac{N_x - N_{x+n}}{D_x}$, to obtain the

annual premium, we have the formula $\pi_x = \dfrac{M_x - M_{x+n} + D_{x+n}}{N_x - N_{x+n}}$.

For an endowment insurance payable in n years or at death, if prior, the premiums being paid annually during m years, m being less than n, we divide the single premium given above by the

temporary annuity of \$1 for m years, $\pi_x = \dfrac{M_x - M_{x+n} + D_{x+n}}{D_x} \div$

$\dfrac{N_x - N_{x+m}}{D_x} = \dfrac{M_x - M_{x+n} - D_{x+n}}{N_x - N_{x+m}}$.

Annual premium during n years to insure a life annuity of a dollars at age $x-n$. $a. A_{x+n} = $ present value of the annuity a at age $x+n$. This is the quantity to be insured on a simple endow-

ment, or $\dfrac{D_{x+n}}{N_x - N_{x+n}} \times a. A_{x+n} = \dfrac{D_{x+n}}{N_x - N_{x+n}} \times \dfrac{a.\, N_{x+n}}{D_{x+n}} = \dfrac{a.\, N_{x+n}}{N_x - N_{x+n}}$

Annual premium to insure b dollars to the age $x+n$, if death occurs within n years, and to insure a life annuity of a dollars during life from age $x+n$. Add the term insurance on b dollars

to the last formula, $\dfrac{a.\, N_{x+n} + b\,(M_x - M_{x+n})}{N_x - N_{x+n}}$.

It is often convenient, especially in computing joint-life premiums, to be able to use only the D and N columns, and a few formulas are given explaining the method.

Since $\Pi_x = \dfrac{v.\, d_x}{l_x} + \dfrac{v^2 d_{x+1}}{l_x} + \dfrac{v^3 d_{x+2}}{l_x}$, etc., and $d_x = l_x - l_{x+1}$,

and $d_{x+1} = l_{x+1} - l_{x+2}$ etc., we have $\Pi_x = \dfrac{v(l_x - l_{x+1})}{l_x} +$

$\dfrac{v^2(l_{x+1} - l_{x+2})}{l_x} + \dfrac{v^3(l_{x+2} - l_{x+3})}{l_x}$, etc. Separating this formula into two parts, we have

$$\Pi_x = \frac{v(l_x + v.l_{x+1} + v.l_{x+2}, \text{ etc.})}{l_x} - \frac{v(l_{x+1} + v.l_{x+2} + v.l_{x+3}, \text{ etc.})}{l_x} =$$

$$v.\Lambda_x - \Lambda_{x+1} = v.\Lambda_x - (\Lambda_x - 1) = 1 - (1-v)\Lambda_x, \text{ and } \pi_x = \frac{1 - (1-v)\Lambda_x}{\Lambda_x} =$$

$$\left[1 - (1-v)\ \Lambda_x\right] \frac{1}{\Lambda_x} = \frac{1}{\Lambda_x} - (1-v)$$

Single premium, life.—Making i the rate per cent,

$$\Pi_x = 1 - (1-v)\Lambda_x = 1 - \left(1 - \frac{1}{1+i}\right).\ \Lambda_x = 1 - \left(\frac{i}{1+i}\right).\ \Lambda_x$$

Annual premium, life.—$\pi_x = \frac{\Pi_x}{\Lambda_x} = \left(1 - \frac{i}{1+i} \times \frac{N_x}{D_x}\right) \frac{D_x}{N_x} =$

$$\frac{D_x}{N_x} - \frac{i}{1+i} = \frac{1}{\Lambda_x} - \frac{i}{1+i}$$

Whole life insurance by n annual premiums.—

$$\frac{\Pi_x}{\Lambda_{xn}} = \frac{1 - (1-v)\Lambda_x}{\Lambda_{xn}} = \left[1 - (1-v)\frac{N_x}{D_x}\right] \times \frac{D_x}{N_x - N_{x+n}} =$$

$$\frac{D_x}{N_x - N_{x+n}} - \frac{(1-v).N_x}{N_x - N_{x+n}} = \frac{D_x - (1-v)N_x}{N_x - N_{x+n}} = \frac{D_x - \left(\frac{i}{1+i}\right)N_x}{N_x - N_{x+n}}$$

Endowment insurance.—The single premium for a temporary insurance of n years is

$$\Pi_x = v \frac{(l_x + v.l_{x+1} + v^2 l_{x+2} + v^3 l_{x+3} \ldots v^n l_{x+n})}{v.l_x}$$

$$- \frac{v.l_{x+1} + v^2.l_{x+2} + v^3.l_{x+3} \ldots v^{n+1}.l_{x+n+1}}{v.l_x} =$$

$v.\left(\frac{N_x - N_{x+n}}{D_x}\right) - v\left(\frac{N_{x+1} - N_{x+n+1}}{D_x}\right)$, divided by the temporary

annuity, $\frac{N_x - N_{x+n}}{D_x}, v - \left(\frac{N_{x+1} - N_{x+n+1}}{N_x - N_{x+n}}\right)$ = annual premium

for temporary insurance. Adding the single premium of simple endowment, $\frac{D_{x+n}}{D_x}$ to the single premium for temporary insurance, and, since $N_{x+n+1} + D_{x+n} = N_{x+n}$, we have the single premium endowment = $v\left(\frac{N_x - N_{x+n}}{D_x}\right) - \left(\frac{N_{x+1} - N_{x+n}}{D_x}\right)$ and dividing by the term annuity, $\frac{N_x - N_{x+n}}{D_x}$ we have, annual premium = $v\left(\frac{N_{x+1} - N_{x+n}}{N_x - N_{x+n}}\right)$ Net annual premium for n years, payable in m payments, $v\left(\frac{N_{x+1} - N_{x+n}}{N_x - N_{x+m}}\right)$.

Joint lives.—We have seen that the general formula for an annuity on a life x is $\Lambda_x = \frac{l_x + v.l_{x+1} + v^2.l_{x+2} + v^3.l_{x+3}}{l_x}$, etc. But if there are two lives, x and y, the result of a combination of them will be their product, and

$$A_{x,y} = \frac{l_x.\,l_y + v.\,l_{x+1}.\,l_{y+1} + v^2.\,l_{x+2}.\,l_{y+2} + v^3\,l_{x+3}.\,l_{y+3}, \text{etc.}}{l_x.\,l_y}, \text{ and mul-}$$

tiplying by v^x, we have

$$A_{x,y} = \frac{v^x\,l_x.\,l_y + v^{x+1}.\,l_{x+1}.\,l_{y+1} + v^{x+2}.\,l_{x+2}.\,l_{y+2} + v^{x+3}.\,l_{x+3}.\,l_{y+3}}{v^x.\,l_x.\,l_y},$$

$$\text{etc.,} = \frac{D_{x,y} + D_{x+1,\,y+1} + D_{x+2,\,y+2} + D_{x+3,\,y+3}}{D_{x,y}}, \text{ etc.,} = \frac{N_{x,y}}{D_{x,y}}.$$

In preparing the column $D_{x,y}$, if $x=15$ and $y=10$ years of age, then we add the logarithm of D_x^{15} to the logarithm of y^{10} or l^{10}, the number of living at the age 10, which gives the logarithm of $D_{x,y}$, and the log. D^{16} + log. y^{11} = log. $D_{x+1,\,y+1}$, and so on throughout the column D_x. The numbers corresponding to these logarithms will be the column $D_{x,y}$. The column $N_{x,y}$ is found by the summation of the column $D_{x,y}$. With the $D_{x,y}$ and $N_{x,y}$ columns of any combination of ages, the operations in joint lives are performed in the same manner as those of single lives.

Return premium plan.—This plan of insurance provides for the return of all the premiums paid when policy becomes a claim. In this kind of policy there are two parts to be considered, the specified sum insured and the part constantly increasing by π_x each year. The first has $\dfrac{M_x}{N_x}$ for the annual premium, and the latter has $\pi_x\left(\dfrac{M_x}{N_x} + \dfrac{M_{x+1}}{N_x} + \dfrac{M_{x+2}}{N_x}, \text{\&c.,}\right) = \pi_x.\dfrac{R_x}{N_x}$ Putting these together, we have $\dfrac{M_x}{N_x} + \pi_x.\dfrac{R_x}{N_x} = \pi_x.$ Clearing of fractions $M_x + \pi_x\,R_x = \pi_x\,N_x$, and $\pi_x = \dfrac{M_x}{N_x - R_x}.$

Loaded annual premium.—Let π_x = net annual premium and ($\$1 +$ loading) $= g$. Multiplying $\dfrac{M_x}{N_x} + \pi_x\,\dfrac{R_x}{N_x} = \pi_x$ by g, we have $g\,\dfrac{M_x}{N_x} + \pi_x\,g.\dfrac{R_x}{N_x} = g.\,\pi_x$, therefore,

$$g.\,\pi_x = \frac{g.\,M_x}{N_x - g.\,R_x} = \frac{M_x}{\dfrac{1}{g}\,N_x - R_x}.$$

Net annual premium for the return of gross premiums.—

$$\pi_x = \frac{M_x}{N_x - g.\,R_x}$$

Limited-payment annual return premium.—

$$\pi_x = \frac{M_x}{N_x - N_{x+n}} + \pi_x \left(\frac{M_x}{N_x - N_{x+n}} + \frac{M_{x+1}}{N_x - N_{x+n}} + \frac{M_{x+2}}{N_x - N_{x+n}}, \right.$$

$$\left. \dots \frac{M_{x+n-1}}{N_x - N_{x+n}} \right) = \frac{M_x}{N_x - N_{x+n}} + \pi_x \left(\frac{R_x - R_{x+n}}{N_x - N_{x+n}} \right)$$

Clearing of fractions, $M_x - \pi_x (R_x - R_{x+n}) = \pi_x (N_x - N_{x+n})$,

$$\pi_x = \frac{M_x}{(N_x - N_{x+n}) - (R_x - R_{x+n})}$$

With loading, g. $\pi_x = \dfrac{g\, M_x}{(N_x - N_{x+n}) - g\, (R_x - R_{x+n})} =$

$$\frac{M_x}{\frac{1}{g} (N_x - N_{x+n})\ (R_x - R_{x+n})}$$

Endowment, $\pi_x \doteq \dfrac{M_x - M_{x+n} + D_{x+n}}{(N_x - N_{x+n}) - (R_x - R_{x+n})}$

With loading, g. $\pi_x = \dfrac{g\, (M_x - M_{x+n} + D_{x+n})}{(N_x - N_{x+n}) - g\, (R_x - R_{x+n})} =$

$$\frac{M_x - M_{x+n} + D_{x+n}}{\frac{1}{g} (N_x - N_{x+n}) - (R_x - R_{x+n})}$$

*Single return premium.—*Let $\Pi_x =$ single return premium,

then $\Pi_x = \dfrac{M_x}{D_x} + \Pi_x \cdot \dfrac{M_x}{D_x}$

$$\Pi_x . D_x = M_x + \Pi_x . M_x$$

$$\Pi_x = \frac{M_x}{D_x - M_x}$$

Net single premium for the return of gross premium.—
Let $(1 + l) = g = \$1 +$ loading ; then

$$\Pi_x = \frac{M_x}{D_x} + g\, \frac{M_x}{D_x} . \Pi_x, \text{ whence } \Pi_x = \frac{M_x}{D_x - g\, M_x}$$

Loaded single return premium.—

$$g . \Pi_x = g\, \frac{M_x}{D_x} + g . \left(\frac{M_x}{D_x} . \Pi_x \right) \text{ whence } g . \Pi_x = \frac{g\, M_x}{D_x - g\, M_x}$$

VALUATION OF POLICIES.

Let π_x be the annual premium payable on a life policy, it is evident that if the policy were not subject to the future payment of this annual premium, the value of it would be the single premium of a policy of assurance on a life aged $x + n = \Pi_{x+n}$. But in consequence of the charge of an annual premium on the policy, the value will be reduced by a sum equal to the value of all the future premiums, or the present value of an annuity of π_x on a life equal to $x + n$, the first payment of which will be made

immediately, and the formula will be $H_{x+n} = \Pi_{+n} - \pi_x \times A_{x+n} =$
$(\pi_{x+n} - \pi_x) A_{x+n}$. But $\pi_{x+n} = \dfrac{1}{A_{x+n}} - (1-v)$ and $\pi_x = \dfrac{1}{A_x} -$
$(1-v)$, $\pi_{x+n} - \pi_x = \dfrac{1}{A_{x+n}} - \dfrac{1}{A_x}$ and $(\pi_{x+n} - \pi_x) A_{x+n} = A_{x+n}$.
$\left(\dfrac{1}{A_{x+n}} - \dfrac{1}{A_x} \right) = 1 - \dfrac{A_{x+n}}{A_x} = H_{x+n}$.

Additional formulæ for the value of whole life policies:

$$H_{x+n} = 1 - \frac{1-\Pi_{x+n}}{1-\Pi_x}; \ H_{x+n} = \frac{\pi_{x+n} - \pi_x}{\pi_{x+n} + (1-v)}$$

Value of a life policy paid up by m premiums is at the end of n years, $\Pi_{x+n} = \Pi_{x+n} - \pi_x \dfrac{N_{x+n} - N_{x+m}}{D_{x+n}}$

Value of an endowment policy payable in m years or at previous death,

$$H_{x+n} = 1 - \left(\frac{N_{x+n} - N_{x+m}}{D_{x+n}} + \frac{N_x - N_{x+n}}{D_x} \right) = 1 - \frac{A_{x+n-m}}{A_m}$$

Also, $\Pi_{x+n} = \Pi_{x+n} - \pi_x \dfrac{N_{x+n} - N_{x+m}}{D_{x+n}}$

Here $\Pi_{x+n} =$ the net single premium of a policy issued at the age $x+n$ and payable at the age $x+m$.

Value of an endowment policy payable at previous death or in m years by m' number of payments.

$$H_{x+n} = \Pi_{x+n} - \pi_x. \frac{N_{x+n} - N_{x+m'}}{D_{x+m}}$$

Value of a term policy to expire at age $x+m$.

$$\Pi_{x+n} = \Pi_{x+n} - \pi_x, \frac{N_{x+n} - N_{x+m}}{D_{x+n}}$$

The explanation of these three last formulæ is found on page 46.

Value of a simple endowment policy. In this form of policy the company does not assume any risk, and the reserve at the end of any given year is the reserve of the previous year increased by the co-efficient of accumulation.

$\Pi_{x+n} = (H_{x+n-1} + \pi_x) u_{x+n-1}$. Also, $H_{x+n} = \Pi_{x+n} - \pi_x$. $\dfrac{N_{x+n} - N_{x+m}}{D_{x+n}}$ in which $\Pi_{x+n} =$ single premium at age $x+n$ to insure policy payable at $x+m$,

$$H_{x+n} = \frac{D_{x+n}}{D_{x+n}} - \frac{D_{x+m}}{N_x - N_{x+m}} \times \frac{N_{x+n} - N_{x+m}}{D_{x+n}}$$

$$H_{x+n} = \frac{D_{x+m}}{D_{x+n}} - \frac{D_{x+m}}{D_{x+n}} \times \frac{N_{x+n} - N_{x+m}}{N_x - N_{x+m}}$$

$$H_{x+n} = \Pi_{x+n} \left(1 - \frac{N_{x+n} - N_{x+m}}{N_x - N_{x+m}} \right)$$

Wright's Accumulation Formula.—Let H_{s+1} = the value of a policy at the end of the first year, $c_s =. v \frac{d_s}{l_s}$, the risk of \$1 at the age x, and π_x = the net premium paid, then we shall have $1 : c_s :: 1 - H_{s+1} : c_s$. H_{s+1} = the value of the actual risk run by the company on \$1 insured. Subtracting this value from the net premium, and accumulating the remainder at the assumed ratio of interest $\frac{1}{v} = r$, we have

$H_{s+1} = r\ (\pi_x - c_s + c_s . H_{s+1})$, which reduces to

$H_{s+1} = \frac{r}{1 - r . c_s}\ (\pi_x - c_x)$.

But $1 - r . c_s = \left(1 - \frac{r . d_x}{l_x}\right) = \frac{l_{x+1}}{l_x}$ and $\frac{r}{\frac{l_{x+1}}{l_x}} = \frac{r . l_x}{l_{x+1}} = \frac{D_x}{D_{x+1}}$.

Representing this last fraction by u_x, we have the formula, $H_{s+1} = u_s\ (\pi_x - c_x)$ = the value of a policy at the end of the first year. The value at the end of the second year is

$H_{s+2} = u_{s+1}\ (H_{s+1} + \pi_x - c_{s+1})$, and generally

$H_{s+n} = u_{s+n-1}\ (H_{s+n-1} + \pi_x - c_{s+n-1})$.

Fackler's Formula.—$H_{s+n+1} = (H_{s+n} + \pi_x)\ u_{s+n} - k_{s+n}$, in which $k_{s+n} = \frac{C_{s+n}}{D_{s+n+1}}$.

McClintock's Formula.—The following formula gives a somewhat shorter process than the two preceding ones.

Let us suppose a group of l_{s+n-1} policyholders assured \$1 each, and having a reserve for each one of H_{s+n-1}, making a total present reserve for the group amount to $l_{x+n-1}\ (H_{s+n-1})$.

A year from the present time, after adding premiums of π_x each now due, and increasing the sum of these reserves and premiums by interest at the rate of $1 + r$, the fund will have amounted to $(1 + r)\ (H_{s+n} - 1 + \pi_x)\ l_{s+n-1}$. There will have died several of the group, reducing the number of living to l_{s+n}, to whose heirs at \$1 each the sum of $l_{s+n-1} - l_{s+n}$ dollars are paid. The fund is then reduced to $1 + r\ (H_{s+n-1} + \pi_x)\ l_{s+n-1} + (l_{s+n-1} - l_{s+n})$ $= l_{s+n} - l_{s+n-1}\ [1 - (1 + r)\ (H_{s+n-1} + \pi_x)]$. Dividing the amount of this reserve by l_{s+n}, the number of policyholders, and putting $\frac{l_{s+n-1}(1 + r)}{l_{s+n}} = u_{x+n-1}$ and $g = v - \pi_x$, the reserve on each policy is found to be $H_{s+n} = 1 - u_{s+n-1}(g - H_{s+n-1})$.

The column c_x or k_x is dispensed with, leaving but one column u_x to be kept on hand and referred to.

Rule.—Subtract the net premium paid on each $1 (and last year's reserve on each $1 assured, if any) from the present value of $1 due one year hence. Multiply the remainder by the value of u_z corresponding to the party's age at the beginning of the year, and subtract the product from unity.

Homans's Contribution Formula.—Let r' = the actual rate of interest received, e = the expenses, and $\dfrac{d'_{z+n}}{l'_{z+n}}(1-\Pi_{z+n+1})$ the actual cost of insurance, then

$$H_{z+n}(1+r') + (\pi_z - e)(1+r') - \frac{d'_{z+n}}{l'_{z+n}}(1-H_{z+n+1}) = X_{z+n} =$$

contribution to surplus.

Formulæ for verifying Commutation Columns.—

$C_z = v.\ D_z - D_{z+1}$ $M_z = v.\ N_{z-1} - N_z = D_z - v.\ N_z$

$R_z = v.\ S_{z-1} - S_z$ $M_{z+n} = v.\ N_{z+n-1} - N_{z+n} =$

$R_{z+n} = v.\ S_{z+n-1} - S_{z+n}.$

Equation of Life.—Let l_x = the number of living at age x, $\dfrac{l_z}{2}$ the number of living at the age of equation, l_{z+n} the number of living at the beginning of the year in which the equation takes place, l_{z+n+1} the number living at the end of the year, f = the fraction of a year, which, added to $x+n$, will make the equation then $\dfrac{l_z}{2} = l_{z+n+f}$ and we have

$$f = \frac{l_{z+n} - l_{z+n+f}}{l_{z+n} - l_{z+n+1}} \text{ substituting } \frac{l_z}{2} \text{ for } l_{z+n+f}$$

$$f = \frac{l_{z+n} - \dfrac{l_z}{2}}{l_{z+n} - l_{z+n+1}}$$

Expectation of Life.—

$$E_z = \frac{1}{2} + \left(\frac{l_{z+1} + l_{z+2} + l_{z+3},\ \text{etc.}}{l_z} \right)$$

WRIGHT'S FORMULA FOR INSURANCE VALUES.

Representing the insurance value at the age $x+n$ by $_{z+n}I_z$, we have the general formula,

$$_{z+n}I_z = \frac{D_z}{_{z+n}N_z} \times \frac{_{z+n}N_{z+1} \times \dfrac{d_z}{l_{z+1}} + _{z+n}N_{z+2} \times \dfrac{d_{z+1}}{l_{z+2}},\ \text{etc.,}\ \dots}{D_z}$$

If we assume $x = 10$, and perform all the multiplications of $\dfrac{d_{10}}{l_{11}}$ into N_{11}, and $\dfrac{d_{11}}{l_{12}}$ into N_{12}, &c., as indicated by the numerator three lines above, the summation of the products, after the manner in which the N column is produced from the D, will produce a column of numerators which we will call Λ, and this will give us $_{z+n}\,I_z = \dfrac{D_z}{_{z+n}\,N_z} \times \dfrac{_{z+n}\Lambda_z}{D_z}$, and $_{z+n}\,I_{z+t} = \dfrac{D_z}{_{z+n}\,N_z} \times \dfrac{_{z+n}\Lambda_{z+t}}{D_{z+t}}$ when the policy has completed t years and the $(t+1)$th premium is just paid.

The formula for the insurance value on a paid-up policy is

$$_{z+n}\,I_{z+t} = (1-v)\,\frac{_{z+n}\Lambda_{z+t}}{D_{z+t}}$$

The formula for any policy payable at age $x+n$, or previous death, including the ordinary whole life policy, is thus modified by Mr. McClintock. Let π_z be the annual premium to be paid q times and when the first premium is just paid, we have

$$_{z+n}\,I_z \,\Big|\; q = d.\,\frac{_{z+n}\Lambda_z}{D_z}\,\pi_z \times \frac{_{z+q}\Lambda_z}{D_z}$$

and when the $(t+1)$th premium has just been paid,

$$_{z+n}\,I_{z+t} \,\Big|\; q = d.\,\frac{_{z+n}\Lambda_{z+t}}{D_{z+t}} + \pi_z\,\frac{_{z+q}\Lambda_{z+t}}{D_{z+t}}$$

PROF. BARTLETT'S FORMULA FOR SURRENDER VALUES.

Prof. Bartlett, actuary of the Mutual Life Insurance Company of New York, has proposed the following formulæ for finding the surrender value of a policy, which is based upon the following assumptions:

A reserve of an individual member of a company is what the company should have to the member's credit at a given epoch after subducting from the amount paid by him, augmented by his interest earnings, his proportion of the death claims that have matured up to the same epoch. A surrender value is the amount the company should pay to abrogate a contract between itself and one of its members.

By the terms of this contract the company promises to pay to the heirs of the assured at his death, whenever that may happen, a certain specified sum of money. And the assured pays, in consideration, another sum down, called, let us suppose, a single net premium, which is the present net value of the assurance. This premium must be such as to amount at compound interest to the sum assured, should the assured live to the greatest age of the tables, and, besides, it must contribute its share to the payment of the death claims, from year to year, of other members who die before attaining to this age; and this obliga. tion to pay death claims must last during the life of the assured, which life is assured in the original agreement to extend to the oldest limit of the tables of mortality employed in computing the premium.

The company and the assured have, therefore, joint interest in the policy of the latter. The present money values of these interests being found at the time of the surrender, their difference will obviously be the surrender value.

The company's interest in any particular policy is the present value of the sums the policy would, if continued in the company in its present condition, contribute from year to year to pay death claims on other policies.

The interest of the assured, or of his heirs, in his policy is the present value of the reversion or sum the latter would receive at the death of the owner, provided he pay nothing more than he has already paid. This interest is the present reserve.

Make

Π_a = Single net premium at age x to insure one dollar at death.

R_s = Net reserve on policy at age x when surrender is made.

m = Number of years the policy has to run to maturity.

n = Difference between the oldest age of tables and that of policyholder at time of surrender.

V_s = Present value of one dollar due in x years.

σ = Sum assured or amount of policy.

Life Single Premium.—Take the life single premium as a standard, we have $R_s = \Pi_z$ and $m = n$.

Denoting the surrender value by Q, the surrender value of σ is found by the formula :

$$Q = \sigma\ \frac{C_x \cdot R_{z+1} + C_{r+1} \cdot R_{z+2} \ldots + C_{z+n} R_{z+n+1}}{D_z}$$

Tabulate the numerator of the second member under the head T, after the manner of the commutation columns N, M, S, &c.

Then will $Q = \sigma\ \dfrac{T_z}{D_z}$ . . . . . . (1)

Life Annual Payments.—In this case

$$Q = \sigma\ \frac{R_z}{\Pi_z} \cdot \frac{T_z}{D_z} \quad \ldots \ldots (2)$$

Life, Limited Payments.—

$$Q_z = \sigma \frac{R_z}{\Pi_z} \cdot \frac{T_z}{D_z} \quad \ldots \ldots \quad (3)$$

this differing from the last case only in the value of R_z.

Temporary Single Premiums.—Here the formula becomes:

$$Q_z = \sigma \frac{C_z \cdot R_{z+1} + C_{z+1} \, R_{z+2} \, \ldots \, C_{z+m-2} \, R_{z+m-1}}{D_z} \quad (4)$$

$$Q = \frac{C_z \cdot R_{z+1}, \overline{m-1}}{D_z}$$

Temporary Annual Premium.

$$Q = \sigma \frac{R_r}{\Pi'_z} \cdot \frac{C_z \cdot R_{z+1}, \overline{m-1}}{D_z} \quad (5)$$

Π'_z being the single premium to purchase temporary insurance of \$1 at the age of surrender.

Simple Endowments—Single Premium.—The company has no interest in the longevity of the holder of this kind of policy. On the contrary, by the principle of the Tontine, its interest is in his early death, at least death before the policy matures.

The reserve being R_z there are l_z chances for and against the company. Of these d_z, d_{z+1}, etc., to d_{z+m-1}, favor lapse by death, and the surrender value is

$$\overline{Q} = \sigma \cdot \overline{R}_z \cdot \left(1 - \frac{d_z + d_{z+1} \ldots d_{z+m-1}}{l_z} \right)$$

$$\overline{Q} = \sigma \cdot \overline{R}_z \frac{l_{z+m}}{l_z} \quad (6)$$

Simple Endowments—Annual Premiums.—

$$\overline{Q} = \sigma \cdot \overline{R}_z \left(1 - \frac{d_r + d_{r+1} \ldots d_{r+m}}{l_z} \right)$$

$$\overline{Q} = \sigma \cdot \overline{R}_z \frac{l_{z+m}}{l_z} \quad (7)$$

Endowment Assurances—Single Payment.—This being a combination of the simple endowment and temporary insurance, the surrender value is found by taking the sum of equations (4) and (6).

$$Q + \overline{Q} = \sigma \cdot \left(\frac{C_z \cdot R_{z+1}, \overline{m-1}}{D_z} + \overline{R}_z \frac{l_{z+m}}{l_z} \right) \quad (8)$$

Endowment Assurances—Annual Payment.—Here take the sum of equations (5) and (7), or

$$Q + \overline{Q} = \sigma \cdot \left(\frac{R_z}{\Pi'_z} \cdot \frac{C_r \cdot R_{r+1}, \overline{m-1}}{D_z} + \overline{R}_z \frac{l_{z+m}}{l_z} \right) \quad (9)$$

The reserves R_z and $\overline{R}_z$ must be: the first for the assurance part of the policy, the second for the endowment.

TABLE No. LX

SURRENDER VALUES. LIFE POLICY FOR $1,000, ENTERED AT AGE 35, PAYABLE AT AGE 100, OR PREVIOUS DEATH.

| | By Mr. Wright's Method: Surrender Charge, 8 per Cent of Insurance Value. | | | | Prof. Bartlett's Method. | |
| | Combined Experience, 4 per cent. Actual Prem.. $26.38. Net Prem . $19 87. | | Combined Experience, 6 per cent. Actual Prem.. $20.45. Net Prem.. $16.49. | | American Experience, 4 per cent. Actual Prem . $26.38. Net. Prem., $18.84. | |
Age.	Surrender Value.	Surrender Charge.	Surrender Value.	Surrender Charge.	Surrender Value.	Surrender Charge.
36	0.00	17.33	0.00	13.26	6.38	4.37
37	5.89	17.45	3.44	13.45	13.14	8.74
38	18.02	17.57	12.31	13.64	20.29	13.14
39	30.56	17.69	21.61	13.84	27.84	17.54
40	43.52	17.82	31.45	14.05	35.81	21.95
41	56.91	17.95	41.51	14.27	44.20	26.36
42	70.75	18.09	52.24	14.50	53.03	30.78
43	85.07	18.22	63.39	14.74	62.30	35.20
44	99.79	18.37	75.14	14.98	72.04	39.62
45	114.90	18.51	87.27	15.23	82.23	44.03
46	130.37	18.65	99.80	15.48	92.90	48.42
47	146.14	18.78	112.77	15.73	104.03	52.79
48	162.21	18.90	126.12	15.98	115.64	57.12
49	178.55	19.01	139.83	16.21	127.72	61.40
50	195.19	19.11	154.01	16.45	140.25	65.62
51	212.07	19.21	168.50	16.68	153.23	69.76
52	229.22	19.28	183.31	16.89	166.66	73.80
53	246.57	19.35	198.50	17.10	180.54	77.72
54	264.14	19.40	214.13	17.30	194.84	81.53
55	281.92	19.43	230.01	17.49	209.57	85.18
56	299.87	19.45	246.23	17.67	224.71	88.68
57	317.98	19.45	262.68	17.82	240.24	92.00
58	336.25	19.44	279.53	17.97	256.16	95.13
59	354.65	19.41	296.75	18.10	272.46	98.03
60	373.18	19.35	314.11	18.21	289.10	100.73
61	391.73	19.29	331.65	18.30	306.07	103.18
62	410.33	19.19	349.43	18.37	323.34	105.37
63	428.90	19.08	367.38	18.42	340.89	107.30
64	447.42	18.94	384.51	18.44	358.71	108.93
65	465.85	18.79	403.56	18.44	376.74	110.29
66	484.17	18.60	421.59	18.41	394.96	111.23
67	502.32	18.40	439.84	18.36	413.34	112.06
68	520.29	18.16	457.93	18.22	431.84	112.46
69	538.04	17.91	475.84	18.16	450.42	112.52

ENDOWMENT POL. OF $1,000, ENTERED AT 35. PAYABLE AT 45 OR PREVIOUS DEATH.

	Actual Prem., $105.58 Net Prem., $85.03.		Actual Prem.. $89.25 Net Prem., $76.71.		Actual Prem.. $105.53. Net Prem.. $84.80.	
36	77.19	2.72	70.05	2.65	72.49	7.47
37	161.38	-2.22	148.13	2.18	149.92	13.82
38	249.57	1.74	231.47	1.74	232.67	18.90
39	342.00	1.30	320.47	1.32	321.13	22.51
40	438.77	.92	415.57	.93	415.74	24.47
41	540.48	.58	517.24	.58	516.97	24.54
42	647.10	.30	625.92	.32	625.38	22.46
43	758.99	.11	742.21	.11	741.55	17.92
44	870.51	.00	866.68	.00	866.17	10.55
45	1,000.00	.00	1,000.00	.00	1,000.00	00.00

VALUATION OF JOINT-LIFE POLICIES.

By Seth C. Chandler, Jr.,

Actuary of the Continental Life Insurance Company, of N. Y.

The following simple modification of the "accumulation" formula offers peculiar facilities for the valuation of all kinds of joint-life and joint-endowment policies, though its application is by no means limited to this class of insurances, but is universal.

By substituting the values of u and k,

$$u_{xy+n} = \frac{1}{v} \cdot \frac{l_{x+n}}{l_{x+n+1}} = \frac{1}{p_{xy+n}} (1+i)$$

$$k_{xy+n} = \frac{d_{x+n}}{l_{x+n+1}} = \frac{1}{p_{xy+n}} - 1$$

in the "accumulation" formula,

$$H_{xy}^{n+1} = u_{xy+n} (H_{xy}^{n} + \pi_{xy}) - k_{xy+n}$$

we obtain the expression,

$$H_{xy}^{n+1} = 1 - \frac{1}{p_{xy+n}} [1 - (H_{xy}^{n} + \pi_{xy}) (1 + i)]$$

where p_{xy+n} is the probability of two lives $x+n$ and $y+n$ or the product of the probabilities of each life living one year.

This formula dispenses with the necessity for the preparation of the auxiliary quantities u and k for different combinations of ages, and requires simply a table of the arithmetical complements of the logarithms of the probability of living one year.

The values of this element, according to the Actuaries' table of mortality, are here inserted, and also an example of the method of computation by the formula.

Example. Required, the net values by the "actuaries'" table 4 per cent interest at the end of the first and second years, of an ordinary joint-life policy issued at ages 46 and 38.

π 46-38 =	.041036
π 46-38 × 1.04 =	.042677
$1 - (\pi$ 46-38 × 1.04) =	.957323
$1 - (\pi$ 46-38 × 1.04) $\times \dfrac{1}{p\,46} \times \dfrac{1}{p\,38} =$	.979477
$H^1$46-38 =	.020523
Second year.—	
$H^1$46-38 + π46-38 =	.051559
× 1.04 =	.064021
$1 - (H^1$46-38 + π46-38)1.04 =	.935979
$\times \dfrac{1}{p\,47} \times \dfrac{1}{p\,39} =$	.958514
$H^2$46-38 =	.041486

TABLE No LXI

VALUATION OF JOINT-LIFE POLICIES, CHANDLER'S FORMULA, COMBINED EXPERIENCE, 4 PER CENT.

Age.	$Log. \frac{1}{p}$	$\frac{1}{p}$	Age.	$Log. \frac{1}{p}$	$\frac{1}{p}$
10	002.9458	1.00681	48	006.2374	1.01447
11	002.9571	1.00683	49	006.5907	1.01529
12	002.9685	1.00686	50	006.9798	1.01620
13	002.9845	1.00690	51	007.4015	1.01719
14	003.0052	1.00694	52	007.8652	1.01828
15	003.0260	1.00699	53	008.3720	1.01946
16	003.0519	1.00705	54	008.9128	1.02073
17	003.0781	1.00711	55	009.5121	1.02215
18	003.1092	1.00718	56	010.1615	1.02367
19	003.1410	1.00726	57	010.8526	1.02530
20	003.1780	1.00735	58	011.6130	1.02710
21	003.2156	1.00743	59	012.4439	1.02907
22	003.2538	1.00752	60	013.3788	1.03128
23	003 2976	1.00762	61	014.3991	1.03371
24	003.3421	1.00772	62	015.5269	1.03640
25	003.3876	1.00783	63	016.7526	1.03943
26	003.4387	1.00795	64	018.1024	1.04256
27	003.4910	1.00807	65	019.5793	1.04611
28	003.5491	1.00821	66	021.1869	1.04999
29	003.6087	1.00834	67	022.9508	1.05427
30	003.6743	1.00849	68	024.8578	1.05891
31	003.7416	1.00865	69	026.9124	1.06393
32	003.8154	1.00882	70	029.1572	1.06944
33	003.8909	1.00900	71	031.5909	1.07545
34	003.9682	1.00918	72	034.2363	1.08202
35	004.0525	1.00937	73	037.1022	1.08919
36	004.1389	1.00957	74	040.2280	1.09700
37	004.2274	1.00978	75	043.6203	1.10566
38	004.3237	1.01001	76	047.2944	1.11505
39	004.4223	1.01024	77	051.3275	1.12545
40	004.5236	1.01047	78	055.7367	1.13694
41	004.6333	1.01073	79	060.5131	1.14951
42	004.7573	1.01101	80	065.7068	1.16334
43	004.9139	1.01136	81	071.3152	1.17846
44	005.1100	1.01186	82	077.3751	1.19502
45	005.3363	1.01234	83	084.0265	1.21346
46	005.6120	1.01301	84	091.3426	1.23408
47	005.9098	1.01370	85	099.6848	1.25801

A NEW METHOD OF VALUING POLICIES.

By Emory McClintock,

Actuary of the Northwestern Mutual Life Insurance Company, Wis.

The following formulæ for valuing whole life policies and endowment policies premiums payable to a certain age, is now published for the first time, and for one who has not the valuation tables at hand, is the easiest method of finding the reserve on a policy at the end of the year.

Having graded the column of "differences" according to the space given for the table, the "values" are found by the following formula.

Let d = the difference.

"Value" = 1000 $[1 - \log^{-1}(0 - 0001 \times d)]$

Example. Let $d = 500$, required the "value."

1,000 $[1 - \log^{-1}(0 - 000\ 1 \times 500)] = 1,000\ [1 - \log^{-1}(0 - 005)] =$ 1,000 $[1 - \log^{-1}(9,9950000)] = 1,000 \times (1 - .98855) = 11.45.$

.98855 is the nearest number corresponding to log. 9,9950000.

Let $d = 4000$, required the "value."

1,000 $[1 - \log^{-1}(0,00001 \times 4000)] = 1000\ [1 - \log^{-1}(0.04)] =$ 1,000 $\times 1 - \log^{-1}(9,960\ 0000) = 1000 \times (1 - .91201) = 87.99.$

This table, which is simply one of the complements of logarithms, and the complements of numbers corresponding to these complements, applies to all the intermediate values of d, *and to any table of mortality and rate of interest.*

The "age numbers" in this table for whole life policies, were obtained by the formula, 100,000 $(\log. A\ 15 - \log. A\ 15 + m)$, and the general formula is 100,000 $[\log. A_z - \log. A_{z+m})$, m denoting the year of the policy in which the value is required.

The formula for "age numbers" on endowments issued at age x, and payable at age $x + n$, is

$$100,000 \left(\log. \frac{N_z - N_{z+n}}{D_z} - \log. \frac{N_{z+m} N_{z+n}}{D_{z+m}} \right)$$

Examples of finding the value of a policy by this method.

Required the value of a whole life policy, age 30, at the end of the 3d year. American Experience 4½ per cent.

Under the column of "age numbers" of whole life policies opposite age 30, is the age number 3,476; opposite 33, the age at valuation, it is 4,531, and the difference of these "age numbers" is 1,055. By inspecting the column of "differences," we find the value opposite to 1,000 to be 22.76, and the difference between 1,055 and 1,000 multiplied by the "multiple of difference" 2.25, gives 55 × 2.25 = 1.23, which added to 22,76, gives 22.76 + 1.23 = 23.09, the value required.

Required the value of the same policy at the end of the 10th year.

The age number at 40 is 7,700, and at 30 is 3,376, difference of age number 4,224; value opposite, 4,200 = 92.18, correction= 4,224−4,200 = 24 × 2.09 = 50, therefore 92.18 + 50 = 92,88, the value.

Required the value of an endowment policy, age 20, 3d year, payable at death or 40. American Experience, 4½ per cent.

The difference in the age numbers in the column "Death, or 40, is 9,426−5,188 = 4,238; value opposite 4,200 = 92.18, correction (4,238−4,200) 2.09 = 80; therefore 92.18 + 80 = 92,98, the value.

This method of valuation applies only to the terminal values of whole life policies and to continued premium endowments maturing at certain ages, but the values of nearly all continued premium endowments can be found by this table in the sufficient exactness for all practical purposes. Thus the reserve on a ten year endowment, age 43, payable at death, or 53, differs but very little from the reserve on an endowment issued at 45 and payable at 55.

With a little practice, the terminal value of any policy given in these tables can be found to the nearest dollar by inspection.

TABLE NO. LXII.

VALUES AND DIFFERENCES FOR McCLINTOCK'S METHOD OF VALUING POLICIES, ADOPTED TO ANY TABLE OF MORTALITY AND RATE OF INTEREST.

Difference.	Value.	Multiple of Difference.	Difference.	Value.	Multiple of Difference.
.100	$2.30	2.29	5.100	$110.80	2.04
.200	4.59	2.29	5.200	112.84	2.04
.300	6.88	2.29	5.300	114.88	2.04
.400	9.17	2.28	5.400	116.92	2.03
.500	11.45	2.27	5.500	118.95	2.03
.600	13.72	2.27	5.600	120.98	2.02
.700	15.99	2.26	5.700	123.00	2.02
.800	18.25	2.26	5.800	125.02	2.01
.900	20.51	2.25	5.900	127.03	2.01
1.000	22.76	2.25	6.000	129.04	2.00
1.100	25.01	2.24	6.200	133.04	1.99
1.200	27.25	2.24	6.400	137.02	1.98
1.300	29.49	2.23	6.600	140.99	1.97
1.400	31.72	2.23	6.800	144.93	1.97
1.500	33.95	2.22	7 000	148.86	1.96
1.600	36.17	2.22	7.200	152.77	1.95
1.700	38.39	2.21	7.400	156.67	1.94
1.800	40 60	2.21	7.600	160.54	1.93
1.900	42.81	2.20	7.800	164 40	1.92
2.000	45.01	2.19	8.000	168.24	1.91
2.100	47.20	2.19	8.200	172.06	1.90
2.200	49.40	2.18	8.400	175.86	1.89
2.300	51.58	2.18	8 600	179.65	1.88
2.400	53.76	2.18	8.800	183.42	1.87
2.500	55.94	2.17	9.000	187.17	1.86
2.600	58.11	2.17	9.200	190.90	1.86
2.700	60.28	2.16	9.400	194.62	1.85
.800	62.44	2.15	9.600	198.32	1.84
2.900	64.59	2.15	9.800	202.01	1.83
3.000	66 75	2.14	10.000	205.67	1.82
3.100	68.89	2.14	10.200	209.32	1.81
3.200	71.03	2.14	10 400	212 95	1.81
3.300	73.17	2.13	10.600	216.57	1.80
3.400	75.30	2.12	10 800	220.17	1.79
3.500	77.43	2.12	11.000	223.75	1.78
3.600	79.55	2.11	11.200	227.32	1.77
3.700	81.67	2.11	11.400	230.87	1.76
3 800	83.78	2.11	11.600	234.40	1.76
3.900	85.89	2.10	11.800	237.92	1.75
4.000	87.99	2.10	12.000	241.42	1.74
4.100	90.09	2.09	12.200	244.91	1.73
4 200	92.18	2.09	12.400	248.38	1.72
4.300	94.27	2.08	12.600	251.83	1.72
4.400	96.35	2.08	12.800	255.27	1.71
4.500	98.43	2.07	13 000	258 69	1.70
4.600	100.50	2.07	13.200	262.10	1.69
4.700	102.57	2.06	13.400	265 49	1.68
4.800	104.63	2.06	13 600	268.86	1.68
4.900	106.69	2.06	13.800	272.22	1.67
5.000	108.75	2.05	14.000	275.56	1.66

TABLE No. LXII.—(CONTINUED.)

VALUES AND DIFFERENCES FOR MCCLINTOCK'S METHOD OF VALUING POLICIES, ADOPTED TO ANY TABLE OF MORTALITY AND RATE OF INTEREST.

Difference.	Value.	Multiple of Difference.	Difference.	Value.	Multiple of Difference.
14.200	278.89	1.66	25.250	440.89	1.28
14.400	282.21	1.65	25.500	444.10	1.27
14.600	285.50	1.64	25.750	447.29	1.27
14.800	288.79	1.63	26.000	450.46	1.26
15.000	292.06	1.62	26.250	453.61	1.26
15.200	295.31	1.61	26.500	456.75	1.25
15.400	298.54	1.61	26.750	459.87	1.24
15.600	301.77	1.60	27.000	462.97	1.23
15.800	304.98	1.59	27.250	466.05	1.22
16.000	308.17	1.58	27.500	469.12	1.21
16.200	311.35	1.58	27.750	472.16	1.21
16.400	314.51	1.57	28.000	475.19	1.20
16.600	317.66	1.57	28.250	478.20	1.20
16.800	320.80	1.56	28.500	481.20	1.19
17.000	323.92	1.55	28.750	484.18	1.18
17.200	327.02	1.55	29.000	487.14	1.18
17.400	330.12	1.54	29.250	490.08	1.17
17.600	333.19	1.53	29.500	493.01	1.16
17.800	336.26	1.52	29.750	495.92	1.15
18.000	339.31	1.51	30.000	498.81	1.15
18.200	342.34	1.51	30.250	501.69	1.14
18.400	345.36	1.50	30.500	504.55	1.14
18.600	348.37	1.50	30.750	507.39	1.13
18.800	351.37	1.49	31.000	510.22	1.12
19.000	354.35	1.48	31.250	513.03	1.12
19.200	357.31	1.48	31.500	515.83	1.11
19.400	360.27	1.47	31.750	518.61	1.10
19.600	363.20	1.46	32.000	521.37	1.10
19.800	366.13	1.45	32.250	524.12	1.09
20.000	369.04	1.45	32.500	526.85	1.08
20.250	372.66	1.44	33.000	532.26	1.07
20.500	376.27	1.43	33.500	537.62	1.06
20.750	379.84	1.42	34.000	542.91	1.05
21.000	383.40	1.41	34.500	548.14	1.04
21.250	386.94	1.41	35.000	553.32	1.02
21.500	390.46	1.40	35.500	558.43	1.01
21.750	393.96	1.39	36.000	563.48	1.00
22.000	397.44	1.38	36.500	568.48	.99
22.250	400.90	1.37	37.000	573.42	.98
22.500	404.34	1.37	37.550	578.30	.97
22.750	407.76	1.36	38.000	583.13	.96
23.000	411.16	1.35	38.500	587.90	.95
23.250	414.54	1.34	39.000	592.62	.94
23.500	417.90	1.33	39.500	597.28	.92
23.750	421.24	1.33	40.000	601.89	.91
24.000	424.56	1.32	40.500	606.45	.90
24.250	427.86	1.31	41.000	610.95	.90
24.500	431.15	1.30	41.500	615.41	.89
24.750	434.41	1.30	42.000	619.81	.88
25.000	437.66	1.29	42.500	624.16	.87

TABLE No. LXII.—(Continued.)

VALUES AND DIFFERENCES FOR McCLINTOCK'S METHOD OF VALUING POLICIES, ADOPTED TO ANY TABLE OF MORTALITY AND RATE OF INTEREST.

Difference.	Value.	Multiple of Difference.	Difference.	Value.	Multiple of Difference.
43.000	$628.46	.86	68.000	$791.07	.48
43.500	632.72	.85	68.500	793.46	.47
44.000	636.92	.83	69.000	795.83	.47
44.500	641.08	.82	69.500	798.16	.46
45.000	645.19	.81	70.000	800.47	.46
45.500	649.25	.80	70.500	802.76	.45
46.000	653.26	.79	71.000	805.02	.45
46.500	657.23	.78	71.500	807.25	.44
47.000	661.15	.78	72 000	809.45	.44
47.500	665.03	.77	72.500	811.64	.43
48.000	668.87	.76	73.000	813.79	.43
48.500	672.66	.75	73.500	815.92	.42
49.000	676.41	.74	74.000	818.03	.42
49.500	680.11	.73	74.500	820.11	.41
50.000	683.77	.72	75.000	822.17	.41
50.500	687.39	.72	75.500	824.21	.40
51.000	690.97	.71	76.000	826.22	.40
51.500	694.51	.70	76.500	828 21	.39
52.000	698.00	.69	77.000	830.18	.39
52.500	701.46	.68	77.500	832.12	.38
53.000	704.88	.68	78.000	834.04	.38
53.500	708.26	.67	78.500	835.94	.38
54.000	711.60	.66	79.000	837.82	.37
54.500	714.90	.65	80.000	841.51	.36
55.000	718.16	.65	81.000	845.12	.35
55.500	721.39	.64	82.000	848.64	.35
56.000	724.58	.63	83.000	852.09	.34
56.500	727.73	.62	84.000	855.46	.33
57.000	730.85	.62	85.000	858.75	.32
57.500	733.93	.61	86.000	861.96	.31
58.000	736 97	.60	87.000	865.10	.31
58 500	739.98	.59	88.000	868.17	.30
59.000	742.96	.59	89.000	871.18	.29
59.500	745.90	.58	90.000	874.11	.286
60.000	748 81	.58	91.000	876 97	.280
60.500	751.69	.57	92.000	879 77	.270
61.000	754.53	.56	94.000	885.18	.259
61.500	757.34	.56	96.000	890.35	.247
62.000	760.12	.55	98.000	895.29	.236
62.500	762.86	.54	100.000	900.00	.225
63.000	765.58	.54	102.000	904.50	.215
63.500	768.26	.53	104.000	908.80	.205
64.000	770.91	.53	106 000	912.90	.196
64.500	773.54	.52	108.000	916.82	.188
65.000	776.13	.51	110 000	920.57	.163
65.500	778.69	.51	120.000	936.90	.130
66.000	781.22	.50	130.000	949.88	.103
66.500	783.73	.49	140.000	960.19	.083
67.000	786.20	.49	150.000	968.38	.065
67.500	788.65	.48	160.000	974 88	.050

TABLE No. LXIII.

McClintock's Method of Valuing Policies; Joint Lives, Age Numbers, Combined Experience, 4 Per Cent.

Younger Age.	Equal Ages.	Diff. in Ages, 5 Years.	Diff. in Ages, 10 Years.	Diff. in Ages, 15 Years.	Diff. in Ages, 20 Years.	Diff. in Ages, 25 Years.	Diff. in Ages, 30 Years.
15	.000	.000	.000	.000	.000	.000	.000
16	.269	.302	.346	.405	.487	.604	.753
17	.550	.616	.706	.828	.996	1.239	1.536
18	.842	.943	1.081	1.269	1.530	1.906	2.350
19	1.147	1.284	1.471	1.729	2.089	2.605	3.195
20	1.464	1.639	1.879	2.210	2.676	3.336	4.073
21	1.794	2.008	2.305	2.713	3.291	4.097	4.985
22	2.138	2.393	2.748	3.238	3.938	4.887	5.931
23	2.496	2.794	3.210	3.788	4.617	5.711	6.112
24	2.868	3.212	3.691	4.363	5.328	6.565	7.928
25	3.256	3.647	4.194	4.966	6.071	7.451	8.983
26	3.660	4.101	4.719	5.599	6.845	8.371	10.073
27	4.080	4.573	5.268	6.264	7.649	9.326	11.207
28	4.519	5.066	5.843	6.962	8.485	10.316	12.381
29	4.976	5.581	6.444	7.692	9.353	11.342	13.598
30	5.452	6.118	7.074	8.455	10.255	12.406	14.858
31	5.948	6.678	7.735	9.251	11.189	13.509	16.161
32	6.466	7.264	8.429	10.077	12.159	14.651	17.506
33	7.006	7.878	9.157	10.936	13.165	15.835	18.893
34	7.569	8.520	9.920	11.827	14.208	17.062	20.324
35	8.159	9.192	10.718	12.754	15.290	18.334	21.797
36	8.775	9.900	11.550	13.717	16.413	19.650	23.313
37	9.421	10.644	12.415	14.717	17.576	21.009	24.870
38	10.098	11.425	13.317	15.757	18.784	22.413	26.470
39	10.808	12.246	14.255	16.836	20.038	23.862	28.113
40	11.555	13.105	15.233	17.958	21.340	25.356	29.800
41	12.342	14.005	16.252	19.124	22.490	26.896	31.533
42	13.171	14.944	17.313	20.337	24.088	28.484	33.312
43	14.046	15.926	18.419	21.600	25.535	30.117	35.138
44	14.963	16.948	19.569	22.912	27.030	31.795	37.012
45	15.922	18.012	20.763	24.272	28.572	33.519	38.939
46	16.922	19.116	22.001	25.679	30.158	35.288	40.894
47	17.958	20.259	23.281	27.131	31.786	37.098	42.902
48	19.032	21.443	24.606	28.627	33.456	38.950	44.954
49	20.144	22.667	25.977	30.166	35.166	40.845	47.047
50	21.297	23.934	27.394	31.750	36.919	42.781	49.186
51	22.490	25.244	28.857	33.376	38.714	44.760	......
52	23.725	26.597	30.364	35.045	40.551	46.783	......
53	25.000	27.966	31.916	36.754	42.428	48.847	......
54	26.318	29.441	33.512	38.504	44.347	50.952	......
55	27.681	30.935	35.152	40.296	46.307	53.100	......
56	29.088	32.474	36.835	42.130	......	......	......
57	30.540	34.059	38.561	44.005	......	......	......
58	32.041	35.691	40.330	45.922	......	......	......
59	33.592	37.371	42.142	47.882	......	......	......
60	35.149	39.097	43.998	49.883	... ..	......	......
61	36.843	40.867	......	......	......	......	......
62	38.538	42.679	......	......	......	......	......
63	40.278	44.531	......	......	......	......	......
64	42.062	46.422	......	......	......	......	......

TABLE No. LXIV.

MCCLINTOCK'S METHOD OF VALUING POLICIES, AGE NUMBERS,
AMERICAN EXPERIENCE, $4\frac{1}{2}$ PER CENT.

Age.	Whole Life.	Endowment at Death, or 40.	Endowment at Death, or 45.	Endowment at Death, or 50.
15	.000	.000	.000	.000
16	.162	.891	.638	.472
17	.332	1.848	1.319	.973
18	.511	2.878	2.047	1.506
19	.698	3.987	2.825	2.072
20	.895	5.188	3.658	2.675
21	1.101	6.486	4.551	3.318
22	1.317	7.884	5.510	4.003
23	1.544	9.426	6.541	4.734
24	1.781	11.098	7.652	5.515
25	2.030	12.929	8.852	6.352
26	2.292	14.944	10.150	7.248
27	2.567	17.169	11.558	8.210
28	2.855	19.642	13.090	9.244
29	3.158	22.405	14.762	10.358
30	3.476	25.518	16.592	11.560
31	3.811	29.055	18.605	12.860
32	4.162	33.120	20.829	14.271
33	4.531	37.856	23.298	15.804
34	4.919	43.475	26.058	17.476
35	5.326	50.304	29.166	19.306
36	5.755	58.893	32.697	21.319
37	6.205	70.271	36.755	23.540
38	6.679	86.750	41.483	26.006
39	7.177	115.708	47.091	28.762
40	7.700	....	53.928	31.863
41	8.250	....	62.482	35.386
42	8.829	....	73.843	39.433
43	9.438	....	90.301	44.148
44	10.079	....	119.235	49.741
45	10.752	....	....	56.538
46	11.460	....	....	65.089
47	12.204	....	....	76.421
48	12.985	....	....	92.844
49	13.804	....	....	121.735
50	14.662	....	....	....
51	15.559	....	....	....
52	16.497	....	....	....
53	17.477	....	....	....
54	18.501	....	....	....
55	19.568	....	....	....
56	20.681	....	....	....
57	21.839	....	....	....
58	23.046	....	....	....
59	24.301	....	....	....
60	25.605	....	....	....
61	26.959	....	....	....
62	28.364	....	....	....
63	29.821	....	....	....
64	31.330	....	....	....

TABLE No. LXIV.—(CONTINUED.)

MCCLINTOCK'S METHOD OF VALUING POLICIES, AGE NUMBERS,
AMERICAN EXPERIENCE, 4½ PER CENT.

Age.	Endowment at Death, or 55.	Endowment at Death, or 60.	Endowment at Death, or 65.	Endowment at Death, or 70.
15	.000	.000	.000	.000
16	.357	.282	.230	.197
17	.757	.579	.472	.403
18	1.139	.893	.670	.621
19	1.565	1.225	.996	.849
20	2.017	1.575	1.279	1.090
21	2.496	1.946	1.576	1.343
22	3.004	2.337	1.892	1.608
23	3.544	2.751	2.223	1.888
24	4.117	3.189	2.573	2.182
25	4.727	3.652	2.942	2.491
26	5.377	4.144	3.332	2.817
27	6 609	4.665	3.743	3.161
28	6.808	5.218	4.179	3.522
29	7.597	5.806	4.638	3.904
30	8.440	6.430	5.125	4.306
31	9.344	7.094	5.640	4.730
32	10.313	7.801	6.186	5.178
33	11.355	8.555	6.764	5.651
34	12.475	9.259	7.378	6.151
35	13 684	10.218	8.029	6.679
36	14.990	11.138	8.722	7.237
37	16.406	12.123	9.458	7.828
38	17.944	13.180	10.242	8.453
39	19.620	14.316	11.076	9.114
40	21.453	15.540	11.967	9.816
41	23.466	16 861	12.917	10.559
42	25.688	18.290	13.934	11.348
43	28.152	19 841	15.023	12.186
44	30.903	21.529	16.191	13.077
45	33 998	23 373	17.447	14.025
46	37.511	25.395	18.800	15.034
47	41.544	27.621	20.259	16.110
48	46.240	30.088	21.837	17.257
49	51.808	32.835	23.549	18.483
50	58.572	35.920	25.412	19.792
51	67.079	39.414	27.445	21.193
52	78.356	43.418	29.675	22.695
53	94.711	48.074	32.135	24.309
52	123.521	53.588	34.876	26.049
55	....	60.385	37.922	27.930
56	....	68.710	41.374	29 972
57	....	79.886	45.322	32.199
58	....	96.123	49.903	34.642
59	....	124.790	55.324	37.342
60	....	....	61.906	40.348
61	....	....	70.191	43.730
62	....	....	81.199	47.583
63	....	....	97.235	52.043
64	....	....	125.666	57.312

TABLE No. LXV.

McClintock's Method of Valuing Policies, Age Numbers, Combined Experience 4 per Cent.

Age.	Whole Life.	Endowment at Death, or 40.	Endowment at Death, or 45.	Endowment at Death, or 50.
15	.000	.000	.000	.000
16	.222	.973	.715	.543
17	.453	2.013	1.473	1.117
18	.694	3.128	2.279	1.723
19	.944	4.324	3.137	2.364
20	1.205	5.609	4.051	3.043
21	1.476	6.994	5.026	3.762
22	1.758	8.490	6.067	4.525
23	2.052	10.112	7.182	5.334
24	2.358	11.874	8.377	6.195
25	2.676	13.795	9.661	7.111
26	3.607	15.901	11.045	8.087
27	3.320	18.218	12.538	9.130
28	3.711	20.782	14.156	10.245
29	4.085	23.638	15.914	11.440
30	4.475	26.843	17.831	12.724
31	4.851	30.471	19.930	14.105
32	5.304	34.628	22.240	15.596
33	5.745	39.456	24.994	17.210
34	6.205	45.166	27.640	18.962
35	6.686	52.086	30.832	20.873
36	7.187	60.766	34.448	22.964
37	7.711	72.234	38.590	25.266
38	8.260	88.803	43.402	27.812
39	8.833	96.588	49.095	30.647
40	9.434	....	55.997	33.829
41	10.065	....	64.656	37.434
42	10.726	....	76.103	41.564
43	11.420	....	92.648	46.364
44	12.147	....	103.716	52.042
45	12.904	....	....	58.923
46	13.694	....	....	67.553
47	14.513	....	....	78.960
48	15.363	....	....	95.453
49	16.245	....	....	110.555
50	17.160	....	....	....
51	18.109	....	....	....
52	19.093	....	....	....
53	20.111	....	....	....
54	21.167	....	....	....
55	22.260	....	....	....
56	23.391	....	....	....
57	24.563	....	....	....
58	25.776	....	....	....
59	27.033	....	....	....
60	28.333	....	....	....
61	29.676	....	....	....
62	31.062	....	....	....
63	32.490	....	....	....
64	33.961	....	....	....
65	35.475	....	....	....

TABLE No. LXV.—(Continued.)

McClintock's Method of Valuing Policies; Age Numbers, Combined Experience, 4 per Cent.

Age.	Endowment at Death, or 55.	Endowment at Death, or 60.	Endowment at Death, or 65.	Endowment at Death, or 70.
15	.000	.000	.000	.000
16	.426	.346	.293	.258
17	.875	.710	.599	.528
18	1.347	1.091	.920	.810
19	1.844	1.491	1.255	1.104
20	2.368	1.911	1.606	1.411
21	2.920	2.351	1.972	1.731
22	3.502	2.814	2.356	2.065
23	4.116	3.300	2.758	2.414
24	4.765	3.810	3.179	2 778
25	5.451	4.348	3.620	3.159
26	6.177	4.913	4.082	3.557
27	6.946	5.509	4.567	3.973
28	7.662	6.138	5.076	4.408
29	8.629	6.800	5.611	4.863
30	9.550	7.500	6.172	5.339
31	10.532	8.240	6.762	5.838
32	11.579	9.024	7.383	6.361
33	12.698	9.853	8.037	6.908
34	13.896	10.733	8.726	7.483
35	15.182	11.669	9.453	8.087
36	16.565	12.665	10.221	8.721
37	18.058	13.726	11.034	9.388
38	19.674	14.861	11.895	10.091
39	21.428	16.075	12.809	10.832
40	23.341	17.379	13.780	11 614
41	25.436	18.782	14.813	12.441
42	27.741	20.296	15.916	13 317
43	30.291	21.934	17.093	14.244
44	33.128	23.710	18.351	15.256
45	36.308	25.641	19.695	16.263
46	39.903	27.747	21.133	17.359
47	44.013	30.053	22.673	18.517
48	48.780	31.592	24.327	19.741
49	54.414	35.408	26.109	21.036
50	61.239	38.556	28.036	22.412
51	69.802	42.109	30.130	23.874
52	81.131	46.167	32.416	25.431
53	97.534	50.872	34.926	27.098
54	117.454	56.430	37.702	28.884
55	....	63.167	40.799	30.806
56	....	71.627	44.288	32.886
57	....	82.836	48.268	35.146
58	....	99.101	52.879	37.619
59	....	124.730	58.328	40.346
60	....	....	64.936	43.378
61	....	....	73.243	46.983
62	....	....	84 272	50.656
63	....	....	100.225	54.752
64	....	....	132.635	60.074
65	....	....	....	66.528

TABLE No. LXVI.

Valuation Columns.

Age.	American Experience, Four and a half per Cent.			
	u_x	c_x	k_x	A_x
15	1.05304	7.305	7.692	18.5509
16	1.05307	7.331	7.720	18.4818
17	1.05310	7.357	7.748	18.4095
18	1.05314	7.394	7.786	18.3339
19	1.05318	7.431	7.826	·18.2550
20	1.05322	7.469	7.826	18.1726
21	1.05328	7.517	7.917	18.0665
22	1.05333	7.566	7.969	17.9968
23	1.05336	7.616	8.022	17.9032
24	1.05344	7.666	8.075	17.8055
25	1.05350	7.717	8.130	17.7036
26	1.05357	7.780	8.196	17.5972
27	1.05364	7.844	8.264	17.4862
28	1.05371	7.909	8.333	17.3705
29	1.05380	7.986	8.415	17.2497
30	1.05388	8.064	8.498	17.1238
31	1.05397	8.144	8.583	16.9926
32	1.05407	8.237	8.681	16.8557
33	1.05419	8.342	8.794	16.7131
34	1.05431	8.451	8.909	16.5646
35	1.05443	8.561	9.027	16.4099
36	1.05458	8.697	8.172	16.2487
37	1.05474	8.837	9.320	16.0811
38	1.05493	9.003	9.497	15.9066
39	1.05512	9.174	9.679	15.7253
40	1.05534	9.373	9.891	15.5669
41	1.05556	9.577	10.109	15.3413
42	1.05583	9.811	10.359	15.1382
43	1.05611	10.064	10.629	14.9275
44	1.05644	10.363	10.947	14.7089
45	1.05680	10.682	11.289	14.4826
46	1.05722	11.064	11.687	14.2484
47	1.05769	11.484	12.146	14.0065

TABLE No. LXVI—(Continued.)

Valuation Columns.

Age.	American Experience, Four and a Half per cent.			
	u_x	c_x	k_x	A_x
48	1.05824	11.771	12.668	13.7569
49	1.05888	12.542	13.280	13.4998
50	1.05960	13.188	13.974	13.2358
51	1.06042	13.915	14.755	12.9651
52	1.06133	14.726	15.629	12.6880
53	1.06235	15.630	16.604	12.4049
54	1.06350	16.647	17.704	12.1160
55	1.06478	17.771	18.922	11.8218
56	1.06620	19.031	20.289	11.5228
57	1.06778	20.416	21.800	11.2194
58	1.06953	21.948	23.474	10.9121
59	1.07149	23.656	25.347	10.6013
60	1.07366	25.544	27.425	10.2877
61	1.07608	27.637	29.739	9.9718
62	1.07876	29.949	32.302	9.6544
63	1.08172	32.481	35.136	9.3360
64	1.08501	35.285	38.285	9.0172
65	1.08869	38.401	41.807	8.6987
66	1.09276	41.825	45.704	8.3814
67	1.09728	45.596	50.031	8.0662
68	1.10232	49.763	54.855	7.7536
69	1.10789	54.318	60.178	7.4446
70	1.11406	59.323	66.090	7.1399
71	1.12084	64.752	72.576	6.8402
72	1.12818	70.557	79.602	6.5460
73	1.13609	76.725	87.167	6.2569
74	1.14461	83.280	95.323	5.9723
75	1.15389	90.307	104.204	5.6914
76	1.16410	97.905	113.971	5.4133
77	1.17556	106.211	124.941	5.1376
78	1.18862	115.621	137.433	4.8640
79	1.20355	126.061	151.720	4.5928
80	1.22156	138.245	168.861	4.3241

PRINCIPLES AND PRACTICE

TABLE No. LXVI—(Continued).

VALUATION COLUMNS.

Age.	American Experience, Six per Cent.			
	u_x	c_x	k_x	A_x
15	1.06813	7.202	7.692	15.1368
16	1.06818	7.227	7.720	15.1003
17	1.06821	7.253	7.747	15.0617
18	1.06825	7.289	7.787	15.0208
19	1.06830	7.326	7.826	14.9778
20	1.06834	7.363	7.866	14.9325
21	1.06839	7.411	7.917	14.8846
22	1.06845	7.459	7.969	14.8342
23	1.06850	7.508	8.022	14.7811
24	1.06856	7.558	8.076	14.7252
25	1.06862	7.608	8.130	14.6662
26	1.06869	7.670	8.197	14.6039
27	1.06877	7.733	8.265	14.5383
28	1.06882	7.797	8.333	14.4694
29	1.06892	7.873	8.415	14.3964
30	1.06901	7.950	8.499	14.3197
31	1.06910	8.029	8.583	14.2388
32	1.06920	8.120	8.682	14.1536
33	1.06932	8.224	8.795	14.0639
34	1.06944	8.331	8.910	13.9695
35	1.06957	8.440	9.027	13.8701
36	1.06972	8.574	9.172	13.7655
37	1.06988	8.711	9.320	13.6555
38	1.07007	8.876	9.498	13.5399
39	1.07026	9.044	9.679	13.4185
40	1.07048	9.240	9.891	13 2911
41	1.07071	9.441	10.109	13.1574
42	1.07098	9.672	10.359	13.0174
43	1.07127	9.922	10.629	12.8701
44	1.07160	10.216	10.947	12.7160
45	1.07197	10.531	11.289	12.5549
46	1.97240	10.907	11.697	12.3865
47	1.07287	11.321	12.146	12.2108

TABLE No. LXVI.—Continued.

Valuation Columns.

Age.	American Experience, Six Per Cent.			
	u_x	c_x	k_x	A_x
48	1.07343	11.801	12.668	12.0278
49	1.07407	12.364	13.280	11.8376
50	1.07481	13.001	13.974	11.6404
51	1.07564	13.717	14.755	11.4365
52	1.07657	14.518	15.629	11.2259
53	1.07760	15.409	16.604	11.0089
54	1.07877	16.411	17.704	10.7859
55	1.08006	17.520	18.922	10.5563
56	1.08150	18.760	20.289	10.3214
57	1.08311	20.128	21.800	10.0811
58	1.08488	21.637	23.474	9.8358
59	1.08687	23.321	25.347	9.5858
60	1.08907	25.182	27.425	9.3317
61	1.09152	27.245	29.739	9.0738
62	1.09424	29.520	32.302	8.8127
63	1.09725	32.022	35.136	8.5490
64	1.10058	34.786	38.285	8.2831
65	1.10431	37.858	41.807	8.0156
66	1.10485	41.233	45.704	7.7475
67	1.11303	44.951	50.031	7.4792
68	1.11815	49.058	54.854	7.2116
69	1.12379	53.549	60.178	6.9455
70	1.13006	58.484	66.090	6.6815
71	1.13693	63.836	72.576	6.4204
72	1.14438	69.559	79.602	6.1626
73	1.15239	75.940	87.167	5.9079
74	1.16104	82.102	95.323	5.6559
75	1.17046	89.029	104.205	5.4057
76	1.18081	96.519	113.971	5.1567
77	1.19244	104.778	124.941	4.9082
78	1.20568	113.988	137.433	4.6603
79	1.22082	124.277	151.720	4.4131
80	1.23899	136.288	168.861	4.1669

TABLE No. LXVI—(Continued.)

Valuation Columns.

Age.	$\dfrac{D_x}{D_{x+1}} = u_x$	$\dfrac{C_x}{D_x} = c_x$	$\dfrac{C_x}{D_{x+1}} = k_x$	$\dfrac{N_x}{D_x} = A_x$
			COMBINED EXPERIENCE, FOUR PER CENT.	
15	1.04727	6.677	6.992	19.9976
16	1.04733	6.733	7.052	19.8937
17	1.04740	6.791	7.113	19.7901
18	1.04757	6.860	7.185	19.6807
19	1,04755	6.929	7.259	19.5675
20	1.04764	7.010	7.344	19.4504
21	1.04773	7.093	7.432	19.3293
22	1.04782	7.177	7.520	19.2041
23	1.04793	7.273	7.622	18.0747
24	1.04803	7.371	7.725	18.9410
25	1.04814	7.471	7.830	18 8027
26	1.04827	7.583	7.949	18.6589
27	1.04839	7.698	8.071	18.5122
28	1.04854	7.826	8.206	18.3597
29	1.04868	7.956	8.344	18.2023
30	1.04884	8.101	8.497	18.0396
31	1.04900	8.248	8.652	17.8718
32	1.04958	8.410	8.824	17.6985
33	1.04936	8.576	8.999	17.5196
34	1.04955	8 746	9.179	17.3350
35	1.04975	8.931	9.375	17.1444
36	1.04996	9.122	9.576	16.9475
37	1.05017	9.313	9.782	16.7443
38	1.05040	9.525	10.005	16.5342
39	1.05064	9.741	10.235	16.3172
40	1.05089	9.963	10.470	16.0929
41	1.05116	10.204	10.726	15.8610
42	1.05146	10.476	11.014	15.6212
43	1.05183	10.818	11.379	15.3736
44	1.05231	11.247	11.836	15.1186
45	1.05286	11.742	12.363	14.8571
46	1.05353	12.345	13.006	14.5896
47	1.05425	12.996	13.701	14.3170

TABLE No. LXVI—(Continued.)

Valuation Columns.

Age.	Combined Experience, Four per Cent.			
	$\dfrac{D_x}{D_{x+1}} = u_x$	$\dfrac{C_x}{D_x} = c_x$	$\dfrac{C_x}{D_{x+1}} = k_x$	$\dfrac{N_x}{D_x} = A_x$
48	1.05504	13.711	14.466	14.0394
49	1.05590	14.482	15.291	13.7571
50	1.05684	15.326	16.197	13.4703
51	1.05788	16.248	17.189	13.1792
52	1.05901	17.257	18.275	12.8841
53	1.06024	18.359	19.464	12.5853
54	1.06156	19.532	20.735	12.2832
55	1.06303	20.831	22.144	11.9779
56	1.06462	22.237	23.674	11.6698
57	1.06632	23.730	25.304	11.3593
58	1.06819	25.371	27.101	11.0463
59	1.07023	27.160	29.068	10.7313
60	1.07254	29.169	31.285	10.4149
61	1.07506	31.357	33.711	10.0977
62	1.07786	33.770	36.399	9.7805
63	1.08090	36.384	39.328	9.4641
64	1.08427	39.255	42.563	9.1489
65	1.08796	42.386	46.115	8.8355
66	1.09199	45.782	49.994	8.5248
67	1.09644	49.494	54.268	8.2170
68	1.10126	53.490	58.907	7.9130
69	1.10648	57.776	63.928	7.6130
70	1.11222	62.436	69.442	7.3172
71	1.11847	67.460	75.452	7.0261
72	1.12530	72.889	82.022	6.7400
73	1.13275	78.734	89.186	6.4593
74	1.14093	85.065	97.054	6.1840
75	1.14988	91.885	105.657	5.9146
76	1.15965	99.211	115.050	5.6512
77	1.17047	107.182	125.453	53.938
78	1.18242	115.812	136.938	5.1428
79	1.19549	125.062	149.511	4.8986
80	1.20987	135.006	163.340	4.6607

INDEX.